D1575561

A CUP OF TEY

A CUP OF TEY

MISS PYM DISPOSES

THE DAUGHTER OF TIME

by
Josephine Tey

DOUBLEDAY LARGE PRINT HOME LIBRARY EDITION
Garden City, New York

This Large Print Book carries the
Seal of Approval of N.A.V.H.

Introduction

BY ROBERT BARNARD

Mystery readers who have never encountered Josephine Tey are in for a delicious treat. Tey belonged to the Golden Age of British crime writing (roughly speaking, 1920–1950), and her place in the pantheon of mystery writers is unassailable.

Josephine Tey (1896 or '97–1952) is a writer who lives by her works alone. Nobody seems to know anything much about her life, in spite of her successful career in the theater, and nobody seems to care. The steady and sustained sale of her novels in the forty-odd years since her death is due to the books themselves, which have proved to have an enduring appeal. And I would hazard the guess that her readers' attitude toward her is different from their attitude toward other classic crime writers: they regard her with love. They give to their favorite

Tey novel what they once gave to their favorite books of childhood, to *The Wind in the Willows, Little Women,* or whatever: unconditional enthusiasm.

This strong bond between novelist and reader is based on trust—trust in someone who is not only a first-rate storyteller but one who is not content with a formula. Tey, in her best books, seeks to tell different sorts of story, in different ways. This marks her off from the usual purveyors of puzzle-plots, brilliant though they often are. Indeed, in her more straight-forward detective stories Josephine Tey often reveals a sort of impatience with the rules and conventions of the whodunit. In *A Shilling for Candles,* for example, two of the three plot strands are unraveled with information that is either not given readers at the time the detective gets it or only revealed just before the unmasking of the criminal. She was, in other words, not interested enough in that kind of game, and preferred to play other, more varied sports.

Three of her novels occupy that hinterland—often uneasy, but not in her hands—between the crime novel and the "novel proper." They all have crime at their hearts, but they are as far as possible from the "body in the library" formula. Impersonation has been at the heart of many detective stories, but it has seldom carried the emotional charge of *Brat Farrar,* and our sympathies are never in a mere puzzle so skillfully and so surprisingly manipulated. *The Daughter of Time* is an almost unrepeatable success (a historical mystery reanimated and investigated by present-day inquirers), and it has aroused a whole new interest in what previously seemed a dusty and rather sordid period of English history—the reign of King Richard III and the murder of the Princes in the Tower. *The Franchise Affair* also has a basis in fact (an eighteenth-century case in which a maid charged her employers with abduction and mistreatment), but in her hands it becomes a sort of parable of the middle class at bay.

Coming at the tail end of the Golden Age of crime fiction, Tey does not escape some of the less attractive attitudes of her contemporaries: anti-Semitism, contempt for the working class, a deep uneasiness about any enthusiasm (for example, Scottish nationalism) that, to her, smacks of crankiness. If Agatha Christie's "Anthony Astor" in

Three Act Tragedy is indeed a hit at Tey, then Christie targets Tey's weaknesses squarely when she talks about "her spiritual home—a boardinghouse in Bournemouth," with the implication of dreary respectability and conventionality.

But that is to seize on the inessentials and to ignore the essence: Josephine Tey's brilliant storytelling; her varied, loving characterization; above all, her control of reader sympathies. These are evident in all her novels, whether whodunits or more unconventional structures. If Ngaio Marsh or Christie had died as young as Tey, we would have a good idea of what they could have gone on writing. We can guess that Tey would have written several more whodunits, but *what* she would have written is beyond our guesswork. That in itself is her best tribute.

ROBERT BARNARD is the author of more than thirty crime novels, including, most recently, *Bad Samaritan,* and a collection of short stories, *The Habit of Widowhood*. A seven-time Edgar nominee, and winner of the Anthony, Agatha, Mcavity, and Nero Wolfe awards, he lives in Leeds, England.

CONTENTS

MISS PYM
DISPOSES

Chapter 1

A bell clanged. Brazen, insistent, maddening.

Through the quiet corridors came the din of it, making hideous the peace of the morning. From each of the yawning windows of the little quadrangle the noise poured out on to the still, sunlit garden where the grass was grey yet with dew.

Little Miss Pym stirred, opened one doubtful grey eye, and reached blindly for her watch. There was no watch. She opened the other eye. There seemed to be no bedside table either. No, of course not; now she remembered. There *was* no bedside table; as she had found last night. Her watch had had of necessity to be put under her pillow. She fumbled for it. Good heavens, what a row that bell was making! Obscene. There seemed to be no watch under the pillow. But it must be there! She lifted the pillow bodily, revealing only one small sheer-linen handkerchief in a saucy pattern of blue-and-white. She dropped the pillow and peered down between the bed and the wall. Yes, there was something that looked like a watch. By lying flat on her front and inserting an arm she could just reach it. Carefully she brought it up, lightly caught between the tips of first and second fingers. If she dropped it now she would have to get out of bed and crawl under for it. She turned on her back with a sigh of relief, holding the watch triumphantly above her.

Half-past five, said the watch.

Half-past five!

Miss Pym stopped breathing and stared in unbelieving fascination. No, really, did any college, however physical and hearty, begin the day at *half-past five!* Anything was possible, of course, in a community which had use for neither bedside tables nor bedside lamps, but—half-past five! She put the watch to her small pink ear. It ticked faithfully. She squinted round her pillow at the garden which was visible from the window behind her bed. Yes, it certainly was early; the world had that unmoving just-an-apparition look of early morning. Well, well!

Henrietta had said last night, standing

large and majestical in the doorway: "Sleep well. The students enjoyed your lecture, my dear. I shall see you in the morning"; but had not seen fit to mention half-past-five bells.

Oh, well. It wasn't her funeral, thank goodness. Once upon a time she too had lived a life regulated by bells, but that was long ago. Nearly twenty years ago. When a bell rang in Miss Pym's life now it was because she had put a delicately varnished fingertip on the bell-push. As the clamour died into a complaining whimper and then into silence, she turned over to face the wall, burrowing happily into her pillow. Not her funeral. Dew on the grass, and all that, was for youth: shining resplendent youth; and they could have it. She was having another two hours' sleep.

Very childlike she looked with her round pink face, her neat little button of a nose, and her brown hair rolled in flat invisible-pinned curls all over her head. They had cost her a spiritual struggle last night, those curls. She had been very tired after the train journey, and meeting Henrietta again, and the lecture; and her weaker self had pointed out that she would in all probability be leav-

ing after lunch on the morrow, that her per-
manent wave was only two months old, and
that her hair might very well be left unpinned
for one night. But, partly to spite her weaker
self with whom she waged a constant and
bitter war, partly so that she might do Henrietta justice, she had seen to it that fourteen pins were pressed to their nightly duty.
She was remembering her strong-minded-
ness now (it helped to cancel out any
twinge of conscience about her self-
indulgence this morning) and marvelling at
the survival of that desire to live up to Henrietta. At school, she, the little fourth-form
rabbit, had admired the sixth-form Henrietta
extravagantly. Henrietta was the born Head
Girl. Her talent lay exclusively in seeing that
other people employed theirs. That was
why, although she had left school to train in
secretarial work, she was now Principal of a
college of physical culture; a subject of
which she knew nothing at all. She had forgotten all about Lucy Pym, just as Lucy had
forgotten about her, until Miss Pym had
written The Book.

That is how Lucy herself thought of it. The
Book.

She was still a little surprised about The

Book herself. Her mission in life had been to teach schoolgirls to speak French. But after four years of that her remaining parent had died, leaving her two hundred and fifty pounds a year, and Lucy had dried her eyes with one hand and given in her resignation with the other. The Headmistress had pointed out with envy and all uncharitableness that investments were variable things, and that two hundred and fifty didn't leave much margin for a civilised and cultured existence such as people in Lucy's position were expected to live. But Lucy had resigned all the same, and had taken a very civilised and cultured flat far enough from Camden Town to be nearly Regents Park. She provided the necessary margin by giving French lessons now and then when gas bills were imminent, and spent all her spare time reading books on psychology.

She read her first book on psychology out of curiosity, because it seemed to her an interesting sort of thing; and she read all the rest to see if they were just as silly. By the time she had read thirty-seven books on the subject, she had evolved ideas of her own on psychology; at variance, of course, with all thirty-seven volumes read to date. In fact, the thirty-seven volumes seemed to her so idiotic and made her so angry that she sat down there and then and wrote reams of refutal. Since one cannot talk about psychology in anything but jargon, there being no English for most of it, the reams of refutal read very learnedly indeed. Not that that would have impressed anyone if Miss Pym had not used the back of a discarded sheet (her typing was not very professional) on which to write:

Dear Mr Stallard,
   I should be so grateful if you would not use your wireless after eleven at night. I find it *so* distracting.
                                    Yours sincerely,
                                    Lucy Pym.

Mr Stallard, whom she did not know (his name was on the card outside his door on the floor below), arrived in person that evening. He was holding her letter open in his hand, which seemed to Lucy very grim indeed, and she swallowed several times before she could make any coherent sound at all. But Mr Stallard wasn't angry about the wireless. He was a publisher's reader, it seemed, and was interested in what she had unconsciously sent him on the back of the paper.

Now in normal times a publisher would have rung for brandy at the mere suggestion of publishing a book on psychology. But the previous year the British public had shaken the publishing world by tiring suddenly of fiction, and developing an interest in abstruse subjects, such as the distance of Sirius from the earth, and the inward meaning of primitive dances in Bechuanaland. Publishers were falling over themselves, therefore, in their effort to supply this strange new thirst for knowledge, and Miss Pym found herself welcomed with open arms. That is to say, she was taken to lunch by the senior partner, and given an agreement to sign. This alone was a piece of luck, but Providence so ordained it that not only had the British public tired of fiction, but the intellectuals had tired of Freud and Company. They were longing for Some New Thing. And Lucy proved to be it. So Lucy woke one morning to find herself not only famous, but a best-seller. She was so shocked that she went out and had three cups of black coffee and sat in the Park looking straight in front of her for the rest of the morning.

She had been a best-seller for several months, and had become quite used to lecturing on "her subject" to learned societies, when Henrietta's letter had come; reminding her of their schooldays together and asking her to come and stay for a while and address the students. Lucy was a little wearied of addressing people, and the image of Henrietta had grown dim with the years. She was about to write a polite refusal, when she remembered the day on which the fourth form had discovered her christened name to be Laetitia; a shame that Lucy had spent her life concealing, the fourth form had excelled themselves, and Lucy had been wondering whether her mother would mind very much about her suicide, and deciding that anyhow she had brought it on herself by giving her daughter such a high-falutin name. And then Henrietta had waded into the humourists, literally and metaphorically. Her blistering comment had withered humour at the root, so that the word Laetitia had never been heard again, and Lucy had gone home and enjoyed jam roly-poly instead of throwing herself in the river. Lucy sat in her civilised and cultured living-room, and felt the old passionate gratitude to Henrietta run over her in waves. She wrote and said that she would be delighted to stay a night with Henrietta (her native caution was not entirely obliterated by her gratitude) and would with pleasure talk on psychology to her students.

The pleasure had been considerable, she thought, pushing up a hump of sheet to shut out the full brilliance of the daylight. Quite the nicest audience she had ever had. Rows of shining heads, making the bare lecture-room look like a garden. And good hearty applause. After weeks of the polite pattering of learned societies it was pleasant to hear the percussion of hollowed palm on hollowed palm. And their questions had been quite intelligent. Somehow, although psychology was a subject on their time-table, as shown in the common-room, she had not expected intellectual appreciation from young women who presumably spent their days doing things with their muscles. Only a few, of course, had asked questions; so there was still a chance that the rest were morons.

Oh well, tonight she would sleep in her

own charming bed, and all this would seem like a dream. Henrietta had pressed her to stay for some days, and for a little she had toyed with the idea. But supper had shaken her. Beans and milk pudding seemed an uninspired sort of meal for a summer evening. Very sustaining and nourishing and all that, she didn't doubt. But not a meal one wanted to repeat. The Staff table, Henrietta had said, always had the same food that the students had; and Lucy had hoped that that remark didn't mean that she had looked doubtfully upon the beans; but perhaps it hadn't been a success.

"Tommy, Tom-*mee!* Oh, Tommy, darling, waken up. I'm *des*perate!"

Miss Pym shot into wakefulness. The despairing cries seemed to be in her room. Then she realised that the second window of her room gave on to the courtyard; that the courtyard was small, and conversation from room to room through the gaping windows a natural method of communication. She lay trying to quiet her thumping heart, peering down over the folds of sheet to where, beyond the hump of her toes, the foreshortened oblong of the window framed a small piece of distant wall. But her bed lay in the angle of the room, one window to her right in the wall behind her, and the court-yard window to her left beyond the foot of her bed, and all that was visible from her pil-low through the tall thin strip of brightness was half of an open window far down the courtyard.

"Tom-*mee! Tom-mee!*"

A dark head appeared in the window Miss Pym could see.

"For God's sake, someone," said the head, "throw something at Thomas and stop Dakers' row."

"Oh, Greengage, darling, you are an un-sympathetic beast. I've bust my garter, and don't know *what* to do. And Tommy took my *only* safety-pin yesterday to pick the win-kles with at Tuppence-Ha'penny's party. She simply *must* let me have it back be-fore—*Tommy!* Oh, *Tommy!*"

"Hey, shut up, will you," said a new voice, in a lowered tone, and there was a pause. A pause, Lucy felt, full of sign language.

"And what does all that semaphoring mean?" asked the dark head.

"Shut up, I tell you. *She's* there!" This in desperate *sotto voce*.

"Who is?"

"The Pym woman."

"What *rubbish*, darling,"—it was the Dakers voice again, high and unsubdued; the happy voice of a world's darling—"she's sleeping in the front of the house with the rest of the mighty. *Do* you think *she* would have a spare safety-pin if I was to ask her?"

"She looks zip-fastener to me," a new voice said.

"Oh, will you be quiet! I tell you she's in Bentley's room!"

There was a real silence this time. Lucy saw the dark head turn sharply towards her window.

"How do you know?" someone asked.

"Jolly told me last night when she was giving me late supper." Miss Joliffe was the housekeeper, Lucy remembered, and appreciated the nickname for so grim a piece of humanity.

"Gawd's truth!" said the "zip-fastener" voice, with feeling.

Into the silence came a bell. The same urgent clamour that had wakened them. The dark head disappeared at the first sound of it, and Dakers' voice above the row could be heard wailing her desperation like a lost thing. Social gaffes were relegated to their proper unimportance, as the business of the day overwhelmed them. A great wave of sound rose up to meet the sound of the bell. Doors were banged, feet drummed in the corridor, voices called, someone remembered that Thomas was still asleep, and a tattoo was beaten on her locked door when objects flung at her from surrounding windows had failed to waken her, and then there was the sound of running feet on the gravel path that crossed the courtyard grass. And gradually there were more feet on the gravel and fewer on the stairs, and the babble of voices swelled to a climax and faded. When the noises had grown faint with distance or died into lecture-room silence, a single pair of feet pattered in flight across the gravel, a voice saying: "Damn, damn, damn, damn, damn—" at each footfall. The Thomas who slept, apparently.

Miss Pym felt sympathetic to the unknown Thomas. Bed was a charming place at any time, but if one was so sleepy that neither riotous bell-ringing nor the wails of a colleague made any impression, then getting up must be torture. Welsh, too, probably. All Thomases were Welsh. Celts hated getting up. Poor Thomas. Poor, poor Thomas. She would like to find poor Thomas a job where she would never have to get up before afternoon.

Sleep ran over her in waves, drawing her deeper and deeper under. She wondered if "looking zip-fastener" was a compliment. Being a safety-pin person couldn't be thought exactly admirable, so perhaps—

She fell asleep.

Chapter 2

She was being beaten with knouts by two six-foot cossacks because she persisted in using the old-fashioned safety-pin when progress decreed a zip-fastener, and the blood had begun to trickle down her back when she woke to the fact that the only thing that was being assaulted was her hearing. The bell was ringing again. She said something that was neither civilised nor cultured, and sat up. No, definitely, not a minute after lunch would she stay. There was a 2.41 from Larborough, and on that 2.41 she would be; her goodbyes said, her duty of friendship done, and her soul filled with the beatitude of escape. She would treat herself to a half-pound box of chocolates on the station platform as a sort of outward congratulation. It would show on the bathroom scales at the end of the week, but who cared?

The thought of the scales reminded her of

the civilised and cultured necessity of having a bath. Henrietta had been sorry about its being so far to the Staff bathrooms; she had been sorry altogether to put a guest into the student block, but Fröken Gustavsen's mother from Sweden was occupying the only Staff guestroom, and was going to stay for some weeks until she had seen and criticized the result of her daughter's work when the annual Demonstration would take place at the beginning of the month. Lucy doubted very much whether her bump of locality—a hollow according to her friends—was good enough to take her back to that bathroom. It would be awful to go prowling along those bright empty corridors, arriving perhaps at lecture-rooms unawares. And still more awful to ask in a crowded corridor of up-since-dawners where one could perform one's belated ablutions.

Lucy's mind always worked like that. It wasn't sufficient for it to visualise one horror; it must visualise the opposite one too. She sat so long considering the rival horrors, and enjoying the sensation of doing nothing, that still another bell rang and still another wave of drumming feet and calling voices rose up and swamped the quiet of the morning. Lucy looked at her watch. It was half-past seven.

She had just decided to be uncivilised and uncultured and "go in her mock," as her daily woman called it—after all, what was this immersion in water but a modern fad, and if Charles the Second could afford to smell a little high, who was she, a mere commoner, to grin at missing a bath?— when there was a knock on her door. Rescue was at hand. Oh, joy, oh, glory, her marooned condition was at an end.

"Come in," she called in the glad tones of a Crusoe welcoming a landing party. Of course Henrietta would come to say good-morning. How silly of her not to have thought of that. She was still at heart the little rabbit who didn't expect Henrietta to bother about her. Really, she must cultivate a habit of mind more suitable to a Celebrity. Perhaps if she were to do her hair differently, or say over something twenty times a day after the manner of Coué—"Come in!"

But it was not Henrietta. It was a goddess.

A goddess with golden hair, a bright blue linen tunic, sea-blue eyes, and the most enviable pair of legs. Lucy always noticed other women's legs, her own being a sad disappointment to her.

"Oh, I'm sorry," said the goddess. "I forgot that you might not be up. In college we keep such odd hours."

Lucy thought that it was nice of this heavenly being to take the blame for her sloth.

"I do apologise for interrupting your dressing." The blue eyes came to rest on a mule which was lying in the middle of the floor, and stayed there as if fascinated. It was a pale blue satin mule; very feminine, very thriftless, very feathery. A most undeniable piece of nonsense.

"I'm afraid it is rather silly," Lucy said.

"If you only knew, Miss Pym, what it is to see an object that is not strictly utilitarian!" And then, as if recalled to her business by the very temptation of straying from it: "My name is Nash. I'm the Head Senior. And I came to say that the Senior students would be very honoured if you would come to tea with them tomorrow. On Sundays we take our tea out into the garden. It is a Senior privilege. And it really is very pleasant out there on a summer afternoon, and we really are looking forward to having you." She smiled with eager benevolence on Miss Pym.

Lucy explained that she would not be there tomorrow; that she was departing this afternoon.

"Oh, no!" protested the Nash girl; and the genuine feeling in her tone caused Lucy a rush of warmth to the heart. "No, Miss Pym, you mustn't! You really mustn't. You have no idea what a god-send you are to us. It's seldom that anyone—anyone interesting comes to stay. This place is rather like a convent. We are all so hard-worked that we have no time to think of an outside world; and this is the last term for us Seniors, and everything is very grim and claustrophobic—Final Exams, and the Demonstration, and being found posts, and what not—and we are all feeling like death, and our last scrap of sense of proportion is gone. And then *you* come, a piece of the outside, a civilised being—" She paused; half laughing, half serious. "You *can't* desert us."

"But you have an outside lecturer *every* Friday," Lucy pointed out. It was the first time in her life she had been a god-send to anyone, and she was determined to take the assertion with a grain of salt. She didn't at all like the gratified feeling that was sniffing round the edge of her emotions.

Miss Nash explained with clarity, point, and no small bitterness that the last three lecturers had been: an octogenarian on Assyrian inscriptions, a Czech on Central Europe, and a bonesetter on scoliosis.

"What is scoliosis?" asked Lucy.

"Curvature of the spine. And if you think that any of them brought sweetness and light into the College atmosphere, you are wrong. These lectures are supposed to keep us in touch with the world, but if I must be both frank and indiscreet"—she was obviously enjoying being both—"the frock you wore last night did us more good than all the lectures we have ever heard."

Lucy had spent a really shocking sum on that garment when first her book became a best-seller, and it still remained her favourite; she had worn it to impress Henrietta. The gratified feeling came a little nearer.

But not near enough to destroy her common sense. She could still remember the beans. And the lack of bedside lamps. And the lack of any bells to summon service. And the everlasting bells that rang to summon others. No, on the 2.41 from Larborough she would be, though every student of the Leys Physical Training College lay down in her path and wept aloud. She murmured something about engagements—leaving it to be inferred that her diary bulged with pressing and desirable appointments—and suggested that Miss Nash might, meanwhile, direct her to the Staff bathrooms. "I didn't want to go prowling through the corridors, and I couldn't find a bell to ring."

Miss Nash, having sympathised with her about the lack of service—"Eliza really should have remembered that there are no bells in the rooms here and come to call you; she's the Staff housemaid"—suggested that, if Miss Pym didn't mind using the students' baths, they were much nearer. "They are cubicles, of course; I mean, they have walls only part of the way; and the floor is a sort of greenish concrete where the Staff have turquoise mosaic with a tasteful design in dolphins, but the water is the same."

Miss Pym was delighted to use the students' bathroom, and as she gathered her bathing things together the unoccupied hall of her mind was busy with Miss Nash's lack of any studentlike reverence for the Staff. It reminded her of something. And presently she remembered what it reminded her of. Mary Barharrow. The rest of Mary Barharrow's form had been meek and admiring young labourers in the field of irregular French verbs, but Mary Barharrow, though diligent and amiable, had treated her French mistress as an equal; and that was because Mary Barharrow's father was "nearly a millionaire." Miss Pym concluded that in the "outside"—strange how one already used Klondyke terms about College—Miss Nash, who had so markedly Mary Barharrow's charming air of social ease and equality, had also a father very like Mary Barharrow's. She was to learn later that it was the first thing that anyone remarked on when Nash's name was mentioned. "Pamela Nash's people are very rich, you know. They have a butler." They never failed to mention the butler. To the daughters of struggling doctors, lawyers, dentists, business men and farmers, he was as exotic as a negro slave.

"Shouldn't you be at some class or other?" asked Miss Pym, as the quietness of the sunlit corridors proclaimed an absorption elsewhere. "I take it that if you are wakened at half-past five you work before breakfast."

"Oh, yes. In the summer we have two periods before breakfast, one active and one passive. Tennis practice and Kinesiology, or something like that."

"What is kin—whatever-it-is?"

"Kinesiology?" Miss Nash considered for a moment the best way of imparting knowledge to the ignorant, and then spoke in imaginary quotation. "I take down a jug with a handle from a high shelf; describe the muscle-work involved." And as Miss Pym's nod showed that she had understood: "But in winter we get up like anyone else at half-past seven. As for this particular period, it is normally used for taking outside certificates—Public Health, and Red Cross, and what not. But since we have finished with these we are allowed to use it as a prep. hour for our Final Exams, which begin next week. We have very little prep time, so we are glad of it."

"Aren't you free after tea, or thereabouts?"

Miss Nash looked amused. "Oh, no. There is afternoon clinic from four o'clock till six; outside patients, you know. Everything from flat feet to broken thighs. And from half-past six to eight there is dancing. Ballet, not folk. We have folk in the morning; it ranks as exercise, not art. And supper doesn't finish much before half-past eight, so we are very sleepy before we begin our prep and it is usually a fight between our sleepiness and our ignorance."

As they turned into the long corridor leading to the stairs, they overtook a small scuttling figure clutching under one arm the head and thorax of a skeleton and the pelvis and legs under the other arm.

"What are you doing with George, Morris?" asked Miss Nash as they drew level.

"Oh, *please* don't stop me, Beau," panted the startled Junior, hitching her grotesque burden more firmly on to her right hip and continuing to scuttle in front of them, "and *please* forget that you saw me. I mean that you saw George. I meant to waken early and put him back in the lecture-room before the half-past-five bell went, but I just slept."

"Have you been up all night with George?"

"No, only till about two. I—"

"And how did you manage about lights?"

"I pinned my travelling rug over the window, of course," said the Junior, in the testy tones of one explaining the obvious.

"A nice atmosphere on a June evening!"

"It was hellish," said Miss Morris, simply. "But it really *is* the only way I can swot up my insertions, so *please*, Beau, just forget that you saw me. I'll get him back before the Staff come down to breakfast."

"You'll never do it, you know. You're bound to meet someone or other."

"Oh, please don't discourage me. I'm terrified enough now. And I really don't know if I can remember how to hook up his middle." She preceded them down the stairs, and disappeared into the front of the house.

"Positively Through-the-Looking-Glass," commented Miss Pym, watching her go. "I always thought insertion was something to do with needlework."

"Insertions? They're the exact place on a bone where a muscle is attached to it. It's much easier to do it with the skeleton in front of you than with just a book. That is why Morris abducted George." She expelled a breath of indulgent laughter. "Very enterprising of her. I stole odd bones from the drawers in the lecture-room when I was a Junior, but I never thought of taking George. It's the dreadful cloud that hangs over a Junior's life, you know. Final Anatomy. It really *is* a Final.

You're supposed to know all about the body before you begin practising on it, so Final Anatomy is a Junior exam, not a Senior one like the other Finals. The bathrooms are along here. When I was a Junior the long grass at the edge of the cricket field was simply stiff on Sundays with hidden Juniors hugging their Gray. It is strictly forbidden to take books out of College, and on Sundays we are supposed to go all social and go out to tea, or to church, or to the country. But no Junior in the summer term ever did anything on a Sunday except find a quiet spot for herself and Gray. It was quite a business getting Gray out of College. Do you know Gray? About the size of those old family Bibles that rested on the parlour table. There was actually a rumour once that half the girls at Leys were pregnant, but it turned out that it was only the odd silhouette that everyone made with Gray stuffed up the front of their Sunday bests."

Miss Nash stooped to the taps and sent a roar of water rushing into the bath. "When everyone in College bathes three or four times a day, in the matter of minutes, you have to have a Niagara of a tap," she explained above the row. "I'm afraid you are going to be very late for breakfast." And as Miss Pym looked dismayed and oddly small-girlish at the prospect: "Let me bring something for you on a tray. No, it won't be any trouble, I'd love to do it. There isn't any need for a guest to appear at eight o'clock breakfast, anyhow. You'd much better have it in peace in your room." She paused with her hand on the door. "And do change your mind about staying. It really would give us pleasure. More pleasure than you can imagine."

She smiled and was gone.

Lucy lay in the warm soft water and thought happily of her breakfast. How pleasant not to have to make conversation among all those chattering voices. How imaginative and kind of that charming girl to carry a tray to her. Perhaps after all it would be nice to spend a day or two among these young—

She nearly leaped from her bath as a bell began its maniacal yelling not a dozen yards from where she lay. That settled it. She sat up and soaped herself. Not a minute later than 2.41 from Larborough, not one minute later.

As the bell—presumably a five-minute warning before the gong at eight o'clock—

died into silence, there was a wild rush in the corridor, the two doors to her left were flung open, and as the water cascaded into the baths, a high familiar voice was heard shrieking: "Oh, darling, I'm going to be so late for breakfast, but I'm in a *muck* sweat, my dear. I know I should have sat down quietly and done the composition of plasma, of which I know *absolutely noth*-ing, my dear, and Final Phys. is on Tuesday. But it is such a lovely morning—Now what *have* I done with my *soap?*"

Lucy's jaw slowly dropped as it was borne in upon her that in a community which began the day at half-past five and ended it at eight in the evening, there were still individuals who had the vitality to work themselves into a muck sweat when they need not.

"Oh, Donnie, *darling*, I've left my soap behind. Do throw me over yours!"

"You'll have to wait till I've soaped myself," said a placid voice that was in marked contrast to Dakers' high emphasis.

"Well, my angel, *do* be *quick*. I've been late twice this week, and Miss Hodge looked dis*tinctly odd* the last time. I say, Donnie, you *couldn't* by any chance take my 'adipose' patient at twelve o'clock clinic, could you?"

"No, I couldn't."

"She really isn't so heavy as she looks, you know. You have only to—"

"I have a patient of my own."

"Yes, but only the little boy with the ankle. Lucas could take him along with her 'tortis colli' girl—"

"No."

"No, I was afraid you wouldn't. Oh, dear, I don't know *when* I'm going to do that plasma. As for the coats of the stomach, they simply *baffle* me, my dear. I don't really believe there are four, anyhow. It's just a conspiracy. Miss Lux says look at tripe, but I don't see that tripe proves anything."

"Soap coming up."

"Oh, *thank* you, darling. You've saved my life. What a *nice smell*, my dear. *Very* expensive." In the momentary silence of soaping she became aware that the bath on her right was occupied. "Who is next door, Donnie?"

"Don't know. Gage, probably."

"Is that you, Greengage?"

"No," said Lucy, startled, "it's Miss Pym." And hoped it wasn't as prim as it sounded.

"No, but really, who is it?"

"Miss Pym."

"It's a very good imitation, whoever you are."

"It's Littlejohn," suggested the placid voice. "She does imitations."

Miss Pym fell back on a defeated silence.

There was the hurr-oosh of a body lifted suddenly from the water, the spat of a wet foot placed firmly on the edge of the bath, tight wet finger-tips appeared on the edge of the partition, and a face peered over it. It was a long pale face, like an amiable pony's with the straight fair hair above it screwed up into a knob with a hasty hairpin. An oddly endearing face. Even in that crowded moment, Lucy understood suddenly how Dakers had managed to reach her final term at Leys without being knocked on the head by exasperated colleagues.

First horror, then a wild flush together with a dawning amusement, invaded the face above the partition. It disappeared abruptly. A despairing wail rose from beyond.

"Oh, Miss *Pym!* Oh, *dear* Miss Pym! I *do* apologise. I *abase* myself. It didn't occur to me even to *think* it might be you—"

Lucy could not help feeling that she was enjoying her own enormity.

"I *hope* you're not offended. Not *terribly*, I mean. We are so used to people's skins that—that—"

Lucy understood that she was trying to say that the gaffe was less important in these surroundings than it would have been elsewhere, and since she herself had been decently soaping a big toe at the operative moment, she had no feelings on the subject. She said kindly that it was entirely her own fault for occupying a students' bathroom, and that Miss Dakers was not to worry about it for a moment.

"You know my *name*?"

"Yes. You woke me in the dawn this morning yelling for a safety-pin."

"Oh, *catastrophe!* Now I shall *never* be able to look you in the face!"

"I expect Miss Pym is taking the first train back to London," said the voice in the further bath, in a now-look-what-you've-done tone.

"That is O'Donnell next door," said Dakers. "She's from Ireland."

"Ulster," said O'Donnell, without heat.

"How d'you do, Miss O'Donnell."

"You must think this is a mad-house, Miss Pym. But don't judge us by Dakers, please.

Some of us are quite grown up. And some of us are even civilised. When you come to tea tomorrow you will see."

Before Miss Pym could say that she was not coming to tea, a low murmur began to invade the cubicles, rising rapidly into the deep roar of a gong. Into the tumult Dakers' banshee wail rose like the voice of a sea-gull in a storm. She was going to be *so* late. And she was *so* grateful for the soap, which had saved her life. And *where* was the girdle of her tunic? And if dear Miss Pym would promise to overlook her failings up to date, she would yet show her that she was a sensible female and a civilised adult. And they were *all* looking forward so much to that tea tomorrow.

With a rush and a bang the students fled, leaving Miss Pym alone with the dying pulse of the gong and the throaty protest of bath water running away.

Chapter 3

At 2.41, when the afternoon fast train to London was pulling out of Larborough prompt to the minute, Miss Pym sat under the cedar on the lawn wondering whether she was a fool, and not much caring anyhow. It was very pleasant there in the sunlit garden. It was also very quiet, since Saturday afternoon was, it appeared, match afternoon, and College *en masse* was down at the cricket field playing Coombe, a rival establishment from the other side of the County. If they had nothing else, these young creatures, they had versatility. It was a far cry from the lining of the stomach to the placing of a cricket field, but they seemingly took it in their stride. Henrietta, coming into her bedroom after breakfast, had said that if she stayed over the weekend she would at least find it a new experience. "They are a very varied and lively crowd, and the work is very interesting." And Hen-

rietta had certainly been right. There was no
moment when some new facet of this odd
existence was not being presented to her.
She had sat through luncheon at the Staff
table, eating unidentifiable dishes that were
"balanced" to a dietetic marvel, and making
the closer acquaintance of the Staff. Henrietta sat in lonely state at the top of the table
and gobbled her food in an abstracted silence. But Miss Lux was talkative. Miss
Lux—angular, plain, and clever—was Mistress of Theory, and as befitted a lecturer on
theory had not only ideas but opinions. Miss
Wragg, on the other hand, the Junior Gymnast—big, bouncing, young, and pink—had
apparently no ideas at all and her only opinions were reflections of Madame Lefevre's.
Madame Lefevre, the ballet mistress, spoke
seldom, but when she did it was a voice like
dark brown velvet and no one interrupted
her. At the bottom of the table, with her
mother by her side, sat Fröken Gustavsen,
the Senior Gymnast, who talked not at all.

It was to Fröken Gustavsen that Lucy
found her eyes going during that lunch.
There was a sly amusement in the handsome Swede's clear pale eyes that Lucy
found irresistible. The heavy Miss Hodge,

the clever Miss Lux, the dumb Miss Wragg, the elegant Madame Lefevre—what did they all look like through the eyes of a tall pale enigma from Sweden?

Now, having spent lunch wondering about a Swede, she was waiting the advent of a South American. "Desterro doesn't play games," Henrietta had said, "so I'll send her to keep you company this afternoon." Lucy had not wanted anyone to keep her company—she was used to her own company and liked it—but the thought of a South American at an English college of physical training teased her. And when Nash, running into her after lunch, had said, "I'm afraid you're going to be deserted this afternoon, if you don't care for cricket," another Senior passing in the crush had said, "It's all right, Beau, The Nut Tart is going to look after her." "Oh, good," Beau had said, apparently so accustomed to the nickname that it had ceased to have either meaning or oddity for her.

But Lucy looked forward to meeting a Nut Tart, and sitting in the sunlit garden digesting the dietetic marvels she pondered the name. "Nut" was Brazil, perhaps. It was also the modern slang for "dippy" or "daft," she believed. But "tart"? Surely not!

A Junior, running past her on the way to the bicycle shed, flashed her a smile, and she remembered that they had met in the corridor that morning. "Did you get George back safely?" she called after her.

"Yes, thank you," beamed little Miss Morris, pausing to dance on one toe, "but I think I'm in a different sort of trouble now. You see, I had my arm round George's waist, sort of steadying him after hanging him up, when Miss Lux came in. I'll never be able to explain away that, I'm afraid."

"Life is difficult," agreed Lucy.

"However, I think I really do know my insertions now," called little Miss Morris, speeding away over the grass.

Nice children, thought Miss Pym. Nice, clean, healthy children. It was really very pleasant here. That smudge on the horizon was the smoke of Larborough. There would be another smudge like that over London. It was much better to sit here where the air was bright with sun and heavy with roses, and be given friendly smiles by friendly young creatures. She pushed her plump little feet a little further away from her, approved the Georgian bulk of the "old house" that glowed in the sunlight across the lawn, regretted the modern brick wings that made a "Mary Ann" back to it, but supposed that as modern blocks go the Leys ensemble was pleasant enough. Charmingly proportioned lecture-rooms in the "old house," and neat modern little bedrooms in the wings. An ideal arrangement. And the ugly bulk of the gymnasium decently hidden behind all. Before she went away on Monday she must see the Seniors go through their gym. There would be a double pleasure in that for her. The pleasure of watching experts trained to the last fine hair of perfection, and the ineffable pleasure of knowing that never, never as long as she lived, would she herself have to climb a ribstall again.

Round the corner of the house, as she gazed, came a figure in a flowered silk dress and a plain, wide-brimmed shady hat. It was a slim, graceful figure; and watching it come Lucy realised that she had unconsciously pictured the South American plump and over-ripe. She also realised where the "tart" came from, and smiled. The outdoor frocks of the austere young students of Leys would not be flowered; neither would they be cut so revealingly; and never, oh never, would their hats be broad-brimmed and shady.

"Good afternoon, Miss Pym. I am Teresa Desterro. I am so sorry that I missed your lecture last night. I had a class in Larborough." Desterro took off her hat with a leisurely and studied grace, and dropped to the grass by Lucy's side in one continuous smooth movement. Everything about her was smooth and fluid: her voice, her drawling speech, her body, her movements, her dark hair, her honey-brown eyes.

"A class?"

"A dancing class; for shop girls. So earnest; so precise; so very bad. They will give me a box of chocolates next week because it is the last class of the season, and because they like me, and because it is after all the custom; and I shall feel like a crook. It is false pretences. No one could teach them to dance."

"I expect they enjoy themselves. Is it usual? I mean, for students to take outside classes?"

"But we all do, of course. That is how we get practice. At schools, and convents, and clubs, and that sort of thing. You do not care for cricket?"

Lucy, rousing herself to this swift change

of subject, explained that cricket was only possible to her in the company of a bag of cherries. "How is it that you don't play?"

"I don't play *any* games. To run about after a little ball is supremely ridiculous. I came here for the dancing. It is a very good dancing college."

But surely, Lucy said, there were ballet schools in London of an infinitely higher standard than anything obtainable at a college of physical training.

"Oh, for that one has to begin young, and to have a métier. Me, I have no métier, only a liking."

"And will you teach, then, when you go back to—Brazil, is it?"

"Oh, no; I shall get married," said Miss Desterro simply. "I came to England because I had an unhappy love affair. He was r-r-ravishing, but quite unsuitable. So I came to England to get over it."

"Is your mother English, perhaps?"

"No, my mother is French. My grandmother is English. I adore the English. Up to here"—she lifted a graceful hand, wrist properly leading, and laid it edge-wise across her neck—"they are full of romance, and from there up, plain horse sense. I went to my grandmother, and I cried all over her best silk chairs, and I said: 'What shall I do? What shall I do?' About my lover, you understand. And she said: 'You can blow your nose and get out of the country.' So I said I would go to Paris and live in a garret and paint pictures of an eye and a seashell sitting on a plate. But she said: 'You will not. You will go to England and sweat a bit.' So, as I always listen to my grandmother, and since I like dancing and am very good at it, I came here. To Leys. They looked a little sideways on me at first when I said I wanted just to dance—"

This is what Lucy had been wondering. How did this charming "nut" find a welcome in this earnest English college, this starting-place of careers?

"—but one of the students had broken down in the middle of her training—they often do, and do you wonder?—and that left a vacant place in the scheme, which was not so nice, so they said: 'Oh, well, let this crazy woman from Brazil have Kenyon's room and allow her to come to the classes. It will not do any harm and it will keep the books straight.' "

"So you began as a Senior?"

"For dancing, yes. I was already a dancer,

you understand. But I took Anatomy with the Juniors. I find bones interesting. And to other lectures I went as I pleased. I have listened to all subjects. All but plumbing. I find plumbing indecent."

Miss Pym took "plumbing" to be Hygiene. "And have you enjoyed it all?"

"It has been a liberal education. They are very naive, the English girls. They are like little boys of nine." Noticing the unbelieving smile on Miss Pym's face: there was nothing naive about Beau Nash. "Or little girls of eleven. They have 'raves.' You know what a 'rave' is?" Miss Pym nodded. "They swoon if Madame Lefevre says a kind word to them. I swoon, too, but it is from surprise. They save up their money to buy flowers for Fröken, who thinks of nothing but a Naval Officer in Sweden."

"How do you know that?" asked Lucy, surprised.

"He is on her table. In her room. His photograph, I mean. And she is Continental. She does not have 'raves.' "

"The Germans do," Lucy pointed out. "They are famous for it."

"An ill-balanced people," said Desterro,

dismissing the Teutonic race. "The Swedes are not like that."

"All the same, I expect she likes the little offerings of flowers."

"She does not, of course, throw them out of the window. But I notice she likes better the ones who do not bring her offerings."

"Oh? There *are* some who do not have 'raves,' then?"

"Oh, yes. A few. The Scots, for instance. We have two." She might have been talking of rabbits. "They are too busy quarrelling to have any spare emotions."

"Quarrelling? But I thought the Scots stuck together the world over."

"Not if they belong to different winds."

"Winds?"

"It is a matter of climate. We see it very much in Brazil. A wind that goes 'a-a-a-ah' "—she opened her red mouth and expelled a soft insinuating breath—"makes one kind of person. But a wind that goes 's-s-s-s-ss' "—she shot the breath viciously out through her teeth—"makes another person altogether. In Brazil it is altitude, in Scotland it is West Coast and East Coast. I observed it in the Easter holidays, and so understood about the Scots. Campbell has a wind that goes 'a-a-a-ah,' and so she is lazy, and tells lies, and has much charm that is all of it quite synthetic. Stewart has a wind that goes 's-s-s-s-ss,' so she is honest, and hardworking, and has a formidable conscience."

Miss Pym laughed. "According to you, the East Coast of Scotland must be populated entirely by saints."

"There is also some personal reason for the quarrel, I understand. Something about abused hospitality."

"You mean that one went home with the other for holidays and—misbehaved?" Visions of vamped lovers, stolen spoons, and cigarette burns on the furniture ran through Lucy's too vivid imagination.

"Oh, no. It happened more than two hundred years ago. In the deep snow, and there was a massacre." Desterro did full justice to the word "massacre."

At this Lucy really laughed. To think that the Campbells were still engaged in living down Glencoe! A narrow-minded race, the Celts.

She sat so long considering the Celts that The Nut Tart turned to look up at her. "Have you come to use us as specimens, Miss Pym?"

Lucy explained that she and Miss Hodge were old friends and that her visit was a holiday one. "In any case," she said, kindly, "I doubt whether as a specimen a Physical Training Student is likely to be psychologically interesting."

"No? Why?"

"Oh, too normal and too nice. Too much of a type."

A faint amusement crossed Desterro's face; the first expression it had shown so far. Unexpectedly, this stung Lucy; as if she too had been found guilty of being naive.

"You don't agree?"

"I am trying to think of someone—some Senior—who is normal. It is not easy."

"Oh, come!"

"You know how they live here. How they work. It would be difficult to go through their years of training here and be quite normal in their last term."

"Do you suggest that Miss Nash is not normal?"

"Oh, Beau. She is a strong-minded creature, and so has suffered less, perhaps. But would you call her friendship for Innes quite normal? *Nice*, of course," Desterro added hastily, "quite irreproachable. But normal, no. That David and Jonathan relationship. It is a very happy one, no doubt, but it"— Desterro waved her arm to summon an appropriate word—"it *excludes* so much. The Disciples are the same, only there are four of them."

"The Disciples?"

"Mathews, Waymark, Lucas, and Little-john. They have come up the College together because of their names. And now, believe me, my dear Miss Pym, they *think* together. They have the four rooms in the roof"—she tilted her head to the four dormer windows in the roof of the wing— "and if you ask any one of them to lend you a pin she says: 'We have not got one.' "

"Well, there is Miss Dakers. What would you say was wrong with Miss Dakers?"

"Arrested development," said Miss Desterro dryly.

"Nonsense!" said Lucy, determined to assert herself. "A happy, simple, uncomplicated human being, enjoying herself and the world. *Quite* normal."

The Nut Tart smiled suddenly, and her smile was frank and unstudied. "Very well,

Miss Pym, I give you Dakers. But I remind you that it is their last term, this. And so everything is e-norrrmously exaggerated. Everyone is just the least little bit insane. No, it is true, I promise you. If a student is frightened by nature, then she is a thousand times more frightened this term. If she is ambitious, then her ambition becomes a passion. *And* so on." She sat up to deliver herself of her summing-up. "It is not a normal life they lead. You cannot expect them to be normal."

Chapter 4

"You cannot expect them to be normal," repeated Miss Pym to herself, sitting in the same place on Sunday afternoon and looking at the crowd of happy and excessively normal young faces clustered below her on the grass. Her eye ran over them with pleasure. If none of them was distinguished, at least none of them was mean. Nor was there any trace of morbidity, nor even of exhaustion, in their sunburnt alertness. These were the survivors of a gruelling course— that was admitted even by Henrietta—and it seemed to Miss Pym that the rigours might perhaps have been justified if the residue were of such excellence.

She was amused to note that the Disciples, by much living together, had begun to look vaguely alike—as husband and wife often do, however different their features. They all seemed to have the same round face with the same expression of pleased expectancy; it was only later that one noticed differences of build and colouring.

She was also amused to observe that the Thomas who slept was most undeniably Welsh; a small, dark aborigine. And that O'Donnell, who had now materialised from a voice in the bath, was equally unmistakably an Irishwoman; the long lashes, the fine skin, the wide grey eyes. The two Scots—separated by the furthest possible distance that still allowed them to be part of the group—were less obvious. Stewart was the red-haired girl cutting up cake from one of the plates that lay about on the grass. ("It's from Crowford's," she was saying, in a pleasant Edinburgh voice, "so you poor creatures who know nothing but Buzzards will have a treat for a change!") Campbell, propped against the bole of the cedar, and consuming bread-and-butter with slow absorption, had pink cheeks and brown hair and a vague prettiness.

Apart from Hasselt, who was the girl with the flat, calm, early-Primitive face and who was South African, the rest of the Seniors were, as Queen Elizabeth said, "mere English."

The only face that approached distinction,

as opposed to good looks, was that of Mary
Innes, Beau Nash's Jonathan. This pleased
Miss Pym in an odd fashion. It was fitting,
she felt, that Beau should have chosen for a
friend someone who had quality as well as
looks. Not that Innes was particularly good-
looking. Her eyebrows, low over her eyes,
gave her face an intensity, a brooding expression, that robbed her fine bones of the
beauty they might have had. Unlike Beau,
who was animated and smiled easily, she
was quiet and so far Miss Pym had not seen
her smile, although they had had what
amounted in the milieu to a lengthy conversation. That was last night, when Miss Pym
was undressing after having spent the
evening in the company of the Staff. There
had come a knock on her door, and Beau
had said: "I just came to see if you had
everything you want. And to introduce you
to your next-door neighbour, Mary Innes.
Any time you want to be rescued, Innes will
see to it." And Beau had said goodnight and
gone away, leaving Innes to finish the interview. Lucy had found her attractive and very
intelligent, but just a shade disconcerting.
She did not bother to smile if she was not
amused, and though friendly and at her

ease made no effort to be entertaining. In the academic and literary circles that Lucy had recently frequented this would not have been remarkable, but in the gay over-accented College world it had the effect almost of a rebuff. Almost. There was certainly nothing of rebuff in Innes's interest in her book—The Book—and in herself.

Looking at her now, sitting in the cedar shade, Lucy wondered if it were just that Mary Innes did not find life very amusing. Lucy had long prided herself on her analysis of facial characteristics, and was beginning nowadays to bet rather heavily on them. She had never, for instance, come across eyebrows beginning low over the nose and ending high up at the outer end without finding that their owner had a scheming, conniving mind. And someone—Jan Gordon, was it?—had observed that of the crowd round a park orator it was the long-nosed people who stayed to listen and the short-nosed people who walked away. So now, looking at Mary Innes's level eyebrows and firm mouth, she wondered whether the concentration of purpose they showed had forbidden any compensating laughter. It was in some way not a contemporary face at all. It was—was what?

An illustration from a history book? A portrait in a gallery?

Not, anyhow, the face of a games mistress at a girls' school. Definitely not. It was round faces like Mary Innes's that history was built.

Of all the faces turning to her so constantly and turning away with chatter and badinage, only two were not immediately likeable. One was Campbell's: too pliant, too soft-mouthed, too ready to be all things to all men. The other belonged to a girl called Rouse; and was freckled, and tight-lipped, and watchful.

Rouse had come late to the tea-party, and her advent had caused an odd momentary silence. Lucy was reminded of the sudden stillness that falls on chattering birds when a hawk hovers. But there was nothing deliberate about the silence; no malice. It was as if they had paused in their talk to note her arrival, but none of them cared sufficiently to welcome her into their own particular group.

"I'm afraid I'm late," she had said. And in the momentary quiet Lucy had caught the monosyllabic comment, "Swot!" and had concluded that Miss Rouse had not been able to drag herself away from her text-books. Nash had introduced her, and she had dropped to the grass with the rest, and the interrupted conversations flowed on. Lucy, always sympathetic to the odd-man-out, had caught herself being sorry for the latecomer; but a further inspection of Miss Rouse's North Country features had con-vinced her that she was wasting good emo-tion. If Campbell, pink and pretty, was too pliant to be likeable, then Rouse was her complement. Nothing but a bulldozer, Lucy felt, would make an impression on Miss Rouse.

"Miss Pym, you haven't had any of *my* cake," said Dakers, who, quite unabashed, had appropriated Lucy as an old acquain-tance, and was now sitting propped against her chair, her legs straight out in front of her like a doll's.

"Which is yours?" asked Lucy, eyeing the various tuckbox products, which stood out from the college bread-and-butter and "Sunday" buns like Creed suits at a country fair.

Dakers' contribution, it seemed, was the

chocolate sandwich with the butter icing. Lucy decided that for friendship's sake (and a little for greed) she would forget her weight this once.

"Do you always bring your own cakes to Sunday tea?"

"Oh, no, this is in *your* honour."

Nash, sitting on her other side, laughed. "What you see before you, Miss Pym, is a collection of skeletons out of cupboards. There is no physical training student who is not a Secret Eater."

"There has been *no* moment in my *whole* college career, my dears, when I wasn't *sick* with hunger. Only *shame* makes me stop eating at breakfast, and half an hour afterwards I'm hungry enough to eat the horse in the gym."

"That is why our only crime is—" Rouse was beginning, when Stewart kicked her so hard in the back that she almost fell forward.

"We have spread our dreams under your feet," mocked Nash, covering Rouse's broken sentence. "And a fine rich carpet of carbohydrate they are, to be sure."

"We also had a *solemn* conclave as to whether we ought to *dress* for you," said

Dakers, cutting up chocolate sandwich for the others and unaware that there had been any gaffe in the offing. "But we decided that you didn't look very particular." As this raised a laugh, she added hastily, "In the very *nicest* sense, I mean. We thought you would like us as we are."

They were wearing all sorts of garments; as the taste of the wearer or the need of the moment dictated. Some were in shorts, some in blue linen games tunics, some in washing-silk dresses of suitably pastel shades. There were no flowered silks; Desterro was taking tea with the nuns of a convent in Larborough.

"Besides," said Gage, who looked like a Dutch doll and who was the dark head that appeared at a courtyard window at five-thirty yesterday morning and prayed someone to throw something at Thomas and so put a period to the wails of Dakers, "besides, much as we would like to do you honour, Miss Pym, every moment counts with our Finals so oppressively near. Even a quick-change artist like a P.T. Senior needs five full minutes to achieve Sunday-bests, and by accepting us in our rags you have contributed"—she paused to count the gathering and do some mental arithmetic—

"you have contributed one hour and twenty minutes to the sum of human knowledge."

"You can subtract *my* five minutes from that, my dear," said Dakers, licking a protuberant piece of butter-icing into safety with an expert tongue. "I've spent the *whole* afternoon doing the cortex of the brain, and the only result is a firm conviction that I personally haven't *got* a cortex."

"You must have a cortex," said Campbell, the literal-minded Scot, in a Glasgow drawl like syrup sliding from a spoon. But no one took any notice of this contribution to the obvious.

"Personally," said O'Donnell, "I think the vilest part of physiology are the villi. Imagine drawing cross-sections of something that has seven different parts and is less than a twentieth of an inch high!"

"But do you have to know the human structure in such detail?" asked Lucy.

"On Tuesday morning we do," said the Thomas who slept. "After that we can forget it for the rest of our lives."

Lucy, remembering the Monday morning visit to the gymnasium which she had promised herself, wondered if physical work ceased during Final Examinations Week. Oh, no, they assured her. Not with the Dem. only a fortnight ahead. The Demonstration, she was given to understand, ranked only a short head behind Final Examinations as a hazard.

"All our parents come," said one of the Disciples, "and—"

"The parents of all of us, she means," put in a fellow Disciple.

"—and people from rival colleges, and all the—"

"And the civic swells of Larborough," put in a third. It seemed that when one Disciple burst into speech the others followed automatically.

"And all the County big-wigs," finished a fourth.

"It's murder," said the first, summing it up for them.

"I *like* the Dem.," said Rouse. And again that odd silence fell.

Not inimical. Merely detached. Their eyes went to her, and came away again, expressionlessly. No one commented on what she had said. Their indifference left her marooned in the moment.

"I think it's fun to show people what we

can do," she added, a hint of defence in her tone.

They let that pass too. Never before had Lucy met that negative English silence in its full perfection; in its full cruelty. Her own edges began to curl up in sympathy.

But Rouse was less easily shrivelled. She was eyeing the plates before her, and putting out her hand for something to eat. "Is there any tea left in the pot?" she asked.

Nash bent forward to the big brown pot, and Stewart took up the talk from where the Disciples had left it.

"What really *is* murder is waiting to see what you pull out of the Post lottery."

"Post?" said Lucy. "You mean jobs? But why a lottery? You know what you apply for, surely?"

"Very few of us need to apply," Nash explained, pouring very black tea. "There are usually enough applications from schools to go round. Places that have had Leys gymnasts before just write to Miss Hodge when they have a vacancy and ask her to recommend someone. If it happens to be a very senior or responsible post, she may offer it to some Old Student who wants a change.

But normally the vacancies are filled from Leaving Students."

"And a very fine bargain they get," said a Disciple.

"No one works so hard as a First Poster does," said a second.

"For less money," supplemented a third.

"Or with a better grace," said a fourth.

"So you see," Stewart said, "the most agonising moment of the whole term is when you are summoned to Miss Hodge's room and told what your fate is going to be."

"Or when your train is pulling out of Larborough and you haven't been summoned at all!" suggested Thomas, who evidently had had visions of being engulfed, jobless, by her native mountains again.

Nash sat back on her heels and smiled at Lucy. "It is not nearly as grim as it sounds. Quite a few of us are provided for already and so are not in the competition at all. Hasselt, for instance, is going back to South Africa to work there. And the Disciples *en masse* have chosen medical work."

"We are going to start a clinic in Manchester," explained one.

"A very rheumaticky place."

"Full of deformities."

"And brass"—supplemented the other three automatically.

Nash smiled benevolently on them. "And I am going back to my old school as Games Coach. And The Nut—and Desterro, of course, doesn't want a post. So there aren't so many of us to find places for."

"I won't even be qualified if I don't go back to the liver pretty soon," Thomas said, her beady brown eyes blinking in the sun. "What a way to spend a summer evening."

They shifted their positions lazily, as if in protest, and fell to chatter again. But the reminder pricked them, and one by one they began to gather up their belongings and depart, trailing slowly across the sunlit grass like disconsolate children. Until presently Lucy found herself alone with the smell of the roses, and the murmur of insects, and the hot shimmer of the sunlit garden.

For half an hour she sat, in great beatitude, watching the slow shadow of the tree creep out from her feet. Then Desterro came back from Larborough; strolling slowly by the drive with a Rue de la Paix elegance that was odd after Lucy's hour of tumbled youth at tea. She saw Miss Pym, and changed her direction.

"Well," she said, "did you have a profitable afternoon?"

"I wasn't looking for profit," said Lucy, faintly tart. "It was one of the happiest afternoons I have ever spent."

The Nut Tart stood contemplating her.

"I think you are a *very* nice person," she said irrelevantly, and moved away, leisurely, to the house.

And Lucy suddenly felt very young, and didn't like the feeling at all. How dare a chit in a flowered frock make her feel inexperienced and foolish!

She rose abruptly and went to find Henrietta and be reminded that she was Lucy Pym, who had written The Book, and lectured to learned societies, and had her name in *Who's Who*, and was a recognised authority on the working of the Human Mind.

Chapter 5

"What is the College crime?" she asked Henrietta, as they went upstairs after supper. They had paused by the big fan-lighted window on the landing to look down on the little quadrangle, letting the others precede them up to the drawing-room.

"Using the gymnasium as a short cut to the field-path," Henrietta said promptly.

"No, I mean real crime."

Henrietta turned to look at her sharply. After a moment she said: "My dear Lucy, when a human being works as hard as these girls do, it has neither the spare interest to devise a crime nor the energy to undertake it. What made you think of that subject?"

"Something someone said at tea this afternoon. About their 'only crime.' It was something to do with being perpetually hungry."

"Oh, that!" Henrietta's brow cleared. "Food

pilfering. Yes, we do now and then have that. In any community of this size there is always someone whose power of resisting temptation is small."

"Food from the kitchen, you mean?"

"No, food from the students' own rooms. It is a Junior crime, and usually disappears spontaneously. It is not a sign of vice, you know. Merely of a weak will. A student who would not dream of taking money or a trinket can't resist a piece of cake. Especially if it is sweet cake. They use up so much energy that their bodies are crying out for sugar; and though there is no limit to what they may eat at table they are forever hungry."

"Yes, they do work very hard. What proportion of any one set finishes the course, would you say?"

"Of this lot"—Henrietta nodded down to where a group of Seniors were strolling out across the courtyard to the lawn—"eighty per cent are finishing. That is about average. Those who fall by the wayside do it in their first term, or perhaps their second."

"But not all, surely. There must be accidents in a life like this."

"Oh, yes, there are accidents." Henrietta turned and began to climb the further flight.

"That girl whose place Teresa Desterro took, was it an accident that overtook her?"

"No," said Henrietta shortly, "she had a breakdown."

Lucy, climbing the shallow steps in the wake of her friend's broad beam, recognised the tone. It was the tone in which Henrietta, the Head Girl, used to say: "And see that no galoshes are left lying about the cloakroom floor." It did not permit of further discussion.

Henrietta, it was to be understood, did not like to think of her beloved College as a Moloch. College was a bright gateway to the future for deserving youth; and if one or two found the gateway a hazard rather than an opening, then it was unfortunate but no reflection on the builders of the gateway.

"Like a convent," Nash had said yesterday morning. "No time to think of an outside world." That was true. She had watched a day's routine go by. She had also seen the students' two daily papers lying unopened in the common-room last night as they went in to supper. But a nunnery, if it was a narrow world, was also a placid one. Uncompetitive. Assured. There was nothing of the nunnery about this over-anxious, wildly strenuous life. Only the self-absorption was the same; the narrowness.

And yet *was* it so narrow, she wondered, considering the gathering in the drawing-room? If this were any other kind of college that gathering would have been homogeneous. If it were a college of science the gathering would consist of scientists; if it were a college of divinity, of theologians. But in this long charming room, with its good "pieces" and its chintzes, with its tall windows pushed up so that the warm evening flowed in through them full of grass and roses, in this one room many worlds met. Madame Lefevre, reclining in thin elegance on a hard Empire sofa and smoking a yellow cigarette in a green holder, represented a world theatrical; a world of greasepaint, art, and artifice. Miss Lux, sitting upright in a hard chair, represented the academical world; the world of universities, textbooks, and discussion. Young Miss Wragg, busy pouring out coffee, was the world of sport; a physical, competitive, unthinking world. And the evening's guest, Dr Enid Knight, one of the "visiting" Staff, stood for the medical world. The foreign world was not present: Sigrid Gustavsen had retired with her mother, who spoke no English, to her own room where they could chatter together in Swedish.

All these worlds had gone to make the finished article that was a Leaving Student; it was at least not the training that was narrow.

"And what do you think of our students, Miss Pym, now that you have had a whole afternoon with them?" Madame Lefevre asked, turning the battery of her enormous dark eyes on Lucy.

A damn-silly question, thought Lucy; and wondered how a good respectable middle-class English couple had produced anything so like the original serpent as Madame Lefevre. "I think," she said, glad to be able to be honest, "that there is not one of them who is not an advertisement for Leys." And she saw Henrietta's heavy face light up. College was Henrietta's world. She lived and moved and had her being in the affairs of Leys; it was her father, mother, lover, and child.

"They *are* a nice lot," agreed Doreen Wragg happily, not yet far removed from her own student days and regarding her pupils with camaraderie.

"They are as the beasts that perish," said Miss Lux incisively. "They think that Botticelli is a variety of spaghetti." She inspected with deep gloom the coffee that Miss Wragg handed to her. "If it comes to that, they don't know what spaghetti is. It's not long since Dakers stood up in the middle of a Dietetic lecture and accused me of destroying her illusions."

"It surprises me to know that anything about Miss Dakers is destructible," observed Madame Lefevre, in her brown velvet drawl.

"What illusion had you destroyed?" the young doctor asked from the window-seat.

"I had just informed them that spaghetti and its relations were made from a paste of flour. That shattered forever, apparently, Dakers' picture of Italy."

"How had she pictured it?"

"Fields of waving macaroni, so she said."

Henrietta turned from putting two lumps of sugar in a very small cup of coffee (*How* nice, thought Lucy wistfully, to have a figure like a sack of flour and not to mind!) and said: "At least they are free from crime."

"Crime?" they said, puzzled.

"Miss Pym has just been enquiring about the incidence of crime at Leys. That is what it is to be a psychologist."

Before Lucy could protest against this version of her simple search for knowledge, Madame Lefevre said: "Well, let us oblige her. Let us turn out the rag-bag of our shameful past. What crime have we had?"

"Farthing was had up last Christmas term for riding her bike without lights," volunteered Miss Wragg.

"Crime," said Madame Lefevre. "Crime. Not petty misdemeanours."

"If you mean a plain wrong-un, there was that dreadful creature who was man-crazy and used to spend Saturday evenings hanging round the barrack gate in Larborough."

"Yes," said Miss Lux, remembering. "What became of *her* when we tossed her out, does anyone know?"

"She is doing the catering at a Seamen Refuge in Plymouth," Henrietta said, and opened her eyes when they laughed. "I don't know what is funny about that. The only real crime we have had in ten years, as you very well know, was the watches affair.

And even that," she added, jealous for her beloved institution, "was a fixation, of course."

"By precedent, I suppose she is now with the Goldsmiths and Silversmiths," said Madame Lefevre.

"I don't know," said Henrietta, seriously. "I think her people kept her at home. They were quite well-to-do."

"Well, Miss Pym, the incidence appears to be point-something per cent." Madame Lefevre waved a thin brown hand. "We are an unsensational crowd."

"Too normal by half," Miss Wragg volunteered. "A little spot of scandal would be nice now and again. A nice change from hand-stands and upward-circlings."

"I should like to see some hand-stands and upward-circlings," Lucy said. "Would it be all right if I came and watched the Seniors tomorrow morning?"

But of course she must see the Seniors, Henrietta said. They were busy with their Demonstration programme, so it would be a private Demonstration all for herself. "They are one of the best sets we ever had," she said.

"Can I have first go of the gym. when the

Seniors are doing their Final Phys. on Tuesday?" Miss Wragg asked; and they began to discuss time-tables.

Miss Pym moved over to the window-seat and joined Dr Knight.

"Are you responsible for the cross-section of something called the villi?" she asked.

"Oh, no; physiology is an ordinary college subject: Catherine Lux takes that."

"Then what do you lecture on?"

"Oh, different things at different stages. Public Health. The so-called 'social' diseases. The even more so-called Facts of Life. Your subject."

"Psychology?"

"Yes. Public Health is my job, but psychology is my specialty. I liked your book so much. So commonsensical. I admired that. It is so easy to be high-falutin about an abstract subject."

Lucy flushed a little. There is no praise so gratifying as that of a colleague.

"And of course I am the College medical advisor," Dr Knight went on, looking amused. "A sinecure if ever there was one. They are a disgustingly healthy crowd."

"But—" Lucy began. It is the outsider, Desterro (she was thinking), who insists on their abnormality. If it is true, then surely this trained observer, also from the outside, must be aware of it.

"They have accidents, of course," the doctor said, misunderstanding Lucy's "but." "Their life is a long series of minor accidents—bruises, and sprains, and dislocated fingers, and what not—but it is very rarely that anything serious happens. Bentley has been the only instance in my time—the girl whose room you have. She broke a leg, and won't be back till next term."

"But—it is a strenuous training, a gruelling life; do they never break down under it?"

"Yes. That's not unknown. The last term is particularly trying. A concentration of horrors from the student's point of view. Crit. classes, and—"

"Crit. classes?"

"Yes. They each have to take a gym. and a dancing class in the presence of the united Staff and their own set, and are judged according to the show they make. Nerve-shattering. These are all over, the crit. classes; but there are still the Finals, and the Demonstration, and being given jobs, and the actual parting from student life, and what not. Yes, it is a strain for them, poor

dears. But they are amazingly resilient. No
one who wasn't would have survived so
long. Let me get you some more coffee. I'm
going to have some."

She took Lucy's cup and went away to the
table; and Lucy leaned back in the folds of
the curtain and looked at the garden. The
sun had set, and the outlines were growing
blurred; there was the first hint of dew in the
soft air that blew up against her face. Somewhere on the other side of the house (in the
students' common-room?) a piano was being played and a girl was singing. It was a
charming voice: effortless and pure, without
professional tricks and without fashionable
dealing in quarter-tones. The song, moreover, was a ballad; old-fashioned and senti-
mental, but devoid of self-pity and posing.
A frank young voice and a frank old song. It
shocked Lucy to realise how long it was
since she had heard any voice raised in
song that was not a product of valves and
batteries. In London at this moment the exhausted air was loud with radios; but here,
in this cool, scented garden, a girl was
singing for the love of it.

I have been too long in London, she
thought; I must have a change. Find a hotel

on the South Coast, perhaps. Or go abroad. One forgets that the world is young.

"Who is singing?" she asked, as her cup was handed to her again.

"Stewart, I think," Dr Knight said, not interested. "Miss Pym, you can save my life if you like to."

Lucy said that to save a doctor's life would give her immense satisfaction.

"I want to go to a medical conference in London," Dr Knight said in a conspiratorial undertone. "It is on Thursday, but that is the day of my psychology lecture. Miss Hodge thinks I am forever going to conferences, so I can't possibly beg off again. But if you were to take that lecture for me, everything would be grand."

"But I am going back to London myself tomorrow after lunch."

"No!" said Dr Knight, much dashed. "Do you have to?"

"Oddly enough, I was just thinking how much I should hate going back."

"Then don't go. Stay on for a day or two, and save my life. Do, Miss Pym."

"And what would Henrietta think of the substitution?"

"That, of course, is sheer affectation, and

you ought to be ashamed of yourself. *I'm*
not a best-seller, *I'm* not a celebrity, *I'm* not
the author of the latest textbook on the subject—"

Lucy made a small gesture acknowledging her fault, but her eyes were on the garden. Why *should* she go back to London
yet? What was there to take her back?
Nothing and nobody. For the first time that
fine, independent, cushioned, celebrated
life of hers looked just a little bleak. A little
narrow and inhuman. Could it be? Was
there, perhaps, a lack of warmth in that existence she had been so content with? Not
a lack of human contact, certainly. She had
her fill of human contact. But it was a very
all-of-a-piece contact, now that she thought
of it. Except for Mrs Montmorency from one
of the suburbs of Manchester, who was her
daily help, and her Aunt Celia down in
Walberswick, who sometimes had her for
weekends, and the tradespeople, she never
talked to anyone who wasn't somehow
connected with the publishing or the academic worlds. And though all the ladies and
gentlemen belonging to these two worlds
were, of course, both intelligent and amusing, there was no denying that their interests

were limited. You couldn't, for instance, talk to one and the same person about Social Security, hill-billy songs, and what won the 3.30. They each had their "subject." And their subject, she found to her cost, was only too likely to be royalties. Lucy herself had only the vaguest idea about royalties; especially her own, and could never keep her end up in this sort of conversation.

Besides, none of them was *young*.

At least, not young as these children here were young. Young in years a few of her acquaintances might be, but they were already bowed down with the weight of the world's wrongs and their own importance. It was nice to meet a morning-of-the-world youngness for a change. Yesterday morning. It was nice to be liked.

There was no good in trying to diddle herself about why she wanted to stay a little longer; why she was seriously prepared to forgo the delights of civilisation that had seemed so desirable—so imperatively desirable—only yesterday morning. It *was nice* to be liked.

In the last few years she had been ignored, envied, admired, kow-towed to, and cultivated; but warm, personal liking was something she had not had since the Lower Fourth said goodbye to her, with a home-made pen-wiper and a speech by Gladys Someone-or-other, shortly after her legacy. To stay in this atmosphere of youth, of liking, of warmth, she was willing to overlook for a space the bells, the beans, and the bathrooms.

"Knight," said young Miss Wragg, raising her voice from the conversation behind them, "did the Disciples ask you about giving them an introduction to some doctor or other in Manchester?"

"Oh, yes, they asked me. In concert. I said yes, of course. As a matter of fact, I was glad to; I think they will be a great success."

"Individually, the Disciples are null and void," Miss Lux said. "But collectively they have a quadruple ruthlessness that will be very useful in Lancashire. It is the only occasion I have ever come across when nothing multiplied by four became something like six-and-a-half. If nobody wants the *Sunday Times* I shall take it to bed with me."

No one apparently wanted it. It had been lying unopened in the drawing-room after lunch when Lucy had been the first to look at it, and as far as she had noticed no one except Miss Lux had picked it up since.

"This set of Seniors are planting themselves out very nicely. Almost without our help," Madame Lefevre said. "There will be less heart-burning than usual." She did not sound very sorry about the heart-burning; just sardonic.

"It continually surprises me," said Miss Hodge, not at all sardonic, "how each year the students slip into their appropriate places in the world's work. The openings come up as the students are ready to fill them. Almost like—like two pieces of the same machine. So surprising and so satisfactory. I don't think we have had a misfit in all my years at Leys. I had a letter from the Cordwainers School, by the way; in Edinburgh, you know. Mulcaster is getting married and they want someone in her place. You will remember Mulcaster, Marie?" She turned to Madame Lefevre, who, except for Henrietta, was the Oldest Inhabitant—and who, incidentally, had been christened plain Mary.

"Of course I remember her. A lump without leaven," said Madame, who judged everyone by their capacity to execute *rondes de jambes*.

"A nice girl," Henrietta said placidly. "I think Cordwainers will be a very good place for Sheena Stewart."

"Have you told her about it?" Miss Wragg asked.

"No, oh, no; I always like to sleep on things."

"Hatch them out, you mean," Madame said. "You must have heard about Cordwainers before lunch-time yesterday because that was the last post, and it is only now we hear about it."

"It was not very important," Henrietta said defensively; and then added with what was nearly a simper: "But I *have* heard rumours of a 'plum,' a really wonderful chance for someone."

"Tell us," they said.

But Henrietta said no; that no official notice had come, that no official notice or application might come at all, and until it did it was better not to talk about it. But she still looked pleased and mysterious.

"Well, I'm going to bed," Miss Lux said, picking up the *Times* and turning her back on Henrietta's elephantine coyness. "You are not going before lunch tomorrow, are you, Miss Pym?"

"Well," said Lucy, pitchforked of a sudden into decision, "I wondered if I might stay on for a day or two? You did ask me to, you know," she reminded Henrietta. "It has been so nice—So interesting to watch a world so different—And it is so lovely here, so—" Oh, dear, why must she sound so idiotic? Would she never learn to behave like Lucy Pym the Celebrity?

But her stammerings were swamped in the loud wave of their approval. Lucy was touched to note a gleam of pleasure even on the face of Miss Lux.

"Stay on till Thursday and take my Senior Psychology lecture, and let me go to a conference in London," Dr Knight suggested, as if it had just occurred to her.

"Oh, I don't know whether—" began Lucy, all artistic doubt, and looked at Henrietta.

"Dr Knight is always running away to conferences," Miss Hodge said, disapproving but without heat. "But of course we would be delighted and honoured, Lucy, if you agreed to give the students a second lecture."

"I should like to. It would be nice to feel

myself a temporary member of the Staff, instead of a mere guest. I should like to very much." She turned in rising to wink at Dr Knight, who was squeezing her arm in a rapture of gratitude. "And now I think I must get back to the student wing."

She said goodnight and went out with Miss Lux.

Lux eyed her sideways as they moved together to the back of the house, but Lucy, catching the glance, thought that there was a friendly gleam in that ice-grey eye.

"Do you really like this menagerie?" Lux asked. "Or are you just looking for things to stick on cardboard with pins?"

That was what The Nut Tart had asked yesterday afternoon. Have you come looking for specimens? Well, she would make the same answer and see what Lux's reaction would be.

"Oh, I'm staying because I like it. A college of Physical Training wouldn't be a very good place to look for the abnormal, anyhow, would it." She made it a statement, not a question; and waited.

"Why not?" asked Miss Lux. "Sweating oneself into a coma may stultify the reason but it doesn't destroy the emotions."

"Doesn't it?" Lucy said, surprised. "If I were dog-tired I'm certain I wouldn't have any feelings about anything but going to sleep quickly."

"Going to sleep dead tired is all right; normal, and pleasant, and safe. It is when one wakens up dead tired that the trouble begins."

"What trouble?"

"The hypothetical trouble of this discussion," Lux said, smoothly.

"And is wakening up dead tired a common thing, would you say?"

"Well, I'm not their medical advisor, so I can't run round with a stethoscope and fond inquiries, but I should say that five Seniors out of six in their last term are so tired that each morning is a mild nightmare. It is when one is as tired as that that one's emotional state ceases to be normal. A tiny obstacle becomes an Everest in the path; a careless comment becomes a grievance to be nursed; a small disappointment is all of a sudden a suicidal affair."

There swam up in Lucy's mind a vision of that circle of faces at tea-time. Brown, laughing, happy faces; careless and for the most part notably confident. Where in that relaxed and healthy crowd had there been the least hint of strain, of bad temper? Nowhere. They had moaned over their hard lot certainly, but it was a humourous and detached complaint.

Tired they might be; in fact tired they certainly were—it would be a miracle if they were not; but tired to the point of abnormality, no. Lucy could not believe it.

"This is my room," Lux said, and paused. "Have you something to read? I don't suppose you brought anything if you meant to go back yesterday. Can I lend you something?"

She opened the door, exhibiting a neat bed-sitting-room of which the sole decorations were one engraving, one photograph, and an entire wainscotting of books. From next-door came the babble of Swedish chat.

"Poor Fröken," Lux said unexpectedly, as Lucy cocked an ear. "She has been so homesick. It must be wonderful to be able to talk family gossip in one's own tongue again." And then, seeing Lucy's eyes on the photograph: "My young sister."

"She is very lovely," Lucy said; and hoped

instantly that there had been no hint of surprise in her tone.

"Yes." Lux was drawing the curtains. "I hate moths. Do you? She was born when I was in my teens, and I have practically brought her up. She is in her third year at Medical school." She came and stood for a moment looking at the photograph with Lucy. "Well, what can I give you to read? Anything from Runyon to Proust."

Lucy took *The Young Visiters*. It was a long time since she had read it last, but she found that she was smiling at the very sight of it. A sort of reflex action; quite involuntary. And when she looked up she found that Lux was smiling too.

"Well, that is one thing I shall never do," Lucy said regretfully.

"What?"

"Write a book that makes all the world smile."

"Not all the world," Lux said, her smile broadening. "I had a cousin who stopped halfway through. When I asked her why, she said: 'So *unlikely*.' "

So Lucy went smiling away towards bed, glad that she was not going to catch that train tomorrow, and thinking about the plain

Miss Lux who loved a beautiful sister and liked absurdity. As she turned into the long corridor of the E-wing she saw Beau Nash standing at the angle of the stairs at the far end, in the act of lifting a hand-bell to shoulder height, and in another second the wild yelling of it filled the wing. She stood where she was, her hands over her ears, while Beau laughed at her and swung the evil thing with a will. Lovely, she was, standing there with that instrument of torture in her hands.

"Is ringing the 'bedroom' bell the Head Girl's duty?" Lucy asked, as Beau at last ceased to swing.

"No, the Seniors take week-about; it just happens to be my week. Being well down the list alphabetically I don't have more than one week each term." She looked at Miss Pym and lowered her voice in mock-confidence. "I pretend to be glad about that—everyone thinks it a frightful bore to have to watch the clock—but I *love* making a row."

Yes, thought Lucy; no nerves and a body brimming with health; of course she would love the row. And then, almost automatically, wondered if it was not the row that she liked but the feeling of power in her hands. But no, she dismissed that thought; Nash was the one that life had been easy for; the one who had, all her life, only to ask, or take, in order to have. She had no need of vicarious satisfactions; her life was one long satisfaction. She liked the wild clamour of the bell; that was all.

"Anyhow," Nash said, falling into step with her, "it isn't the 'bedroom bell.' It's 'Lights Out.' "

"I had no idea it was so late. Does that apply to me?"

"Of course not. Olympus does as it likes."

"Even a boarded-out Olympus?"

"Here is your hovel," Nash said, switching on the light and standing aside to let Lucy enter the bright little cell, so gay and antiseptic in the unshaded brilliance. After the subtleties of the summer evening and the grace of the Georgian drawing-room, it was like an illustration from one of the glossier American magazines. "I am glad I happened to see you because I have a confession to make. I won't be bringing your breakfast tomorrow."

"Oh, that is all right," Lucy was beginning, "I ought to get up in any case—"

"No, I don't mean that. Of *course* not. It is just that young Morris asked if she might do it—she is one of the Juniors—and—"

"The abductor of George?"

"Oh, yes, I forgot you were there. Yes, that one. And she seemed to think that her life would not be complete unless she had brought up your breakfast on your last morning, so I said that as long as she didn't ask for your autograph or otherwise make a nuisance of herself, she could. I hope you don't mind. She is a nice child, and it would really give her pleasure."

Lucy, who didn't mind if her breakfast was brought by a wall-eyed and homicidal negro so long as she could eat the leathery toast in peace and quiet, said she was grateful to young Morris, and anyhow it wasn't going to be her last morning. She was going to stay on and take a lecture on Thursday.

"You *are!* Oh, that's wonderful. I'm so glad. Everyone will be glad. You are so *good* for us."

"A medicine?" Lucy wrinkled her nose in protest.

"No, a tonic."

"Somebody's Syrup," Lucy said; but she was pleased.

So pleased that even pushing little hair-pins into their appointed places did not bore her with the customary frenzy of boredom. She creamed her face and considered it, unadorned and greasy in the bright hard light, with unaccustomed tolerance. There was no doubt that being a little on the plump side kept the lines away; if you had to have a face like a scone it was at least comforting that it was a smooth scone. And, now she came to think of it, one was given the looks that were appropriate; if she had Garbo's nose she would have to dress up to it, and if she had Miss Lux's cheek-bones she would have to live up to them. Lucy had never been able to live up to any-thing. Not even The Book.

Remembering in time that there was no bedside light—students were discouraged from working in bed—she switched the light off and crossed to pull aside the curtains of the window looking out on the courtyard. She stood there by the wide-open window, smelling the cool scented night. A great stillness had settled on Leys. The chatter, the bells, the laughter, the wild protests, the drumming of feet, the rush of bath water, the coming and going, had crystallised into this great silent bulk, a deeper darkness in the quiet dark.

"Miss Pym."

The whisper came from one of the windows opposite.

Could they see her, then? No, of course not. Someone had heard the small noise of her curtains being drawn back.

"Miss Pym, we are so glad you are staying."

So much for the college grape-vine! Not fifteen minutes since Nash said goodnight, but already the news was in the opposite wing.

Before she could answer, a chorus of whispers came from the unseen windows round the little quadrangle. Yes, Miss Pym. We are glad. Glad, Miss Pym. Yes. Yes. Glad, Miss Pym.

"Goodnight, everyone," Lucy said.

Goodnight, they said. Goodnight. So glad. Goodnight.

She wound her watch and pulled up a chair to put it on—*the* chair, rather: there was only one—so that there should be no burrowing under pillows for it in the morning; and thought how odd it was that only yesterday morning she could not wait to get out of this place.

And perhaps it was because no self-respecting psychologist would have anything to do with a thing so outmoded as Premonition that no small helpful imp from the Unexplainable was there to whisper in her drowsy ear, "Go away from here. Go away while the going is good. Go away. Away from here."

Chapter 6

The chairs scraped on the parquet floor as the students rose from their kneeling position and turned to wait while the Staff filed out of morning prayers. Lucy, having become "temporary Staff," had made the gesture of attending this 8.45 ceremony as an off-set to the un-Staff-like indulgence of breakfast in bed; and she had spent the last few minutes considering the collective legs of College as spread before her in kneeling rows and marvelling at their individuality. Dress was uniform at this hour of the morning, and heads were bowed in dutiful hands, but a pair of legs were as easy to identify as a face, she found. There they were: stubborn legs, frivolous legs, neat legs, dull legs, doubtful legs—already she needed only a turn of calf and piece of ankle to say: Dakers, or Innes, or Rouse, or Beau, as the case might be. Those elegant ones at the end of the first row were The Nut Tart. Did the nuns not mind that their protégée should listen to Anglican prayers, then? And those rather stick-like ones were Campbell, and those—

"Amen," said Henrietta, with unction.

"Amen," murmured the students of Leys, and rose to their feet with the scraping of chairs. And Lucy filed out with the Staff.

"Come in and wait while I arrange this morning's post," Henrietta said, "and then I'll go over to the gymnasium with you," and she led the way into her own sitting-room, where a meek little part-time secretary was waiting for instructions. Lucy sat down on the window-seat with the *Telegraph*, and listened with only half an ear to the professional conversation that followed. Mrs So-and-so had written to ask the date of the Demonstration, Mrs Someone-else wanted to know whether there was a hotel near-by where she and her husband could stay when they came to see their daughter perform, the receipt for the butcher must be looked at and presented to his disbelieving eyes, the special lecturer for the last Friday of term had cried off, three Prospective Parents wanted prospectuses.

"All quite straightforward, I think," Henrietta said.

"Yes," agreed the meek little secretary. "I'll get on with them at once. There was a letter from Arlinghurst. It doesn't seem to be here."

"No," Henrietta said. "That can be answered later in the week."

Arlinghurst, Lucy's mind said. Arlinghurst. The school for girls, of course. A sort of female Eton. "I was at Arlinghurst," they said, and that settled it. She took her attention from the *Telegraph* leader for a moment and thought that if the "plum" that Henrietta had been waiting for was Arlinghurst then indeed it was going to create more than the usual stir among the interested Seniors. She was on the point of asking whether Arlinghurst was in fact that "plum," but was stopped partly by the presence of the meek little secretary but more immediately by the expression on Henrietta's face. Henrietta—there was no denying it—Henrietta had a wary, a sort of guilty, look. The look of a person who is Up To Something.

Oh, well, thought Lucy, if she is merely hugging her lovely secret to herself, let her. I shan't spoil it for her. She followed her friend down the long corridor that ran the length of the wing, and out to the covered way that continued the corridor to the gymnasium. The gymnasium lay parallel to the house and to the right-angled wing, so that from the air the buildings made a complete letter E; the three horizontal strokes being "old house," the right-angled wing, and the gymnasium; the vertical stroke being the connecting wing and the covered way.

The door to which the covered way led was open, and from inside the gymnasium came the sounds of uncoordinated activity; voices, laughter, thudding feet. Henrietta paused by the open door and pointed through to the door on the other side, now closed. "*That* is the College crime," she said. "Crossing the gymnasium to the field-path instead of using the appointed covered way round the building. That is why we have had to lock it up. One wouldn't think that a few extra steps would mean much to students who took so many in the day, but there was no argument or threat which would stop them using the short cut through. So we removed the temptation altogether."

She turned from the open door and led the way to the other end of the building, where a small porch held the stairway to the gallery. As they climbed the stairs Henrietta paused to point to a piece of mechanism on a low trolley, which filled the well of the staircase. "That," she said, "is the most famous College character of all. That is our vacuum-cleaner; known from here to New Zealand as The Abhorrence."

"Why abhorrence?" Lucy asked.

"It used to be Nature's Abhorrence, but it became shortened to The Abhorrence. You remember the tag one is taught at school: Nature abhors a vacuum." She looked a moment longer at the monstrous object, caressing it with her eyes. "It cost us a deplorable sum, The Abhorrence, but it was money well spent. However well the gymnasium was cleaned in the old days, there was always a residue of dust, which was beaten into the air by the students' feet and sucked up, of course, by the students' respiratory passages; and the result was catarrh. Not universal, of course, but there never was a time, summer or winter, when some student or other was not having a bout of catarrh. It was Dr Knight's predecessor who suggested that it might be invisible dust that was responsible, and she was right. Since we squandered that immense sum on The

Abhorrence there has been no more catarrh. And of course," she added happily, "it
was a saving in the end since it is Giddy the
gardener's job to vacuum the gymnasium
now, and we don't have to pay cleaners."

Lucy stopped as they reached the top of
the stairs, and looked over the railings into
the well again. "I don't think I like it. It is very
well named, it seems to me. There is something obscene about it."

"It is unbelievably powerful. And very easy
to work. It takes Giddy only about twenty
minutes every morning, and when he has
finished there is, as he says himself, 'nothing left but the fixtures.' He is very proud of
The Abhorrence. He grooms it as if it were
an animal." Henrietta opened the door at
the top of the stairs and they entered the
gallery.

A gymnasium as a building does not permit of architecture. It is purely functional. It
is an oblong box, lit by windows which are
either in the roof or high up the walls. The
gymnasium at Leys had windows where the
walls met the roof, which is not a beautiful
arrangement; but through their far-away
panes at no hour of any day could direct
sunlight blind a student's eyes, and so

cause an accident. The great oblong box of a building was filled with the reflected radiance of a summer morning; golden and soft. Across the floor were scattered the Senior students, limbering up, practising, criticising, and in a few happy instances playing the fool.

"Do they mind an audience?" Lucy asked as they sat down.

"They are very used to one. Hardly a day goes by without a visitor of some kind."

"What is under the gallery? What is it they watch all the time?"

"Themselves," said Henrietta succinctly. "The whole wall below the gallery is one long mirror."

Lucy admired the impersonal interest on the faces of the students as they watched their reflected performances. To be able to view one's physical entity with such critical detachment was surely no bad thing.

"It is one of the griefs of my life," the Dutch-doll Gage was saying, looking at her up-stretched arms, "that my arms have that kink at the elbow."

"If you listened to that Friday-friend and used your willpower, you'd have them straight by now," Stewart observed, not pausing in her own contortions.

"Probably bent back the other way," Beau Nash mocked, from a double-up position at the ribstalls.

Lucy deduced that a Friday-friend was the "interest" lecturer who appeared on Friday evenings; and wondered idly whether that particular one had called his subject "faith" or "mind-over-matter"; was it Lourdes or was it Coué?

Hasselt, the South African with the flat Primitive face, was clutching Innes's ankles in the air while Innes stood on her hands. "*Reeeee*-ly on thee *arrrrms*, Mees Innes," Hasselt was saying, in a would-be Swedish accent that was evidently a quotation from Fröken; and Innes laughed and collapsed. Looking at them, flushed and smiling (this, she thought, is the first time I have seen Mary Innes smile), Lucy felt again how out-of-place these two faces were. Hasselt's belonged above a Madonna-blue robe, with a tiny landscape of hills and castles and roads somewhere at her left ear. And Innes's to a portrait on some ancestral staircase—seventeenth century, perhaps? No, too gay, too adaptable, too arched-of-

eyebrow. Sixteenth century, rather. Withdrawn, uncompromising, unforgiving; the-
stake-or-nothing.

Away by herself in a far corner was Rouse,
painstakingly stretching her ham-strings by
walking her palms up to her feet. She
couldn't really *need* to stretch her ham-
strings, not after years of continued stretching, so presumably this was merely a North
Country example of "makking siccar." There
was no fooling about for Miss Rouse; life
was real, life was earnest; life was long
ham-strings and a good post in the offing.
Lucy wished she liked Miss Rouse better,
and looked round for Dakers as a sort of an-
tidote. But there was no tow-head and
cheerful pony-face among the collection.

And then, suddenly, the desultory noise
and the chatter faded.

No one had come in by the open door at
the far end, but there was beyond doubt a
Presence in the place. Lucy could feel it
coming up through the gallery floor at her
feet. She remembered that there was a door
at the foot of the stairway; where The Abhorrence stood. Someone had come in
down there.

There was no audible word of command,

but the students, who a moment before had been scattered over the floor like beads from a broken string, were now, as if by magic, standing in a still, waiting line.

Fröken Gustavsen walked out from under the gallery, and surveyed them.

"Unt wvere ess Mees Dakers?" she asked in a cool small voice. But even as she said it a flustered Dakers ran in through the open door, and stopped short as she saw the picture that waited her.

"Oh, *catastrophe!*" she wailed, and darted to the gap that someone had accommodatingly left for her. "Oh, I *am* sorry, Fröken. *Abyssmally* sorry. It was just that—"

"Ees eet proposed to be laate at the Demonstraation?" asked Fröken, with almost scientific interest.

"Oh, *no*, of *course* not, Fröken. It was just that—"

"We know. We know. Something was lost, or broke. Eef eet wass possible to come to thees plaace naakid, Mees Dakers would still find something to lose or break. Attention!"

They came to attention, and were motionless except for their quick breathing.

"Eef Mees Thomas were to pull een her

stow-mach the line would be improved, I theenk."

Thomas obliged instantly.

"Unt Mees Appleyard shows too much cheen."

The plump little girl with the red cheeks pulled her chin further into her neck. "So!"

They right-turned into file, covered, and marched in single file down the gymnasium; their feet falling so lightly on the hard wood floor that they were almost inaudible.

"Quieter, quieter. Lightly, lightly!"

Was it possible?

But it was possible, apparently. Still more quietly fell those long-trained feet, until it was unbelievable that a collection of solid young females weighing individually anything up to ten stones were marching, marching, round the hall.

Lucy slid an eye round to Henrietta; and almost instantly switched it away again. The fond pride on Henrietta's large pale countenance was startling, almost painful, to see; and for a little Lucy forgot the students below and thought about Henrietta. Henrietta of the sack-line figure and the conscientious soul. Henrietta, who had had elderly parents, no sisters, and the instincts of a mother hen. No one had ever lain awake at night over Henrietta; or walked back and fore in the darkness outside her house; or even, perhaps, sent her flowers. (Which reminded her to wonder where Alan was nowadays; there had been several weeks, one spring, when she had thought quite seriously of accepting Alan, in spite of his Adam's apple. It would be nice, she had thought, to be cherished for a change. What had stopped her was the realisation that the cherishing would have to be mutual. That she would inevitably have to mend socks, for instance. She didn't like feet. Even Alan's.) Henrietta had been apparently doomed to a dull if worthy life. But it had not turned out like that. If the expression on her unguarded face had been any criterion, Henrietta had built for herself a life that was full, rich, and satisfying. She had said, in her first re-union gossip with Lucy, that when she took over Leys a decade ago it had been a small and not very popular college, and that she and Leys had flourished together; that she was, in fact, a partner now as well as Principal, and partner in a flourishing concern. But until she had surprised that look on Henrietta's face, Lucy had not realised how much her old friend identified herself with her work. That College was her world, she knew; Henrietta talked of little else. But absorption in a business was one thing, and the emotion on Henrietta's face was quite another.

She was roused from her speculations by the sound of apparatus being dragged out. The students had stopped arching themselves into bows at the ribstalls, puffed out like figureheads on a ship, and were now bringing out the booms. Lucy's shins ached with remembered pain; how often had she barked her bones against that unyielding piece of wood; certainly one of the compensations of middle-age was not having to do uncomfortable things.

The wooden upright was now standing in the middle of the floor, and the two booms were fitted into its grooved sides and hoisted as high as hands could reach. The iron pins with wooden handles shot home through their appointed holes in the upright to hold the booms up, and there was the instrument of torture ready. Not that it was shin-barking time yet; that would come later. Just now it was only "travelling." Two by two, one at each end, the students proceeded along the boom, hanging by their hands, monkey-wise. First sideways, then backwards, and lastly with a rotary movement, like a travelling top. All this was done with monotonous perfection until it was Rouse's turn to rotate. Rouse had bent her knees for the spring to the boom, and then dropped her hands and looked at her instructor with a kind of panic on her tight, freckled face.

"Oh, Fröken," she said, "I'm not going to be able to do it."

"*Nonsense*, Mees Rouse," Fröken said, encouraging but not surprised (this was apparently a repetition of some previous scene), "you have done eet perfectly since you were a Junior. You do it now of course."

In a strained silence Rouse sprang to the boom and began her progress along it. For half its length she performed with professional expertness, and then for no apparent reason her hand missed the boom as she turned, and her body swung away, suspended by her other hand. She made an effort to recover herself, pulling up with her sustaining hand, but the rhythm had broken and she dropped to her feet.

"I knew it," she said. "I'm going to be like Kenyon, Fröken. Just like Kenyon."

"*Mees* Rouse; you are not going to be like *anyone*. It is knack, that. And for a moment you haf lost the knack, that is all. You will try again."

Rouse sprang once more to the boom above her head.

"*No!*" said the Swede with emphasis; and Rouse came back to the ground looking inquiring.

"*Not* saying: Oh dear, I cannot do eet. But saying: This I do often, with ease, and now also. So!"

Twice more Rouse tried, and failed.

"Ve-ry well, Mees Rouse. That will do. One half of the boom will be put up last thing at night, as it is now, and you will come een the morning early and practise, until the knack has come back."

"Poor Rouse," Lucy said, as the booms were being reversed for balance exercises, flat side up instead of rounded.

"Yes, such a pity," Henrietta said. "One of our most brilliant students."

"Brilliant?" said Lucy, surprised. It was not an adjective she would have applied to Rouse.

"In physical work, anyhow. Most brilliant. She finds written work a difficulty, but makes up for it by hard work. A model student, and a great credit to Leys. Such a pity about this little nervous development. Overanxiety, of course. It happens sometimes. Usually over something quite simple, strangely enough."

"What did she mean by 'being like Kenyon'? That is the girl whose place Teresa Desterro took, isn't it?"

"Yes. How clever of you to remember. That was a case in point. Kenyon suddenly decided that she could not balance. She had always had abnormally good balance, and there was no reason why she should lose it. But she began by being wobbly, took to jumping off in the middle of an exercise, and ended by being unable to get up from sitting position on the boom. She sat there and clung to the boom like a frightened child. Sat there and cried."

"Some inner insufficiency."

"Of course. It was not the balance that she was frightened of. But we had to send her home. We are hoping that she will come back to finish her training when she has had a long rest. She was very happy here."

Was she? thought Lucy. So happy that she broke down. What had reduced the girl who was good at balance to a crying, shivering piece of misery, clutching at the boom?

She watched with a new interest the progress of the balancing that had been poor Kenyon's Waterloo. Two by two the students somersaulted upwards on to the high boom, turned to a sitting position sideways, and then slowly stood up on the narrow ledge. Slowly one leg lifted, the muscles rippling in the light, the arms performed their appointed evolution. The faces were calm, intent. The bodies obedient, sure, and accustomed. When the exercise was finished they sank until they were sitting on their heels, upright and easy, put forward blind hands to seize the boom, descended to sideways sitting once more, and from there to a forward somersault and to the ground again.

No one fluffed or failed. The perfection was unblemished. Even Fröken found no word to say. Lucy found that she had been holding her breath. She sat back and relaxed and breathed deeply.

"That was lovely. At school the balance

was much lower, wasn't it, and so it was not exciting."

Henrietta looked pleased. "Sometimes I come in just to see the balance and nothing else. So many people like the more spectacular items. The vaulting and so on. But I find the quiet control of the balance very satisfying."

The vaulting, when it came, was spectacular enough. The obstacles were, to Lucy's eyes, horrific; and she looked with uncomprehending wonder at the delighted faces of the students. They *liked* this. They liked launching themselves into nothingness, flying through the air to problematical landings, twisting and somersaulting. The restraint that had characterised their attitude up to now had vanished; there was verve in their every movement, a sort of laughter; living was good and this was a physical expression of their joy in living. Amazed, she watched the Rouse who had stumbled and failed over the simple boom exercise, performing hair-raising feats of perfection that must require the maximum of courage, control, and "knack." (Henrietta had been right, her physical performance was brilliant. She was also, no doubt, a brilliant games player;

her timing was excellent. But still that "brilliant" stuck in Lucy's throat. "Brilliant" meant someone like Beau; an all-round fineness; body, mind, and spirit.)

"*Mees* Dakers! Take the left hand off at *wons*. Is eet *mountaineering* you are?"

"I didn't mean to leave it so long, Fröken. Really I didn't."

"That is understood. It is the not meaning to that ees rrreprehensible. Come again, after Mees Mathews."

Dakers came again, and this time managed to make her rebellious hand release its grip at the appropriate moment.

"Ha!" she said, delighted with her own success.

"Ha indeed," agreed Fröken, a smile breaking. "Co-ordination. All is co-ordination."

"They like Fröken, don't they," Lucy said to Henrietta, as the students tidied away the implements of their trade.

"They like all the Staff," Henrietta said, with a faint return of her Head Girl tone. "It is not advisable to keep a mistress who is unpopular, however good she may be. On the other hand it is desirable that they should be just a little in awe of their preceptors." She smiled in her senior-clergy-making-a-joke manner; Henrietta did not make jokes easily. "In their different ways, Fröken, Miss Lux, and Madame Lefevre all inspire a healthy awe."

"Madame Lefevre? If I were a student, I don't think it would be awe that would knock my knees together, but sheer terror."

"Oh, Marie is quite human when you know her. She likes being one of the College legends."

Marie and The Abhorrence, thought Lucy; two College legends. Each with identical qualities; terrible and fascinating.

The students were standing in file, breathing deeply as they raised their arms and lowered them. Their fifty minutes of concentrated activity had come to an end, and there they were: flushed, triumphant, fulfilled.

Henrietta rose to go, and as she turned to follow Lucy found that Fröken's mother had been sitting behind them in the gallery. She was a plump little woman with her hair in a bun at the back, and reminded Lucy of Mrs Noah, as portrayed by the makers of toy Arks. Lucy bowed and smiled that extra-wide-for-foreigners smile that one uses to bridge the gap of silence, and then, remembering that although this little woman spoke no English she might speak German, she tried a phrase, and the little woman's face lit up.

"To speak with you, Fräulein, is such pleasure that I will even speak German to do it," she said. "My daughter tells me that you are very distinguished."

Lucy said that she had had a success, which was not the same thing as being distinguished unfortunately; and expressed her admiration for the work she had just witnessed. Henrietta, who had taken Classics instead of Modern Languages at school, washed her hands of this exchange of civilities, and preceded them down the stairs. As Lucy and Fru Gustavsen came out into the sunlight the students were emerging from the door at the other end, running or dawdling across the covered way to the house. Last of the group came Rouse, and Lucy could not help suspecting that her emergence was timed to coincide with the passing of Henrietta. There was no need for her to linger a yard or two behind the others like that; she must see out of the tail of her eye that Henrietta was bearing down on her.

In similar circumstances Lucy would have bolted, but Rouse was lingering. She liked Miss Rouse even less than usual.

Henrietta overtook the girl and paused to speak to her; and as Lucy and her companion passed them Lucy saw the expression on the tight freckled face turned up to receive the Principal's words of wisdom, and remembered what they had called that at school. "Being smarmy." And laying it on with a trowel, too, she thought with vulgar satisfaction.

"And I've always liked freckles, too," she said regretfully.

"Bitte?"

But this was not a subject that could be done justice to in German. The Significance of Freckles. She could see it: a thick tome full of portmanteau words and portentousness. No, it would need French to do it justice. Some distilled essence of amiable cynicism. Some pretty little blasting phrase.

"Is this your first visit to England?" she asked; and instead of entering the house with the others they strolled together through the garden toward the front of the house.

Yes, this was Fru Gustavsen's first visit to

England, and it amazed her that a people who created gardens like this should also create the buildings in them. "Not this, of course," she said, "this old house is very pleasant. It is of a period that was good, yes? But what one sees from train and taxi; after Sweden it is horrible. Please do not think that I am Russian about things. It is—"

"Russian?"

"Yes. Naive, and ignorant, and sure that no one can do anything as well as my own country can do it. It is just that I am used to modern houses that are good to look at."

Lucy said that she might as well get over the subject of our cooking while she was at it.

"Ach, no," said the little woman surprisingly, "it is not so, that. My daughter has told me. Here in College it is according to regime"—Lucy thought that "according to regime" was tact of the most delicate—"and so is not typical. Nor in the hotels is it typical, my daughter says. But she has stayed in private houses in holiday time, and the dishes of the country, she says, are delicious. Not everything she liked. Not everyone likes our raw herring, after all. But the joint roasted in the oven, and the apple tart with cream, and the cold ham very pink and tender, all that is most admirable. Most admirable."

So, walking through the summer garden Lucy found herself expatiating on herrings fried in oatmeal, and parkins, and Devonshire splits, and hot-pot, and collops, and other regional delicacies. She concealed the existence of the pork pie, which she privately considered a barbarism.

As they turned the corner of the house towards the front door, they passed the windows of a lecture-room where the Seniors were already engaged in listening to Miss Lux. The windows were pushed up from the bottom as far as they would go, so that the room was visible in all its details, and Lucy cast an idle glance at the assembled profiles presented to her.

She had looked away before she realised that these were not the faces she had seen only ten minutes ago. She looked back again, startled. Gone was the excitement, the flush of exercise, the satisfaction of achievement. Gone for the moment was even the youth. The faces were tired and spiritless.

Not all of them, of course. Hasselt still had

her air of calm well-being. And Beau Nash's face had still its bright indestructible good looks. But the majority looked sunken; indescribably weary. Mary Innes, seated nearest the window, had a marked line from nostrils to chin; a line that had no business there for thirty years yet.

A little saddened and uncomfortable, as one is at the unexpected discovery of an unhappiness in the middle of delight, Lucy turned her head away, and her last glimpse as she walked past was the face of Miss Rouse. And the expression on the face of Miss Rouse surprised her. It reminded her of Walberswick.

Now why Walberswick?

The wary freckled countenance of Miss Rouse had nothing in common with that formidable grande dame who was Lucy's aunt.

Certainly not.

Then why—but stop! It wasn't her aunt; it was her aunt's cat. The expression on that North Country face in the lecture-room was the expression on the face of Philadelphia when she had had cream instead of milk in her saucer. And there was only one word for that expression. The word smug.

Lucy felt, not unreasonably, that someone

who had just failed to perform a routine exercise had no right to be looking smug. And the last faint lingering inclination to be sorry for Miss Rouse died in her.

Chapter 7

"Miss Pym," said The Nut Tart, materialising at Lucy's elbow, "let us run away together."

It was Wednesday morning, and College was sunk in the thick silence of Final Examinations. Lucy was leaning over a five-barred gate behind the gymnasium, staring at a field of buttercups. It was here at the end of the Leys garden that the country began; the real country, free of the last tentacles of Larborough, unraped and unlittered. The field sloped to a stream, beyond which was the cricket field; and beyond that into the far distance stretched the unbroken pattern of hedge and tree and pasture; yellow, and white, and green; asleep in the morning sunshine.

Lucy took her eyes with difficulty from the shimmering yellow of the buttercups that had been mesmerising her, and wondered how many flowered silk frocks the Brazilian possessed. Here was yet another one,

shaming the English subtleties with its brilliance.

"Where do you propose that we run to?"
she asked.

"Let's go to the village."

"Is there a village?"

"There is always a village in England; it is
that kind of country. But more especially
there is Bidlington. You can see the weather
thing of the church steeple just over those
trees there."

"It looks a long way," said Lucy, who was
no great walker and was greatly content
where she was; it was a long time since she
had had a field of buttercups to look at and
all time to do it in. "Is it much of a place?"

"Oh yes. It is a two-pub village," Desterro
said, as one quoting a calibre. "Besides, it
has everything a village in England should
have. Queen Elizabeth slept there, and
Charles the Second hid there; and Cru-
saders are buried in the church—there is
one just like the manager of our ranch in
Brazil—and all the cottages are obtainable
on postcards at the shop; and it appears in
books, the village does—"

"Guide books, you mean?"

"No, no. It has an author who specialised

in it, you understand. I read one of his books when I came first to Leys. *Rain Over the Sky* it was called. All breasts and incest. And it has the Bidlington Martyrs—that is six men who threw stones at the police station last century some time and got put in jail. Imagine a country that remembers a thing like that! In my country they use knives—when they can't afford revolvers—and we smother the corpses with flowers, and cry a lot, and forget all about it next week."

"Well—"

"We can have some coffee at The Teapot."

"A little Hibernian, surely?"

But that was too much for even an intelligent stranger to these shores. "It is *real* coffee, I may tell you. It both smells and tastes. Oh, come on, Miss Pym. It is a small fifteen minutes away, and it is not yet ten o'clock. And there is nothing to do in this place until we are summoned to eat beans at one o'clock."

"Are you not taking any of the examinations?" Lucy asked, passing meekly through the gate that was held open for her.

"Anatomy I shall take, I think. Just, as you say, for the hell of it. I have taken all the lec-

tures, so it will be fun to find out how much
I know. It is worth knowing anatomy. It is a
great labour, of course; it is a subject in
which imagination is not appreciated, but it
is worth learning."

"I suppose so. One wouldn't feel a fool in
an emergency."

"Emergency?" said Desterro, whose mind
had apparently not been running along
these lines. "Oh, yes, I see. But what I
meant is that it is a subject that does not get
out of date. Now *your* subject, if you will forgive me, Miss Pym, is continually getting
out of date, no? To listen to it is charming,
but to work at it would be very foolish. An
idea today may be nonsense tomorrow, but
a clavicle is a clavicle for all time. You see?"

Lucy saw, and envied such economy of
effort.

"So tomorrow, when the Juniors take their
Final Anatomy, I take it too. It is a respect-
worthy thing; my grandmother would approve of it. But today they are busy about
conundrums, and so me, I walk to Bidlington with the charming Miss Pym and we
have coffee."

"Conundrums?"

The Nut Tart fished a folded paper from

the minute pocket of her frock and read from it: "If the ball is over the touch line but has not reached the ground and a player standing inside hits or catches the ball and brings it into the court again, what decision would you give?"

In a silence more eloquent than speech she folded up the cyclostyled sheet and put it away again.

"How did you get a copy of their paper if they are still busy on the subject of games?"

"Miss Wragg gave me one. She said it might amuse me. It does."

Down between the yellow field and the may-white hedge the path led them to the stream. They paused by the small bridge to stare at the shadowed water under the willows.

"Over there," Desterro said, pointing at the level ground across the stream, "is the games field. In winter it is deep in mud, and they have bars across their shoes to keep them from slipping in it." Lucy thought that if she were saying, "They wear rings through their noses to add to their attraction," the tone would be identical. "Now we walk down-stream to the next little bridge and get on to the road there. It is not a road; just a lane." She moved in silence down the shaded path, a bright dragon-fly of a creature, graceful and alien; and Lucy was surprised to find that she was capable of so unbroken a quiet.

As they came up on to the road at last she said: "Have you any money, Miss Pym?"

"No," said Lucy, stopping in dismay.

"Neither have I. But it is all right. Miss Nevill will finance us."

"Who is Miss Nevill?"

"The lady who runs the tea-house."

"That is rather unusual, isn't it?"

"Not with me. I am always forgetting my money. But Miss Nevill is charming. Do not feel bad about it, dear Miss Pym, I am in good standing in the village, you will see."

The village was all that Desterro had claimed for it; and so was Miss Nevill. So, indeed, was The Teapot. It was one of those tea-shops so much despised by the bread-and-cheese-and-beer school, and so gladly welcomed by a generation of tea-drinkers who remember the fly-blown rooms behind village bakers' shops, the primitive buns with currants like dead insects, the cracked and ill-washed cups, and the black evil tea.

It had all the properties stigmatised by the

literary frequenters of village inns: the Indian-tree-pattern china, the dark oak tables, the linen curtains in a Jacobean design, the herbaceous bouquets in unglazed brown jugs; yes, even the arts and crafts in the window. But to Lucy, who in the Alan period had had her share of undusted "snugs," it was quite frankly charming. There was a rich scent of spiced cakes straight from the oven; there was, as well as the long window on the street, a further window that gave on a garden bright with colour; there was peace, and coolness, and welcome.

Miss Nevill, a large lady in a chintz apron, received Desterro as an old and valued acquaintance, and asked if she were "playing hookey, as you say on your side of the Atlantic." The Nut Tart ignored this identification with the back streets of Brooklyn. "This is Miss Pym, who writes books about psychology and is our guest at Leys," she said, politely introducing Lucy. "I have told her that here one can drink real coffee, and be in general civilised. We have no money at all, either of us, but we will have a great deal to eat and pay you back later."

This appeared to Miss Nevill to be quite a

normal proposition, and she went away to the kitchen to get the coffee with neither surprise nor demur. The place was empty at this hour of the morning, and Lucy wandered round inspecting the old prints and the new crafts—she was pleased to observe that Miss Nevill drew the line at Brummagem brass door-knockers even if there were raffia mats—and then sat down with Desterro at the table looking on to the village street. Before their coffee arrived, they were joined by a middle-aged couple, husband and wife, who drove up in a car as if they were searching for the place. The car was the kind that a provincial doctor might use; low in petrol consumption and in its third or fourth year of wear. But the woman who came round from the further seat with a laughing remark to her husband was not a typical doctor's wife. She was grey, and slim, with long legs and narrow feet in good shoes. Lucy watched her with pleasure. It was not often nowadays that one saw good bones; smartness had taken the place of breeding.

"In *my* country," said Desterro, looking with a considering eye at the woman and with a contemptuous eye on the car, "that woman would have a chauffeur *and a foot-man*."

It was not often, moreover, that one saw a middle-aged husband and wife so pleased with each other, Lucy thought, as she watched them come in. They had a holiday air. They came in and looked about them expectantly, questioningly.

"Yes, this is it," the woman said. "That is the window on the garden that she talks about, and there is the print of Old London Bridge."

They moved about looking at things, quietly, unself-consciously, and then took the table at the other window. Lucy was relieved to see that the man was the mate she would have chosen for such a woman; a little saturnine, perhaps, more self-absorbed than the woman; but quite admirable. He reminded her of someone, but she could not think of whom; someone whom she admired. The eyebrows, it was. Dark level brush-marks low over the eyes. His suit was very old, she noticed; well-pressed and kept, but with that much-cleaned air that overtakes a garment in its old age. The woman's suit, a tweed, was frankly shabby, and her stockings were darned—very neatly darned—at the heels. Her hands, too, looked as if they were accustomed to household tasks, and her fine grey hair was washed at home and unwaved. What had she got to look so happy about, this woman who struggled with straitened means? Was it just being on holiday with a husband she loved? Was it that that gave her grey luminous eyes their almost childlike happiness?

Miss Nevill came in with the coffee and a large plate of spiced cakes shining with newness and crisp at the edges. Lucy decided to forget her weight just this once and enjoy herself. This was a decision she made with deplorable frequency.

As she poured the coffee she heard the man say: "Good morning. We have come all the way from the West Country to taste your griddle cakes. Do you think you could make us some, or are you too busy at this hour of the morning?"

"If you are too busy it doesn't matter," said the woman with the hard-worked hands. "We shall have some of the cakes that smell so good."

But Miss Nevill would not be a minute in preparing the griddle cakes. She had no batter standing, she said, so the griddle cakes would not be as wonderful as when the batter was allowed to stand; but she was not often asked for them in summer time.

"No, I expect not. But our daughter at Leys has talked so often of them, and this may be our only chance of tasting them." The woman smiled, half it seemed at the thought of her daughter, half at their own childish desire.

So they were College parents.

Whose? Lucy wondered, watching them over the rim of her coffee cup.

Beau's, perhaps. Oh, no; Beau was rich, of course. Then whose?

She wouldn't mind giving them to Dakers, but there were objections. That tow-head could not be sired by that dark grave man; nor could that adult and intelligent woman have given birth to the through-other piece of nonsense that was Dakers.

And then, quite suddenly, she knew whose eyebrows those were.

Mary Innes's.

They were Mary Innes's parents. And in some odd way they explained Mary Innes. Her gravity; her air of belonging to a century other than this one; her not finding life very amusing. To have standards to live up to, but to have little money to live up to them with, was not a happy combination for a girl burdened with the need to make a success of her training.

Into the silence that had succeeded Miss Nevill's departure, Lucy heard her own voice saying, "Forgive me, but is your name Innes?"

They turned to her, puzzled for a moment; then the woman smiled. "Yes," she said. "Have we met somewhere?"

"No," said poor Lucy, growing a little pink as she always did when her impulsiveness had led her into an unexpected situation. "But I recognised your husband's eyebrows."

"My *eyebrows*," said Mr Innes.

But his wife, quicker-witted, laughed. "Of course," she said. "Mary! Are you from Leys, then? Do you know Mary?" Her face lit and her voice sang as she said it. Do you know Mary? Was it because she was going to see her daughter that she was happy today?

Lucy explained who she was, and introduced Desterro, who was pleased to find that this charming couple knew all about her. "There is very little we don't know about Leys," Mrs Innes said, "even if we have never seen the place."

"Not seen it? Won't you come over and have your coffee with us, by the way?"

"It was too far for us to inspect it before Mary went there. So we decided that we would wait until her training was finished and then come to the Demonstration." Lucy deduced that if fares had not been a problem, Mary Innes's mother would not have had to wait these years before seeing Leys; she would have come if only so that she could picture her daughter in her setting.

"But you are going there now, surely?"

"No. Oddly enough, we are not. We are on our way to Larborough, where my husband—he's a doctor—has to attend a meeting. We *could* go to Leys, of course, but it is the week of the Final Examinations, and it would only distract Mary to have her parents descending suddenly on her for no reason. It is a little difficult to pass by when we are so near, but we have waited so long that we can wait another ten days or so. What we couldn't resist was turning off the main West road as far as Bidlington. We didn't expect to run into any College people at this hour of the morning, especially in Examination Week, and we did want to see the place that Mary had talked so much about."

"We knew that we shouldn't have time on Demonstration Day," Dr Innes said. "There will be so much to see then. A surprisingly varied training, isn't it?"

Lucy agreed, and described her first impression of the staffroom with its varying worlds.

"Yes. We were a little puzzled when Mary chose that for her career—she had never shown any great interest in games, and I had thoughts that she might take a medical training—but she said she wanted a career with a great many facets; and she seems to have found it!"

Lucy remembered the concentration of purpose in those level brows; she had been right in her face-reading; if Mary Innes had an ambition it would not lightly be given up. Really, eyebrows were the most *helpful* things. If psychology ever went out of fashion she would write a book about face-reading. Under another name, of course. Face-reading was not well seen among the intelligentsia.

"She is very beautiful, your daughter," said

Desterro unexpectedly. She polished off a large mouthful of spice cake, and then, feeling the surprise in their silence, looked up at them. "Is it not a proper thing in England to compliment parents on their daughter's looks?"

"Oh, yes," Mrs Innes said hastily, "it is not that, it is just that we had not thought of Mary as beautiful. She is nice to look at, of course; at least we think so, but then parents are apt to be fatuous about an only daughter. She—"

"When I came first to this place," Desterro said, reaching out for another cake from the plate (how *did* she keep that figure!), "it was raining, and all the dirty leaves were hanging down from the trees like dead bats and dripping on everyone, and everyone was rushing round College and saying: 'Oh *darling*, how *are* you? Did you have nice hols? Darling, you won't believe it but I left my new hockey stick on *Crewe platform!*' And then I saw a girl who was *not* running about and *not* talking, and who looked a little like my great-grandmother's grandmother who is in the dining-room at the house of my grandmother's great-nephew, so I said: 'It is not after all a barbarism. If it were as it seems to be that girl would not be here. I shall stay.' Is there more coffee, Miss Pym, please? She is not only beautiful, your daughter, she is the only beautiful person at Leys."

"What about Beau Nash?" asked Lucy loyally.

"In England at Christmas time—*very* little milk, Miss Pym, please—the magazines go all gay and give away bright pretty pictures that one can frame and hang above the kitchen mantelpiece to make glad the hearts of the cook and her friends. Very shiny, they are, with—"

"Now that," said Mrs Innes, "is sheer libel! Beau is lovely, quite lovely, and you know it. I forgot that you would know Beau, too," she turned to Lucy, "that you would know them all, in fact. Beau is the only one we know because she came to us for the holidays once; at Easter time when the West is kinder than the rest of England; and Mary went to them once for some weeks in the summer. We admired Beau so much." She looked to her husband for confirmation; he had been too withdrawn.

Dr Innes roused himself—he had the wrung-out look of the overworked G.P.

when he sank into repose—and the saturnine face took on a boyish and faintly malicious, if tender, amusement. "It was very
odd to see our competent and self-reliant
Mary being looked after," he said.

Mrs Innes evidently felt that this was not
the contribution she had been looking for,
but decided to make the best of it. "Perhaps," she said, as if thinking of it for the
first time, "we have always taken Mary's
self-reliance so much for granted that she
finds it pleasant to be looked after." And to
Miss Pym: "It is because they are comple-
mentary, I think, that they are such great
friends. I am glad about it because we like
Beau so much, and because Mary has
never made intimate friends easily."

"It is a very strenuous training, isn't it?" Dr
Innes said. "I sometimes look at my daughter's notebooks and wonder why they
bother with stuff that even a doctor forgets
as soon as he leaves medical school."

"The cross-section of the villi," remembered Lucy.

"Yes; that sort of thing. You seem to have
picked up a remarkable amount of physical
lore in four days."

The crumpets came, and even without the

ritual standing of the batter they were worth coming even from the West Country for, supposing that had been true. It was a happy party. Indeed, Lucy felt that the whole room was soaked in happiness; that happiness bathed it like a reflexion from the sunlight outside. Even the doctor's tired face looked content and relaxed. As for Mrs Innes, Lucy had rarely seen such happiness on the face of a woman; merely being in this room that her daughter had used so often was, it seemed, a sort of communion with her, and in a few days' time she would see her in the flesh and share her achievement.

If I had gone back to London, Lucy thought, I would have had no share in this. What would I be doing? Eleven o'clock. Going for a walk in the Park, and deciding how to get out of being guest of honour at some literary dinner. Instead I have this. And all because Dr Knight wanted to go to a medical conference tomorrow. No, because once long ago Henrietta stood up for me at school. It was odd to think that this sun-lit moment in an English June began to take shape thirty years ago in a dark crowded school cloakroom filled with little girls putting on their goloshes. What were first causes, anyhow?

"This has been *very* pleasant," said Mrs Innes, as they stood once more in the village street. "And it is nice to think that we shall meet again so soon. You will still be at Leys when the Demonstration comes off, won't you?"

"I hope so," Lucy said, and wondered if she could cadge a bed from Henrietta for so long.

"And you have both promised, solemnly and on your word of honour, not to tell anyone that you saw us today," Dr Innes said.

"We have," they said, waiting to see their new friends get into their car.

"Do you think I can turn the car in one swoop without hitting the Post Office?" Dr Innes said, consideringly.

"I should hate to make any more Bidlington martyrs," his wife said. "A tiresome breed. On the other hand, what is this life without some risk?"

So Dr Innes encouraged his engine and swung into this risky evolution. The hub of his off front wheel left a faint smudge on the Post Office's virgin white-wash.

"Gervase Innes, his mark," said Mrs Innes,

and waved her hand to them. "Till Demonstration Day, and pray for fine weather for it! Au revoir!"

They watched the car grow small up the village street, and turned towards the field-path and Leys.

"*Nice* people," Desterro said.

"Charming. Odd to think that we should never have met them if you had not had a craving for good coffee this morning."

"That is the kind of English, let me tell you in confidence, Miss Pym, that make every other nation on earth sick with envy. So quiet, so well-bred, so good to look at. They are poor, too, did you notice? Her blouse is quite washed-out. It used to be blue, the blouse; you could see when she leaned forward and her collar lifted a little. It is wrong that they should be so poor, people like that."

"It must have cost her a lot not to see her daughter when she was so near," Lucy said reflectively.

"Ah, but she has character, that woman. She was right not to come. None of the Seniors has one little particle of interest to spare this week. Take away even one little particle, and *woops!* the whole thing comes crashing down." She plucked an ox-eyed daisy from the bank by the bridge and gave the first giggle Lucy had ever heard from her. "I wonder how my colleagues are getting on with their one-leg-over-the-line puzzles."

Lucy was wondering how she herself would appear in Mary Innes's Sunday letter home. "It will be amusing," Mrs Innes had said, "to get back home and read all about you in Mary's Sunday letter. Something to do with relativity. Like coming back the previous night."

"It was strange that Mary Innes should have reminded you of someone in a portrait," she said to Desterro. "That is how she seemed to me, too."

"Ah yes, my great-grandmother's grandmother." Desterro dropped the daisy on to the surface of the water and watched the stream bear it down under the bridge and away out of sight. "I did not say it to the nice Inneses, but my great-grandmother's grandmother was a little unpopular with her generation."

"Oh? Shy, perhaps. What we call nowadays an inferiority complex."

"I would not know about that. Her husband died too conveniently. It is always sad for a woman when her husband dies too conveniently."

"You mean that she murdered him!" Lucy said, standing stock-still in the summer landscape, appalled.

"Oh, no. There was no *scandal*." Desterro sounded reproving. "It was just that her husband died too conveniently. He drank too much, and was a great gambler, and *not* very attractive. And there was a loose tread at the top of the stairs. A long flight of stairs. And he stepped on it one day when he was drunk. That was all."

"And did she marry again?" Lucy asked, having absorbed this information.

"Oh, no. She was not in love with anyone else. She had her son to bring up, and the estates were safe for him now that there was no one to gamble them away. She was a very good estate manager. That is where my grandmother got her talent from. When my grandmother came out from England to marry my grandfather she had never been further from her own county than Charles Street, West One; and in six months she was running the estate." Desterro sighed with admiration. "They are wonderful the English."

Chapter 8

Miss Pym was invigilating at the Senior Pathology Final, so as to give Miss Lux more time for the correction and marking of previous papers, when Henrietta's meek little secretary tiptoed in and laid the day's letters reverently on the desk in front of her. Miss Pym had been frowning over a copy of the examination paper, and thinking how badly words like *arthritis gonorrhoica* and *suppurative tenosynovitis* went with the clean air of a summer morning after breakfast. *Emphysema* was not so bad; it might be the gardener's name for a flower. A sort of columbine. And *kyphosis* she could picture as something in the dahlia line. *Myelitis* would be a small creeping plant, very blue, with a tendency to turn pink if not watched. And *tabes dorsalis* was obviously an exotic affair of the tiger lily persuasion, expensive and very faintly obscene.

Chorea. Sclerosis. Pes Varus.

Dear goodness. Did those young things know all that? Differentiate the treatment of something-or-other according to whether it is (a) congenital (b) traumatic (c) hysterical. Well, well. How had she ever erred so far as to feel patronizing about these young creatures?

She looked down from her dais with affection on them; all writing away for dear life. The faces were sober but not on the whole anxious. Only Rouse looked worried, and Lucy decided that her face looked better worried than smug, and withheld her sympathy. Dakers was ploughing steadily over the paper with her tongue protruding and an automatic sigh as she came to the end of each line and began a new one. Beau was confident and detached as if she were writing invitations; doubt was something that had never entered her life; neither her present standing nor her future life was in jeopardy. Stewart's face under the bright red hair was pale, but a faint smile played around her mouth; Stewart's future, too, was assured; she was going to the Cordwainers School, going home to Scotland bringing her sheaves with her, and Lucy was going to the party she was giving in her room on Saturday night to celebrate. ("We don't ask Staff to individual parties, but since you are not quite Staff you could rank as just a friend.") The Four Disciples, spread across the front row, cast each other communal and encouraging glances now and then; this was their own particular subject and obviously what they did not know about it was not worth mentioning; Manchester was going to get its money's worth. Innes, by the window, lifted her head every now and then to look out at the garden, as if seeking refreshment; that it was not inspiration she sought was apparent from her unhurried progress through the questions; she turned to the garden for some spiritual comfort; it was as if she said: "Ah yes, you are still there, Beauty; there is a world outside this lecture-room." Innes was beginning to look as if College might be too much with her. That tired line from nostril to mouth was still there.

Lucy picked up the paper-knife from Miss Lux's neat desk, and considered her post. Three bills, which she need not disturb the holy hush by opening. A receipt. An Annual Report. A large, square, deep-blue, and very stiff and expensive envelope with

MILLICENT CRAYE embossed in scarlet across the flap (really there was no end to the self-advertising instinct in actresses) which would be five lines of thanks with a broad nib and outsize capitals for her contribution to the Benevolent Fund. That left only Mrs Montmorency. So into Mrs Mont-morency she inserted the paper-knife.

Maddam (wrote Mrs Montmorency),
I as done as you sed an sent the urgent by passel post. Registered. Fred put it into Wigmore Street on is way to work receit enclosed I as packed the blue and the blouses also underclose as per in-struxions your pink nitie not having come back from the laundry I as put in the hedge instead hopping this will be all rite.
Maddam, please dont think that I pre-soom but this is a good thing. It is no life for a woman writin books and not havin no young company please dont think I presoom but I as your welfare at heart you ben one of the nicest ladies I ever worked for Fred says the same. A nice lady like that he says when look at the

things thats around not write it isnt
please dont think I presoom
                              yrs respectfully
                         Mrs Montmorency.
    P.S. Wire brush in toe of swede shoe

Lucy spent the next fifteen minutes being
touched by Mrs Montmorency's concern for
her, being furious with the laundry, and
wondering why she paid education rates. It
wasn't public schools for everyone that was
needed but a great many elementary school
classes of not more than a dozen, where the
future Mrs Montmorencys could be ade-
quately taken care of in the matter of the
Three Rs. Old McLean, their jobbing gardener at home, had left school when he was
twelve, but he could write as good a letter
as any University acquaintance of hers; and
why? Because he came from a small village
school with small classes and a good
schoolmaster.

And of course because he lived in an age
when the Three Rs were more important
than Free Milk. They made him literate and
left the rest to him. He lived on white-flour
scones and stewed tea and died hale and
hearty at the age of ninety-two.

She was roused from her musings by Miss Rouse. There was a new expression on Miss Rouse's face, and Lucy didn't like the new expression at all. She had seen Miss Rouse look despairing, smarmy, smug, and worried, but till now she had never seen her look furtive.

Why should she be looking furtive?

She watched her for a moment or two, curiously.

Rouse looked up and caught her gaze and looked quickly away again. Her furtive expression had gone; what had taken its place was one labelled Consciously Carefree. Lucy knew all about that expression. She had not been Form Mistress of the Lower Fourth for nothing. Every eater of illicit sweets wore that expression. So did those who were doing their arithmetic in French lesson.

So did those who were cheating at an examination.

What was it Henrietta had said? "She finds written work difficult."

So.

Emphysema and all those flowery sounding things were too much for Miss Rouse, and so she had provided some aids to memory. The question was what kind of aids and where were they? Not on her knee. The desks were open in front, so that a lap was no safe billet for a crib. And one could hardly write enough pathology on one's fingernails to be of much help; fingernails were useful only for formula. The obvious solution would be the notes up the sleeve, with or without an arrangement of elastic, but these girls had no sleeves below the elbow. Then, what? Where? Or was it that she was just having glimpses of O'Donnell's paper in front of her? Or Thomas's to her right?

Lucy went back to her letters for a moment or two, and waited. All school-mistresses know this gambit. She looked up casually at the Seniors in general and again went back to her letters. When next she looked up it was straight at Rouse. Rouse's head was low over her paper and in her left hand she held a handkerchief. Now even on a handkerchief it is not possible to write anything that is helpful on so large a subject as pathology, nor is it an easy affair to manipulate; on the other hand, handkerchiefs were not common objects at Leys, and certainly no one else was clutching one and dabbing a nose occasionally with it. Lucy decided that whatever sources of information Rouse had lay in her left hand. Her desk was at the back on the window side, so that the wall was to her left; whatever she did with her left hand was not overlooked by anyone.

Well, thought Lucy, what does A do?

Walk down the room and demand the handkerchief and find that it is a square piece of white linen, nine inches by nine inches, with the owner's initials properly marked in one corner, and as candid as a good laundry can make it?

Demand the handkerchief and unearth a scandal that will blast the Senior set like a hurricane at their least stable moment?

See that Rouse gets no chance to use her source of information, and say nothing?

The last was certainly the most sensible. She couldn't have obtained very much aid from anything so far; it would be doing no injustice to anyone to make her a present of that small amount.

Lucy left the desk and strolled down the room to the back, where she stood leaning against the wall, Thomas to her right and Rouse to her left. Thomas stopped writing for a moment and looked up at her with a quick smile. But Rouse did not look up. And Lucy watched the hot blood dye her sandy neck a dull red. And presently she put away the handkerchief—and whatever else that hand contained—in her tunic pocket.

Well, she had foiled the machinations of the evil-intended, but she could feel no satisfaction about it. For the first time it occurred to her that what was very naughty and deplorable in the fourth form was quite sickening in a Senior Final. She was glad that it was Rouse and not anyone else. Presently she strolled back to her desk on the dais, and as far as she could see Rouse made no further effort to obtain help with her paper. On the contrary, she was very obviously in deep waters. And Lucy was infuriated to find herself feeling sorry for her. Yes, *sorry*. Sorry for *Rouse*. After all, the girl had worked. Worked like a madman, if all reports were true. It was not as if she had been taking an easy way out to save herself effort. It was just that she found acquiring theoretical knowledge difficult almost to the point of impossibility, and had succumbed to temptation in her desperation.

This point of view made Lucy feel much better about it, and she spent the rest of her

invigilating time speculating quite undis-
tressedly about the nature of the crib. She
would look again at the examination paper,
and consider the enormous range of material it covered, and wonder how Rouse had
devised anything at once helpful and invisible. She longed to ask her.

The most likely explanation was that there
were two or three particular subjects that
Rouse was afraid of, and that help with
them was scribbled on a piece of paper.

Innes was the first to shuffle the written
sheets together and slip the waiting clip
over the upper edge. She read through the
pages, making a correction now and then,
laid the sheaf down on her desk, sat for a
few relaxed moments taking in the beauty
of the garden, and then rose quietly and
came forward to leave her work on the desk
in front of Miss Pym.

"Oh, *catastrophe!*" wailed Dakers; "is
somebody *finished?* And I have a whole
question and a half to do yet!"

"Hush, Miss Dakers," said Lucy, as in duty
bound.

Dakers favoured her with a radiant smile,
and went back to her steady plodding.

Stewart and Beau Nash followed Innes

very shortly; and presently the pile of papers in front of Miss Pym began to grow. With five minutes of the allotted time still to go there were only three students left in the examination room: the little dark Welsh Thomas, who presumably slept too much to be a good "study"; the imperturbable Dakers still plodding steadily; and a flushed and unhappy Rouse, who was plainly making heavy weather of it. With two minutes still to go there was only Rouse; she was looking confused and desperate; making hasty little excursions back and fore through her papers, deleting, amending, and adding.

The distant yelling of the bell put an end to her indecisions and to her chances; whatever she had done must now abide. She shoved her papers hastily together, aware that the bell meant an instant appearance in the gymnasium and that Fröken would not consider the ordeal of an examination paper any excuse for being late, and brought them up to Lucy at the double. Lucy had expected her to avoid her eye, or otherwise to display symptoms of awkwardness or self-consciousness. But Rouse surprised her by a frank smile and a still franker remark.

"Whoo!" said Rouse, blowing her breath

out expressively, "that was a horror." And she ran out to join the rest of her set.

Lucy opened the much-scored offering and looked at it with compunction. She had been imagining things. Rouse had not been cheating after all. Or at least not systematically. That furtive look might have been the guilt of inadequacy, now she came to think of it; or perhaps, at the worst, a hope of hints from her neighbour's paper. And that flush that had dyed her neck was due to her awareness of being suspected; Lucy could remember very well even yet times at school when the very knowledge that her innocent act was capable of sinister interpretation was enough to make her face burn with false guilt. Really, she owed Rouse an apology. She would find some way of making it up to her.

She stacked the papers neatly together, put them in alphabetical order from sheer force of habit, checked their number, and carried them upstairs to Miss Lux's room, glad that it would not be her chore to correct them. There was no one in the room, so she left them on the desk and stood for a moment wondering what to do with the hour before lunch. She toyed with the thought of watching the gymnastics, but decided that she must not allow the performance to become familiar, and consequently devoid of wonder, before Demonstration Day. Having induced Henrietta to keep her until then—Henrietta had not required much inducement, it is true—she was not going to mar her own pleasure in the day by too many tastings beforehand. She went downstairs, lingering by the tall window on the landing—how well eighteenth-century architects had understood how to build houses; nowadays landings were not things to linger on, but breakneck little corners lit, if at all, by a small circular light like a ship's port-hole—and from there, beyond the courtyard and the opposite wing she could see the elms of the field that led to the stream. She would go and look at the buttercups for a little. There was no better way of wasting a summer hour than staring at a field of buttercups. So down she went, and along the wing, and so out to the covered path to the gymnasium, for beyond the gymnasium were the buttercups.

As she went down the covered way her eye caught a spot of colour in the grass that bordered the path. At first she took it for a flower petal and was going to ignore it, when she noticed that it was square, and certainly not a petal. She turned back and picked it up. It was a tiny address-book in faded red leather. It looked as if it had formed part of the fittings of a handbag; an old-fashioned handbag probably since one did not see leather nor workmanship like that nowadays. Idly, with her thoughts on the femininity of that vanished bag with its miniature fittings—there would of course have been a little tube of scent, and a gold pencil, and one of those ivory tablets to scribble engagements on—she opened it, and read, on a page crowded with writing in a tiny script: "Path. anat. changes as in traumatic. Fibrin in synov. memb. Tissues contr. by fibr. and fold of caps. joined to bone. Anchylosis. Fever."

It meant nothing to Lucy as information but its meaning was obvious. She turned the pages, finding nearly all of them crowded with the same succinct information. Even the X page—devoted by the keepers of address-books to measurements for new curtains or that good story that would do for the W.R.I. speech next Tuesday—even the X page had cryptic remarks about rays. What bowled Lucy over was the comprehensiveness of it; the premeditation. This was no product of a last-minute panic; it was a cold-blooded insurance against failure. By the neatness and method shown in the compiling, it looked as though the entries had been made as each subject was studied. Had the notebook been of a normal size, in fact, it would have been nothing more than a legitimate précis of a subject. But no one making a précis would have chosen a book not much larger than a good-sized postage stamp when an equally portable but normal-sized notebook could be had for a few pence. The use of a book so tiny that a mapping pen had been necessary in order to make the entries legible could have only one explanation.

Lucy knew very well what had happened. Rouse had pulled out her handkerchief as she ran. She had never before carried the little book in a pocket, and her mind was divided urgently between the bad paper she had done and the fear of being late for gymnastics, so there was no care in the pulling out of the handkerchief. And so the little book dropped on to the grass at the edge of the path.

She walked on beyond the gymnasium

and through the five-barred gate into the field, but she had no eye for the buttercups. She walked on slowly down the field to the coolness under the willows and the quiet green water. She hung over the rail of the bridge watching the weeds trail and the occasional fish dart, and thought about Rouse. There was no name on the flyleaf, nor as far as she could see any means of identification in the book itself. Most schools taught script as well as current form in writing nowadays; and script was much less easily recognisable than current writing. A handwriting expert would no doubt be easily able to trace the author, but to what end? There was no evidence that the book had been used for any illegitimate purpose; no evidence even that it had been compiled with any sinister intent—although the presumption was strong. If she handed it over to Henrietta as lost property what would happen? No one would claim it, and Henrietta would be faced with the fact that one of her Seniors had prepared a précis that could be conveniently palmed at an examination.

If nothing was ever said about the book, then Rouse's punishment would be a perpetual and lifelong doubt as to what had become of it. Lucy felt that such a punishment fitted the crime admirably. She thumbed the tiny India-paper pages once more, wondered again what Edwardian elegancy had given it birth, and leaning over, dropped it into the water.

As she walked back to the house she wondered how Rouse had managed the other Final Examinations. Pathology could be no less easy to memorise than Kinesiology or any of the other obscurities studied by the budding P.T.I. How had Rouse, the difficult "study," managed with these? Was the little red leather book only one of five or six? Did one invest in a mapping pen for one subject only? One *could*, she supposed, buy very tiny address-books if one searched long enough; though not perhaps so fine or so tiny as the little red one. It may have been the possession of the little red one which first put the thought of insurance against failure into Rouse's mind.

She remembered that the result of the previous examinations would be exhibited on the letter-board by the students' entrance, so instead of walking round to the front of the house as she had meant to she turned in at the quadrangle door. There were several

Junior lists pinned to the green baize, and three Senior lists. Lucy read them with interest.

FINAL PHYSIOLOGY

Honours
  Mary Innes   93

First Class
  Wilhelmina Hasselt   87
  Pamela Nash   86
  Sheena Stewart   82
  Pauline Lucas   79
  Janet Gage   79
  Barbara Rouse   77

Second Class
  Dorothy Littlejohn   74
  Beatrice Appleyard   71
  Joan Dakers   69
  Eileen O'Donnell   68
  Margaret Campbell   67
  Ruth Waymark   66
  Lilian Mathews   65

and the rest, below that mark, mere Passes.

Well, Rouse had scraped into a First by two marks, it seemed.

Lucy turned to the next list.

FINAL MEDICALS

First Class

Pauline Lucas	89
Pamela Nash	89
Mary Innes	89
Dorothy Littlejohn	87
Ruth Waymark	85
Wilhelmina Hasselt	82
Sheena Stewart	80
Lilian Mathews	79
Barbara Rouse	79

Second Class

Jenny Burton	73
Janet Gage	72
Eileen O'Donnell	71
Joan Dakers	69

and the rest mere Passes.

And again Rouse managed to scrape a First.

FINAL KINESIOLOGY

Honours

Mary Innes	96

First Class

Pauline Lucas	89

Pamela Nash	88
Sheena Stewart	87
Wilhelmina Hasselt	85
Ruth Waymark	80
Janet Gage	79
Joan Dakers	78
Barbara Rouse	78

Another First! Three Firsts out of three tries. The girl who found written work so difficult? There was surely a strong case for the existence of more little notebooks?

Oh, well; this being Friday, tomorrow would see the end of examinations and it was not likely that Rouse would, after this morning's experience, bring any extraneous help to the test tomorrow morning. The little book prepared for tomorrow, if it existed, would be still-born.

While she mused over the lists (it was nice to see that Dakers had managed at least one First) Miss Lux arrived with the results of yesterday's Final.

"Thank you for bringing up the Path. papers," she said. "And thank you for invigilating. It helped me to get these done."

She thumbed the drawing-pin into the board and stood back to look at the list.

FINAL HYGIENE

Honours
Mary Innes	91

First Class
Pamela Nash	88
Wilhelmina Hasselt	87
Sheena Stewart	86
Pauline Lucas	81
Barbara Rouse	81

"Barbara Rouse, eighty-one," Lucy said, before she thought.

"Yes, surprising, isn't it?" Miss Lux said placidly. "But she works like a black. She is so brilliant in her physical work that I think it maddens her to be far down any list."

"Innes seems to make a habit of heading the lists."

"Oh, Innes is wasted here."

"Why? The more intelligence one brings to a profession the better surely?"

"Yes, but with an intelligence like Innes's one could head much more thrilling lists than these. It's a waste."

"I somehow don't think that Rouse will get eighty-one in today's paper," Lucy said, as they moved away from the board.

"Why? Was she in difficulties?"

"Bogged down," said Lucy; and hoped that she did not sound too pleased. "*What* a life it is," she added, as the five-minute bell rang, and the dripping Seniors came running in from the gymnasium, ripping off their tunics as they tore into the bathrooms for a shower before the gong went. "When you think of the leisurely way we acquired knowledge. At university, I mean. If we sat a Final Examination, the rest of the day would almost certainly be our own to recover in. But these young creatures do it as part of their time-table."

From the bathrooms came cursing and chaos. "Oh, Donnie, you *swine*, that was *my* shower!" "Mark, you brute, get off my foot!" "Oh, no, you don't, my girl; these are *my* tights!" "God, look at my blisters!" "Kick over my shoe, Greengage, the floor's sopping." "*Must* you shoot the cold water round like that, you chump!"

"They like it, you know," Lux said. "In their heart they like the rush and the overwork. It makes them feel important. Very few of them will ever have any legitimate reason for feeling important, and so it is comforting for them to have the image of it at least."

"Cynic," said Lucy.

"No, psychologist." She inclined her head towards the row as they moved away. "It sounds like a free fight, doesn't it? Everyone sounds desperate and furious. But it is all play-acting. In five minutes they will be sitting like good children in the dining-room with not a hair out of place."

And so they were. When the Staff filed in to the top table five minutes later, there were the scramblers of the bathroom, standing dutifully behind their chairs, calm, and combed, and neat, their interest already absorbed by the thought of food. Truly, they *were* children. Whatever heartbreaks they suffered would be forgotten in tomorrow's toy. It was absurd to think of them as harassed adults, trembling on the precipice edge of breakdown. They were volatile children; their griefs were loud, and vocal, and transient. For five days now, ever since The Nut Tart had been so knowing under the cedar tree last Saturday afternoon, she had looked for some hint of abnormality, of aberration, of lack of control, and what had she found? One very normal and highly controlled piece of dishonesty; unremarkable except for its neatness.

"Isn't it nice," Henrietta said, helping out something that looked like cheese-and-vegetable pie, "I've got a post in Wales for little Miss Thomas. Near Aberystwyth. I am so delighted."

"A very soporific atmosphere, Wales," Madame Lefevre said, consideringly; blasting Henrietta's whole conception with five gentle words.

"Yes," said Miss Lux, "who is going to keep her awake?"

"It's not who is going to *keep* her awake, it's who is going to wake her in the first place," Wragg said, with a greedy eye on the pie. Wragg was still near enough her College days to be possessed of a large hunger and no gastronomic judgment.

"Wales is her native atmosphere," Henrietta said, repressive, "and I have no doubt she will know how to deal with it. In any case she is not likely to have any great success *outside* Wales; the Welsh are extraordinarily provincial, using the word in its literal sense. I have noticed before how they gravitated back to their own province. It is as well for them to go there in the first place if the chance offers. And luckily, in this case, it has offered very conveniently. The junior gymnast of three. That will suit Miss Thomas very nicely. She has no great initiative, I'm afraid."

"Is Thomas's the only new post?" Wragg asked, falling on the pie.

"No, there was one that I wanted to discuss with you."

Aha, thought Lucy, here comes Arlinghurst at last.

"Ling Abbey wants someone to be wholly responsible for the younger children, and to take dancing as well all through the school. That is to say, the dancing would have to be of a high standard. I wanted to give the post to Miss Dakers—she is very good with small children—but I wanted to know what you thought of her dancing, Marie."

"She is a cow," said Madame.

"She *is* very good with little ones, though," Wragg said.

"A *heavy* cow," said Madame.

"It isn't her personal performance that is important," Henrietta said. "It is her power to inspire performance in others. Does she understand the subject sufficiently, that is the point?"

"Oh, she knows the difference between three-four time and four-four, certainly."

"I saw Dakers teaching the babies at West

Larborough their dances for their do last Christmas," Wragg said, "and she was wonderful. I was there to crit. her, and I was so fascinated I forgot to make any notes at all. I think she would be just right for that post."

"Well, Marie."

"I can't imagine why anyone bothers," Madame said. "The dancing at Ling Abbey is quite frightful anyhow."

This Pilatian washing of hands, in spite of its negative quality, seemed positive enough to all concerned. It was apparent that Dakers was going to Ling Abbey. And since Ling Abbey was a good place to be going to—if one had to be going to a school—Lucy was glad for her. She glanced down the room to where, even above this babel, Dakers' high voice could be heard italicising her opinion of the Pathology paper. "I said that a joint went *gummy*, my dear, and I'm certain that's not the *technical* word."

"Shall I warn them both, Miss Hodge?" Wragg asked, later.

(Warn?)

"No, just Miss Thomas today, I think. I shall tell Miss Dakers tomorrow. It is better to spread the excitement out."

As the Staff rose from their table and filed

out, Wragg turned to the politely standing and temporarily silent students and said: "Miss Hodge will see Miss Thomas in her office when luncheon is over."

This was apparently a ritual pronouncement, for the buzz broke out almost before the Staff had reached the door. "A post, Tommy!" "Congrats., Tommy." "Hoorah, old Thomas." "Up the Welsh!" "Hope it's a thousand a year, Tom." "Iss nott thatt the lucky thing, now!" "Cheers, Tommy!"

And still no one had mentioned Arlinghurst.

Chapter 9

When Lucy first heard Arlinghurst mentioned it was not by any of the Staff but by
the students themselves. She had spent
Saturday afternoon with Fröken and her
mother, helping to finish the Swedish folk
costumes which the Juniors would wear for
some of the country dances at the Demonstration. It was a lovely day and they had
taken the piles of bright primitive colour to
the furthest corner of the garden, where they
could sit and look over the English countryside. Both cricket and tennis matches were
"away" this week, so the garden was deserted, and no toiling figures marred the virgin green of the field beyond the stream.
They had sewed in great beatitude, and Fru
Gustavsen seemed to have reported well of
Lucy to her daughter, for Fröken's reticence
had largely vanished, and Lucy was delighted to find that a young woman who had
always reminded her of sunlight on snow

was the possessor of a rich warm chuckle
and a sense of humour to match. (It is true
that Lucy's sewing considerably shook Fru
Gustavsen's faith in her, but much must be
forgiven the English.) Fru Gustavsen had
gone back to the subject of food, and held
forth at great length on the virtues of something called "frikadellar"; which, it appeared,
was a kind of mince. Lucy (whose cooking
consisted of chopping up a few tomatoes in
a pan at the last moment, adding whatever
was to be cooked, and pouring some cream
over the lot) thought it a very lengthy and
complicated affair, and decided to have
nothing to do with it.

"Are you doing anything tonight?" Fröken
had asked. "My mother and I are going into
Larborough to the theatre. She has not yet
seen an English company. We would be delighted if you would care to come with us."

Lucy explained that tonight she was going
to a party in Stewart's room to celebrate her
post. "I understand that Staff don't usually
go, but I am not real Staff."

Fröken slid an eye round at her and said:
"You ought to be. You are very good for
them."

That medicinal phrase again. As if she were a prescription.

"How?"

"Oh, in ways too subtle for my English—and *much* too subtle for the German language. It is, a little, that you wear heels; a little, that you have written a book; a little, that they don't have to be just a tiny bit afraid of you; a little, that—oh, a thousand littles. You have come at a good time for them; a time when they need a distraction that is not—distracting. Oh, dear, I wish my English was better."

"You mean, I am a dose of alkali on an acid stomach."

Fröken gave her unexpected chuckle. "Yes, just that. I am sorry you will not be coming to the theatre, but it is a great mark of favour to be invited to a students' party, and you will enjoy it, I think. Everyone will be happy tonight, now that the examinations are over. Once they come back from the match they are free for the week-end. So they will be gay this Saturday. Off the chain," she added, in English.

And off the chain they certainly were. As Lucy came in by the quadrangle door, leaving Fröken and her mother to go round to the front of the house where they lived, a blast of sound rose up round her. The rush of bath water on two floors, the calling of innumerable voices, the drum-fire of feet on bare oak stairs, singing, whistling, crooning. Both teams had apparently come back—victorious to judge by the atmosphere—and the place was alive. The place was also excited, and one word was woven like a leit-motif through the babble. Arlinghurst. Arlinghurst. As she walked past the ground-floor bathrooms on her way to the stairs, she heard the first of it. "*Have you heard*, my dear! *Arlinghurst!*"

"What?"

"*Arling-hurst!*"

A tap was turned off.

"I can't hear with the blasted water. Where, did you say?"

"Arlinghurst!"

"I don't believe it."

"But yes," said another voice, "it's true."

"It can't be; they don't send First Posters to Arlinghurst."

"No, really it's true. Miss Hodge's sec. told Jolly in confidence and Jolly told her sister in the village and *she* told Miss Nevill at The Teapot, and Miss Nevill talked about it to

The Nut Tart when she was there to tea this afternoon with that cousin of hers."

"Is that gigolo here again?"

"I say, *Arlinghurst!* Who would believe it! Whom do you think they'll give it to?"

"Oh, that's easy."

"Yes, Innes of course."

"Lucky Innes."

"Oh, well, she deserves it."

"Just imagine. *Arlinghurst!*"

And on the first floor it was the same; the rushing of bath water, the splashing, the babble, and Arlinghurst.

"But who told you?"

"The Nut Tart."

"Oh, my dear, she's dippy, everyone knows."

"Well, it's a cert for Innes, anyhow, so it's nothing to do with me. I'll probably wind up in the L.C.C."

"She may be dippy, but she's not M.D., and she'd got it pat. She didn't even know what Arlinghurst *was*, so she wasn't making it up. She said: 'Is it a school?'"

"*Is it a school!* My hat!"

"I say, won't The Hodge be just dizzy with pride, my dears!"

"D'you suppose she'll be dizzy enough to

give us tart for supper instead of that milk pudding?"

"I expect Jolly made the puddings yesterday and they're all standing waiting in rows on the hatch."

"Oh, well, they can wait as far as I'm concerned. I'm for Larborough."

"Me, too. I say, is Innes there?"

"No, she's finished. She's dressing."

"I say, let's throw Innes a party, all of us, instead of letting her give a little private one. After all, it's—"

"Yes. Let's do that, shall we? After all, it isn't every day that someone gets a post like that, and Innes deserves it, and everyone will be glad about it, and—"

"Yes, let's have a do in the common-room."

"After all, it's a sort of communal honour. A decoration for Leys."

"Arlinghurst! Who'd have believed it?"

"Arlinghurst!"

Lucy wondered if the meek little secretary's indiscretion had been prompted by the knowledge that the news was about to be made public. Even the cautious and secretive Henrietta could not sit on such a piece of information much longer; if for no other reason than that Arlinghurst would be expecting an answer. Lucy supposed that Henrietta had been waiting until the "bad" week was over before providing her sensation; she could not help feeling that it was a very neat piece of timing.

As she walked along the corridor to her cell at the end, she met Innes, buttoning herself into a fresh cotton frock.

"Well," said Lucy, "it seems to have been a successful afternoon."

"The row, you mean?" Innes said. "Yes, we won. But the row is not a war chant. It's a paean of praise that they will never have to live this week again."

Lucy noticed how unconsciously she had used the word "they." She wondered for a moment at the girl's calm. Had she, possibly, not yet heard about the Arlinghurst vacancy? And then, as Innes moved from the dimness of the corridor into the light from Dakers' wide-open door, Lucy saw the radiance on her face. And her own heart turned over in sympathy. *That* was how it felt, was it? Like seeing Heaven opened.

"*You* look happy, anyhow," she said, falling back on bald platitude since there were no words to describe what was shining in Innes's eyes.

"To use a phrase of O'Donnell's, I wouldn't call the king my cousin," Innes said, as they moved apart. "You are coming to Stewart's party, aren't you? That's good. We'll meet again there."

Lucy powdered her nose, and decided to go over to the "old house" and see how the Staff were reacting to the news of Arlinghurst. Perhaps there would still be some tea; she had forgotten all about tea and so apparently had the Gustavsens. She rearranged the bottle of champagne which was waiting for Stewart's party in the ice she had begged from Miss Joliffe, regretted yet once more that the Larborough wine merchant had not been able to supply a better year, but trusted (rightly) that Rheims and all its products were simply "champagne" to a student.

To go over to the "old house" one had to pass both the Seniors' bedrooms and the first-floor bathrooms again, and it seemed to Lucy that the orchestration of sound had reached a new pitch of intensity, as more and more students heard the news and passed it on and commented on it above the roar of water, and banging of doors, and the thudding of feet. It was strange to come from that blare of sound and excitement into the quiet, the cream paint and mahogany, the tall windows and space, the waiting peace of the "house." She crossed the wide landing and opened the door of the drawing-room. Here too there was quiet, and she had shut the door behind her and come forward into the room before becoming aware of the exact quality of that quiet. Before realising, in fact, that the quiet was electric, and that she had walked into the middle of a Staff row. A row, moreover, if one was to judge from the faces, of most unholy proportions. Henrietta was standing, flushed and defensive and stubborn, with her back to the fireplace, and the others were staring at her, accusing and angry.

Lucy would have beaten a retreat, but someone had automatically poured out a cup of tea and thrust it at her, and she could hardly put it down again and walk out. Though she would have liked to for more reasons than one. The tea was almost black and quite cold.

No one took any notice of Lucy. Either they accepted her as one of themselves, or they were too absorbed in their quarrel to realise her fully. Their eyes had acknowledged her presence with the same absent acquiescence that greets a ticket collector in a railway carriage; a legitimate intruder but not a partaker in discussion.

"It's monstrous," Madame was saying. "Monstrous!" For the first time within Lucy's experience she had discarded her Récamier pose and was sitting with both slender feet planted firmly on the floor.

Miss Lux was standing behind her, her bleak face even bleaker than usual, and two very unusual spots of bright red high on her cheek-bones. Fröken was sitting back in one of the chintz-covered chairs looking contemptuous and sullen. And Wragg, hovering by the window, looked as much confused and embarrassed as angry; as if, having so lately come up from the mortal world, she found this battling of Olympians disconcerting.

"I fail to see anything monstrous about it," Henrietta said with an attempt at her Head Girl manner; but even to Lucy's ears it had a synthetic quality. Henrietta was obviously in a spot.

"It is more than monstrous," Madame said, "it is very nearly criminal."

"Marie, don't be absurd."

"Criminal from more than one point of view. You propose to palm off an inferior product on someone who expects the best; and you propose at the same time to lower the credit of Leys so that it will take twenty years to recover it, if it ever recovers. And for what, I ask you? For what? Just to satisfy some whim of your own!"

"I fail to see where the whim comes in," Henrietta snapped, dropping some of her Great Dane dignity at this thrust. "No one here can deny that she is a brilliant student, that she has worked hard and deserved her reward. Even her theoretical work has been consistently good this term."

"Not consistently," said Miss Lux in a voice like water dropping on to a metal pan. "According to the paper I corrected last night, she could not even get a Second in Pathology."

It was here that Lucy stopped wondering what to do with her tea, and pricked up her ears.

"Oh, dear, that is a pity," Henrietta said, genuinely distracted from the main point by this news. "She was doing so well. So much better than I had dared to hope."

"The girl is a moron, and you know it," Madame said.

"But that is nonsense. She is one of the most brilliant students Leys has ever—"

"For God's sake, Henrietta, stop saying that. You know as well as any of us what they mean by brilliant." She flourished a sheet of blue note-paper in her thin brown hand, and holding it at arm's length (she was "getting on" was Madame, and she hated to wear glasses), read aloud. "'We wondered if, among your Leaving Students, you had one brilliant enough to fill this place. Someone who would be "Arlinghurst" from the beginning, and so more part of the school and its traditions than a migrant can ever be, and at the same time continue the Leys connection that has been so fortunate for us.' The Leys connection that has been so fortunate! And you propose to end it by sending them Rouse!"

"I don't know why you are all so stubbornly against her. It can be nothing but prejudice. She has been a model student, and no one has ever said a word against her until now. Until I am prepared to give her the rewards of her work. And then you are all suddenly furious. I am entirely at a loss. Fröken! Surely you will bear me out. You can never have had a better pupil than Miss Rouse."

"Mees Rouse is a very good gymnast. She is also, I understand from Mees Wragg, a very fine games player. But when she goes out from thees plaace it will not matter any longer that she can do a handstand better than anyone else and that she ees a good half-back. What will matter then is character. And what Mees Rouse has of character is neither very much nor very admirable."

"Fröken!" Henrietta sounded shocked. "I thought you liked her."

"Did you?" The two cold, disinterested little words said: I am expected to like all my students; if you had known whom I liked or disliked I should be unworthy.

"Well, you *asked* Sigrid, and you've certainly been told," Madame said, delighted. "I could not have put it better myself."

"Perhaps—" began Miss Wragg. "I mean, it *is* for gymnastics they want her. They are separate departments at Arlinghurst: the gym., and the games, and the dancing; one person for each. So perhaps Rouse wouldn't be too bad."

Lucy wondered whether this tentative offering was inspired by Rouse's performance for Miss Wragg's department at half-back, or by a desire to smooth things over and draw the two edges of the yawning gap even a little nearer.

"Doreen, my pet," said Madame, in the tolerant tones that one uses to a half-wit, "what they are looking for is not someone who 'wouldn't be too bad'; what they are looking for is someone so outstanding that she can step straight from College to be one of the gymnasts at the best girls' school in England. Does that sound to you like Miss Rouse, do you think?"

"No. No, I suppose not. It does sound like Innes, I must admit."

"Quite so. It does sound like Innes. And it is beyond the wit of man why it doesn't sound like Innes to Miss Hodge." She fixed Henrietta with her enormous black eyes, and Henrietta winced.

"I've told you! There is a vacancy at the Wycherley Orthopaedic Hospital that would be ideal for Miss Innes. She is excellent at medical work."

"God give me patience! The Wycherley Orthopaedic Hospital!"

"Doesn't the unity of the opposition persuade you that you are wrong, Miss Hodge?" It was Miss Lux, incisive even in her anger. "Being a minority of one is not a very strong position."

But that was the wrong thing to say. If Henrietta had ever been open to persuasion, she was by now far past that stage. She reacted to Miss Lux's logic with a spurt of fury.

"My position as a minority may not be very strong, Miss Lux, but my position as Principal of this college is unquestioned, and what you think or do not think of my decisions is immaterial. I took you into my confidence, as I always have, about the disposal of this vacancy. That you do not agree with me is, of course, regrettable, but of no consequence. It is for me to make decisions here, and in this case I have made it. You are free to disapprove, of course; but not to interfere, I am glad to say."

She picked up her cup with a hand that shook, and put it away on the tea-tray, as was her habit; and then made for the door.

Lumbering and hurt, like a wounded elephant, thought Lucy.

"Just a minute, Henrietta!" Madame said, her eyes having lighted on Lucy and a spark of amused malice appearing therein. "Let us ask the outsider and the trained psychologist."

"But I am *not* a trained psychologist," said poor Lucy.

"Just let us hear what Miss Pym thinks."

"I don't know what Miss Pym has to do with the vacancies—"

"No, not about the appointment. Just what she thinks of these two students. Come along, Miss Pym. Give us your frank opinion. After a mere week among us you cannot be accused of bias."

"You mean Rouse and Innes?" asked Lucy, playing for time. Henrietta had paused with her hand on the door. "I don't know them of course; but it certainly surprises me that Miss Hodge should think of giving that appointment to Rouse. I don't think she is at all—in fact I think she would be *quite* the wrong person."

Henrietta, to whom this was apparently the last straw, cast her an *et tu Brute* look and blundered out of the room, with a muttered remark about it being "surprising what a pretty face can do to influence people." Which Lucy took to refer to Innes, not to herself.

In the drawing-room was a very crowded silence.

"I thought I knew all about Henrietta," Madame said at last, reflective and puzzled.

"I thought one could trust her to do justice," Miss Lux said, bitter.

Fröken got to her feet without a word, and still looking contemptuous and sullen, walked out of the room. They watched her go with gloomy approbation; her silence was comment enough.

"It is a pity that this should have happened, when everything was going so well," Wragg said, producing another of her unhelpful offerings. She was like someone running round with black-currant lozenges to the victims of an earthquake. "Everyone has been so pleased with their posts, and—"

"Do you think she will come to her senses when she has had time to think it over?" Lux asked Madame.

"She has been thinking it over for nearly a week. Or rather she has had it settled in her mind for nearly a week; so that by now it has become established fact and she will not be able to see it any other way."

"And yet she couldn't have been sure about—I mean, sure of our reaction—or she would not have kept it to herself until now. Perhaps when she thinks it over—"

"When she thinks it over she will remember that Catherine Lux questioned the Royal Prerogative—"

"But there is a Board in the background. There is no question of Divine Right. There must be someone who can be appealed to against her decision. An injustice like this can't be allowed to happen just because—"

"Of course there is a Board. You met them when you got the job here. You see one of them when she comes to supper on the Friday nights when the lecture happens to be on Yoga, or Theosophy, or Voodoo, or what not. A greedy slug in amber beads and black satin, with the brains of a louse. She thinks Henrietta is wonderful. So do the rest of the Board. And so, let me say it here and now, do I. That is what makes it all so shocking. That Henrietta, the shrewd Henrietta who built this place up from something not much better than a dame's school, should be so blind, so suddenly devoid of the most elementary judgment—it's fantastic. Fantastic!"

"But there must be *something* we can do—"

"My good if tactless Catherine," Madame said, rising gracefully to her feet, "all we can do is go to our rooms and pray." She reached for the scarf that even in the hottest weather draped her thin body as she moved from one room to another. "There are also the lesser resorts of aspirin and a hot bath. They may not move the Almighty but they are beneficial to the blood pressure." She floated out of the room; as nearly without substance as a human being can be.

"If Madame can't do anything to influence Miss Hodge, I don't see that anyone else can," Wragg said.

"I certainly can't," Lux said. "I just rub her the wrong way. Even if I didn't, even if I had the charm of Cleopatra and she hung on my every word, how can one reduce a mental astigmatism like that? She is quite honest about it, you see. She is one of the most honest persons I have ever met. She really *sees* the thing like that; she really sees Rouse as everything that is admirable and deserving, and thinks we are prejudiced and oppositious. How can one alter a thing like that?" She stared a moment, blankly, at the bright window, and then picked up her book. "I must go and change, if I can find a free bathroom."

Her going left Lucy alone with Miss Wragg, who obviously wanted to go too but did not know how to make her departure sufficiently graceful.

"It is a mess, isn't it?" she proffered.

"Yes, it seems a pity," Lucy said, thinking how inadequately it summed up the situation; she was still stunned by the new aspect presented to her. She became aware that Wragg was still in her outdoor clothes. "When did you hear about it?"

"I heard the students talking about it downstairs—when we came in from the match, I mean—and I bolted up here to see if it was true, and I walked straight into it. Into the row, I mean. It *is* a pity; everything was going so well."

"You know that the students take it for granted that Innes will get the post," Lucy said.

"Yes." Wragg sounded sober. "I heard them in the bathrooms. It was a natural thing to think. All of us would take it for granted that Innes would be the one. She is not very good for me—in games, I mean—but she is a good coach. She understands what she is doing. And of course in other things she is brilliant. She really should have been a doctor or something brainy like that. Oh, well, I suppose I must go and get out of these things." She hesitated a moment. "Don't think we do this often, will you, Miss Pym? This is the first time I have seen the Staff het up about anything. We are all such good friends as a rule. That's what makes this such a pity. I wish someone could change Miss Hodge's point of view. But if I know her no one can do that."

Chapter 10

No one can do that, they said; but it was just possible that she, Lucy, might. When the door closed behind Wragg she found herself faced with her own dilemma. She had reason to know that Miss Lux's first view of Henrietta's reaction was much truer than her second. That mental astigmatism that Lux talked about was not great enough to exclude a doubt of her own judgment; Lucy had not forgotten the odd guilty look on Henrietta's face last Monday morning when her secretary had tried to bring up the subject of the Arlinghurst letter. It had been an up-to-something look. Not a Father Christmas up-to-something, either. Quite definitely it was something she was a little ashamed of. Astigmatic enough she might be to find Rouse worthy, but not cock-eyed enough to be unaware that Innes had a prior claim.

And that being so, then it was Lucy's duty

to put certain facts before her. It was a great pity about the little red book now dissolving into pulp among the weeds—she had been altogether too impulsive about its disposal—but book or no book, she must brave Henrietta and produce some cogent reasons for her belief that Rouse was not a suitable person to be appointed to Arlinghurst.

It surprised her a little to find that an interview with Henrietta on this footing brought back a school-girl qualm that had no place in the bosom of any adult; least of all one who was a Celebrity. But she was greatly fortified by that remark of Henrietta's about "pretty faces." That was a remark that Henrietta really should not have made.

She got up and put the cup of black, cold tea on the tray; noticing regretfully that they had had almond-fingers for tea; she would have very much liked an almond-finger ten minutes ago, but now she could not have eaten even an éclair. It would not be true to say that she had discovered feet of clay in Henrietta, since she had never made any sort of image in Henrietta's likeness. But she *had* looked up to Henrietta as a person of superior worth to her own, and the habit of mind acquired at school had stayed with her. She was therefore shocked to find her capable of what was at worst cheating, and at the very least a *bêtise*. She wondered what there had been in Rouse to unseat so solid a judgment as Henrietta's. That remark about "pretty faces." That unconsidered, blurted remark. Was there something in that plain, North Country face that had touched a woman so used to good looks in her students? Was there something in the plain, unloved, hardworking, ambitious Rouse that Henrietta identified with herself? Was it like seeing some old struggle of her own? So that she adopted, and championed, and watched over her unconsciously. Her disappointment over Rouse's comparative failure in Pathology had been so keen that it had distracted her even from the urgent quarrel with her Staff.

Or was it just that Rouse had made good use of those admiring—not to say adoring—looks that she had sampled on the covered way the other morning?

No, not that. Henrietta had her faults but silliness was not one of them. She had, moreover, like everyone else in the scholastic world, served a long apprenticeship to adoration, both real and synthetic. Her interest in Rouse might be heightened by Rouse's obvious discipleship, but the origin of that interest was elsewhere. It was most likely that the Henrietta who had been plain, and unloved, and ambitious, had viewed the plain, and unloved, and ambitious young Rouse with a kindliness that was half recognition.

Lucy wondered whether to go to Henrietta at once, or to wait until she simmered down. The snag was that as Henrietta simmered down, so would her own determination to beard Henrietta on the subject. All things considered, and with the memory of previous fiascos, she thought that she had better go now while her feet would still carry her in the proper direction.

There was no immediate answer to her tap at the office door, and for a moment she hoped that Henrietta had retired to her own room upstairs and so reprieved her from her plain duty for a few hours longer. But no; there was her voice bidding her come in, and in went Lucy, feeling horribly like a culprit and furious with herself for being such a rabbit. Henrietta was still flushed and wounded-looking, and if she had not been

Henrietta, Lucy would have said that there were tears in her eyes; but that was manifestly impossible. She was very busy about some papers on her desk, but Lucy felt that until she had knocked Henrietta's only activity had been mental.

"Henrietta," she began, "I'm afraid you thought it presumptuous of me to express an opinion about Miss Rouse." (Oh dear, that sounded very pompous!)

"A little uncalled-for," Henrietta said coldly.

Of all the Henrietta phrases! "Uncalled-for!" "But it *was* called for," she pointed out. "That is just what it was. I should never have dreamed of offering my opinion unasked. The point is, that opinion—"

"I don't think we need discuss it, Lucy. It is a small matter, anyhow, and not one to—"

"But it *isn't* a small matter. That is why I've come to see you."

"We pride ourselves in this country, don't we, that everyone has a right to his opinion, and a right to express it. Well, you expressed it—"

"When I was asked to."

"When you were asked to. And all I say is that it was a little tactless of you to take sides in a matter of which you can know very little, if anything at all."

"But that is just it. I *do* know something about it. You think I am just prejudiced against Miss Rouse because she is not very attractive—"

"Not very attractive to *you*, perhaps," amended Henrietta quickly.

"Shall we say not very obviously attractive," Lucy said, annoyed and beginning to feel better. "You think I have judged her merely on her social graces, but that is not so."

"On what else could you judge her? You know nothing of her work."

"I invigilated at one of her examinations."

Lucy observed with satisfaction that this brought Henrietta up short.

There was silence while one could count five.

"And what quality of a student could you possibly test by invigilating at an examination?"

"Her honesty."

"Lucy!" But the tone was not shocked. It was a warning. It meant, if it meant anything: Do-you-know-what-the-punishment-for-slander-is?

"Yes, I said her honesty."

"Are you trying to tell me that you found Miss Rouse—obtaining help during an examination?"

"She did her best. I haven't spent the best years of my life in fourth-form circles without knowing the routine. It was at the beginning that I noticed what she was about, and since I didn't want to make a scandal of it I thought the best way was to prevent her from using it."

"Using it? Using what?"

"The little book."

"You mean that you saw a student using a small book at an examination, and *said nothing about it?*"

"No, of course not. It was only afterwards that I knew about the book. All that I knew at the time was that there was something she was trying to refer to. She had a handkerchief in her left hand—although she hadn't a cold, and seemed to have no legitimate use for the thing—and she had that bag-of-sweets-under-the-desk look that you know as well as I do. There wasn't anything under her desk, so I deduced that whatever she had was in her hand with the handkerchief. As I had no proof—"

"Ah! You had no proof."

"No. I had no proof, and I didn't want to upset the whole room by demanding any, so I invigilated from the back of the room, where I was directly behind her, and could see to it that she got no help from anything or anybody."

"But if you did not ask her about the affair, how did you know about a book?"

"I found the book lying by the path to the gymnasium. It was—"

"You mean the book was not in her desk? Not *in the room at all?*"

"No. If it had been in her desk you would have known about it five minutes later. And if I had found such a book in the examination room I would have brought it to you at once."

"Such a book? What kind of book?"

"A tiny address-book filled with Pathology notes."

"An address-book?"

"Yes. A, arthritis—and so on."

"You mean that the book was merely a book of reference compiled by a student in the course of her study?"

"Not 'merely.' "

"And *why* not 'merely'?"

"Because the whole thing was not much bigger than an outsize postage stamp."

Lucy waited for this to sink in.

"And what connection is there between this book you found and Miss Rouse?"

"Only that no one else in the room had a bag-of-sweets-under-the-desk expression; in fact, no one else seemed to be particularly worried about the paper. And that Rouse was the last to leave the room."

"What has that to do with it?"

"If the book had been dropped before Rouse came out of the examination room it would almost certainly have been picked up by one of the other students. It was a sort of dahlia red, and was lying very obviously on the grass at the edge of the path."

"Not *on the path?*"

"No," said Lucy, reluctantly. "About half an inch off it."

"So that it could have been passed many times by a crowd of chattering students excited over an examination, and anxious not to be late for their next class?"

"Yes, I suppose it could."

"And was there a name on the book?"

"No."

"No name? No means of identification?"

"Nothing except the script. It was in script, not current form."

"I see." One could see Henrietta bracing herself. "Then you had better bring me the book and we will take the proper steps to have the owner identified."

"I haven't got it," said poor Lucy. "I drowned it."

"You what?"

"I mean, I dropped it into the stream by the games field."

"That was surely a very extraordinary thing to do!" *Was* there a spark of relief in Henrietta's eye?

"Not really. I suppose it was impetuous. But what was I to do with it? It was a précis of Pathology, and the Pathology Final was over and the book had not been used. Whatever had been planned had not been carried out. Why, then, worry you by bringing the book to you? It seemed to me that the best punishment for whoever had compiled the thing was never to know what had become of it. To live the rest of her days with a question at the back of her mind."

" 'Whoever had compiled it.' That describes the situation, doesn't it? There is not one iota of evidence to connect the book with Miss Rouse."

"If there had been evidence, as I said before, I would have brought it to you. There is only presumption. But the presumption is very strong. A great many people are ruled out altogether."

"Why?"

"Those who don't consider themselves likely to be at a loss don't waste time insuring against it. That is to say, those who are good on the theoretical side are innocent. But you yourself told me that Rouse finds written work extraordinarily difficult."

"So do a great many others."

"Yes. But there is another factor. A great many no doubt find difficulty with theory but don't particularly care as long as they struggle through. But Rouse is brilliant at practical work, and it galls her to be also-ran in examinations. She is ambitious, and a hard worker. She wants the fruits of her labours, and she is very doubtful of getting them. Hence the little book."

"That, my dear Lucy, is psychological theorising."

"Maybe. But psychological theorising is what Madame asked me to do, in the drawing-room. You thought I had based my opinion on a mere prejudice. I thought you ought to know that I had some better foundation for my theorising." She watched Henrietta's flushed face, and wondered if she might venture into the minefield again, now that she had proved that she was not merely wantonly trespassing. "As one friend to another, Henrietta, I don't understand why you even consider sending Rouse to Arlinghurst when you have someone as suitable as Innes." And she waited for the explosion.

But there was no explosion. Henrietta sat in heavy silence, making a dotted pattern with her pen on the fine clean blotting-paper; a measure of her troubled state, since neither doodling nor wasting paper was a habit of Henrietta's.

"I don't think you know much about Innes," she said at length, in a reasonably friendly tone. "Because she has a brilliant mind and good looks you credit her with all the other virtues. Virtues that she quite definitely does not possess. She has no sense of humour, and she does not make friends easily—two serious disabilities in anyone who plans to live the communal life of a res-

idential school. Her very brilliance is a draw-
back in that it makes it difficult for her to
suffer fools gladly. She has a tendency—
quite unconscious, I am sure—to look down
her nose at the rest of the world." (Lucy remembered suddenly how, this very afternoon, Innes had automatically used the
word "they" in referring to the students. Old
Henrietta was shrewd enough.) "In fact,
ever since she came here she has left me
with the impression that she despises Leys,
and is using it only as a means to an end."

"Oh, surely not," Lucy protested mechan-
ically, while her inner self was wondering
whether that were indeed so, and whether
that accounted for a great deal that had
puzzled her about Mary Innes. If being at
Leys had indeed been a secret purgatory, a
trial endured as a means to an end, that
might explain that too-adult reticence, that
air of concentration in a person who had no
natural need of concentration, that inability
to smile.

She remembered, irrelevantly, Desterro's
lighthearted account of how she changed
her mind and decided to stay at Leys when
she saw Innes. It was because Innes was
not "of" Leys that Desterro had noticed her

on that dreary autumn afternoon, picking her out from the milling crowd as someone from an alien, more adult world.

"But she is very popular with her colleagues," Lucy said aloud.

"Yes, her own set like her well enough. They find her aloofness—intriguing I think. She is not so popular with children, unfortunately; they find her intimidating. If you look at her crit. book—the book that the Staff use for reports when they go to outside classes with students—you would find that the word 'antagonistic' appears again and again in describing her attitude."

"Perhaps it is just those eyebrows," Lucy said. She saw that Henrietta, uncomprehending, thought this a mere frivolousness, and added: "Or perhaps like so many people she has an inner doubt about herself, in spite of all appearances to the contrary. That is the usual explanation of antagonism as an attitude."

"I find psychologists' explanations a little too glib," Henrietta said. "If one has not the natural graces to attract friendship, one can at least make an *effort* to be friendly. Miss Rouse does."

(I bet! thought Lucy.)

"It is a great tragedy to lack the natural graces; one is not only denied the ready friendship of one's colleagues but one has to overcome the unreasoning prejudice of those in office. Miss Rouse has fought hard to overcome her natural disabilities: her slowness of mind and her lack of good looks; she goes more than halfway to meet people and puts herself to great pains to be adaptable and pleasant and—and—and acceptable to people. And with her pupils she succeeds. They like her and look forward to seeing her; her reports from her classes are excellent. But with the Staff in their private capacity she has failed. They see only her personal—unattractiveness, and her efforts to be friendly and adaptable have merely annoyed them." She looked up from her pen-patterns and caught Lucy's expression. "Oh, yes, you thought my preference for Rouse as a candidate was the result of blind prejudice, didn't you? Believe me, I have not brought up Leys to its present position without understanding something of how the human mind works. Rouse has worked hard during her years here and has made a success of them; she is popular with her pupils and sufficiently adaptable to make herself acceptable to her colleagues; she has the friendliness and the adaptability that Innes so conspicuously lacks; and there is no reason why she should not go to Arlinghurst with my warm recommendation."

"Except that she is dishonest."

Henrietta flung the pen down on its tray with a clatter.

"That is a sample of what the unattractive girl has to struggle against," she said, all righteousness and wrath. "You think that one out of a score of girls has tried to cheat at an examination, and you pick on Rouse. Why? Because you don't like her face—or her expression, if one must be accurate."

So it had been no use. Lucy drew her feet under and prepared to go.

"There is nothing at all to connect the little book you found with any particular student. You just remembered that you hadn't liked the looks of Miss Rouse; and so she was the culprit. The culprit—if there is one; I should be sorry to think that any Senior student of mine would stoop to such a subterfuge—the culprit is probably the prettiest and most innocent member of the set. You should know enough of human nature, as distinct from psychology, to know that."

Lucy was not sure whether it was this last thrust or the accusation of fastening crime on to plain faces, but she was very angry by the time she reached the door.

"There is just one point, Henrietta," she said, pausing with the door-knob in her hand.

"Yes?"

"Rouse managed to get a First in all her Finals so far."

"Yes."

"That is odd, isn't it?"

"Not at all odd. She had worked very hard."

"It's odd, all the same; because on the occasion when someone was prevented from using the little red book she could not even get a Second."

And she closed the door quietly behind her.

"Let her stew over that," she thought.

As she made her way over the wing her anger gave way to depression. Henrietta was, as Lux said, honest, and that honesty made arguing with her hopeless. Up to a point she was shrewd and clear-minded, and beyond that she suffered from Miss Lux's "astigmatism"; and for mental astigmatism nothing could be done. Henrietta was not consciously cheating, and therefore could not be reasoned, frightened, nor cajoled into a different course. Lucy thought with something like dismay of the party she was to attend presently. How was she going to face a gathering of Seniors, all speculating about Arlinghurst and rejoicing openly over Innes's luck?

How was she going to face Innes herself, with the radiance in her eyes? The Innes who "wouldn't call the king her cousin."

Chapter 11

Supper at Leys was the formal meal of the day, with the Seniors in their dancing silks and the rest in supper frocks, but on Saturdays when so many had "Larborough leave" it was a much more casual affair. Students sat where they pleased, and, within the bounds of convention, wore what they pleased. Tonight the atmosphere was even more informal than usual since so many had departed to celebrate the end of Examination Week elsewhere, and still more were planning celebration on the spot after supper. Henrietta did not appear—it was understood that she was having a tray in her room—and Madame Lefevre was absent on concerns of her own. Fröken and her mother were at the theatre in Larborough, so Lucy shared the top table with Miss Lux and Miss Wragg, and found it very pleasant. By tacit consent the burning question of Arlinghurst was not referred to.

"One would think," said Miss Lux, turning over with a fastidious fork the vegetable mysteries on her plate, "that on a night of celebration Miss Joliffe would have provided something more alluring than a scran-bag."

"It's *because* it's a celebration night that she doesn't bother," said Wragg, eating heartily. "She knows quite well that there is enough good food waiting upstairs to sink a battleship."

"Not for us, unfortunately. Miss Pym must put something in her pocket for us when she is coming away."

"I bought some cream puffs in Larborough on the way home from the match," Wragg confessed. "We can have our coffee in my room and have a gorge."

Miss Lux looked as if she would have preferred cheese straws, but in spite of her chill incisiveness she was a kind person, so she said: "I take that very kindly of you, so I do."

"I thought you would be going to the theatre, or I would have suggested it before."

"An out-moded convention," said Miss Lux.

"Don't you like the theatre?" asked the

surprised Lucy, to whom the theatre was still a part of childhood's magic.

Miss Lux stopped looking with a questioning revulsion at a piece of carrot, and said: "Have you ever considered what you would think of the theatre if you were taken to it for the first time, now, without the referred affection of childhood pantomimes and what not? Would you really find a few dressed-up figures posturing in a lighted box *entertaining?* And the absurd convention of intervals—once devoted to the promenade of toilettes and now perpetuated for the benefit of the bar. What other entertainment would permit such arbitrary interruption? Does one stop in the middle of a symphony to go and have a drink?"

"But a play is made that way," Lucy protested.

"Yes. As I said; an out-moded convention."

This dashed Lucy a little, not because of her lingering affection for the theatre, but because she had been so wrong about Miss Lux. She would have said that Miss Lux would be a passionate attender of try-out performances in the drearier suburbs of plays devoted to a Cause and Effects.

"Well, I nearly went tonight myself," Wragg said, "just to see Edward Adrian again. I had a terrific rave on him when I was a student. I expect he's a bit passé now. Have you ever seen him?"

"Not on the stage. He used to spend his holidays with us when he was a boy." Miss Lux ran her fork once more through the heap on her plate and decided that there was nothing further worth her attention.

"*Used to spend the holidays!* At your *house?*"

"Yes, he went to school with my brother."

"Good heavens! How absolutely incredible!"

"What is incredible about it?"

"I mean, one just doesn't think of Edward Adrian as being an ordinary person that people *know*. Just a schoolboy like anyone else."

"A very horrid little boy."

"Oh, *no!*"

"A quite revolting little boy. Always watching himself in mirrors. And possessed of a remarkable talent for getting the best of everything that was going." She sounded calm, and clinical, and detached.

"Oh, Catherine, you shatter me."

"No one I have ever met had the same genius for leaving someone holding the baby as Teddy Adrian."

"He has other kinds of genius though, surely," Lucy ventured.

"He has talent, yes."

"Do you still see him?" asked Wragg, still a little dazzled to be getting first-hand news of Olympus.

"Only by accident. When my brother died we gave up the house that our parents had had, and there were no more family gatherings."

"And you've never seen him on the stage?"

"Never."

"And you didn't even go to a sixpenny bus-ride into Larborough to see him play tonight."

"I did not. I told you, the theatre bores me inexpressibly."

"But it's Shakespeare."

"Very well, it's Shakespeare. I would rather sit at home and read him in the company of Doreen Wragg and her cream puffs. You won't forget to put something in your pocket for us when you leave your feast, will you, Miss Pym? Anything gratefully received by the starving proletariat. Macaroons, Mars bars, blood oranges, left-over sandwiches, squashed sausage rolls—"

"I'll put a hat round," promised Lucy. "I'll pass the hat and quaver: 'Don't forget the Staff.' "

But as she lifted the champagne bottle out of its melting ice in her wash-bowl she did not feel so gay about it. This party was going to be an ordeal, there was no denying it. She tied a big bow of ribbon to the neck of the bottle, to make it look festive and to take away any suggestion of "bringing her own liquor"; the result was rather like a duchess in a paper cap, but she didn't think that the simile would occur to the students. She had hesitated over her own toilette, being divided between a rough-and-tumble outfit suitable to a cushions-on-the-floor gathering, and the desire to do her hosts honour. She had paid them the compliment of putting on her "lecture" frock, and doing an extra-careful make-up. If Henrietta had taken away from this party by her vagaries, she, Lucy, would bring all she could to it.

Judging by the noise in other rooms, and the running back and fore with kettles, Stewart's was not the only party in Leys that evening. The corridors smelt strongly of coffee, and waves of laughter and talk rose and died away as doors were opened and shut. Even the Juniors seemed to be entertaining; if they had no posts to celebrate they had the glory of having their first Final behind them. Lucy remembered that she had not found out from The Nut Tart how she had fared in that Anatomy Final. ("Today's idea may be nonsense tomorrow, but a clavicle is a clavicle for all time.") When she passed the students' notice-board again she must look for Desterro's name.

She had to knock twice at the door of Number Ten before the sound penetrated, but when a flushed Stewart opened the door and drew her in a sudden shyness fell on the group, so that they got to their feet in polite silence like well-brought-up children.

"We are so glad to have you," Stewart was beginning, when Dakers sighted the bottle and all formality was at an end.

"*Drink!*" she shrieked. "As I live and breathe, *drink!* Oh, Miss Pym, you are a *poppet!*"

"I hope that I am not breaking any rules," Lucy said, remembering that there had been an expression in Miss Joliffe's eye that she had still not accounted for, "but it seemed to me an occasion for champagne."

"It's a triple occasion," Stewart said. "Dakers and Thomas are celebrating too. It couldn't be *more* of an occasion. It was lovely of you to think of the champagne."

"It will be sacrilege to drink it out of tooth-glasses," Hasselt said.

"Well, anyhow, we drink it now, as aperitif. A course by itself. Pass up your glasses everyone. Miss Pym, the chair is for you."

A basket-chair had been imported and lined with a motley collection of cushions; except for the hard chair at the desk it was the only legitimate seat in the room, the rest of the party having brought their cushions with them and being now disposed about the floor or piled in relaxed heaps like kittens on the bed. Someone had tied a yellow silk handkerchief over the light so that a golden benevolence took the place of the usual hard brightness. The twilight beyond the wide-open window made a pale blue back-cloth that would soon be a dark one. It was like any student party of her own college days, but as a picture it had more brilliance than her own parties had had. Was it just that the colours of the cushions were gayer? That the guests were better physical types, without lank hair, spectacles, and studious pallor?

No, of course it wasn't that. She knew what it was. There was no cigarette smoke.

"O'Donnell isn't here yet," Thomas said, collecting tooth-glasses from the guests and laying them on the cloth that covered the desk.

"I expect she's helping Rouse to put up the boom," a Disciple said.

"She can't be," a second Disciple said, "it's Saturday."

"Even a P.T.I. stops work on a Sunday," said a third.

"Even Rouse," commented a fourth.

"Is Miss Rouse still practising rotatory travelling?" Lucy asked.

"Oh, yes," they said. "She will be, up to the day of the Dem."

"And when does she find time?"

"She goes when she is dressed in the morning. Before first class."

"Six o'clock," said Lucy. "Horrible."

"It's no worse than any other time," they said. "At least one is fresh, and there is no hurry, and you can have the gym to yourself.

Besides, it's the only possible time. The boom has to be put away before first class."

"She doesn't have to go," Stewart said, "the knack has come back. But she is terrified she will lose it again before the Dem."

"I can understand that, my dear," Dakers said. "Think what an *immortal* fool one would feel hanging like a sick monkey from the boom, with all the élite looking on, and Fröken simply *stabbing* one with that eye of hers. My dear, *death* would be a happy release. If Donnie isn't doing her usual chore for Rouse, *where* is she? She's the only one not here."

"Poor Don," Thomas said, "she hasn't got a post yet." Thomas with her junior-of-three in Wales was feeling like a millionaire.

"Don't worry over Don," Hasselt said, "the Irish always fall on their feet."

But Miss Pym was looking round for Innes, and not finding her. Nor was Beau there.

Stewart, seeing her wandering eye, interpreted the question in it and said: "Beau and Innes wanted me to tell you how sorry they were to miss the party, and to hope that you would be their guest at another one before the end of term."

"Beau will be giving one for Innes," Hasselt said. "To celebrate Arlinghurst."

"As a matter of fact, we're *all* giving a party for Innes," a Disciple said.

"A sort of general jamboree," said a second Disciple.

"It's an honour for College, after all," said a third.

"You'll come to that, won't you, Miss Pym," said a fourth, making it a statement rather than a question.

"Nothing would please me more," Lucy said. And then, glad to skate away from such thin ice: "What has happened to Beau and Innes?"

"Beau's people turned up unexpectedly and took them off to the theatre in Larborough," Stewart said.

"That's what it is to own a Rolls," Thomas said, quite without envy. "You just dash around England as the fit takes you. When *my* people want to move they have to yoke up the old grey mare—a brown cob, actually—and trot twenty miles before they reach any place at all."

"Farmers?" Lucy asked, seeing the lonely narrow Welsh road winding through desolation.

"No, my father is a clergyman. But we have to keep a horse to work the place, and we can't have a horse and a car too."

"Oh, well," said a Disciple arranging herself more comfortably on the bed, "who wants to go to the theatre anyhow?"

"Of all the boring ways of spending an evening," said a second.

"Sitting with one's knees in someone's back," said a third.

"With one's eyes to opera glasses," said a fourth.

"Why opera glasses?" asked Lucy, surprised to find Miss Lux's attitude repeated in a gathering where sophistication had not yet destroyed a juvenile thirst for entertainment.

"What would you see without them?"

"Little dolls walking about in a box."

"Like something on Brighton pier."

"Except that on Brighton pier you can see the expression on the faces."

They were rather like something from Brighton pier themselves, Lucy thought. A turn. A sort of extended Tweedledum and Tweedledee. They were apparently not moved to speech unless one of their number made a remark; when the others felt called upon to produce corroborative evidence.

"Me, I'm only too glad to put my feet up and do nothing for a change," Hasselt said. "I'm breaking in a new pair of ballet shoes for the Dem. and my blisters are spectacular."

"Miss Hasselt," said Stewart, obviously quoting, "it is a student's business to preserve her body in a state of fitness at all times."

"That may be," said Hasselt, "but I'm not standing in a bus for five miles on a Saturday night to go anywhere, least of all to a theatre."

"Anyhow, it's only Shakespeare, my dears," Dakers said. " 'It is the cause, my soul!' " she burlesqued, clutching at her breast.

"Edward Adrian, though," volunteered Lucy, feeling that her beloved theatre must have one champion.

"Who is Edward Adrian?" Dakers asked, in genuine inquiry.

"He's that weary-looking creature who looks like a moulting eagle," Stewart said, too busy about her hostess's duties to be aware of the reaction on Lucy: that was a horribly vivid summing-up of Edward Adrian, as seen by the unsentimental eyes of modern youth. "We used to be taken to see him when I was at school in Edinburgh."

"And didn't you enjoy it?" Lucy asked, remembering that Stewart's name headed the lists on the notice-board along with Innes's and Beau's, and that mental activity would not be for her the chore that it probably was for some of the others.

"Oh, it was better than sitting in a classroom," Stewart allowed. "But it was all terribly—old-fashioned. Nice to look at, but a bit dreary. I'm a tooth-glass short."

"Mine, I suppose," O'Donnell said, coming in on the words and handing over her glass. "I'm afraid I'm late. I was looking for some shoes that my feet would go into. Forgive these, won't you, Miss Pym." She indicated the bedroom slippers she was wearing. "My feet have died on me."

"Do *you* know who Edward Adrian is?" Lucy asked her.

"Certainly I do," O'Donnell said. "I've had a rave on him ever since I went to see him at the age of twelve in Belfast."

"You seem to be the only person in this room either to know or to admire him."

"Ah, the heathen," said O'Donnell, casting a scornful eye on the gathering—and it seemed to Lucy that O'Donnell was suspiciously bright about the eyes, as if she had been crying. "It's in Larborough I would be this minute, sitting at his feet, if it wasn't practically the end of term and I lacked the price of a seat."

And if, thought Lucy pitying, you hadn't felt that backing out of this party would be put down to your being the only one present not yet to have a post. She liked the girl who had dried her eyes and thought of the bedroom slipper excuse and come gaily to the party that was none of hers.

"Well," said Stewart, busy with the wire of the cork, "now that O'Donnell is here we can open the bottle."

"Good heavens, champagne!" O'Donnell said.

The wine came foaming into the thick blunt tooth-glasses, and they turned to Lucy expectantly.

"To Stewart in Scotland, to Thomas in Wales, to Dakers at Ling Abbey," she said.

They drank that.

"And to all our friends between Capetown and Manchester," Stewart said.

And they drank that too.

"Now, Miss Pym, what will you eat?"

And Lucy settled down happily to enjoy herself. Rouse was not going to be a guest; and she was by some special intervention of Providence in the shape of rich parents in a Rolls-Royce going to be spared the ordeal of sitting opposite an Innes bursting with happiness that had no vestige of foundation.

Chapter 12

But by noon on Sunday she was much less happy, and was wishing that she had had the foresight to invent a luncheon engagement in Larborough and so removed herself out of the area of the explosion that was coming. She had always hated explosions, literal and metaphorical; people who blew into paper bags and then burst them had always been regarded by Lucy with a mixture of abhorrence and awe. And the paper bag that was going to be burst after lunch was a particularly nasty affair; an explosion whose reverberations would be endless and unpredictable. At the back of her mind was the faint hope that Henrietta might have changed her mind; that the silent witness of those tell-tale lists on the notice-board might have proved more eloquent than her own poor words. But no amount of encouragement could make this hope anything but embryonic. She remembered only too clearly that a shaking of Henrietta's faith in Rouse would not mean a corresponding access of belief in Innes as a candidate. The best that could be hoped for was that she might write to the Head at Arlinghurst and say that there was no Leaving Student good enough for so exalted a post; and that would do nothing to save Innes from the grief that was coming to her. No, she really should have got herself out of Leys for Sunday lunch and come back when it was all over. Even in Larborough, it was to be supposed, there were people that one might conceivably be going to see. Beyond those over-rich villas of the outskirts with their smooth sanded avenues and their pseudo everything, somewhere between them and the soot of the city there must be a belt of people like herself. Doctors, there must be, for instance. She could have invented a doctor friend—except that doctors were listed in registers. If she had thought in time she could have invited herself to lunch with Dr Knight; after all, Knight owed her something. Or she could have taken sandwiches and just walked out into the landscape and not come home till bed-time.

Now she sat in the window-seat in the drawing-room, waiting for the Staff to assemble there before going down to the dining-room; watching the students come back from church and wondering if she had sufficient courage and resolution to seek out Miss Joliffe even yet and ask for sandwiches; or even just walk out of College with no word said—after all, one didn't starve in the English country even on a Sunday. As Desterro said, there were always villages.

Desterro was the first to come back from church; leisured and fashionable as always. Lucy leant out and said: "Congratulations on your knowledge of the clavicle." For she had looked at the board on the way to bed last night.

"Yes, I surprised myself," said The Nut Tart. "My grandmother will be so pleased. A 'First' sounds so well, don't you think? I boasted about it to my cousin, but he said that was most unseemly. In England one waits to be asked about one's successes."

"Yes," agreed Lucy, sadly, "and the worst of it is so few people ask. The number of lights under bushels in Great Britain is tragic."

"Not Great Britain," amended Desterro. "He says—my cousin—that it is all right north of the river Tweed. That is the river between England and Scotland, you know. You can boast in Dunbar but not in Berwick, Rick says."

"I should like to meet Rick," Lucy said.

"He thinks you are quite adorable, by the way."

"*Me?*"

"I have been telling him about you. We spent all the intervals talking about you."

"Oh you went to the theatre, did you?"

"He went. I was taken."

"Did you not enjoy it, then?" asked Lucy, mentally applauding the young man who made The Nut Tart do anything at all that she did not want to do.

"Oh, it was as they say, 'not too bad.' A little of the grand manner is nice for a change. Ballet would have been better. He is a dancer manqué, that one."

"Edward Adrian?"

"Yes." Her mind seemed to have strayed away. "The English wear all one kind of hat," she said reflectively. "Up at the back and down in front."

With which irrelevance she trailed away round the house, leaving Lucy wondering whether the remark was occasioned by last night's audience or Dakers' advent up the avenue. Dakers' Sunday hat was certainly a mere superior copy of the hat she had worn at school, and under its short brim her pleasant, waggish, pony's face looked more youthful than ever. She took off the hat with a gesture when she saw Miss Pym, and loudly expressed her delight in finding Lucy alive and well after the rigours of the night before. This was the first morning in *all* her college career, it seemed, when she had positively *failed* to eat a fifth slice of bread and marmalade.

"Gluttony is one of the seven deadly sins," she observed, "so I had need of shriving this morning. I went to the Baptist place because it is nearest."

"And do you feel shriven?"

"I *don't* know that I *do*, now you come to mention it. It was all very *conversational*."

Lucy took it that a shamed soul demanded ritual.

"Very friendly, though, I understand."

"Oh, *frightfully*. The clergyman began his sermon by leaning on one elbow and remarking: 'Well, my friends, it's a very fine day.' And everyone shook hands with everyone coming out. And they had some fine warlike hymns," she added, having thought over the Baptist good points. She looked thoughtful for a moment longer and then said: "There are some Portsmouth Brothers on the Larborough road—"

"Plymouth."

"Plymouth what?"

"Plymouth Brethren, I suppose you mean."

"Oh, yes; I know it had something to do with the Navy. And I'm Pompey by inclination. Well, I think I shall sample *them* next Sunday. You don't suppose they're *private* or anything like that?"

Miss Pym thought not, and Dakers swung her hat in a wide gesture of burlesque farewell and went on round the house.

By ones and twos, and in little groups, the students returned from their compulsory hour out of College. Waving or calling a greeting or merely smiling, as their temperaments were. Even Rouse called a happy "Good morning, Miss Pym!" as she passed. Almost last came Beau and Innes; walking slowly, serene and relaxed. They came to rest beneath the window looking up at her.

"Heathen!" said Beau, smiling at her.

They were sorry they missed the party, they said, but there would be others.

"I shall be giving one myself when the

Dem. is over," Beau said. "You'll come to that, won't you?"

"I shall be delighted. How was the theatre?"

"It might have been worse. We sat behind Colin Barry."

"Who is he?"

"The All-England hockey 'half.' "

"And I suppose that helped *Othello* a lot."

"It helped the intervals, I assure you."

"Didn't you want to see *Othello*?"

"Not us! We were dying to go to Irma Ireland's new film—*Flaming Barriers*. It sounds very sultry but actually, I believe, it's just a good clean forest fire. But my parents' idea of a night out is the theatre and a box of chocolates for the intervals. We couldn't disappoint the old dears."

"Did *they* like it?"

"Oh, they *loved* it. They spent the whole of supper talking about it."

"You're a fine pair to call anyone 'heathen,' " Lucy observed.

"Come to tea with the Seniors this afternoon," Beau said.

Lucy said hastily that she was going out to tea.

Beau eyed her guilty face with something

like amusement, but Innes said soberly: "We should have asked you before. You are not going away before the Dem., are you?"

"Not if I can help it."

"Then will you come to tea with the Seniors next Sunday?"

"Thank you. If I am here I should be delighted."

"My lesson in manners," said Beau.

They stood there on the gravel looking up at her, smiling. That was how she always remembered them afterwards. Standing there in the sunlight, easy and graceful; secure in their belief in the world's rightness and in their trust in each other. Untouched by doubt or blemish. Taking it for granted that the warm gravel under their feet was lasting earth, and not the precipice edge of disaster.

It was the five-minute bell that roused them. As they moved away, Miss Lux came into the room behind, looking grimmer than Lucy had ever seen her.

"I can't imagine why I'm here," she said. "If I had thought in time I wouldn't be taking part in this Godforsaken farce at all."

Lucy said that that was exactly what she herself had been thinking.

"I suppose there has been no word of Miss Hodge having a change of heart?"

"Not as far as I know. I'm afraid it isn't likely."

"What a pity we didn't *all* go out for lunch. If Miss Hodge had to call Rouse's name from a completely deserted table, College would at least be aware that we had no part in this travesty."

"If you didn't have to mark yourself 'out' on the slate before eleven, I would go now, but I haven't the nerve."

"Oh well, perhaps we can do something with our expressions to convey that we consider the whole thing just a bad smell."

It's the being there to countenance it she minds, thought Lucy; while I just want to run away from unpleasantness like a child. Not for the first time, she wished she was a more admirable character.

Madame Lefevre came floating in wearing a cocoa-brown silk affair that was shot with a metallic blue in the high-lights; which made her look more than ever like some exotic kind of dragon-fly. It was partly those enormous headlamps of eyes, of course; like some close-up of an insect in half-remembered Nature "shorts"; the eyes and the thin brown body, so angular yet so graceful. Madame, having got over her immediate rage, had, it seemed, recovered her detached contempt for the human species, and was regarding the situation with malicious if slightly enjoyable distaste.

"Never having attended a wake," she said, "I look forward with interest to the performance today."

"You are a ghoul," Lux said; but without feeling, as if she were too depressed to care greatly. "Haven't you done anything to alter her mind?"

"Oh, yes, I have wrestled with the Powers of Darkness. Wrestled very mightily. Also very cogently, may I say. With example and precept. Who was it who was condemned to push an enormous stone up a hill for ever? Extraordinary how appropriate these mythological fancies still are. I wonder if a ballet of Punishment would be any good? Sweeping out stables, and so forth. To Bach, perhaps. Though Bach is not very inspirational, choreographically speaking. And a great many people rise up and call one damned, of course, if one uses him."

"Oh, stop it," Lux said. "We are going to

connive at an abomination and you specu-
late about choreography!"

"My good, if too earnest, Catherine, you
must learn to take life as it comes, and to
withdraw yourself from what you cannot alter. As the Chinese so rightly advise: When
rape is inevitable, relax and enjoy it. We
connive at an abomination, as you so ex-
quisitely put it. True. But as intelligent human beings we concern ourselves with the
by-products of the action. It will be interesting to see how, for instance, the little Innes
reacts to the stimulus. Will the shock be a
mortal one, will it galvanise her into action,
or will it send her into crazy throes of gal-
vanic activity that has no meaning?"

"Damn your metaphors. You are talking
nonsense and you know it. It is someone
else's rape we are invited to countenance;
and as far as I know there is nothing in the
history of philosophy, Chinese or otherwise,
to recommend that."

"Rape?" said Fröken, coming in followed
by her mother. "Who is going to be raped?"

"Innes," Lux said dryly.

"Oh." The twinkle died out of Fröken's
eye, leaving it cold and pale. "Yes," she
said, reflectively. "Yes."

Fru Gustavsen's round "Mrs Noah" face looked troubled. She looked from one to another, as if hoping for some gleam of assurance, some suggestion that the problem was capable of being resolved. She came over to Lucy in the window-seat, ducked her head in a sharp Good-morning, and said in German:

"You know about this thing the Principal does? My daughter is very angry. Very angry my daughter is. Not since she was a little girl have I seen her so angry. It is very bad what they do? You think so too?"

"Yes, I'm afraid I do."

"Miss Hodge is a very good woman. I admire her very much. But when a good woman makes a mistake it is apt to be much worse than a bad woman's mistake. More colossal. It is a pity."

It was a great pity, Lucy agreed.

The door opened and Henrietta came in, with a nervous Wragg in tow. Henrietta appeared serene, if a little more stately than usual (or than circumstances demanded), but Wragg cast a placatory smile round the gathering as if pleading with them to be all girls together and look on the bright side. Their close-hedged antagonism dismayed

her, and she sent an appealing glance at
Madame, whose dogs-body she normally
was. But Madame's wide sardonic gaze
was fixed on Henrietta.

Henrietta wished them all good-morning
(she had breakfasted in her own room) and
she had timed her entrance very neatly, for
before her greeting was finished, the murmur of the distant gong made the moment
one for action, not conversation.

"It is time for us to go down, I think," Henrietta said, and led the way out.

Madame rolled her eye at Lux in admiration of this piece of generalship, and fell in
behind.

"A wake indeed!" Lux said to Lucy as
they went downstairs. "It feels more like
Fotheringay."

The demure silence waiting them in the
dining-room seemed to Lucy's heightened
imagination to be charged with expectation, and certainly during the meal College
seemed to be more excited than she had
ever seen it. The babble of conversation deepened to a roar, so that Henrietta,
coming-to between her busy gobbling of
the meat course and her expectation of
the pudding, sent a message by Wragg to

Beau, asking that College should contain themselves.

For a little they were circumspect, but soon they forgot and the talk and laughter rose again.

"They are excited to have Examinations Week over," Henrietta said indulgently, and let them be.

This was her only contribution to conversation—she never did converse while eating—but Wragg served up brave little platitudes at regular intervals, looking from one to the other of the shut faces round the table hopefully, like a terrier which has brought a bone to lay at one's feet. One could almost see her tail wag. Wragg was to be the innocent means of execution, the passive knife in the guillotine, and she felt her position and was tacitly apologising for it. Oh, for Pete's sake, she seemed to be saying, I'm only the Junior Gymnast in this set-up, it's not my fault that I have to tag along in her rear; what do you expect me to do?—tell her to announce the damned thing herself?

Lucy was sorry for her, even while her pious pieces of the obvious made her want to scream. Be quiet, she wanted to say, do be quiet, there is nothing for a situation like this but silence.

At last Henrietta folded up her napkin, looked round the table to make sure that all her Staff had finished eating, and rose. As the Staff rose with her, College came to its feet with an alacrity and a unanimity that was rare. It was apparent that they had been waiting for this moment. Against her will, Lucy turned to look at them; at the rows of bright expectant faces, half-smiling in their eagerness; it did nothing to comfort her that they looked as if at the slightest provocation they would break into a cheer.

As Henrietta turned to the door and the Staff filed after her, Wragg faced the delighted throng and said the words that had been given her to say.

"Miss Hodge will see Miss Rouse in her office when luncheon is over."

Chapter 13

Lucy could no longer see the faces, but she felt the silence go suddenly blank. Become void and dead. It was the difference between a summer silence full of bird-notes and leaves and wind in the grasses, and the frozen stillness of some Arctic waste. And then, into the dead void just as they reached the door, came the first faint sibilant whisper as they repeated the name.

"Rouse!" they were saying. "Rouse!"

And Lucy, stepping over the warm sunlight, shivered. The sound reminded her of frozen particles being swept over a snow surface by a bitter wind. She even remembered where she had seen and heard those particles: that Easter she had spent on Speyside when they had missed the Grantown bus and they were a long way from home and they had to walk it every foot of the way, under a leaden sky into a bitter wind over a frozen world. She felt a long way from home now, crossing the sunny courtyard to the quadrangle door, and the sky seemed to her as leaden as any Highland one in a March storm. She wished for a moment that she were at home, in her own quiet little sitting-room, settling down for a Sunday afternoon of unbroken peace, untouched by human problems and unhurt by human griefs. She toyed with the idea of inventing an excuse to go when tomorrow morning's post would give her a chance; but she had looked forward like a child to the Demonstration on Friday, and she had now a quite personal interest in what had promised to be for her merely something new in spectacles. She knew all the Seniors personally and a great many of the Juniors; she had talked "Dem." with them, shared their half-fearful anticipation of it, even helped to make their costumes. It was the summit, the triumphant flower, the resounding full-stop of their College careers, and she could not bear to go without seeing it; without being part of it.

She had dropped the rest of the Staff, who were bound for the front of the house, but Wragg, coming behind her to pin a notice on the students' board, mopped her forehead in frank relief and said: "Thank heaven that is over. I think it was the worst thing I have ever had to do. I couldn't eat my lunch with thinking of it." And Lucy remembered that there had indeed been the phenomenon of a large piece of tart unfinished on Miss Wragg's plate.

That was life, that was. Innes had Heaven's door shut in her face, and Wragg couldn't finish her pudding!

No one had yet come out of the dining-room—College appetites being so much larger than Staff ones, their meals lasted at least ten or fifteen minutes longer—so the corridors were still deserted as Lucy went up to her room. She resolved to get away from Leys before the crowd of students overran the countryside. She would go away deep into the green and white and yellow country-side, and smell the may and lie in the grass and feel the world turning on its axis, and remember that it was a very large world, and that College griefs were wild and bitter but soon over and that in the Scale of Things they were undeniably Very Small Beer.

She changed her shoes to something more appropriate to field-paths, crossed to the "old house" and ran down the front stairs and out by the front door so as to avoid the students who would now be percolating out of the dining-room. The "old house" was very silent and she deduced that there had been no lingering in the drawing-room after lunch today. She skirted the house and made for the field behind the gymnasium, with vague thoughts of Bidlington and The Teapot stirring in her mind. The hedge of may was a creamy foam on her right and on her left the buttercups were a golden sea. The elms, half-floating in the warm light, were anchored each to its purple shadow, and daisies patterned the short grass under her feet. It was a lovely world, a fine round gracious world, and no day for— Oh, poor Innes! *Poor* Innes!—no day for the world to turn over and crush one.

It was when she was debating with herself whether to cross the little bridge, to turn down-stream to Bidlington, or up-stream to the unknown, that she saw Beau. Beau was standing in the middle of the bridge watching the water, but with her green linen dress and bright hair she was so much a part of the sunlight-and-shadow under the willows that Lucy had been unaware that anyone was there. As she came into the shade herself and could see more clearly, Lucy saw that Beau was watching her come, but she gave her no greeting. This was so unlike Beau that Lucy was daunted.

"Hullo," she said, and leaned beside her on the wooden rail. "Isn't it beautiful this afternoon?" *Must* you sound so idiotic? she asked herself.

There was no answer to this, but presently Beau said: "Did you know about this appointment?"

"Yes," said Lucy. "I—I heard the Staff talking about it."

"When?"

"Yesterday."

"Then you knew this morning when you were talking to us."

"Yes. Why?"

"It would have been kind if someone had warned her."

"Warned whom?"

"Innes. It isn't very nice to have your teeth kicked in in public."

She realised that Beau was sick with rage. Never before had she seen her even out of temper, and now she was so angry that she could hardly talk.

"But how could I have done that?" she asked reasonably, dismayed to be taken personally to task for something that she considered none of her business. "It would have been disloyal to mention it before Miss Hodge had announced her decision. For all I knew she might have altered that decision; when I left her it was still possible that she might see things from—" She stopped, realising where she was headed. But Beau too had realised. She turned her head sharply to look at Miss Pym.

"Oh. You argued with her about it. You didn't approve of her choice, then?"

"Of course not." She looked at the angry young face so near her own and decided to be frank. "You might as well know, Beau, that no one approves. The Staff feel about it very much as you do. Miss Hodge is an old friend of mine, and I owe her a great deal, and admire her, but where this appointment is concerned she is 'on her own.' I have been desolated ever since I first heard of it, I would do anything to reverse it, to waken up tomorrow and find that it is just a bad dream; but as to warning anyone—" She lifted her hand in a gesture of helplessness.

Beau had gone back to glaring at the water. "A clever woman like you could have thought of something," she muttered.

The "clever woman" somehow made Beau

of a sudden very young and appealing; it was not like the confident and sophisticated Beau to look for help or to think of her very ordinary Pym self as clever. She was after all a child; a child raging and hurt at the wrong that had been done her friend. Lucy had never liked her so well.

"Even a hint," Beau went on, muttering at the water. "Even a suggestion that there might be someone else in the running. *Anything* to warn her. To make the shock less shattering. To put her on her guard, so that she wasn't wide open. It had to be punishment, but it needn't have been a massacre. You could have sacrificed a little scruple in so good a cause, couldn't you?"

Lucy felt, belatedly, that perhaps she might have.

"Where is she?" she asked. "Where is Innes?"

"I don't know. She ran straight out of College before I could catch her up. I know she came this way, but I don't know where she went from here."

"She will take it very badly?"

"Did you expect her to be brave and noble about the hideous mess?" Beau said savagely, and then, instantly: "Oh, I'm sorry. I do beg your pardon. I know you're sorry about it too. I'm just not fit to be spoken to just now."

"Yes, I am sorry," Lucy said. "I admired Innes the first time I saw her, and I think she would have been an enormous success at Arlinghurst."

"Would have been," muttered Beau.

"How did Miss Rouse take the news? Was she surprised, do you think?"

"I didn't wait to see," Beau said shortly. And presently: "I think I shall go up-stream. There is a little thorn wood up there that she is very fond of, she may be there."

"Are you worried about her?" Lucy asked; feeling that if it were merely comforting that Beau planned, Innes would surely prefer solitude at the moment.

"I don't think she is busy committing suicide, if that is what you mean. But of course I am worried about her. A shock like that would be bad for anyone—especially coming now, at the end of term when one is tired. But Innes—Innes has always cared too much about things." She paused to look at the water again. "When we were Juniors and Madame used to blister us with her sarcasm—Madame can be simply unspeakable, you know—the rest of us just came up in weals but Innes was actually flayed; just raw flesh. She never cried, as some of the others did when they'd had too much for one go. She just—just burned up inside. It's bad for you to burn up inside. And once when—" She stopped, and seemed to decide that she had said enough. Either she had been on the verge of an indiscretion or she came to the conclusion that discussing her friend with a comparative stranger, however sympathetic, was not after all the thing to do. "She has no oil on her feathers, Innes," she finished.

She stepped off the bridge and began to walk away up the path by the willows. "If I was rude," she said, pausing just before she disappeared, "do forgive me. I didn't mean to be."

Lucy went on looking at the smooth silent water, wishing passionately that she could recover the little red book which she had consigned so smugly to the brook two days ago, and thinking of the girl who had no "duck's back"—no protective mechanism against the world's weather. The girl who could neither whimper nor laugh; who "burned up inside" instead. She rather hoped that Beau would not find her until the worst was over; she had not run to Beau for sympathy, she had run as far and as fast from human company as she could, and it seemed only fair to let her have the solitude she sought.

It would do Beau no harm at any rate, Lucy thought, to find that the world had its snags and its disappointments; life had been much too easy for Beau. It was a pity that she had to learn at Innes's expense.

She crossed the bridge into the games field, turned her face to open country and took the hedge gaps as they came; hoping that she might not overtake Innes, and determined to turn a blind eye in her direction if she did. But there was no Innes. No one at all moved in the Sunday landscape. Everyone was still digesting roast beef. She was alone with the hedges of may, the pasture, and the blue sky. Presently she came to the edge of a slope, from which she could look across a shallow valley to successive distances, and there she sat with her back against an oak, while the insects hummed in the grass, and the fat white clouds sailed up and passed, and the slow shadow of the tree circled round her feet. Lucy's capacity for doing nothing was almost endless, and had been the despair of both her preceptors and friends.

It was not until the sun was at hedge level that she roused herself to further decision. The result of her self-communing was a realisation that she could *not* face College supper tonight; she would walk until she found an inn, and in the half-dark she would come back to a College already hushed by the "bedroom" bell. She made a wide circle round, and in half an hour saw in the distance a steeple she recognised, whereupon she jettisoned her thoughts of an inn and wondered if The Teapot was open on Sundays. Even if it wasn't perhaps she could persuade Miss Nevill to stay her pangs with something out of a can. It was after seven before she reached the outskirts of Bidlington, and she looked at the Martyr's Memorial—the only ugly erection in the place—with something of a fellow interest, but the open door of The Teapot restored her. *Dear* Miss Nevill. Dear large clever business-like accommodating Miss Nevill.

She walked into the pleasant room, already shadowed by the opposite cottages, and found it almost empty. A family party occupied the front window, and in the far corner were a young couple who presumably owned the expensive coupé which was backed in at the end of the garden. She thought it clever of Miss Nevill to manage that the room should still look spotless and smell of flowers after the deluge of a Sunday's traffic in June.

She was looking round for a table when a voice said: "Miss Pym!"

Lucy's first instinct was to bolt: she was in no mood for student chat at the moment; and then she noticed that it was The Nut Tart. The Nut Tart was the female half of the couple in the corner. The male half was undoubtedly "my cousin"; the Rick who thought her adorable and who was referred to in College parlance as "that gigolo."

Desterro rose and came over to meet her—she had charming manners on formal occasions—and drew her over to their table. "But this is lovely!" she said. "We were talking of you, and Rick was saying how much he would like to meet you, and here you are. It is magic. This is my cousin, Richard Gillespie. He was christened Riccardo, but he thinks it sounds too like a cinema star."

"Or a band leader," Gillespie said, shaking

hands with her and putting her into a chair. His unaccented manner was very English, and did something to counteract his undoubted resemblance to the more Latin types of screen hero. Lucy saw where the "gigolo" came from; the black smooth hair that grew so thick, the eyelashes, the flare of the nostrils, the thin line of dark moustache were all according to the recipe; but nothing else was, it seemed to Lucy. Looks were what he had inherited from some Latin ancestor; but manner, breeding, and character seemed to be ordinary public school. He was considerably older than Desterro—nearly thirty, Lucy reckoned—and looked a pleasant and responsible person.

They had just ordered, it seemed, and Richard went away to the back premises to command another portion of Bidlington rarebit. "It is a cheese affair," Desterro said. "But not those Welsh things you get in London teashops. It is a very rich cheese sauce on very soft buttery toast, and it is flavoured with odd things like nutmeg—I think it is nutmeg—and things like that, and it tastes divine."

Lucy, who was in no state to care what

food tasted like, said that it sounded delicious. "Your cousin is English, then?"

"Oh, yes. We are not what you call first cousins," she explained as Richard came back. "The sister of my father's father married his mother's father."

"In simpler words," Richard said, "our grandparents were brother and sister."

"It may be simpler, but it is not explicit," Desterro said, with all the scorn of a Latin for the Saxon indifference to relationships.

"Do you live in Larborough?" Lucy asked Richard.

"No, I work in London, at our head office. But just now I am doing liaison work in Larborough."

In spite of herself Lucy's eye swivelled round to Desterro, busy with a copy of the menu.

"One of our associated firms is here, and I am working with them for a week or two," Rick said smoothly; and laughed at her with his eyes. And then, to put her mind completely at rest: "I came with a chit to Miss Hodge, vouching for my relationship, my respectability, my solvency, my presentability, my orthodoxy—"

"Oh, be quiet, Rick," Desterro said, "it is

not my fault that my father is Brazilian and my mother French. What is saffron dough-cake?"

"Teresa is the loveliest person to take out to a meal," Rick said. "She eats like a starved lion. My other women friends spend the whole evening reckoning the calories and imagining what is happening to their waists."

"Your other women friends," his cousin pointed out a trifle astringently, "have not spent twelve months at Leys Physical Training College, being sweated down to vanishing point and fed on vegetable macédoine."

Lucy, remembering the piles of bread wolfed by the students at every meal, thought this an overstatement.

"When I go back to Brazil I shall live like a lady and eat like a civilised person, and it will be time then to consider my calories."

Lucy asked when she was going back.

"I am sailing on the last day of August. That will give me a little of the English summer to enjoy between the last day of College and my going away. I like the English summer. So green, and gentle, and kind. I like everything about the English except their clothes, their winter, and their teeth. Where is Arlinghurst?"

Lucy, who had forgotten Desterro's abrupt hopping from one subject to another, was too surprised by the name to answer immediately and Rick answered for her. "It's the best girls' school in England," he finished, having described the place. "Why?"

"It is the College excitement at the moment. One of our students is going there straight from Leys. One would think she had at least been made a Dame, to listen to them."

"A legitimate reason for excitement, it seems to me," Rick observed. "Not many people get professional plums straight out of college."

"Yes? It really is an honour, then, you think?"

"A very great one, I imagine. Isn't it, Miss Pym?"

"Very."

"Oh, well. I am glad of it. It is sad to think of her wasting the years in a girls' school, but if it is an honour for her, then I am glad."

"For whom?" Lucy asked.

"For Innes, of course."

"Were you not at lunch today?" asked Lucy, puzzled.

"No. Rick came with the car and we went over to the Saracen's Head at Beauminster. Why? What has that to do with this school affair?"

"It isn't Innes who is going to Arlinghurst."

"Not Innes! But they all said she was. Everyone said so."

"Yes, that is what everyone expected, but it didn't turn out like that."

"No? Who is going, then?"

"Rouse."

Desterro stared.

"Oh, no. No, that I refuse to believe. It is quite simply not possible."

"It is true, I am afraid."

"You mean that—that someone—that they have preferred that *canaille*, that *espèce d'une*—!"

"Teresa!" warned Rick, amused to see her moved for once.

Desterro sat silent for a space, communing with herself.

"If I were not a lady," she said at length in clear tones, "I would *spit!*"

The family party looked over, surprised and faintly alarmed. They decided that it was time they were going, and began to collect their things and reckon up what they had had.

"Now look what you have done," Rick said. "Alarmed the lieges."

At this moment the rarebits arrived from the kitchen, with Miss Nevill's large chintz presence behind them; but The Nut Tart, far from being distracted by the savoury food, remembered that it was from Miss Nevill that she had first had news of the Arlinghurst vacancy, and the subject took a fresh lease of life. It was Rick who rescued Lucy from the loathed subject by pointing out that the rarebit was rapidly cooling; Lucy had a strong feeling that he himself cared nothing for the rarebit, but that he had somehow become aware of her tiredness and her distaste for the affair; and she felt warm and grateful to him and on the point of tears.

"After all," pointed out Rick as The Nut Tart at last turned her attention to her food, "I don't know Miss Innes, but if she is as wonderful as you say she is bound to get a very good post, even if it isn't exactly Arlinghurst."

This was the argument with which Lucy had sought to comfort herself all the long afternoon. It was reasonable, logical, and balanced; and as a sort of moral belladonna-plaster it was so much red flannel. Lucy understood why The Nut Tart rejected it with scorn.

"How would *you* like to have *that* preferred to you?" she demanded through a large mouthful of rarebit. "That" was Rouse. "How would you like to believe that they were going to pay you honour, a fine public honour, and then have them slap your face in front of everyone?"

"Having your teeth kicked in," Beau had called it. Their reactions were remarkably similar. The only difference was that Desterro saw the insult, and Beau the injury.

"And we had such a lovely happy morning in this very room the other day with Innes's father and mother," Desterro went on, her fine eyes wandering to the table where they had sat. This, too, Lucy had been remembering. "Such nice people, Rick; I wish you could see them. We were all nice people together: me, and Miss Pym, and the Inneses *père et mère*, and we had an interval of civilisation and some good coffee. It was charming. And now—"

Between them, Lucy and Rick steered her

away from the subject; and it was not until
they were getting into the car to go back to
Leys that she remembered and began to
mourn again. But the distance between
Bidlington and Leys as covered by Rick's
car was so short that she had no time to
work herself up before they were at the
door. Lucy said goodnight and was going to
withdraw tactfully, but The Nut Tart came
with her. "Goodnight, Rick," she said, casually. "You are coming on Friday, aren't you?"

"Nothing will stop me," Rick assured her.
"Three o'clock, is it?"

"No, half-past two. It is written on your invitation card. The invitation I sent you. For a
business person you are not very accurate."

"Oh, well, my business things I naturally
keep in files."

"And where do you keep my invitation?"

"On a gold chain between my vest and my
heart," Rick said, and went the winner out of
that exchange.

"Your cousin is charming," Lucy said, as
they went up the steps together.

"You think so? I am very glad. I think so
too. He has all the English virtues, and a little spice of something that is not English

virtue at all. I am glad he is coming to see me dance on Friday. What makes you smile?"

Lucy, who had been smiling at this typically Desterro view of her cousin's presence on Friday, hastened to change the subject.

"Shouldn't you be going in by the other door?"

"Oh, yes, but I don't suppose anyone will mind. In a fortnight I shall be free to come up these steps if I like—I shall not like, incidentally—so I might as well use them now. I do not take well to tradesmen's entrances."

Lucy had meant to pay her respects to the Staff before going to her room in the wing, but the hall was so quiet, the air of the house so withdrawn, that she was discouraged and took the line of least resistance. She would see them all in the morning.

The Nut Tart paid at least a token obedience to College rules, and it was apparent from the hush in the wing corridor that the "bedroom" bell must have gone some minutes ago; so they said goodnight at the top of the stairs, and Lucy went away to her room at the far end. As she undressed she found that her ear was waiting for a sound from next door. But there was no sound at all; nor was there any visible light from the window, as she noticed when she drew her own curtains. Had Innes not come back?

She sat for a while wondering whether she should do something about it. If Innes had not come back, Beau would be in need of comfort. And if Innes had come back and was silent, was there perhaps some impersonal piece of kindness, some small service, that she could do to express her sympathy without intrusion?

She switched off her light and drew back the curtains, and sat by the open window looking at the brightly lit squares all round the little quadrangle—it was considered an eccentricity to draw a curtain in this community—watching the separate activities of the now silent and individual students. One was brushing her hair, one sewing something, one putting a bandage on her foot (a Foolish Virgin, that one; she was hopping about looking for a pair of scissors instead of having begun with the implement already laid out, like a good masseuse), one wriggling into a pyjama jacket, one swatting a moth.

Two lights went out as she watched. Tomorrow the waking bell would go at half-past five again, and now that examinations were over they need no longer stay awake till the last moment over their notebooks.

She heard footsteps come along her own corridor, and got up, thinking they were coming at her. Innes's door opened quietly and shut. No light was switched on, but she heard the soft movements of someone getting ready for bed. Then bedroom slippers in the corridor, and a knock. No answer.

"It's me: Beau," a voice said; and the door was opened. The murmur of voices as the door closed. The smell of coffee and the faint chink of china.

It was sensible of Beau to meet the situation with food. Whatever demons Innes had wrestled with during the long hours between one o'clock and ten she must now be empty of emotion and ready to eat what was put in front of her. The murmur of voices went on until the "lights out" bell sounded; then the door opened and closed again, and the silence next-door merged into the greater silence that enveloped Leys.

Lucy decided to stay awake a little and think of some way in which she could express to poor Innes how great was her own sympathy and how deep her own indignation; and fell instantly asleep.

Chapter 14

Monday was an anti-climax. Lucy came back into a community that had talked itself out on the subject of Arlinghurst. Both Staff and students had had a whole day's leisure in which to spread themselves over the sensation, and by night-time there was nothing more to be said; indeed every possible view had already been repeated *ad nauseam*; so that with the resumption of routine on Monday the affair had already slipped into the background. Since she still had her breakfast brought to her by the devoted Miss Morris, she was not there to see Innes's first public appearance; and by the time she came face to face with the students as a body, at lunch, habit had smoothed over the rough places and College looked much as usual.

Innes's face was composed, but Lucy thought that its normal withdrawn expression had become a shut-down look; whatever emotions she still wrestled with, they were under hatches and battened down. Rouse looked more than ever like Aunt Celia's cat, Philadelphia, and Lucy longed to shut her out-of-doors and let her mew. The only curiosity she had had about the affair was to know how Rouse took that unexpected announcement; she had even gone the length of asking Miss Lux on the way down to lunch.

"What did Rouse look like when she heard the news?"

"Ectoplasm," said Miss Lux.

"Why ectoplasm?" Lucy had asked, puzzled.

"It is the most revolting thing I can think of."

So her curiosity remained unsatisfied. Madame twitted her about her desertion of them yesterday, but no one wanted to harp on the probable reason for it. Already the shadow of the Demonstration, only four days away, loomed large over them all; Arlinghurst was yesterday's sensation and already a little stale. College was once more into its stride.

Indeed only two small incidents livened

the monotony of routine between Monday and Friday.

The first was Miss Hodge's offer to Innes of the post at the Wycherley Orthopaedic Hospital, and Innes's refusal of it. The post was then offered to and gratefully accepted by a much-relieved O'Donnell. ("*Darling*, how *nice!*" Dakers had said. "Now I can sell you my clinic overalls which I shall *never* use again, my dear." And sell them she did; and was so delighted to have good hard cash in her purse so near the end of term that she instantly began to hawk the rest of her belongings round the wing, and was only dissuaded when Stewart asked caustically if the safety-pins were standard equipment.)

The second incident was the arrival of Edward Adrian, thespian.

This unlooked-for occurrence took place on Wednesday. Wednesday was swimming afternoon, and all the Juniors and such Seniors as had no afternoon patients were down at the pool. Lucy, who by prayer, counting, and determination, could just get across the bath, took no part in this exercise in spite of warm invitations to come in and be cool. She spent half an hour watching the gambols, and then walked back to the house for tea. She was crossing the hall to the stairs when one of the Disciples—she thought it was Luke, but she was still not quite certain about them—dashed out of the clinic door and said:

"Oh, Miss Pym, would you be an angel and sit on Albert's feet for a moment?"

"Sit on Albert's feet?" repeated Lucy, not quite sure that she had heard aright.

"Yes, or hold them. But it's easier to sit on them. The hole in the strap has given way, and there isn't another that isn't in use." She ushered the dazed Lucy into the quiet of the clinic, where students swathed in unfamiliar white linen superintended their patients' contortions, and indicated a plinth where a boy of eleven or so was lying face down. "You see," she said, holding up a leather strap, "the thing has torn away from the hole, and the hole in front is too tight and the one behind too loose. If you would just hang on to his feet for a moment; if you wouldn't rather sit on them."

Lucy said hastily that she would prefer to hang on.

"All right. This is Miss Pym, Albert. She is going to be the strap for the nonce."

"Hullo, Miss Pym," said Albert, rolling an eye round at her.

Luke—if it was she—seized the boy under the shoulders and yanked him forward till only his legs remained on the plinth. "Now clamp a hand over each ankle and hang on, Miss Pym," she commanded, and Lucy obeyed, thinking how well this breezy bluntness was going to suit Manchester and how extremely heavy a small boy of eleven was when you were trying to keep his ankles down. Her eyes strayed from what Luke was doing to the others, so strange and remote in this new guise. Was there no end to the facets of this odd life? Even the ones she knew well, like Stewart, were different, seen like this. Their movements were slower, and there was a special bright artificially-interested voice that they used to patients. There were no smiles and no chatter; just a bright hospital quiet. "Just a *little* further. *That's* right." "That is looking much better today, isn't it!" "Now, we'll try that once more and then that will be all for today."

Through a gap in Hasselt's overall as she moved, Lucy caught a glimpse of silk, and realised that she was already changed for dancing, there being no interval between finishing her patient and appearing in the gym. Either she had already had tea, or would snatch a cup en route.

While she was thinking of the oddity of this life of dancing silks under hospital clothes, a car passed the window and stopped at the front door. A very fashionable and expensive car of inordinate length and great glossiness, chauffeur-driven. It was so seldom nowadays that one saw anyone but an invalid driven by a chauffeur that she watched with interest to see who might emerge from it.

Beau's mother, perhaps? That was the kind of car that went with a butler, undoubtedly.

But what came out of the car was a youngish man—she could see only his back—in the kind of suit one sees anywhere between St. James's Street and the Duke of York's Steps any time between October and the end of June. What with the chauffeur and the suit Lucy ran through in her mind the available Royalties, but could not find an appropriate one; Royalty drove itself nowadays, anyhow.

"Thank you very much, Miss Pym. You've

been an enormous help. Say thank you, Albert."

"Thank you, Miss Pym," Albert said dutifully; and then, catching her eye, winked at her. Lucy winked back, gravely.

At this moment O'Donnell erupted into the room clutching the large sifter of talcum powder that she had been having refilled by Fröken in the further room, and hissed in an excited whisper: "What do you think! *Edward Adrian!* In the car. *Edward Adrian!*"

"Who cares?" Stewart said, relieving her of the sifter. "You were a damned long time getting the talc."

Lucy closed the clinic door behind her and emerged into the hall. O'Donnell had spoken truth. It was Edward Adrian who was standing in the hall. And Miss Lux had also spoken truth. For Edward Adrian was examining himself in the mirror.

As Lucy climbed the stairs she met Miss Lux coming down, and as she turned to the second flight could see their meeting.

"Hullo, Teddy," Miss Lux said, without enthusiasm.

"Catherine!" Adrian said, with the most delighted enthusiasm, going forward to meet her as if about to embrace her. But her cool solitary hand, outstretched in conventional greeting, stopped him.

"What are you doing here? Don't tell me you have developed a 'niece' at Leys."

"Don't be a beast, Cath. I came to see you, of course. Why didn't you tell me you were here? Why didn't you come to see me, so that we could have had a meal together, and a talk about old—"

"Miss Pym," Miss Lux's clear accents came floating up the staircase, "don't run away. I want you to meet a friend of mine."

"But Catherine—" she heard him say in quick low protest.

"It's the *famous* Miss Pym," Miss Lux said, in a you'll-like-that-you-silly-creature tone, "and a great admirer of yours," she added as a final snare.

Does he realise how cruel she is being? she wondered as she waited for them to come up to her, or is his self-satisfaction too great to be pierced by her rating of him?

As they went together into the deserted drawing-room, she remembered suddenly Stewart's description of him as a "weary-looking creature who looked like a moulting eagle" and thought how apt it was. He had good looks of a sort, but although he could

not be much older than forty—forty-three or
-four, perhaps—they already had a pre-
served air. Without his paints and his pen-
cils and his toupees, he looked tired and
worn, and his dark hair was receding. Lucy
felt suddenly sorry for him. With the youth
and strength and beauty of Desterro's Rick
fresh in her mind, she found the spoiled and
famous actor somehow pitiful.

He was being charming to her—he knew
all about her book; he read all the best-
sellers—but with one eye on Miss Lux while
she examined what was left of tea, inspected the contents of the tea-pot, and apparently deciding that a little more hot water
would meet the case, lit the burner under the
tea-kettle again. There was something in
that consciousness of Catherine Lux's presence that puzzled Lucy. It wasn't in the part,
as she had imagined the part for him. The
successful star calling on the humble lecturer at a girls' college should surely show
more detachment; more willingness to peacock in front of the stranger, after the matter
of actors. He was "doing his act" for her, of
course; all his charm was turned full on, and
it was a very considerable charm; but it was
mere reflex action. All his interest was cen-

tered round the cool scraggy woman who rated him at some washy tea. It couldn't be very often, Lucy thought with amusement, that Edward Adrian arrived on any doorstep without trumpets; for nearly twenty years— ever since that first heart-breaking Romeo had brought tears to the eyes of critics sick of the very name of Montague—his comings and goings had been matters of moment, he had moved in a constant small eddy of importance; people ran to do his bidding and waited for his pleasure; they gave him things and asked nothing in return; they gave up things for him and expected no thanks. He was Edward Adrian, household word, two feet high on the bills, national possession.

But he had come out this afternoon to Leys to see Catherine Lux, and his eyes followed her round like an eager dog's. The Catherine whose estimate of him was a little hot water added to the tea-pot. It was all very strange.

"I hope you are doing well in Larborough, Teddy?" Lux asked, with more politeness than interest.

"Oh, yes; fair. Too many schools, but one must put up with that when one plays Shakespeare."

"Don't you like playing to young people?" Lucy asked, remembering that the young people she had met lately had not greatly liked having to listen to him.

"Well—they don't make the best audience in the world, you know. One would prefer adults. And they get cut rates, of course; which doesn't help the takings. But we look on it as an investment," he added with generous tolerance. "They are the future theatre-goers, and must be trained up in the way they should go."

Lucy thought that the training, if judged by results, had been singularly unsuccessful. The way the young went was in a bee-line to something called *Flaming Barriers*. It wasn't even true to say that they "didn't go" to the theatre; it was much more positive than that: they fled from it.

However, this was a polite tea-party and no time for home truth. Lucy asked if he was coming to the Demonstration—at which Miss Lux looked annoyed. He had never heard of a Demonstration and was all eagerness. It was years since he had seen anyone do any more P.T. than putting their toes under the wardrobe and waving their torso about. Dancing? Goodness, was there dancing? But of course he would come. And what was more, they should come back with him to the theatre and have supper with him afterwards.

"I know Catherine hates the theatre, but you could stand it for once, couldn't you, Catherine? It's *Richard III* on Friday night, so you wouldn't have to put up with me in a romantic effort. It isn't a good play, but the production is wonderful, even if it is I who say it that shouldn't."

"A criminal libel on a fine man, a blatant piece of political propaganda, and an extremely silly play," Lux opined.

Adrian smiled broadly, like a schoolboy. "All right, but sit through it and you shall see how good a supper the Midland at Larborough can provide when egged on by a miserable actor. They even have a Johannisberger."

A faint colour showed in Lux's cheek at that.

"You see I remember what you like. Johannisberger, as you once remarked, tastes of flowers, and will take the stink of the theatre out of your nostrils."

"I never said it stank. It creaks."

"Of course it does. It has been on its last legs for quite two hundred years."

"Do you know what it reminds me of? The Coronation Coach. A lumbering anachronism; an absurd convention that we go on making use of because of inherited affection. A gilded relic—"

The kettle boiled, and Miss Lux poured the hot water into the pot.

"Give Miss Pym something to eat, Teddy."

An almost nursery tone, Lucy thought, taking one of the curled-up sandwiches from the plate he offered her. Was that what attracted him? Was it a sort of nostalgia for a world where he was taken for granted? He would not like such a world for long, that was certain, but it was quite possible that he wearied sometimes of the goldfish life he led, and would find a refreshment in the company of someone to whom he was just Teddy Adrian who used to come in the holidays.

She turned to say something to him, and surprised the look in his eyes as he watched Catherine spurning the various eatables. The amusement, the affection, that lit them might be a brother's, but there was something else. A—hopelessness, was it? Something like that. Something, anyhow, that had nothing to do with brotherliness; and that was very odd in a Great Star looking at the plain and ironic Mistress of Theory at Leys.

She looked across at the unconscious Catherine, and for the first time saw her as Edward Adrian saw her. As a woman with the makings of a *belle laide*. In this scholastic world one accepted her "good" clothes, her simple hairdressing, her lack of make-up, as the right and appropriate thing, and took her fine bones and lithe carriage for granted. She was just the plain and clever Miss Lux. But in the theatre world how different she would be! That wide supple mouth, those high cheek-bones with the hollow under them, the short straight nose, the good line of the lean jaw—they cried aloud for make-up. From the conventional point of view Lux had the kind of face that, as errand boys say, would "stop a clock"; but from any other view-point it was a face that would stop them eating at the Iris if she walked in at lunch-time properly dressed and made-up.

A combination of *belle laide* and someone who knew him "when" was no inconsiderable attraction. For the rest of tea-time Lucy's mind was busy with revision.

As soon as she decently could she retired, leaving them to the tête-à-tête that he had so obviously sought; the tête-à-tête that Miss Lux had done her best to deny him. He pleaded once more for a theatre party on Friday night—his car would be there and the Dem. would be over by six o'clock and College supper would be nothing but an anti-climax, and *Richard III* might be a lot of nonsense but it *was* lovely to look at, he promised them, and the food at the Midland was really wonderful since they had lured the chef away from Bono in Dover Street, and it was a very long time since he had seen Catherine and he had not talked half enough to the clever Miss Pym who had written that wonderful book, and he was dead sick anyhow of the company of actors who talked nothing but theatre and golf, and just to please him they might come— and although what with his practised actor's charm and his genuine desire that they should say yes, it was agreed that on Friday night they should go back to Larborough with him, witness his production of *Richard*

III, and be rewarded with a good supper and a lift home.

As she crossed to the wing, however, Lucy found herself a little depressed. Yet once more she had been wrong about Miss Lux. Miss Lux was not an unwanted plain woman who found compensation in life by devoting herself to a beautiful younger sister. She was a potentially attractive creature who so little needed compensation that she couldn't be bothered with one of the most successful and handsome men in the world today.

She had been all wrong about Miss Lux. As a psychologist she began to suspect she was a very good teacher of French.

Chapter 15

The only person who was moved by Edward Adrian's incursion into the College world was Madame Lefevre. Madame, as the representative of the theatre world in College, evidently felt that her own share in this visit should have been a larger one. She also gave Miss Lux to understand that she had, in the first place, no right to know Edward Adrian, but that, in the second place, having known him she had no right to keep him to herself. She was comforted by the knowledge that on Friday she would see him in person, and be able to talk to him in his own language, so to speak. He must have felt greatly at sea, she gave them to understand, among the aborigines of Leys Physical Training College.

Lucy, listening to her barbed silkinesses at lunch on Thursday, hoped that she would not ingratiate herself sufficiently with Adrian to be included in the supper party; she was looking forward to Friday night, and she most certainly would not look forward any more if Madame was going to be watching her all evening with those eyes of hers. Perhaps Miss Lux would put a spoke in her wheel in time. It was not Miss Lux's habit to put up with something that was not to her mind.

Still thinking of Madame and Miss Lux and tomorrow night, she turned her eyes absently on the students, and saw Innes's face. And her heart stopped.

It was three days, she supposed, since she had seen Innes for more than a moment in passing; but could three days have done this to a young girl's face? She stared, trying to decide where the change actually lay. Innes was thinner and very pale, certainly, but it was not that. It was not even the shadows under her eyes and the small hollow at the temple. Not even the expression; she was eating her lunch with her eyes on the plate in apparent calm. And yet the face shocked Lucy. She wondered if the others saw; she wondered that no one had mentioned it. The thing was as subtle and as obvious as the expression on the face of the

Mona Lisa; as indefinable and as impossible to ignore.

So that is what it is to "burn up inside," she thought. "It is bad to burn up inside," Beau had said. Verily it must be bad if it ravaged a face like that. How could a face be at the same time calm and—and look like that? How, if it came to that, could one have birds tearing at one's vitals and still keep that calm face?

Her glance went to Beau, at the head of the nearer table, and she caught Beau's anxious look at Innes.

"I hope you gave Mr Adrian an invitation card?" Miss Hodge said to Lux.

"No," said Lux, bored with the subject of Adrian.

"And I hope you have told Miss Joliffe that there will be one more for tea."

"He doesn't eat at tea-time, so I didn't bother."

Oh, stop talking little sillinesses, Lucy wanted to say, and look at Innes. What is happening to her? Look at the girl who was so radiant only last Saturday afternoon. *Look* at her. What does she remind you of? Sitting there so calm and beautiful and all wrong inside. What does she remind you of? One of those brilliant things that grow in the woods, isn't it? One of those apparently perfect things that collapse into dust at a touch because they are hollow inside.

"Innes is not looking well," she said in careful understatement to Lux as they went upstairs.

"She is looking very ill," Lux said bluntly. "And would you wonder?"

"Isn't there something one can do about it?" Lucy asked.

"One could find her the kind of post she deserves," Lux said dryly. "As there is no post available at all, that doesn't seem likely to materialise."

"You mean that she will just have to begin to answer advertisements?"

"Yes. It is only a fortnight to the end of term, and there are not likely to be any more posts in Miss Hodge's gift now. Most places for September are filled by this time. The final irony, isn't it? That the most brilliant student we have had for years is reduced to application-in-own-handwriting-with-five-copies-of-testimonials-not-returnable."

It was damnable, Lucy thought; quite damnable.

"She *was* offered a post, so that lets Miss Hodge out."

"But it was a medical one, and she doesn't want that," Lucy said.

"Oh, yes, yes! You don't have to convert me; I'm enlisted already."

Lucy thought of tomorrow, when the parents would come and radiant daughters would show them round, full of the years they had spent here and the new achievement that was theirs. How Innes must have looked forward to that; looked forward to seeing the two people who loved her so well and who had by care and deprivation managed to give her the training she wanted; looked forward to putting Arlinghurst in their laps.

It was bad enough to be a Leaving Student without a post, but that was a matter susceptible to remedy. What could never be remedied was the injustice of it. It was Lucy's private opinion that injustice was harder to bear than almost any other inflicted ill. She could remember yet the surprised hurt, the helpless rage, the despair that used to consume her when she was young and the victim of an injustice. It was the helpless rage that was worst; it consumed one like a slow fire. There was no outlet, because there was nothing one could do about it. A very destructive emotion indeed. Lucy supposed that she had been like Innes, and lacked a sense of humour. But did the young ever have the detachment necessary for a proper focusing of their own griefs? Of course not. It was not people of forty who went upstairs and hanged themselves because someone had said a wrong word to them at the wrong moment, it was adolescents of fourteen.

Lucy thought she knew the passion of rage and disappointment and hate that was eating Innes up. It was enormously to her credit that she had taken the shock with outward dignity. A different type would have babbled to all and sundry, and collected sympathy like a street singer catching coins in a hat. But not Innes. A sense of humour she might lack—oil on her feathers, as Beau said—but the suffering that lack entailed was her affair; not to be exhibited to anyone—least of all to people she unconsciously referred to as "them."

Lucy had failed to think of a nice noncommittal way of expressing her sympathy; flowers and sweets and all the conventional marks of active friendship were not to be considered, and she had found no substitute; and she was disgusted with herself now to realise that Innes's trouble, even though it was next-door to her all night, had begun to fade into the background for her. She had remembered it each night as Innes came to her room after the "bedroom" bell, and while the small noises next-door reminded her of the girl's existence. She had wondered and fretted about her for a little before falling to sleep. But during the crowded many-faceted days she had come near forgetting her.

Rouse had made no move to give a post party on Saturday night; but whether this was due to tact, an awareness of College feeling on the subject, or the natural thrift with which, it seemed, she was credited, no one knew. The universal party that had been so triumphantly planned for Innes was no more heard of; a universal party for Rouse was something that was apparently not contemplated.

Although, even allowing for the fact that Lucy had not been present at the height of the excitement when presumably tongues would have wagged with greater freedom,

College had been strangely reticent about the Arlinghurst appointment. Even little Miss Morris, who chattered with a fine lack of inhibition every morning as she planked the tray down, made no reference to it. In this affair Lucy was for College purposes "Staff"; an outsider; perhaps a sharer in blame. She did not like the idea at all.

But what she liked least of all, and now could not get out of her mind, was Innes's barren tomorrow. The tomorrow that was to have been such a triumph. Lucy longed to provide her with a post at once, instantly, here and now; so that when tomorrow that tired happy woman with the luminous eyes came at last to see her daughter she would not find her empty-handed.

But of course one could not hawk a P.T.I. from door to door like a writing-pad; nor offer her to one's friends like a misfit frock. Goodwill was not enough. And goodwill was practically all she had.

Well, she would use the goodwill and see where it got her. She followed Miss Hodge into her office as the others went upstairs, and said: "Henrietta, can't we *invent* a post for Miss Innes? It seems all wrong that she should be jobless."

"Miss Innes will not be long jobless. And I can't imagine what consolation an imaginary post would be to her meanwhile."

"I didn't say imagine, I said invent; manufacture. There must be dozens of places all up and down the country that are still vacant. Couldn't we bring the job and Innes together somehow without her going through the slow suspense of applying? That waiting, Henrietta. Do you remember what it used to be like? The beautifully written applications and the testimonials that never came back."

"I have already offered Miss Innes a post and she has refused it. I don't know what more I can do. I have no more vacancies to offer."

"No, but you could get in touch with some of those advertised vacancies on her behalf, couldn't you?"

"I? But that would be most irregular. And quite unnecessary. She naturally gives my name as a reference when she applies; and if she were not commendable—"

"But you could—oh, you could ask for particulars of the post since you have a particularly brilliant student—"

"You are being absurd, Lucy."

"I know, but I want Innes to be very much sought-after by five o'clock this afternoon."

Miss Hodge, who did not read Kipling—or indeed, acknowledge his existence—stared.

"For a woman who has written such a note-worthy book—Professor Beatock praised it yesterday at the University College tea—you have an extraordinarily impulsive and frivolous mind."

This defeated Lucy, who was well aware of her mental limitations. Punctured, she stood looking at Henrietta's broad back in the window.

"I am greatly afraid," Henrietta said, "that the weather is going to break. The forecast this morning was anything but reassuring, and after so long a spell of perfect summer we are due for a change. It would be a tragedy if it decided to change tomorrow of all days."

A tragedy, would it! My God, you big lumbering silly woman, it is you who have the frivolous mind. I may have a C_3 intelligence and childish impulses but I know tragedy when I see it and it has nothing to do with a lot of people running to save their party frocks or the cucumber sandwiches getting wet. No, by God, it hasn't.

"Yes, it would be a pity, Henrietta," she said meekly, and went away upstairs.

She stood for a little at the landing window watching the thick black clouds massing on the horizon, and hoping evilly that tomorrow they would swamp Leys in one grand Niagara so that the whole place steamed with damp people drying like a laundry. But she noticed almost immediately the heinousness of this, and hastily revised her wish. Tomorrow was their great day, bless them; the day they had sweated for, borne bruises and sarcasm for, been pummelled, broken, and straightened for, hoped, wept, and lived for. It was plain justice that the sun should shine on them.

Besides, it was pretty certain that Mrs Innes had only one pair of "best" shoes.

Chapter 16

Each successive day of her stay at Leys saw Lucy a little more wide awake in the mornings. When the monstrous clamour of the 5.30 bell had first hurled her into wakefulness, she had turned on her other side as soon as the noise stopped and had fallen asleep again. But habit was beginning to have its way. Not only did she not fall asleep again after the early waking, but for the last day or two she had been sufficiently conscious to know in some drowsy depths of her that the waking bell was about to ring. On Demonstration morning she made history by wakening before the reveille.

What woke her was a faint fluttering under the point of her sternum: a feeling that she had not had since she was a child. It was associated with prize-giving days at school. Lucy had always had a prize of sorts. Never anything spectacular, alas—2nd French, 3rd Drawing, 3rd Singing—but she was definitely in the money. Occasionally, too, there was a "piece" to be played—the Rachmaninoff Prelude, for one; not the DA, DA, DA one but the Da-de-de-de; with terrific concentration on the de-de-de—and consequently a new frock. Hence the tremor under the breastbone. And today, all those years afterwards, she had recaptured the sensation. For years any flutterings in that region had been mere indigestion—if indigestion can ever be mere. Now, because she was part of all the young emotion round her, she shared the thrill and the anticipation.

She sat up and looked at the weather. It was blank and grey, with a cool mist that might later lift on a blazing day. She got up and went to the window. The silence was absolute. Nothing stirred in the still greyness but the College cat, picking its way in an annoyed fashion over the dew-wet stones, and shaking each foot in turn as protest against the discomfort. The grass was heavy with dew, and Lucy, who had always had a perverted affection for wet grass, regarded it with satisfaction.

The silence was ripped in two by the bell. The cat, as if suddenly reminded of urgent business, sprang into wild flight. Giddy crunched past on his way to the gymnasium; and presently the faint whine of his vacuum-cleaner could be heard, like some far-distant siren. Groans and yawns and inquiries as to the weather came from the little rooms all round the courtyard, but no one came to a window to look; getting up was an agony to be postponed to the last moment.

Lucy decided to dress and go out into the dew-grey morning, so cool and damp and beneficent. She would go and see how the buttercups looked without the sun on them. Wet gamboge, probably. She washed sketchily, dressed in the warmest things she had with her, and slinging a coat over her shoulders went out into the silent corridor and down the deserted stairs. She paused by the quadrangle door to read the notices on the students' board; cryptic, esoteric, and plain. "Students are reminded that parents and visitors may be shown over the bedroom wings and the clinic, but not the front of the house." "Juniors are reminded that it is their duty to wait on the guests at tea and so help the domestic staff." And, by itself, in capitals, the simple statement:

DIPLOMAS WILL BE PRESENTED ON TUESDAY MORNING AT 9 O'CLOCK

As she moved on towards the covered way, Lucy visualised the diploma as an imposing roll of parchment tied up with ribbon, and then remembered that even in the matter of diplomas this place was a law unto itself. Their diploma was a badge to stick in their coat; a little enamel-and-silver affair that, pinned to the left breast of their working garment, would tell all and sundry where they had spent their student years and to what end.

Lucy came out into the covered way and dawdled along it to the gymnasium. Giddy had long since finished his cleaning operations—she had seen him from her window before she left her room contemplating his roses at the far side of the lawn—and it was apparent that Rouse had already performed her morning routine—the faint damp marks of her gym. shoes were visible on the concrete path—so the gymnasium was deserted. Lucy paused as she was about to turn along the path by its side wall, and stepped in at the wide-open door. Just as a race-course is more dramatic before the crowds blur it or an arena before its traffic writes scribbles over it, so the great waiting hall had a fascination for her. The emptiness, the quiet, the green subaqueous light, gave it a dignity and a mysteriousness that did not belong to its daytime personality. The single boom that Rouse used swam in the shadows, and the liquid light of the mirrors under the gallery wavered at the far end in vague repetition.

Lucy longed to shout a command so as to hear her voice in this empty space; or to climb a ribstall and see if she could do it without having heart-failure; but she contented herself with gazing. At her age gazing was enough; and it was a thing that she was good at.

Something winked on the floor halfway between her and the boom; something tiny and bright. A nailhead or something, she thought; and then remembered that there were no nailheads in a gymnasium floor. She moved forward, idly curious, and picked the thing up. It was a small filigree rosette, flat, and made of silvery metal; and as she put it absently into her jersey pocket and turned away to continue her walk, she smiled. If the quiver under her sternum this morning had reminded her of school days, that small metal circle brought back even more clearly the parties of her childhood. Almost before her conscious mind had recognised it for what it was she was back in the atmosphere of crackers-and-jellies and white silk frocks, and was wearing on her feet a pair of bronze leather pumps with elastic that criss-crossed over the ankle and a tiny silver filigree rosette on each toe. Going down the path to the field gate, she took it out again and smiled over it, remembering. She had quite forgotten those bronze pumps; there were black ones too, but all the best people wore bronze ones. She wondered who in College possessed a pair. College wore ballet shoes for dancing, with or without blocked toes; and their gymnasium shoes were welted leather with an elastic instep. She had never seen anyone wear those pumps with the little ornament at the toe.

Perhaps Rouse used them for running down to the gymnasium in the mornings. It was certainly this morning the ornament had been dropped, since The Abhorrence under Giddy's direction was guaranteed to

abstract from the gymnasium everything
that was not nailed down.

She hung over the gate for a little but it
was chilly there and disappointing; the trees
were invisible in the mist, the buttercups a
mere rust on the grey meadow, and the may
hedges looked like dirty snow. She did not
want to go back to the house before breakfast, so she walked along to the tennis
courts where the Juniors were mending
nets—this was odd-job day for everyone,
they said, this being the one day in the year
when they conserved their energies against
a greater demand to come—and with them
she stayed, talking and lending a hand, until they went up to College for breakfast.
When they marvelled at her early rising little
Miss Morris had suggested that she was
tired of cold toast in her room, but when she
said frankly that she could not sleep for excitement they were gratified by so proper an
emotion in an alien breast, and promised
that the reality would beggar expectation.
She had not seen anything yet, it seemed.

She changed her wet shoes, suffered the
friendly gibes of the assembled Staff at her
access of energy, and went down with them
to breakfast.

It was when she turned to see how Innes was looking this morning that she became aware of a gap in the pattern of bright heads. She did not know the pattern well enough to know who was missing, but there was certainly an empty place at one of the tables. She wondered if Henrietta knew. Henrietta had cast the usual critical eye over the assembly as she sat down, but as the assembly was also at that moment in the act of sitting down the pattern was blurred and any gap not immediately visible.

Hastily, in case Henrietta did not in fact know about the gap, she withdrew her gaze without further investigation. It was none of her wish to call down retribution on the head of any student, however delinquent. Perhaps, of course, someone had just "gone sick"; which would account for the lack of remark where their absence was concerned.

Miss Hodge, having wolfed her fish-cake, laid down her fork and swept the students with her small elephant eye. "Miss Wragg," she said, "ask Miss Nash to speak to me."

Nash got up from her place at the head of the nearest table and presented herself.

"Is it Miss Rouse who is missing from Miss Stewart's table?"

"Yes, Miss Hodge."

A stolid amiable Junior called Tuttle, who was always having to take the can back, was sent on the mission, and came back to say that Rouse was not in her room; which report Beau bore to the head table.

"Where was Miss Rouse when you saw her last?"

"I can't remember actually seeing her at all, Miss Hodge. We were all over the place this morning doing different things. It wasn't like sitting in class or being in the gym."

"Does anyone," said Henrietta addressing the students as a whole, "know where Miss Rouse is?"

But no one did, apparently.

"Has anyone seen her this morning?"

But no one, now they came to think of it, had seen her.

Henrietta, who had put away two slices of toast while Tuttle was upstairs, said, "Very well, Miss Nash," and Beau went back to her breakfast. Henrietta rolled up her napkin and caught Fröken's eye, but Fröken was already rising from table, her face anxious.

"You and I will go to the gymnasium,

Fröken," Henrietta said, and they went out together, the rest of the Staff trailing after them but not following them out to the gymnasium. It was only on the way upstairs to make her bed that it occurred to Lucy to think: "I could have told them that she wasn't in the gymnasium. How silly of me not to think of it." She tidied her room—a task that the students were expected to perform for themselves and which she thought it only fair that she likewise should do for herself—wondering all the time where Rouse could have disappeared to. And why. Could she suddenly have failed again this morning to do that simple boom exercise and been overtaken by a *crise des nerfs?* That was the only explanation that would fit the odd fact of any College student missing a meal; especially breakfast.

She crossed into the "old house" and went down the front stairs and out into the garden. From the office came Henrietta's voice talking rapidly to someone on the telephone, so she did not interrupt her. There was still more than half an hour before Prayers; she would spend it reading her mail in the garden, where the mist was rapidly lifting and a shimmer had come into the atmosphere that had been so dead a grey. She went to her favourite seat at the far edge of the garden overlooking the countryside, and it was not until nine o'clock that she came back. There was no doubt about the weather now: it was going to be a lovely day; Henrietta's "tragedy" was not going to happen.

As she came round the corner of the house an ambulance drove away from the front door down the avenue. She looked at it, puzzled; but decided that in a place like this an ambulance was not the thing of dread that it was to the ordinary civilian. Something to do with the clinic, probably.

In the drawing-room, instead of the full Staff muster demanded by two minutes of nine o'clock, there was only Miss Lux.

"Has Rouse turned up?" Lucy asked.

"Yes."

"Where was she?"

"In the gymnasium, with a fractured skull."

Even in that moment of shock Lucy thought how typical of Lux that succinct sentence was. "But *how?* What happened?"

"The pin that holds up the boom wasn't properly in. When she jumped up to it it came down on her head."

"Good heavens!" Lucy could feel that inert

log crash down on her own skull; she had always hated the boom.

"Fröken has just gone away with her in the ambulance to West Larborough."

"That was smart work."

"Yes. West Larborough is not far, and luckily at this hour of the morning the ambulance hadn't gone out and once it was on the way there was no traffic to hold it up."

"What dreadful luck for everyone. On Demonstration Day."

"Yes. We tried to keep it from the students but that was hopeless, of course. So all we can do is to minimise it."

"How bad is it, do you think?"

"No one knows. Miss Hodge has wired to her people."

"Weren't they coming to the Dem.?"

"Apparently not. She has no parents; just an aunt and uncle who brought her up. Come to think of it," she added after a moment's silence, "that is what she looked like: a stray." She did not seem to notice that she had used the past tense.

"I suppose it was Rouse's own fault?" Lucy asked.

"Or the student who helped her put up the thing last night."

"Who was that?"

"O'Donnell, it seems. Miss Hodge has sent for her to ask her about it."

At that moment Henrietta herself came in, and all the vague resentments that Lucy had been nursing against her friend in the last few days melted at sight of Henrietta's face. She looked ten years older, and in some odd fashion at least a stone less heavy.

"They have a telephone, it seems," she said, continuing the subject that was the only one in her mind, "so I shall be able to talk to them perhaps before the telegram reaches them. They are getting the trunk call for me now. They should be here before night. I want to be available for the telephone call, so will you take Prayers, Miss Lux. Fröken will not be back in time." Fröken was, as Senior Gymnast, second in rank to Miss Hodge. "Miss Wragg may not be at Prayers; she is getting the gymnasium put to rights. But Madame will be there, and Lucy will back you up."

"But of course," said Lucy. "I wish there was something more that I could do."

There was a tap at the door, and O'Donnell appeared.

"Miss Hodge? You wanted to see me?"

"Oh, in my office, Miss O'Donnell."

"You weren't there, so I—"

"Not that it matters, now that you are here. Tell me: when you put up the boom with Miss Rouse last night—It *was* you who helped her?"

"Yes, Miss Hodge."

"When you put up the boom with her, which end did you take?"

There was a tense moment of silence. It was obvious that O'Donnell did not know which end of the boom had given way and that what she said in the next few seconds would either damn her or save her. But when she spoke it was with a sort of despairing resolution that stamped what she said with truth.

"The wall end, Miss Hodge."

"You put the pin into the upright that is fixed to the wall?"

"Yes."

"And Miss Rouse took care of the upright in the middle of the floor."

"Yes, Miss Hodge."

"You have no doubt as to which end you attended to?"

"No, none at all."

"Why are you so certain?"

"Because I always did do the end by the wall."

"Why was that?"

"Rouse is taller than I am and could shove the boom higher than I could. So I always took the end by the wall so that I could put a foot in the ribstalls when I was putting the pin in."

"I see. Very well. Thank you, Miss O'Donnell, for being so frank."

O'Donnell turned to go, and then turned back.

"Which end came down, Miss Hodge?"

"The middle end," Miss Hodge said, looking with something like affection on the girl though she had been on the point of letting her go without putting her out of suspense.

A great wave of colour rushed into O'Donnell's normally pale face. "Oh, thank you!" she said, in a whisper, and almost ran out of the room.

"Poor wretch," said Lux. "That was a horrible moment for her."

"It is most unlike Miss Rouse to be careless about apparatus," Henrietta said thoughtfully.

"You are not suggesting that O'Donnell is not telling the truth?"

"No, no. What she said was obviously true. It was the natural thing for her to take the wall end where she would have the help of the ribstalls. But I still cannot see how it happened. Apart from Miss Rouse's natural carefulness, a pin would have to be very badly put in indeed for it to be so far *not* in that it let the boom come down. And the hoisting rope so slack that it let the boom fall nearly three feet!"

"I suppose Giddy couldn't have done something to it accidentally!"

"I don't know what he could have done to it. You can't alter a pin put in at that height without stretching up deliberately to it. It is not as if it were something he might possibly touch with his apparatus. And much as he prides himself on the strength of The Abhorrence there is no suction that will pull a pin out from under a boom."

"No." Lux thought a little. "Vibration is the only kind of force that would alter a pin's position. Some kind of tremor. And there was nothing like that."

"Not inside the gymnasium, certainly. Miss Rouse locked it as usual last night and gave the key to Giddy, and he unlocked it just after first bell this morning."

"Then there is no alternative to the theory that for once Rouse was too casual. She was the last to leave the place and the first to come back to it—you wouldn't get anyone there at that hour of the morning who wasn't under the direct compulsion—so the blame is Rouse's. And let us be thankful for it. It is bad enough as it is, but it would be far worse if someone else had been careless and had to bear the knowledge that she was responsible for—"

The bell rang for Prayers, and downstairs the telephone shrilled in its own hysterical manner.

"Have you marked the place in the Prayer book?" Lux asked.

"Where the blue ribbon is," Miss Hodge said, and hurried out to the telephone.

"Has Fröken not come back?" asked Madame, appearing in the doorway. "Ah, well, let us proceed. Life must go on, if I may coin a phrase. And let us hope that this morning's ration of uplift is not too apposite. Holy Writ has a horrible habit of being apposite."

Not for the first time, Lucy wished Madame Lefevre on a lonely island off Australia.

It was a silent and subdued gathering that awaited them, and Prayers proceeded in an atmosphere of despondency that was foreign and unprecedented. But with the hymn they recovered a little. It was Blake's and had a fine martial swing, and they sang it with a will. So did Lucy.

"Nor shall the sword sleep in my hand," she sang, making the most of it. And stopped suddenly, hit in the wind.

Hit in the wind by a jolt that left her speechless.

She had just remembered something. She had just remembered why she had been so sure that Rouse would not be found in the gymnasium. Rouse's damp footprints had been visible on the concrete path, and so she had taken it for granted that Rouse had already been and gone. But Rouse had not been. Rouse had come later, and had sprung to the insecure boom and had lain there until after breakfast when she was searched for.

Then—whose footprints were they?

Chapter 17

"Students," said Miss Hodge, rising in her place after lunch and motioning the rest of the Staff to remain seated, "you are all aware of the unfortunate accident which occurred this morning—entirely through the carelessness of the student concerned. The first thing a gymnast learns is to examine apparatus before she uses it. That a student as responsible and altogether admirable as Miss Rouse should have failed in so simple and fundamental a duty is a warning to you all. That is one point. This is the other. This afternoon we are entertaining guests. There is no secret about what happened this morning—we could not keep it secret even if we wanted to—but I do ask you not to make it a subject of conversation. Our guests are coming here to enjoy themselves; and to know that this morning an accident took place sufficiently serious to send one of our students to hospital would undoubtedly take the edge off their pleasure; if indeed it did not fill them with a quite unnecessary apprehension when watching gymnastics. So if any of you have a desire to dramatise today's happenings, please curb it. It is your business to see that your guests go away happy, without reservations or regrets. I leave the matter to your own good sense."

It had been a morning of adjustment; physical, mental, and spiritual. Fröken had come back from the West Larborough hospital to put a worried lot of Seniors through a routine that would allow for the fact that they were one short. Under her robust calm they took the alterations, and necessity for them, with a fair degree of equanimity; although she reported that at least a third of them shied like nervous colts each time they handled the right-hand front boom, or passed the place where it had fallen. It was going to be a miracle, Fröken said with resignation, if they got through this afternoon's performance without someone or other making a fool of themselves. As soon as Fröken had released them Madame Lefevre took them over for a much lengthier session. Thanks to her physical prowess, Rouse had been part of almost every item on the ballet programme; which meant that almost every item had to undergo either patching or reconstruction. This thankless and wearisome business had lasted until nearly lunchtime, and the echoes of it were still audible. Most of the lunch-table conversation appeared to consist of remarks like "Is it you I give my right hand to when Stewart passes in front of me?" and Dakers lightened the universal anxiety by being overtaken by one of those sudden silences common to all gatherings, which left her announcing loudly that my *dears*, the last hour had *proved* that one could be in two places at the same time.

The most fundamental adjustment, however, occurred when both Fröken and Madame had finished their respective revisions. It was then that Miss Hodge had sent for Innes and offered her Rouse's place at Arlinghurst. Hospital had confirmed Fröken's diagnosis of a fracture, and there was no chance that Rouse would be able for work until many months had passed. How Innes had taken this no one knew; all that anyone knew was that she had accepted. The appointment, having all the qualities of anti-climax and being overshadowed by an authentic sensation, was taken as a matter of course; and as far as Lucy could see neither Staff nor students gave it a thought. Madame's sardonic "The Deity disposes" was the solitary comment.

But Lucy was less happy about it. A vague uneasy stirring plagued her like some mental indigestion. The patness of the thing worried her. The accident had happened not only opportunely but at the last available moment. Tomorrow there would have been no need for Rouse to go to the gymnasium and practise; there would have been no boom set up and no pin to be insecurely placed. And there were those damp footmarks in the early morning. If they were not Rouse's own, whose were they? As Lux had very truly observed, no one could be dragged anywhere near the gymnasium at that hour by anything less compelling than wild horses.

It was possible that they were Rouse's prints and that she had done something else before going into the gymnasium for her few minutes on the boom. Lucy could not swear that footprints actually went into the building; she could remember no actual print on either of the two steps. She had merely seen the damp marks on the covered way and concluded, without thinking about it at all, that Rouse was ahead of her. The prints may have continued round the building, for all she knew. They may have had nothing to do with the gymnasium at all. Nothing to do with the students, even. It was possible that those heelless impressions, so vague and blurred, were made by a maid-servant's early-morning shoes.

All that was possible. But allied to the steps that were not likely to be Rouse's was the oddity of a small metal ornament lying on a floor that had been swept twenty minutes before by a powerful vacuum-cleaner. An ornament lying directly between the door and the waiting boom. And whatever was conjecture, one thing was certain: the ornament was not lost by Rouse. Not only had she almost certainly not been in the gymnasium this morning before Lucy entered it, but she did not possess a pair of pumps. Lucy knew, because one of her helpful chores today had been to pack poor Rouse's things. Miss Joliffe, whose task it would nominally have been, was overwhelmed by preparations for the afternoon's entertainment, and had passed the duty on to Wragg. Wragg had no student to enlist as substitute, since they were all busy with Madame, and it was not a duty that could be entrusted to a Junior. So Lucy had willingly taken over the job, glad to find a way to be of use. And her first action in Number Fourteen had been to take Rouse's shoes out of the cupboard and look at them.

The only pair that were not there were her gymnastic shoes, which presumably had been what she wore this morning. But to be sure she summoned O'Donnell when she heard the Seniors come back from the gymnasium and said: "You know Miss Rouse very well, don't you? Would you cast your eye over these shoes and tell me whether they are all she had, before I begin packing them?"

O'Donnell considered, and said yes, these were all. "Except her gym. shoes," she added. "She was wearing those."

That seemed to settle it.

"Nothing away being cleaned?"

"No, we clean our own—except for our hockey boots in winter."

Well, that seemed to be that. What Rouse had worn this morning were regulation College gym. shoes. It was not off any shoes of

Rouse's that the little filigree rosette had come.

Then from where? Lucy had asked herself as she packed Rouse's belongings with a care she never accorded her own. From where?

She was still asking herself that as she changed her dress for the party. She put the rosette into one of the small drawers of the dress-table-desk affair, and dully looked over her scanty collection of clothes for something that would be suitable to a garden-party afternoon. From her second window, the one looking out on the garden, she could see the Juniors busy with small tables and basket-chairs and tea-umbrellas. Their ant-like running about was producing a gay border of colour round three sides of the lawn. The sun streamed down on them, and the picture in its definition and variety of detail was like a Brueghel gone suddenly gay.

But Lucy, looking down at the picture and remembering how she had looked forward to this occasion, felt sick at heart; and could not bring herself yet to acknowledge why she should be heartsick. Only one thing was clear to her. Tonight she must go to Henrietta with the little rosette. When all the excitement was over and Henrietta had time to be quiet and consider, then the problem—if there was a problem—must be handed over to her. She, Lucy, had been wrong last time when she had tried to save Henrietta suffering by dropping the little red book into the water; this time she must do her duty. The rosette was no concern of hers.

No. It was no concern of hers. Certainly not.

She decided that the blue linen with the narrow red belt was sufficiently Hanover Square to satisfy the most critical of parents from the provinces, brushed the suede shoes with the brush so dutifully included by Mrs Montmorency, and went down to help wherever she could be useful.

By two o'clock the first guests were arriving; going into the office to pay their respects to Miss Hodge, and then being claimed by excited offspring. Fathers prodded doubtfully at odd gadgets in the clinic, mothers prodded the beds in the wing, and horticultural uncles prodded Giddy's roses in the garden. She tried to find distraction in "pairing" the parents she met with the appropriate student. She noticed that she was searching unconsciously for Mr and Mrs Innes and anticipating their meeting with something that was half dread. Why dread? she asked herself. There was nothing in the world to dread, was there? Certainly not. Everything was lovely. Innes had after all got Arlinghurst; the day was after all a triumph for her.

She came upon them unexpectedly, round the corner of the sweet-pea hedge; Innes walking between them with her arms through theirs and a light on her face. It was not the radiance that had shone in her eyes a week ago, but it was a good enough substitute. She looked worn but at peace; as if some inner battle was over, the issue settled for good or bad.

"You knew them," she said to Miss Pym, indicating her parents, "and you never told me."

It was like meeting old friends, Lucy thought. It was unbelievable that her only traffic with these people had been across a coffee table for an hour on a summer morning. She seemed to have known them all her life. And she felt that they in their turn felt like that about her. They really were glad to see her again. They remembered things and asked about them, referred to things she had said, and generally behaved as if she not only was of importance in their scheme of things, but was actually part of that scheme. And Lucy, used to the gushing indifference of literary parties, felt her heart warm afresh to them.

Innes left them together and went away to get ready for the gymnastic display that would open the afternoon's programme, and Lucy walked over to the gymnasium with them.

"Mary is looking very ill," her mother said. "Is there anything wrong?"

Lucy hesitated, wondering how much Innes had told them.

"She has told us about the accident, and about falling heir to Arlinghurst. I don't suppose she is very happy at profiting by another student's bad luck, but it can't be just that."

Lucy thought that the more they understood about the affair the better it would be if—well, the better it would be anyhow.

"Everyone took it for granted that she would get the appointment in the first place.

I think it was a shock to her when she didn't."

"I see. Yes," said Mrs Innes, slowly; and Lucy felt that more explanation was not necessary; the whole tale of Innes's suffering and fortitude was clear to her mother in that moment.

"I think she might not approve of my having told you that, so—"

"No, we will not mention it," said Innes's mother. "How lovely the garden is looking. Gervase and I struggle along with our patch but only his bits look like the illustration; mine always turn out to be something else. Just look at those little yellow roses."

And so they came to the gymnasium door, and Lucy showed them up the stairs and introduced them to The Abhorrence—with pricking thought of a little metal rosette—and they found their seats in the gallery, and the afternoon had begun.

Lucy had a seat at the end of the front row. From there she looked down with affection on the grave young faces waiting, with such tense resolution, Fröken's word of command. "Don't worry," she had heard a Senior say, "Fröken will see us through," and one could see the faith in their eyes.

This was their ordeal, and they came to it shaken, but Fröken would see them through.

She understood now the love that had filled Henrietta's eyes when she had watched with her on that other occasion. Less than a fortnight ago, that was, and already she had a proprietorial interest and pride in them. When the autumn came the very map of England would look different to her because of these two weeks at Leys. Manchester would be the place where the Disciples were, Aberystwyth the place where Thomas was trying to stay awake, Ling the place where Dakers was being good with the babies, and so on. If she felt like that about them after a matter of days, it was not much wonder that Henrietta, who had seen them come untried into their new life, had watched them grow and improve, struggle, fail, and succeed, not much wonder that she looked on them as daughters. Successful daughters.

They had got through their preliminaries, and a little of the strain had gone from their faces; they were beginning to settle down. The applause that marked the end of their free-standing work broke the silence and warmed them and made the affair more human.

"What a charming collection," said a dowager with lorgnettes who was sitting next to her (now who owned that? she couldn't be a parent) and turning to her confidentially asked: "Tell me, are they hand-picked?"

"I don't understand," murmured Lucy.

"I mean, are these all the Seniors there are?"

"You mean, are these just the best? Oh, no; that is the whole set."

"Really? Quite wonderful. So attractive, too. Quite amazingly attractive."

Did she think we had given the spotty ones half a crown to take themselves off for the afternoon? wondered Lucy.

But of course the dowager was right. Except for a string of two-year-olds in training, Lucy could think of nothing more attractive to mind and eye than that set of burnished and controlled young creatures busy dragging out the booms below her. The ropes rushed down from their looped position near the roof, the window-ladder came to vertical, and over all three pieces of apparatus the Seniors swarmed in easy mastery.

The applause as they put ropes and ladder away and turned the booms for balance was real and loud; the spectacular had its appeal.

Very different the place looked from that mysterious vault of greenish shadows that she had visited this morning. It was golden, and matter-of-fact, and alive; the reflected light from the sunlit roof showering down on the pale wood and making it glow. Seeing once more in her mind's eye that dim empty space with the single waiting boom, she turned to see whose lot it might be to perform her balance on the spot where Rouse had been found. Who had the inner end of the right-hand front boom?

It was Innes.

"Go!" said Fröken; and eight young bodies somersaulted up to the high booms. They sat there for a moment, and then rose in unison to a standing position, one foot in front of the other, facing each other in pairs at opposite ends of each boom.

Lucy hoped frantically that Innes was not going to faint. She was not merely pale; she was green. Her opposite number, Stewart, made a tentative beginning, but, seeing that Innes was not ready, waited for her. But

Innes stood motionless, apparently unable to move a muscle. Stewart cast her a glance of wild appeal. Innes remained paralysed. Some wordless message passed between them, and Stewart went on with her exercise; achieving a perfection very commendable in the circumstances. All Innes's faculties were concentrated on keeping her standing position on the boom long enough to be able to return to the floor with the rest, and not to ruin the whole exercise by collapsing, or by jumping off. The dead silence and the concentration of interest made her failure painfully obvious; and puzzled sympathy settled on her as she stood there. Poor dear, they thought, she was feeling ill. Excitement, no doubt. Positively green, she was. Poor dear, poor dear.

Stewart had finished, and now waited, looking at Innes. Slowly they sank together to the boom, and sat down on it; turned together to lean face-forward on it; and somersaulted forward on to the ground.

And a great burst of applause greeted them. As always, the English were moved by a gallant failure where an easy success left them merely polite. They were expressing at once their sympathy and their admiration. They had understood the strength of purpose that had kept her on the boom, paralysed as she was.

But the sympathy had not touched Innes. Lucy doubted if she actually heard the applause. She was living in some tortured world of her own, far beyond the reach of human consolation. Lucy could hardly bear to look at her.

The bustle of the following items covered up her failure and put an end to drama. Innes took her place with the others and performed with mechanical perfection. When the final vaulting came, indeed, her performance was so remarkable that Lucy wondered if she were trying to break her neck publicly. The same idea, to judge by her expression, had crossed Fröken's mind; but as long as what Innes did was controlled and perfect there was nothing she could do. And everything that Innes did, however breathtaking, was perfect and controlled. Because she seemed not to care, the wildest flights were possible to her. And when the students had finished their final go-as-you-please and stood breathless and beaming, a single file on an empty floor as they had begun, their guests stood up as one man and cheered.

Lucy, being at the end of the row and next to the door, was first to leave the hall, and so was in time to see Innes's apology to Fröken.

Fröken paused, and then moved on as if not interested, or not willing to listen.

But as she went she lifted a casual arm and gave Innes a light friendly pat on the shoulder.

Chapter 18

As the guests moved out to the garden and the basket-chairs round the lawn, Lucy went with them, and while she was waiting to see if sufficient chairs had been provided before taking one for herself, she was seized upon by Beau, who said: "Miss Pym! There you are! I've been hunting for you. I want you to meet my people."

She turned to a couple who were just sitting down and said: "Look, I've found Miss Pym at last."

Beau's mother was a very lovely woman; as lovely as the best beauty parlours and the most expensive hairdressers could make her—and they had good foundation to work on since when Mrs Nash was twenty she must have looked very like Beau. Even now, in the bright sunlight, she looked no older than thirty-five. She had a good dressmaker too, and bore herself with the easy friendly confidence of a woman who has been a beauty all her life; so used to the effect she had on people that she did not have to consider it at all and so her mind was free to devote itself to the person she happened to be meeting.

Mr Nash was obviously what is called an executive. A fine clear skin, a good tailor, a well-soaped look, and a general aura of mahogany tables with rows of clean blotters round them.

"I should be changing. I must fly," said Beau, and disappeared.

As they sat down together Mrs Nash looked quizzically at Lucy and said: "Well, now that you are here in the flesh, Miss Pym, we can ask you something we are dying to know. We want to know *how you do it?*"

"Do what?"

"Impress Pamela."

"Yes," said Mr Nash, "that is just what we should like to know. All our lives we have been trying to make some impression on Pamela, but we remain just a couple of dear people who happen to be responsible for her existence and have to be humoured now and then."

"Now *you*, it seems, are quite literally

something to write home about," Mrs Nash said, and raised an eyebrow and laughed.

"If it is any consolation to you," Lucy offered, "I am greatly impressed by your daughter."

"Pam *is* nice," her mother said. "We love her very much; but I wish we impressed her more. Until you turned up no one has made any impression on Pamela since a Nanny she had at the age of four."

"And that impression was a physical one," Mr Nash volunteered.

"Yes. The only time in her life that she was spanked."

"What happened?" Lucy asked.

"We had to get rid of the Nanny!"

"Didn't you approve of spanking?"

"Oh yes, but Pamela didn't."

"Pam engineered the first sit-down strike in history," Mr Nash said.

"She kept it up for seven days," Mrs Nash said. "Short of going on dressing and forcibly feeding her for the rest of her life, there was nothing to do but get rid of Nanny. A first-rate woman she was, too. We were devastated to lose her."

The music began, and in front of the high screen of the rhododendron thicket ap-

peared the bright colours of the Juniors'
Swedish folk dresses. Folk-dancing had begun. Lucy sat back and thought, not of
Beau's childish aberrations, but of Innes,
and the way a black cloud of doubt and
foreboding was making a mockery of the
bright sunlight.

It was because her mind was so full of
Innes that she was startled when she heard
Mrs Nash say, "Mary, darling. There you are.
How nice to see you again," and turned to
see Innes behind them. She was wearing
boys' things; the doublet and hose of the fifteenth century; and the hood that hid all her
hair and fitted close round her face accen-
tuated the bony structure that was so individual. Now that the eyes were shadowed
and sunk a little in their always-deep sock-
ets, the face had something it had not had
before: a forbidding look. It was—what was
the word?—a "fatal" face. Lucy remembered her very first impression that it was
round faces like that that history was built.

"You have been overworking, Mary," Mr
Nash said, eyeing her.

"They all have," Lucy said, to take their attention from her.

"Not Pamela," her mother said. "Pam has never worked hard in her life."

No. Everything had been served to Beau on a plate. It was miraculous that she had turned out so charming.

"Did you see me make a fool of myself on the boom?" Innes asked, in a pleasant conversational tone. This surprised Lucy, somehow; she had expected Innes to avoid the subject.

"My dear, we sweated for you," Mrs Nash said. "What happened? Did you turn dizzy?"

"No," said Beau, coming up behind them and slipping an arm into Innes's, "that is just Innes's way of stealing publicity. It is not inferior physical powers, but superior brains the girl has. None of us has the wit to think up a stunt like that."

Beau gave the arm she was holding a small reassuring squeeze. She too was in boys' clothes, and looked radiant; even the quenching of her bright hair had not diminished the glow and vivacity of her beauty.

"That is the last of the Juniors' efforts— don't they look gay against that green background?—and now Innes and I and the rest of our put-upon set will entertain you with

some English antics, and then you shall
have tea to sustain you against the real
dancing to come."

And they went away together.

"Ah, well," said Mrs Nash, watching her
daughter go, "I suppose it is better than being seized with a desire to reform natives in
Darkest Africa or something. But I wish she
would have just stayed at home and been
one's daughter."

Lucy thought that it was to Mrs Nash's
credit that, looking as young as she did, she
wanted a daughter at home.

"Pam was always mad on gym. and
games," Mr Nash said. "There was no holding her. There never was any holding her,
come to that."

"Miss Pym," said The Nut Tart, appearing
at Lucy's elbow, "do you mind if Rick sits
with you while I go through this rigmarole
with the Seniors?" She indicated Gillespie,
who was standing behind her clutching a
chair, and wearing his habitual expression
of grave amusement. The wide flat hat
planked slightly to the back of her head on
top of her wimple—Wife of Bath fashion—
gave her an air of innocent astonishment
that was delightful. Lucy and Rick ex-

changed a glance of mutual appreciation, and he smiled at her as he sat down on her other side.

"Isn't she lovely in that get-up," he said, watching Desterro disappear behind the rhododendrons.

"I take it that a rigmarole doesn't count as dancing."

"Is she good?"

"I don't know. I have never seen her, but I understand she is."

"I've never even danced ballroom stuff with her. Odd, isn't it. I didn't even know she existed until last Easter. It maddens me to think she has been a whole year in England and I didn't know about it. Three months of odd moments isn't very long to make any effect on a person like Teresa."

"Do you want to make an effect?"

"Yes." The monosyllable was sufficient.

The Seniors, in the guise of the English Middle Ages, ran out on to the lawn, and conversation lapsed. Lucy tried to find distraction in identifying legs and in marvelling over the energy with which those legs ran about after an hour of strenuous exercise. She said to herself: "Look, you have to go to Henrietta with the little rosette tonight. All right. That is settled. There is nothing you can do, either about the going or the result of the going. So put it out of your mind. This is the afternoon you have been looking forward to. It is a lovely sunny day, and everyone is pleased to see you, and you should be having a grand time. So relax. Even if—if anything awful happens about the rosette, it has nothing to do with you. A fortnight ago you didn't know any of these people, and after you go away you will never see any of them again. It can't matter to you what happens or does not happen to them."

All of which excellent advice left her just where she was before. When she saw Miss Joliffe and the maids busy about the tea-table in the rear she was glad to get up and find some use for her hands and some occupation for her mind.

Rick, unexpectedly, came with her. "I'm a push-over for passing plates. It must be the gigolo in me."

Lucy said that he ought to be watching his lady-love's rigmaroles.

"It is the last dance. And if I know anything of my Teresa her appetite will take more appeasing than her vanity, considerable as it is."

He seemed to know his Teresa very well, Lucy thought.

"Are you worried about something, Miss Pym?"

The question took her by surprise.

"Why should you think that?"

"I don't know. I just got the impression. Is there anything I can do?"

Lucy remembered how on Sunday evening when she had nearly cried into the Bidlington rarebit he had known about her tiredness and tacitly helped her. She wished that she had met someone as understanding and as young and as beautiful as The Nut Tart's follower when she was twenty, instead of Alan and his Adam's apple and his holey socks.

"I have to do something that is right," she said slowly, "and I'm afraid of the consequences."

"Consequences to you?"

"No. To other people."

"Never mind; do it."

Miss Pym put plates of cakes on a tray. "You see, the proper thing is not necessarily the right thing. Or do I mean the opposite?"

"I'm not sure that I know what you mean at all."

"Well—there are those awful dilemmas about whom would you save. You know. If you knew that by saving a person from the top of a snow slide you would start an avalanche that would destroy a village, would you do it? That sort of thing."

"Of course I would do it."

"You would?"

"The avalanche might bury a village without killing a cat—shall I put some sandwiches on that tray?—so you would be one life to the good."

"You would always do the right thing, and let the consequences take care of themselves?"

"That's about it."

"It is certainly the simplest. In fact I think it's too simple."

"Unless you plan to play God, one has to take the simple way."

"Play God? You've got two lots of tongue sandwiches there, do you know?"

"Unless you are clever enough to 'see before and after' like the Deity it's best to stick to rules. Wow! The music has stopped and here comes my young woman like a hunting leopard." He watched Desterro come with a smile in his eyes. "Isn't that hat a knockout!"

He looked down at Lucy for a moment. "Do the obvious right thing, Miss Pym, and let God dispose."

"Weren't you watching, Rick?" she heard Desterro ask, and then she and Rick and The Nut Tart were overwhelmed by a wave of Juniors come to do their duty and serve tea. Lucy extricated herself from the crush of white caps and Swedish embroidery, and found herself face to face with Edward Adrian, alone and looking forlorn.

"Miss Pym! You are just the person I wanted to see. Have you heard that—"

A Junior thrust a cup of tea into his hand, and he gave her one of his best smiles, which she did not wait to see. At the same moment little Miss Morris, faithful even in the throes of a Dem., came up with tea and a tray of cakes for Lucy.

"Let us sit down, shall we?" Lucy said.

"Have you heard of the frightful thing that has happened?"

"Yes. It isn't very often, I understand, that a serious accident happens. It is just bad luck that it should be Demonstration Day."

"Oh, the accident, yes. But do you know that Catherine says she can't come to Larborough tonight? This has upset things, she says. She must stay here. But that is absurd. Did you ever hear anything more absurd? If there has been some kind of upset that is all the more reason why she should be taken out of herself for a little. I have arranged everything. I even got special flowers for our table tonight. *And* a birthday cake. It's her birthday next Wednesday."

Lucy wondered if any other person within the bounds of Leys knew when Catherine Lux's birthday was.

Lucy did her best to sympathise, but said gently that she saw Miss Lux's point of view. After all, the girl was seriously injured, and it was all very worrying, and it would no doubt seem to her a little callous to go merrymaking in Larborough.

"But it isn't merrymaking! It is just a quiet supper with an old friend. I really can't see why because some student has had an accident she should desert an old friend. You talk to her, Miss Pym. You make her see reason."

Lucy said she would do her best but could offer no hope of success since she rather shared Miss Lux's ideas on the subject.

"You, too! Oh, my God!"

"I know it isn't reasonable. It's even absurd. But neither of us would be happy and the evening would be a disappointment and you don't want that to happen? Couldn't you have us tomorrow night instead?"

"No, I'm catching a train directly after the evening performance is over. And of course, it being Saturday, I have a matinée. And anyhow, I'm playing Romeo at night and that wouldn't please Cath at all. It takes her all her time to stand me in *Richard III*. Oh dear, the whole thing is absurd."

"Cheer up," Lucy said. "It stops short of tragedy. You will be coming to Larborough again, and you can meet as often as you like now that you know she is here."

"I shall never get Catherine in that pliant mood again. Never. It was partly your doing, you know. She didn't want to appear too much of a Gorgon in front of you. She was even going to come to see me act. Something she has never done before. I'll never get her back to that point if she doesn't come tonight. Do persuade her, Miss Pym."

Lucy promised to try. "How are you enjoying your afternoon, apart from broken appointments?"

Mr Adrian was enjoying himself vastly, it appeared. He was not sure which to admire

most: the students' good looks or their efficiency.

"They have charming manners, too. I have
not been asked for an autograph once, all
the afternoon."

Lucy looked to see if he was being ironic.
But no; the remark was "straight." He really
could not conceive any reason for the lack
of autograph hunters other than that of
good manners. Poor silly baby, she thought,
walking all his life through a world he knew
nothing about. She wondered if all actors
were like that. Perambulating spheres of atmosphere with a little actor safely cocooned
at the heart of each. How nice it must be, so
cushioned and safe from harsh reality. They
weren't really born at all; they were still
floating in some pre-natal fluid.

"Who is the girl who fluffed at the balance
exercise?"

Was she not going to get away from Innes
for two minutes together?

"Her name is Mary Innes. Why?"

"What a wonderful face. Pure Borgia."

"Oh, no!" Lucy said, sharply.

"I've been wondering all the afternoon
what she reminded me of. I think it is a portrait of a young man by Giorgione, but

which of his young men I wouldn't know. I should have to see them again. Anyhow, it's a wonderful face, so delicate and so strong, so good and so bad. Quite fantastically beautiful. I can't imagine what anything so dramatic is doing at a girls' Physical Training College in the twentieth century."

Well, at least she had the consolation of knowing that someone else saw Innes as she did; exceptional, oddly fine, out of her century, and potentially tragic. She remembered that to Henrietta she was merely a tiresome girl who looked down her nose at people less well endowed with brains.

Lucy wondered what to offer Edward Adrian by way of distraction. She saw coming down the path a floppy satin bow-tie against a dazzling collar and recognized Mr Robb, the elocution master; the only member of the visiting Staff, apart from Dr Knight, that she knew. Mr Robb had been a dashing young actor forty years ago—the most brilliant Lancelot Gobbo of his generation, one understood—and she felt that to hoist Mr Adrian with his own petard would be rather pleasant. But being Lucy her heart softened at the thought of the wasted preparations he had made—the flowers, the cake, the plans for showing off—and she decided to be merciful. She saw O'Donnell, gazing from a discreet distance at her one-time hero, and she beckoned to her. Edward Adrian should have a real, authentic, dyed-in-the-wool fan to cheer him; and he need never know that she was the only one in College.

"Mr Adrian," she said, "this is Eileen O'Donnell, one of your most devoted admirers."

"Oh, Mr Adrian—" she heard O'Donnell begin.

And she left them to it.

Chapter 19

When tea was over (and Lucy had been introduced to at least twenty different sets of parents) the drift back from the garden began, and Lucy overtook Miss Lux on the way to the house.

"I'm afraid that I am going to cry off tonight," she said. "I feel a migraine coming."

"That is a pity," Lux said without emotion. "I have cried off too."

"Oh, why?"

"I'm very tired, and upset about Rouse, and I don't feel like going junketing in town."

"You surprise me."

"I surprise you? In what way?"

"I never thought I should live to see Catherine Lux being dishonest with herself."

"Oh. And what am I fooling myself about?"

"If you have a look at your mind you'll find that that's not why you're staying at home."

"No? Why, then?"

"Because you get such pleasure out of telling Edward Adrian where he gets off."

"A deplorable expression."

"Descriptive, though. You simply jumped at the chance of being high and mighty with him, didn't you?"

"I own that breaking the engagement was no effort."

"And a little unkind?"

"A deplorable piece of self-indulgence by a shrew. That's what you're trying to say, isn't it?"

"He is looking forward so much to having you. I can't think why."

"Thanks. I can tell you why. So that he can cry all over me and tell me how he hates acting—which is the breath of life to him."

"Even if he bores you—"

"If! My God!"

"—you can surely put up with him for an hour or so, and not use Rouse's accident as a sort of ace from your sleeve."

"Are you trying to make an honest woman of me, Lucy Pym?"

"That is the general idea. I feel so sorry for him, being left—"

"My—good—woman," Lux said, stabbing

a forefinger at Lucy with each word, "*never* be sorry for Edward Adrian. Women spend the best years of their lives being sorry for him, and end by being sorry for it. Of all the self-indulgent, self-deceiving—"

"But he *has* got a Johannisberger."

Lux stopped, and smiled at her.

"I could do with a drink, at that," she said reflectively.

She walked on a little.

"Are you really leaving Teddy high and dry?" she asked.

"Yes."

"All right. You win. I was just being a beast. I'll go. And every time he trots out that line about 'Oh, Catherine, how weary I am of this artificial life' I shall think with malice: That Pym woman got me into this."

"I can bear it," Lucy said. "Has anyone heard how Rouse is?"

"Miss Hodge has just been on the telephone. She is still unconscious."

Lucy, seeing Henrietta's head through the window of her office—it was known as the office but was in reality the little sitting-room to the left of the front door—went in to compliment her on the success of the afternoon and so take her mind for at least a moment or two off the thing that oppressed it, and Miss Lux walked on. Henrietta seemed glad to see her, and even glad to have repeated to her the platitudes she had been listening to all the afternoon, and Lucy stayed talking to her for some time; so that the gallery was almost filled again when she took her seat to watch the dancing.

Seeing Edward Adrian in one of the gangway seats she paused and said:

"Catherine is coming."

"And you?" he said, looking up.

"No, alas; I am having a migraine at six-thirty sharp."

Whereupon he said, "Miss Pym, I adore you," and kissed her hand.

His next-door neighbour looked startled, and someone behind tittered, but Lucy liked having her hand kissed. What was the good of putting rose-water and glycerine on every night if you didn't have a little return now and then?

She went back to her seat at the end of the front row, and found that the dowager with the lorgnettes had not waited for the dancing; the seat was empty. But just before the lights went down—the hall was curtained and artificially lit—Rick appeared from behind and said: "If you are not keeping that seat for anyone, may I sit there?"

And as he sat down the first dancers appeared.

After the fourth or fifth item Lucy was conscious of a slow disappointment. Used to the technical standards of international ballet, she had not allowed in her mind for the inevitable amateurism of dancing in this milieu. In everything she had seen the students do so far they had been the best of their line in the business; professionals. But it was obviously not possible to give to other subjects the time and energy that they did and still reach a high standard as dancers. Dancing was a whole-time job.

What they did was good, but it was uninspired. On the best amateur level, or a little above. So far the programme had consisted of the national and period dances beloved of all dancing mistresses, and they had been performed with a conscientious accuracy that was admirable but not diverting. Perhaps the need for keeping their minds on the altered track took some of the spontaneity from their work. But on the whole Lucy thought that it was that neither training nor temperament was sufficient. Their audience too lacked spontaneity; the eagerness with which they had watched the gymnastics was lacking. Perhaps they had too much tea; or perhaps it was the cinema had brought to their remotest doors a standard of achievement that made them critical. Anyhow their applause was polite rather than enthusiastic.

A piece of Russian bravura roused them for a moment, and they waited hopefully for what might come next. The curtains parted to reveal Desterro, alone. Her arms raised above her head and one slim hip turned to the audience. She was wearing some sort of native dress from her own hemisphere, and the "spot" made the bright colours and the barbaric jewels glitter so that she looked like one of the brilliant birds from her Brazilian forests. Her little feet in their high-heeled shoes tapped impatiently under the full skirt. She began to dance; slowly, almost absent-mindedly, as if she were putting in time. Then it became evident that she was waiting for her lover and that he was late. What his lateness meant to her also became rapidly apparent. By this time the audience were sitting up. From some empty space she conjured a lover. One could almost see the hang-dog look on his swarthy face. She dealt with him: faithfully. By this time the audience were sitting on the edge of their seats. Then, having dealt with him, she began to show off to him; but did he not realise his luck in having a girl like her, a girl who had a waist, an eye, a hip, a mouth, an ankle, a total grace like hers? Was he a boor that he could not see? She therefore showed him; with a wit in every movement that brought smiles to every face in the audience. Lucy turned to look at them; in another minute they would be cooing. It was magic. By the time she began to relent and let her lover have a word in, they were her slaves. And when she walked away with that still invisible but undoubtedly subdued young man, they cheered like children at a Wild West matinée.

Watching her as she took her bow, Lucy remembered how The Nut Tart had chosen Leys because for the proper dancing schools "one must have a métier."

"She was modest about her dancing after all," she said aloud. "She could have been a professional."

"I am glad she didn't," Rick said. "Coming here she has learned to love the English countryside. If she had trained in town she would have met only the international riff-raff that hang around ballet."

And Lucy thought that he was probably right.

There was a distinct drop in temperature when the conscientious students reappeared to continue their numbers. Stewart had a Celtic verve that was refreshing, and Innes had grace and moments of fire, but the moment Desterro came among them even Lucy forgot Innes and all the others. Desterro was enchanting.

At the end she had an ovation all to herself.

And Miss Pym, catching the look on Rick's face, felt a small pang.

It was not enough to have one's hand kissed.

"Nobody told me that Desterro could dance like that," she said to Miss Wragg as they went over to supper together when the guests had at last taken their departure with much starting up of engines and shouted goodbyes.

"Oh, she is Madame's little pet," Wragg said in the unenthusiastic voice of Madame's follower speaking of a creature so far gone in sin that she did not play games. "I think she is stagey, myself. Out of place here, somehow. I honestly think that first dance wasn't quite nice. Did you think that?"

"I thought it delightful."

"Oh, well," Wragg said, resignedly; and added: "She must be good, or Madame wouldn't be so keen on her."

Supper was a quiet meal. Exhaustion, anti-climax, and the recollection (now that they were idle) of this morning's accident all served to damp the students' spirits and clog their tongues. The Staff, too, were tired after their shocks, exertions, social efforts, and anxieties. Lucy felt that the occasion called for a glass of good wine, and thought with a passing regret of the Johannisberger that Lux was drinking at that moment. Her heart had begun to thud in a horrid way when she thought that in a few moments she must take that little rosette into the office, and tell Henrietta where she found it.

She had still not taken it out of the drawer where she had left it, and after supper she was on the way up to fetch it when she was overtaken by Beau, who slid an arm into hers and said:

"Miss Pym, we are brewing cocoa in the

common-room, the whole shoot of us. Do come and cheer us up. You don't want to go and sit in that morgue upstairs"—the morgue was presumably the drawing-room—"do you? Come and cheer us up."

"I don't feel particularly cheerful myself," Lucy said, thinking with loathing of the cocoa, "but if you put up with my gloom I shall put up with yours."

As they turned towards the common-room a great wind out of nowhere swept down the corridor through all the wide-open windows, dashing the green branches of the trees outside against one another and tearing the leaves upward so that their backs showed. "The end of the good weather," Lucy said, pausing to listen. She had always hated that restless destroying wind that put paid to the golden times.

"Yes, it's cold too," Beau said. "We've lit a wood fire."

The common-room was part of the "old house" and had an old brick fireplace; and it certainly looked cheerful with the flame and crackle of a freshly lit fire, the rattle of crockery, the bright dresses of the students lying about in exhausted heaps, and their still brighter bedroom slippers. It was not only

O'Donnell who had had recourse to odd footwear tonight; practically everyone was wearing undress shoes of some sort or another. In fact Dakers was lying on a settee with her bare bandaged toes higher than her head. She waved a cheerful hand at Miss Pym, and indicated her feet.

"Haemostosis!" she said. "I bled into my *best* ballet shoes. I suppose no one would like to *buy* a pair of ballet shoes, slightly soiled? No, I was afraid not."

"There's a chair over by the fire, Miss Pym," Beau said, and went to pour out the cocoa. Innes, who was sitting curled up on the hearth superintending a Junior's efforts with a bellows, patted the chair and made her welcome in her usual unsmiling fashion.

"I've cadged the rest of the tea stuff from Miss Joliffe," Hasselt said, coming in with a large plate of mixed left-overs.

"How did you do that?" they asked. "Miss Joliffe never gives away even a smell."

"I promised to send her some peach jam when I got back to South Africa. There isn't really very much though it looks a plateful. The maids had most of it after tea. Hullo, Miss Pym. What did you think of us?"

"I thought you were all wonderful," Lucy said.

"Just like London policemen," Beau said. "Well, you bought that, Hasselt."

Lucy apologised for the cliché, and sought by going into further detail to convince them of her enthusiasm.

"Desterro ran away with the evening, didn't she, though?" they said; and glanced with friendly envy at the composed figure in the bright wrap sitting upright in the inglenook.

"Me, I do only one thing. It is easy to do just one thing well."

And Lucy, like the rest of them, could not decide if the cool little remark was meant to be humble or reproving. On the whole she thought humble.

"That's enough, March, it's going beautifully," Innes said to the Junior, and moved to take the bellows from her. As she moved, her feet came out from under her and Lucy saw that she was wearing black pumps.

And the little metal ornament that should have been on the left one was not there.

Oh, *no,* said Lucy's mind. No. No. No.

"That is your cup, Miss Pym, and here is

yours, Innes. Have a rather tired macaroon, Miss Pym."

"No, I have some chocolate biscuits for Miss Pym."

"No, she is going to have some Ayrshire shortbread, out of a tin, and *fresh*. None of your pawed-over victuals."

The babble went on round her. She took something off a plate. She answered what was said to her. She even took a sip of the stuff in the cup.

Oh, no. No.

Now that the thing was here—the thing she had been afraid of, so afraid that she would not even formulate it in her mind—now that it was here, made concrete and manifest, she was appalled. It had all suddenly become a nightmare: the bright noisy room with the blackening sky outside where the storm was rushing up, and the missing object. One of those nightmares where something small and irrelevant has a terrifying importance. Where something immediate and urgent must be done about it but one can't think what or why.

Presently she must get up and make polite leave-taking and go to Henrietta with her story and end by saying: "And I know whose shoe it came from. Mary Innes's."

Innes was sitting at her feet, not eating but drinking cocoa thirstily. She had curled her feet under her again, but Lucy had no need for further inspection. Even her faint hope that someone else might be wearing pumps had gone overboard. There was a fine colourful variety of footgear present but not a second pair of pumps.

In any case, no one else had a motive for being in the gymnasium at six o'clock this morning.

"Have some more cocoa," Innes said presently, turning to look at her. But Miss Pym had hardly touched hers.

"Then I must have some more," Innes said, and began to get up.

A very tall thin Junior called Farthing, but known even to the Staff as Tuppence-Ha'penny, came in.

"You're late, Tuppence," someone said. "Come and have a bun." But Farthing stood there, uncertainly.

"What is the matter, Tuppence?" they asked, puzzled by her shocked expression.

"I went to put the flowers in Fröken's room," she said slowly.

"Don't tell us there were some there already?" someone said; and there was a general laugh.

"I heard the Staff talking about Rouse."

"Well, what about her? Is she better?"

"She's dead."

The cup Innes was holding crashed on the hearth. Beau crossed over to her to pick up the pieces.

"Oh, nonsense," they said. "You heard wrong, young Tuppence."

"No, I didn't. They were talking on the landing. She died half an hour ago."

This was succeeded by a dismayed silence.

"I *did* put up the wall end," O'Donnell said loudly, into the silence.

"Of course you did, Don," Stewart said, going to her. "We all know that."

Lucy put down her cup and thought that she had better go upstairs. They let her go with murmured regrets, their happy party in pieces round them.

Upstairs, Lucy found that Miss Hodge had gone to the hospital to receive Rouse's people when they arrived, and that it was she who had telephoned the news. Rouse's people had come, and had taken the blow unemotionally, it seemed.

"I never liked her, God forgive me," said Madame, stretched at full length on the hard sofa; her plea to the Deity for forgiveness had a genuine sound.

"Oh, she was all right," Wragg said, "quite nice when you knew her. And the most marvellous centre-half. This is frightful, isn't it. Now it will be a matter of inquiry, and we'll have police, an inquest, and appalling publicity, and everything."

Yes, police and everything.

She should not do anything about the little rosette tonight. And anyhow she wanted to think about it.

She wanted to get away by herself and think about it.

Chapter 20

Bong! Bong! The clock in that far-away steeple struck again. Two o'clock.

She lay staring into the dark, while the cold rain beat on the ground outside and wild gusts rose every now and then and rioted in anarchy, flinging her curtains out into the room so that they flapped like sails and everything was uncertainty and turmoil.

The rain wept with steady persistence, and her heart wept with it. And in her mind was a turmoil greater than the wind's.

"Do the obvious right thing, and let God dispose," Rick had said. And it had seemed a sensible ruling.

But that was when it had been a hypothetical affair of "causing grievous bodily harm" (that was the phrase, wasn't it?) and now it had ceased to be hypothesis and it wasn't any longer mere bodily harm. It was—was *this*.

It wouldn't be God who would dispose

this, in spite of all the comforting tags. It would be the Law. Something written with ink in a statute book. And once that was invoked God Himself could not save a score of innocent persons being crushed under the juggernaut wheels of its progress.

An eye for an eye and a tooth for a tooth, said the old Mosaic law. And it sounded simple. It sounded just. One saw it against a desert background, as if it involved two people only. It was quite different when one put it in modern words and called it "being hanged by the neck until you are dead."

If she went to Henrietta in the—

If?

Oh, all right, of course she was going.

When she went to Henrietta in the morning, she would be putting in motion a power over which neither she nor anyone else had control; a power that once released would catch up this, that, and the next one from the innocent security of their peaceful lives and fling them into chaos.

She thought of Mrs Innes, happily asleep somewhere in Larborough; bound home tomorrow to wait for the return of the daughter in whom she had her life. But her daughter would not come home—ever.

Neither will Rouse, a voice pointed out.

No, of course not, and Innes must somehow pay for that. She must not be allowed
to profit by her crime. But surely, surely
there was some way in which payment
could be made without making the innocent
pay even more bitterly.

What was justice?

To break a woman's heart; to bring ruin
and shame on Henrietta and the destruction
of all she had built up; to rub out for ever the
radiance of Beau, the Beau who was un-
conditioned to grief. Was that a life for a
life? That was three—no, four lives for one.

And one not worth—

Oh, no. That she could not judge. For that
one had to "see before and after," as Rick
said. A curiously sober mind, Rick had, for a
person with a play-boy's face and a Latin
lover's charm.

There was Innes moving about again next-
door. As far as Lucy knew she had not slept
yet either. She was very quiet, but every now
and then one heard a movement or the tap in
her room ran. Lucy wondered whether the
water was to satisfy a thirst or to cool tem-
ples that must be throbbing. If she, Lucy,
was lying awake with her thoughts running

round and round inside her skull like trapped mice, what must Innes be going through? Humourless she might be, unenamoured of the human species she probably was, but insensitive she most certainly was not. Whether it was thwarted ambition, or sheer anger and hate, that had driven her down to the gymnasium through the misty morning, she was not the sort to be able to do what she had done with impunity. It might well be indeed, that given her temperament it was herself she had destroyed when she tampered with that boom. In the case-histories of crime there were instances of women so callous that they had come to a fresh blooming once the obstacle to their desires was out of the way. But they were not built like Mary Innes. Innes belonged to that other, and rarer, class who found too late that they could not live with themselves any more. The price they had paid was too high.

Perhaps Innes would provide her own punishment.

That, now she came to think of it, was how she had first thought of Innes, on that Sunday afternoon under the cedar. The stake or nothing. A self-destroyer.

That she had destroyed a life that stood in her way was almost incidental.

It had not, in any case, been intended as destruction; Lucy was quite sure of that. That is what made this business of starting the machine so repellent, so unthinkable. All that the insecure pin was meant to achieve was a temporary incapacity. An assurance that Rouse would not go to Arlinghurst in September—and that she would.

Had she had that in mind, Lucy wondered, when she refused the appointment at the Wycherley Orthopaedic Hospital? No, surely not. She was not a planner in cold blood. The thing had been done at the very last moment, in desperation.

At least, it had been *achieved* at the very last moment.

It was possible that its lateness was due to lack of previous opportunity. The way to the gymnasium might never have been clear before; or Rouse may have got there first.

"A Borgia face," Edward Adrian had said, delightedly.

And Teresa's great-grandmother's grand-mother, whom she resembled, *she* had planned. And had lived a long, secure, and successful life as a widow, administering rich estates and bringing up a son, without apparently any signs of spiritual suicide.

The wind flung itself into the room, and Innes's window began to rattle. She heard Innes cross the room to it, and presently it stopped.

She wished she could go next-door, now, at this minute, and put her hand down. Show Innes the ace she held and didn't want to play. Together they could work something out.

Together? With the girl who loosened that pin under the boom?

No. With the girl she had talked to in the corridor last Saturday afternoon, so radiant, so full of dignity and wisdom. With the girl who could not sleep tonight. With her mother's daughter.

Whatever she had done, even if she had planned it, the result had been something she had neither planned nor foreseen. The result was catastrophe for her.

And who in the first place had brought that catastrophe?

Henrietta. Henrietta with her mule-like preference for her inferior favourite.

She wondered if Henrietta was sharing Innes's vigil. Henrietta who had come back from West Larborough so strangely thin and old-looking. As if the frame she was strung on had collapsed and the stuffing had shifted. Like a badly stuffed toy after a month in the nursery. That is what Henrietta had looked like.

She had been truly sorry for her friend, bereft of someone she had—loved? Yes, loved, she supposed. Only love could have blinded her to Rouse's defects. Bereft; and afraid for her beloved Leys. She had been truly moved by her suffering. But she could not help the thought that but for Henrietta's own action none of this would have happened.

The operative cause was Innes's vulnerability. But the button that had set the whole tragedy in motion was pressed by Henrietta.

And now she, Lucy, was waiting to press another button which would set in motion machinery even more monstrous. Machinery that would catch up in its gears and meshes, and maim and destroy, the innocent with the guilty. Henrietta perhaps had bought her punishment, but what had the Inneses done to have this horror unloaded on them? This unnameable horror.

Or *had* they contributed? How much had

Innes's upbringing been responsible for her lack of resilience? Given that she had been born without "oil on her feathers," had they tried to condition her to the lack? Who could ever say where first causes lay?

Perhaps after all, even through the Law, it was the Deity who disposed. If you were a Christian you took that for granted, of course. You took for granted that nothing ever happened that there was no cause for. That everyone who would be tortured incidentally by Innes's trial for murder had in some way "bought" their punishment. It was a fine comfortable theory, and Lucy wished that she could subscribe to it. But she found it difficult to believe that any deficiency on the part of parents as responsible and as devoted as the Inneses could warrant the bringing down on their heads of a tragedy so unspeakable.

Or perhaps—

She sat up, to consider this new thought.

If God did dispose—as undoubtedly He did in the latter end—then perhaps the disposing was already at work. Had begun to work when it was she and not someone else who found the little rosette. It had not been found by a strong-minded person who would go straight to Henrietta with it as soon as she smelt a rat, and so set the machinery of man-made Law in motion. No. It had been found by a feeble waverer like herself, who could never see less than three sides to any question. Perhaps that made sense.

But she wished very heartily that the Deity had found another instrument. She had always hated responsibility; and a responsibility of this magnitude was something that she could not deal with at all. She wished that she could throw away the little rosette—toss it out of the window now and pretend that she had never seen it. But of course she could not do that. However rabbity and inadequate she was by nature, there was always her other half—the Laetitia half—which stood watching her with critical eyes. She could never get away from that other half of herself. It had sent her into fights with her knees knocking, it had made her speak when she wanted to hold her tongue, it had kept her from lying down when she was too tired to stand up. It would keep her from washing her hands now.

She got up and leaned out into the wet, lashing, noisy night. There was a puddle of rain water on the wood floor inside the window. The cold shock of it on her bare feet was somehow grateful; a physical and understandable discomfort. At least she did not have to mop it up, or wonder about a carpet. All the elements came into this place at their will and everyone took it for granted. One of Innes's few volunteered remarks had been how lovely it had been one morning to waken and find her pillow crusted with snow. That had happened only once, she said, but you could always tell the season by what you found on your pillow in the morning: spiders in the autumn and sycamore seeds in June.

She stayed so long cooling her burning head that her feet grew cold, and she had to wrap them in a jersey to warm them when she got back into bed. That completes it, she thought: cold feet mentally and physically. You're a poor thing, Lucy Pym.

About three o'clock when she was growing sleepy at last, she was shot wide awake by the realisation of what she was proposing to do. She was seriously considering keeping back evidence in a capital charge. Becoming an accessory after the fact. A criminal.

She, respectable, law-abiding Lucy Pym.

How had she got to that point? What could she have been thinking of?

Of course she had no choice in the matter at all. Who disposed or did not dispose was no concern of hers. This was a matter of public inquiry, and she had a duty to do. A duty to civilisation, to the State, to herself. Her private emotions had nothing to do with it. Her views on justice had nothing to do with it. However unequal and wrong-headed the Law might be, she could not suppress evidence.

How in the name of all that was crazy had she ever thought that she could?

Rick was right: she would do the obvious right thing, and let God dispose.

About half-past four she really did fall asleep.

Chapter 21

The morning was bleary and sodden, and Lucy regarded it with distaste. The waking-bell had sounded as usual at five-thirty, although on the morning after the Demonstration there were no classes before breakfast. College might make concessions but it did not discard its habits. She tried to fall asleep again, but reality had come with the daylight, and what had been feverish theory in the dark hours was now chill fact. In an hour or two she would have pressed that button, and altered beyond computing lives of whose existence she was not even aware. Her heart began to thud again.

Oh, dear, why had she ever come to this place!

It was when she had finished dressing and was sticking a few invisible hairpins into appropriate places that she realised that she could not go to Henrietta about the rosette without first going to Innes. She was not sure whether this was a remnant of some childish conception of "playing fair" or whether she was just trying to find a way of breaking the matter that would make her own personal responsibility less absolute.

She went to Innes's door, quickly before the impulse to action should evaporate, and knocked. She had heard Innes come back from her bath and reckoned that by now she must be dressed.

The Innes who opened the door looked tired and heavy-eyed but composed. Now that she was face to face with her Lucy found it difficult to identify her with the Innes of her disturbed thoughts last night.

"Do you mind coming into my room for a moment?" she asked.

Innes hesitated, looked uncertain for a second, and then recovered herself. "Yes, of course," she said; and followed Lucy.

"What a night of rain it was," she said brightly.

It was unlike Innes to bother with remarks about the weather. And it was exceedingly unlike Innes to be bright.

Lucy took the little silver rosette out of her drawer and held it out on her palm for Innes to see.

"Do you know what that is?" she asked.

In a second the brightness had disappeared and Innes's face was hard and wary.

"Where did you get that?" she snapped.

It was only then that Lucy realised how, deep down, she had counted on Innes's reaction being different. How, unconsciously, she had expected Innes to say: "It looks like something off a dancing pump; lots of us have them." Her heart stopped thudding and sank into her stomach.

"I found it on the gymnasium floor very early yesterday morning," she said.

The hard wariness melted into a slow despair.

"And why do you show it to me?" Innes said dully.

"Because I understand that there is only one pair of those old-fashioned pumps in College."

There was silence. Lucy laid the little object down on the table and waited.

"Am I wrong?" she asked at last.

"No."

There was another silence.

"You don't understand, Miss Pym," she said in a burst, "it wasn't meant to be— I know you'll think I'm just trying to white-wash it, but it was never meant to be—to be the way it turned out. It was because I was so sick about missing Arlinghurst—I practically lost my reason over that for a time—I behaved like an idiot. It got so that I couldn't think of anything in the world but Arlinghurst. And this was just to be a way of—of letting me have a second chance at it. It was never meant to be more than that. You must believe that. You must—"

"But of course I believe it. If I didn't I don't suppose I should be sharing the knowledge of this with you." She indicated the rosette.

After a moment Innes said: "What are you going to do?"

"Oh, dear God, I don't know," said poor Lucy, helpless now that she was face to face with reality. All the crimes she had met with were in slick detective stories where the heroine, however questionable, was invariably innocent, or in case-histories where the crime was safely over with and put away and a matter only for the scalpel. All those subjects of case-history record had had friends and relations whose stunned disbelief must have been very like her own, but the knowledge was neither comfort nor guide to her. This was the kind of thing that happened to other people—happened daily if one could believe the Press—but could not possibly happen to oneself.

How *could* one believe that someone one had laughed and talked with, liked and admired, shared a communal life with, could be responsible for another's death?

She found herself beginning to tell Innes of her sleepless night, of her theories about "disposing," of her reluctance to destroy half a dozen lives because of one person's crime. She was too absorbed in her own problem to notice the dawning hope in Innes's eyes. It was only when she heard herself saying, "Of course you cannot possibly be allowed to profit by Rouse's death," that she realised how far she had already come along the road that she had had no intention of travelling.

But Innes pounced on this. "Oh, but I won't, Miss Pym. And it has nothing to do with your finding the little ornament. I knew last night when I heard that she was dead that I couldn't go to Arlinghurst. I was going to tell Miss Hodge this morning. I was awake too last night. Facing a lot of things. Not only my responsibility for Rouse's death—my inability to take defeat and like it. But—oh, well, a lot of things that wouldn't interest you." She paused a moment, considering Lucy. "Look, Miss Pym, if I were to spend the rest of my life atoning for yesterday morning will you—would you—" She could not put so brazen a suggestion into words, even after Lucy's dissertation on justice.

"Become an accessory after the fact?"

The cold legality of the phrase discouraged Innes.

"No, I suppose it is too much to expect anyone to do. But I *would* atone, you know. It wouldn't be any halfhearted affair. It would be my life for—hers. I would do it gladly."

"I believe you, of course. But how do you plan to atone?"

"I thought of that last night. I began with leper colonies and things like that, but they were rather unreal and didn't make much sense in connection with a Leys training. I have a better idea. I decided that I would work alongside my father. I hadn't planned to do medical work, but I am good at it and there is no orthopaedic clinic in our home town."

"It sounds admirable," Lucy said, "but where is the penance?"

"My one ambition since I was a little girl has been to get away from living in a little market town; coming to Leys was my passport to freedom."

"I see."

"Believe me, Miss Pym, it would be penance. But it wouldn't be a barren one. It wouldn't be just personal flagellation. I would be doing something useful with my life, something that would—would make it good value for exchange."

"Yes, I see."

There was another long silence.

The five-minute bell rang, but for the first time since she came to Leys Lucy was unconscious of a bell.

"Of course you have nothing but my word for it—"

"I would accept your word."

"Thank you."

It seemed too easy a way out, she was thinking. If Innes was to be punished, the living of a dull and useful life hardly seemed a sufficient exaction. She had forfeited Arlinghurst of course; that would cost her something. But would it pay for a death?

What, in any case, would pay for a death? Except a death.

And Innes was offering what she obviously considered a living death. Perhaps after all it was not so poor an exchange.

What she, Lucy, was faced with was the fact that her deliberations, her self-communing and comparing of arguments, fused at this moment into one single and simple issue. Was she going to condemn to death the girl who was standing in front of her?

It was, after all, as simple as that. If she took that little rosette to Henrietta this morning, Innes would die before the first students came back to Leys in the autumn. If she did not die she would spend her twenties in a living death that would indeed be "barren."

Let her spend her years in the prison of her choice, where she could be useful to her fellows.

Certainly she, Lucy Pym, was quite unequal to the task of condemning her.

And that was that.

"I am entirely in your hands," she said slowly to Innes, "because I am quite incapable of sending anyone to the gallows. I know what my plain duty is and I can't do it." Odd, she thought, that I should be in her reverence rather than she in mine.

Innes stared at her, doubtfully.

"You mean—" Her tongue came out and ran along her dry lips. "You mean that you won't tell about the rosette?"

"No. I shall never tell anyone."

Innes went suddenly white.

So white that Lucy realised that this was a phenomenon that she had read about but never seen. "White as a sheet," they said. Well, it was perhaps an unbleached sheet but it certainly was "going white."

Innes put her hand out to the chair by the dressing-table and sat down abruptly. Seeing Lucy's anxious expression she said: "It's all right, I'm not going to faint. I've never fainted in my life. I'll be all right in a minute."

Lucy, who had been antagonised by her self-possession, her ready bargaining—Innes had been far too lucid on the subject, she felt—was seized with something like compunction. Innes had not after all been self-possessed. It had been the old story of emotion clamped down and taking a mean revenge when it found escape.

"Would you like a drink of water?" Lucy said, moving to the wash-basin.

"No, thank you, I'm all right. It's just that for the last twenty-four hours I've been so afraid, and seeing that silver thing on your hand was the last straw, and then suddenly it is all over, you've let me buy a reprieve, and—and—"

Sobs came up in her throat and choked the words. Great rending sobs without a single tear. She put her hands over her mouth to stop them, but they burst through and she covered her face and struggled for composure. It was no use. She put both arms on the desk with her head between them and sobbed her heart out.

And Lucy, looking at her, thought: Another girl would have begun with this. Would have used it as a weapon, a bid for my sympathy. But not Innes. Innes comes self-contained and aloof, offering hostages. Without the breakdown no one would have guessed that she was suffering. Her present aban-donment was the measure of her previous torture.

The first low murmur of the gong began in a slow crescendo.

Innes heard it and struggled to her feet. "If you'll forgive me," she said, "I'll go and dash some cold water on myself. That will stop it."

Lucy thought it remarkable that a girl so racked with sobs that she could hardly speak should prescribe for herself with such detachment; as if she were another person from this hysterical individual who had taken possession of her and was making such an exhibition of herself.

"Yes, do," Lucy said.

Innes paused with her hand on the door-knob.

"Some day I'll be able to thank you properly," she said, and disappeared.

Lucy dropped the little silver rosette into her pocket and went down to breakfast.

Chapter 22

It was a horrible week-end.

The rain poured down. Henrietta went about looking as though she had had a major operation that had not proved a success. Madame was at her worst and not at all helpful, either actually or verbally. Fröken was furious that such a thing should have happened in "her" gymnasium. Wragg was an ever-present Cassandra scattering depressing truisms. Lux was quiet and tired.

Lux had come back from Larborough bearing a small pink candle wrapped in pale green tissue paper. "Teddy said I was to give you this," she said. "I can't think why."

"Oh? From a cake?"

"Yes. It's my birthday about now."

"How nice of him to remember."

"Oh, he keeps a birthday diary. It's part of his publicity. It is his secretary's duty to send telegrams to all the appropriate people on the appropriate days."

"Don't you ever give him credit for anything?" Lucy asked.

"Teddy? Not for a real emotion, I don't. I've known him since he was ten, don't forget. He can't fool me for more than five seconds together."

"My hairdresser," Lucy said, "who lectures to me while he is doing my hair, says that one should allow everyone three faults. If one makes that allowance, one finds that the rest is surprisingly nice, he says."

"When you allow for Teddy's three faults there is nothing left, unfortunately."

"Why?"

"Because his three faults are vanity, selfishness, and self-pity. And any one of the three is totally destructive."

"Whew!" said Lucy. "I give up."

But she stuck the silly little candle on her dressing-table, and thought kindly of Edward Adrian.

She wished she could think as kindly of her beloved Beau, who was making things as difficult as possible by being furious with Innes for giving up Arlinghurst. In fact Lucy understood that things had come as near a quarrel between them as was possible between two people so mutually devoted.

"Says she wouldn't be happy in dead men's shoes," said Beau, positively giving off sparks with wrath. "Can you imagine anything more ridiculous? Turning down Arlinghurst as if it were a cup of tea. After nearly dying of chagrin because she didn't get it in the first place. For God's sake, Miss Pym, you talk to her and make her see sense before it is too late. It isn't just Arlinghurst, it's her whole future. Beginning at Arlinghurst means beginning at the top. You talk to her, will you? Talk her out of this absurd notion!"

It seemed to Lucy that she was always being implored to "talk to" people. When she wasn't being a dose of soothing syrup she was being a shot of adrenaline, and when she wasn't being that she was being just a spoonful of alkaline powder for general consumption.

When she wasn't being a *deus ex machina;* a perverter of justice. But she tried not to think of that.

There was nothing she could say to Innes, of course, but other people had said it. Miss Hodge had wrought with her long and faithfully; dismayed by the defection of the girl she had not wanted to appoint in the first place. Now she had no one to send to Arlinghurst; she must write and tell them so and see the appointment go elsewhere. Perhaps when the news of the fatal accident leaked round the academic world Arlinghurst would decide to look elsewhere next time they wanted a gymnast. Accidents shouldn't happen in well-conducted gymnasiums; not fatal accidents, anyhow.

That, too, was the police point of view. They had been very nice, the police, very considerate. Very willing to consider the harm that undesirable publicity would do the establishment. But there had to be an inquest, of course. And inquests were painfully public and open to misconstruction. Henrietta's lawyer had seen the local Press and they had promised to play down the affair, but who knew when a clipping might catch the eye of a sub-editor at a temporary loss for a sensation? And then what?

Lucy had wanted to go away before the inquest, to get away from the perpetual reminders of her guilt in the eyes of the Law, but Henrietta had begged her to stay. She had never been able to say no to Henrietta, and this pathetic aged Henrietta was someone whom she could not refuse. So Lucy stayed; doing odd jobs for Henrietta and generally leaving her free to deal with the crowd of extraneous duties that the accident had saddled her with.

But to the inquest she would not go.

She could not sit there with all her load of knowledge and not at some point be tempted to stand up and tell the truth and have the responsibility off her soul.

Who knew what rat the police might smell out? They had come and viewed the gymnasium, and measured things, and reckoned the weight of the boom, and interviewed all and sundry, and consulted the various experts on the subject, and listened and said nothing. They had taken away the pin that had been so fatally insecure; and that may have been mere routine, but who could tell? Who could tell what suspicions they might be entertaining in their large calm breasts and behind their polite expressionless faces?

But as it turned out, a quite unexpected saviour appeared at the inquest. A saviour in the person of Arthur Middleham, tea importer, of 59 West Larborough Road; that is to say, a resident in one of the villas which lined the highroad between West Larborough and the gates of Leys. Mr Middleham knew nothing about College except that it was there, and that the scantily attired young women who flew about the district on bicycles belonged to it. But he had heard about the accident. And it had struck him as odd that a pin in the gymnasium at Leys had moved out of place on the same morning, and presumably about the same time, as a pane of glass had been shaken out of his drawing-room window by a passing convoy of tanks from the works at South Larborough. His theory was, in fact, the same as Miss Lux's: vibration. Only Miss Lux's had been a hit in the dark and of no value. Mr Middleham's was reasonable and backed by three-dimensional evidence: a pane of broken glass.

And as always when someone has given a lead, there were gratuitous followers. (If someone invented a story and wrote to the Press that they had seen a green lion in the sky at 5.30 the previous evening, at least six people would have seen it retrospectively.) An excited woman, hearing Mr Middleham's evidence, got up from the body of the hall and said that her ginger jar that she had had for years had dropped off the little table in her window of its own accord at the same time.

"Where do you live, madam?" the coroner

asked, when he had winkled her out of the crowd and installed her as evidence.

She lived in the cottages between Leys and Bidlington, she said. On the highroad? Oh, yes, much too much on the highroad; in the summer the dust was a fair sickener, and when the traffic was them there tanks— No, she had no cat. No, there had been no one in the room. She had just come in after breakfast and found it on the floor. It had never happened before.

Poor O'Donnell, very nervous but clear and decided, gave evidence that she had put up the end by the wall and that Rouse had attended to the middle end. "Puting it up" meant hoisting the boom by the pulley rope and pushing the pin under it to keep it up. It was also kept up, to a certain extent, by the rope, the hanging end of which was given a turn round a cleat on the upright. No, they had not tested the apparatus before going.

Fröken, asked about the rope which had not proved a substitute for the pin, said that it had not been wound tightly enough to prevent sagging when the pin was removed. The twisting of the rope round the cleat was an automatic gesture, and no student thought of it as a precautionary measure. It was that, in fact, of course. The metal of the pin might break through some fault, and the rope in that case took the strain. Yes, it was possible that a rope, unaccustomed to a greater strain than the weight of a boom, stretched under the sudden addition of a ten-stone burden, but she thought not. Gymnasium ropes were highly tested and guaranteed. It was much more likely that the twist Miss Rouse gave it had been inadequate.

And that seemed to be all. It was an unfortunate accident. The pin the police had abstracted had been used by all and sundry during the Demonstration, and was no evidence of anything.

It was obviously Death by Misadventure.

Well, that was the end of it, Lucy thought, when she heard the news. She had waited in the drawing-room, looking out at the rainy garden, not able to believe that something would not go wrong. No crime was ever committed without a slip-up somewhere; she had read enough case-histories to know that.

There had been one slip-up already, when that little ornament came loose from a shoe. Who knew what else the police might have unearthed? And now it was over, and Innes was safe. And she knew now that it was for Innes that she had put herself in the Law's reverence. She had thought it was for Innes's mother, for Henrietta, for absolute justice. But in the latter end it was because whatever Innes had done she had not deserved what the Law would do to her. She had been highly tried, and her breaking-point was lower than normal. She lacked some alloy, some good coarse reinforcing stuff, that would have helped her to stand tension without giving way. But she was too fine to throw away.

Lucy noticed with interest the quality of the cheer that greeted her as she went up to receive her diploma on Wednesday morning. The cheers for the various Seniors varied not only in intensity but in quality. There was laughter, for instance, and affection in the reception they gave Dakers. And Beau got a Head Senior's tribute; the congratulations of her inferiors to a highly popular Senior. But there was something in the cheer that they gave Innes that was remarkable; a warmth of admiration, a sympathy, and a well-wishing, that was accorded to no one else. Lucy wondered if it was merely that her inability to take the Arlinghurst appointment had moved them. Henrietta had said, during that conversation about Rouse and her examination tactics, that Innes was not popular. But there was something more in that cheer than mere popularity. They admired her. It was their tribute to quality.

The giving of diplomas, postponed from Tuesday to Wednesday because of the inquest, was the last event of Lucy's stay at Leys. She had arranged to catch the twelve o'clock train to London. She had been touched during the last few days to receive an endless string of small presents, which were left in her room with written messages attached. She hardly ever returned to her room without finding a new one there. Very few people had given Lucy presents since she grew up, and she still had a child's pleasure in being given something, however small. And these gifts had a spontaneity that was heart-warming; it was no concerted effort, no affair of putting the hat round; they had each given her something as it occurred to them. The Disciples' offering was a large white card which said:

THIS WILL ADMIT
MISS LUCY PYM

TO THE FOUR DISCIPLES CLINIC
AT MANCHESTER
AND WILL PROVIDE
A COURSE OF TREATMENTS
OF ANY KIND WHATEVER
AT ANY TIME WHATEVER.

Dakers had contributed a small untidy parcel, labelled "To remind you every morning of our first meeting!" which on being opened proved to be one of those flat loofahs for back-scrubbing. It was surely in some other life that she had been peered at over the bathroom partition by that waggish pony's-face. It was certainly not this Lucy Pym who had sat in the bath.

The devoted Miss Morris had made her a little felt purse—Heaven alone knew when the child had found time to fabricate it—and at the other end of the scale of worldly magnificence was Beau's pigskin case, which bore the message "You will have so many parting gifts that you will need something to put them in," and was stamped with her initials. Even Giddy, with whom she had spent odd half hours talking about rheumatism and rats, had sent up a plant in a pot. She had no idea what it was—it looked fleshy and faintly obscene—but was relieved that it was small. Travelling with a pot plant was not her idea of what was fitting.

Beau had come in between breakfast and Diploma-giving to help her pack, but all the serious packing was done. Whether anything would close once everything was in was another matter.

"I'll come back and sit on them for you before morning clinic," Beau said. "We are free until then. Except for clinic there is nothing much to do until we go home on Friday."

"You'll be sorry to finish at Leys?"

"Dreadfully. I've had a wonderful time. However, summer holidays are a great consolation."

"Innes told me some time ago that you were going to Norway together."

"Yes, we were," Beau said, "but we're not any more."

"Oh."

"Innes has other plans."

It was evident that this relationship was not what it had been.

"Well, I'd better go and see that the Juniors haven't hogged all the best seats at the Diploma Do," she said, and went.

But there was one relationship that showed satisfactory progress.

The Nut Tart knocked at her door and said that she had come to give dear Miss Pym a luck-piece. She came in, looked at the piled cases, and said with her customary frankness: "You are not a very good packer, are you? Neither am I. It is a pedestrian talent."

Lucy, whose luck-pieces in the last few days had ranged from a Woolworth monkey-on-a-stick to a South African halfpenny, waited with some curiosity to see what The Nut Tart's idea of the thing might be.

It was a blue bead.

"It was dug up in Central America a hundred years ago and it is almost as old as the world. It is very lucky."

"But I can't take that from you," Lucy protested.

"Oh, I have a little bracelet of them. It was the bracelet that was dug up. But I have taken out one of the beads for you. There are five left and that is plenty. And I have a piece of news for you. I am not going back to Brazil."

"No?"

"I am going to stay in England and marry Rick."

Lucy said that she was delighted to hear it.

"We shall be married in London in October, and you will be there and you will come to the wedding, no?"

Yes, Lucy would come to the wedding with pleasure.

"I am so glad about it," she said. She needed some contact with happiness after the last few days.

"Yes, it is all very satisfactory. We are cousins but not too near, and it is sensible to keep it in the family. I always thought I should like to marry an Englishman; and of course Rick is a parti. He is senior partner although he is so young. My parents are very pleased. And my grandmother, of course."

"And I take it that you yourself are pleased?" Lucy said, a shade dashed by this matter-of-fact catalogue.

"Oh yes. Rick is the only person in the world except my grandmother who can make me do things I don't want to do. That will be very good for me."

She looked at Lucy's doubtful face, and her great eyes sparkled.

"And of course I like him very much," she said.

When the diplomas had been presented, Lucy had mid-morning coffee with the Staff and said goodbye to them. Since she was leaving in the middle of the morning no one was free to come to the station with her. Henrietta thanked her, with undoubted tears in her eyes this time, for the help she had been. (But not in her wildest imaginings would Henrietta guess how much the help amounted to.) Lucy was to consider Leys as her home any time she wanted to come and stay, or if she ever wanted a lecturer's job, or if—or if—

And Lucy had to hide the fact that Leys, where she had been so happy, was the one place in the world that she would never come back to. A place that she was going, if her conscience and the shade of Rouse would let her, to blot out of her mind.

The Staff went to their various duties and Lucy went back to her room to finish packing. She had not spoken to Innes since that so-incredible conversation on Saturday morning; had hardly seen her, indeed, except for the moment when she had taken her diploma from Miss Hodge's hands.

Was Innes going to let her go without a word?

But when she came back to her room she found that word on her table. A written word. She opened the envelope and read:

Dear Miss Pym,

Here it is in writing. For the rest of my life I shall atone for the thing I can't undo. I pay forfeit gladly. My life for hers.

I am sorry that this has spoiled Leys for you. And I hope that you will not be unhappy about what you have done for me. I promise to make it worth while.

Perhaps, ten years from today, you will come to the West Country and see what I have done with my life. That would give me a date to look forward to. A landmark in a world without them.

Meanwhile, and always, my gratitude—my unspeakable gratitude.

                              Mary Innes.

"What time did you order the taxi for?" Beau asked, coming in on top of her knock.

"Half-past eleven."

"It's practically that now. Have you everything in that is going in? Hot water bottle? You hadn't one. Umbrella downstairs? You don't possess one. What do you do? Wait in doorways till it's over, or steal the nearest one? I had an aunt who always bought the cheapest she could find and discarded it in the nearest waste-paper-bin when the rain stopped. More money than sense, as my Nanny used to say. Well, now. Is that all? Consider well, because once we get those cases shut we'll never get them open again. Nothing left in the drawers? People always leave things stuck at the back of drawers." She opened the small drawers of the table and ran her hands into the back of them. "Half the divorces in the Western Hemisphere start through the subsequent revelations."

She withdrew her right hand, and Lucy saw that she was holding the little silver rosette; left lying at the back of the drawer because Lucy had not been able to make up her mind what to do with it.

Beau turned it over in her fingers.

"That looks like the little button thing off my shoe," she said.

"*Your* shoe?"

"Yes. Those black pump things that one wore at dancing class. I hung on to them because they are so lovely when one's feet are tired. Like gloves. I can still wear the shoes I wore when I was fourteen. I always had enormous feet for my age, and believe me it was no consolation to be told that you were going to be tall." Her attention went back to the thing she was holding. "So *this* is where I lost it," she said. "You know, I wondered quite a lot about that." She dropped it into her pocket. "You'll have to sit on the case, I'm afraid. You sit on it and I'll wrestle with the locks."

Automatically Lucy sat on it.

She wondered why she had never noticed before how cold those blue eyes were. Brilliant and cold and shallow.

The bright hair fell over her lap as Beau wrestled with the locks. The locks would do what she wanted, of course. Everything and everyone, always, since the day she was born, had done what she wanted. If they hadn't, she took steps to see that they did. At the age of four, Lucy remembered, she had defeated a whole adult world because her will to have things her way was greater than all the wills combined against her. She had never known frustration.

She could not visualise the possibility of frustration.

If *her* friend had the obvious right to Arlinghurst, then to Arlinghurst she should go.

"There! That's done it. Stand by to sit on the other if I can't manage it. I see Giddy's given you one of his loathsome little plants. What a bore for you. Perhaps you can exchange it for a bowl at the back door one day."

How soon, Lucy wondered, had Innes begun to suspect? Almost at once? Certainly before the afternoon, when she had turned green on the spot where it had happened.

But she had not been sure until she saw the silver rosette on Lucy's palm, and learned where it had been found.

Poor Innes. Poor Innes, who was paying forfeit.

"*Tax-i!*" yelled a voice along the corridor.

"There's your cab. I'll take your things. No, they're quite light; you forget the training I've had. I wish you weren't going, Miss Pym. We shall miss you so much."

Lucy heard herself saying the obvious things. She even heard herself promising Beau that she might come to them for Christmas, when Beau would be home for her first "working" holidays.

Beau put her into the cab, took a tender

farewell of her, and said, "The station" to the driver, and the taxi slid into motion and Beau's face smiled a moment beyond the window, and was gone.

The driver pushed back the glass panel and asked: "London train, lady?" Yes, Lucy said, to London.

And in London she would stay. In London was her own, safe, nice, calm, collected existence, and in future she would be content with it. She would even give up lecturing on psychology.

What did she know about psychology anyhow?

As a psychologist she was a first-rate teacher of French.

She could write a book about character as betrayed by facial characteristics. At least she had been right about that. Mostly.

Eyebrows that sent people to the stake.

Yes, she would write a book about face-reading.

Under another name, of course. Face-reading was not well seen among the intelligentsia.

THE
DAUGHTER
OF TIME

RALPH NEVILL
1st Earl of Westmorland

RICHARD ≈ CICELY NEVILL
Duke of York | *(The Rose of Raby)*

RICHARD NEVILL
1st Earl of Salisbury

ELIZABETH
m.
John de la
Pole, *Duke of*
Suffolk

EDWARD ≈ Elizabeth ≈ Sir John
IV | Woodville | Grey

GEORGE
Duke of
Clarence
m.
Isabel Nevill

MARGARET
m.
Charles
Duke of
Burgundy

RICHARD III
m.
Anne Nevill

RALPH NEVILL
Earl of Warwick
(The Kingmaker)

Thomas   Sir Richard
Lord Dorset   Grey

JOHN
Earl of
Lincoln

EDWARD
Prince of
Wales

RICHARD
Duke of
York

ELIZABETH
m.
Henry VII

EDWARD
Earl of
Warwick

Margaret

EDWARD
Prince of
Wales

ISABEL
m.
George
Duke of
Clarence

ANNE
m.
Richard
III

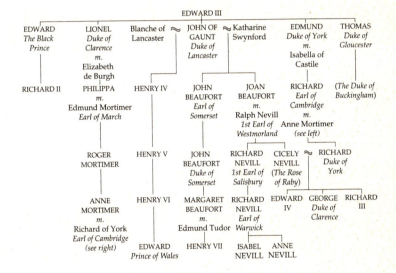

EDWARD III

EDWARD — *The Black Prince*

LIONEL — *Duke of Clarence* — m. Elizabeth de Burgh

Blanche of Lancaster ≈ JOHN OF GAUNT — *Duke of Lancaster* ≈ Katharine Swynford

EDMUND — *Duke of York* — m. Isabella of Castile

THOMAS — *Duke of Gloucester*

RICHARD II

PHILIPPA — m. Edmund Mortimer *Earl of March*

HENRY IV

JOHN BEAUFORT — *Earl of Somerset*

JOAN BEAUFORT — m. Ralph Nevill *1st Earl of Westmorland*

RICHARD — *Earl of Cambridge* — m. Anne Mortimer *(see left)*

(The Duke of Buckingham)

ROGER MORTIMER

HENRY V

JOHN BEAUFORT — *Duke of Somerset*

RICHARD NEVILL — *1st Earl of Salisbury*

CICELY NEVILL *(The Rose of Raby)* ≈ RICHARD — *Duke of York*

ANNE MORTIMER — m. Richard of York *Earl of Cambridge (see right)*

HENRY VI

MARGARET BEAUFORT — m. Edmund Tudor

RICHARD NEVILL — *Earl of Warwick*

EDWARD IV

GEORGE — *Duke of Clarence*

RICHARD III

EDWARD — *Prince of Wales*

HENRY VII

ISABEL NEVILL

ANNE NEVILL

Truth is the daughter of time.

— *Old Proverb*

Chapter 1

Grant lay on his high white cot and stared at the ceiling. Stared at it with loathing. He knew by heart every last minute crack on its nice clean surface. He had made maps of the ceiling and gone exploring on them; rivers, islands, and continents. He had made guessing games of it and discovered hidden objects; faces, birds, and fishes. He had made mathematical calculations of it and rediscovered his childhood; theorems, angles, and triangles. There was practically nothing else he could do but look at it. He hated the sight of it.

He had suggested to The Midget that she might turn his bed around a little so that he could have a new patch of ceiling to explore. But it seemed that that would spoil the symmetry of the room, and in hospitals symmetry ranked just a short head behind cleanliness and a whole length in front of Godliness. Anything out of the parallel was hospital profanity. Why didn't he read? she asked. Why didn't he go on reading some of those expensive brand-new novels that his friends kept on bringing him?

"There are far too many people born into the world, and far too many words written. Millions and millions of them pouring from the presses every minute. It's a horrible thought."

"You sound constipated," said The Midget.

The Midget was Nurse Ingham, and she was in sober fact a very nice five-feet-two, with everything in just proportion. Grant called her The Midget to compensate himself for being bossed around by a piece of Dresden china which he could pick up in one hand. When he was on his feet, this is to say. It was not only that she told him what he might or might not do, but she dealt with his six-feet-odd with an off-hand ease that Grant found humiliating. Weights meant nothing, apparently, to The Midget. She tossed mattresses around with the absent-minded grace of a plate spinner. When she was off duty he was attended to by The Amazon, a goddess with arms like the limb of a beech tree. The Amazon was Nurse Darroll, who came from Gloucestershire and was homesick each daffodil season. (The Midget came from Lytham St. Anne's, and there was no daffodil nonsense about her.) She had large soft hands and large soft cow's eyes and she always looked very sorry for you, but the slightest physical exertion set her breathing like a suction-pump. On the whole Grant found it even more humiliating to be treated as a dead weight than to be treated as if he were no weight at all.

Grant was bed-borne, and a charge on The Midget and The Amazon, because he had fallen through a trap-door. This, of course, was the absolute in humiliation; compared with which the heavings of The Amazon and the light slingings of The Midget were a mere corollary. To fall through a trap-door was the ultimate in absurdity; pantomimic, bathetic, grotesque. At the moment of his disappearance from the normal level of perambulation he had been in hot pursuit of Benny Skoll, and the fact that Benny had careened round the next corner slap into the arms of Sergeant Williams provided the one small crumb of comfort in an intolerable situation.

Benny was now "away" for three years,

which was very satisfactory for the lieges, but Benny would get time off for good behaviour. In hospitals there was no time off for good behaviour.

Grant stopped staring at the ceiling, and slid his eyes sideways at the pile of books on his bedside table; the gay expensive pile that The Midget had been urging on his attention. The top one, with the pretty picture of Valetta in unlikely pink, was Lavinia Fitch's annual account of a blameless heroine's tribulations. In view of the representation of the Grand Harbour on the cover, the present Valerie or Angela or Cecile or Denise must be a naval wife. He had opened the book only to read the kind message that Lavinia had written inside.

The Sweat and the Furrow was Silas Weekley being earthly and spade-conscious all over seven hundred pages. The situation, to judge from the first paragraph, had not materially changed since Silas's last book: mother lying-in with her eleventh upstairs, father laid-out after his ninth downstairs, eldest son lying to the Government in the cow-shed, eldest daughter lying with her lover in the hayloft, everyone else lying low in the barn. The rain dripped from the thatch, and the manure steamed in the midden. Silas never omitted the manure. It was not Silas's fault that its steam provided the only uprising element in the picture. If Silas could have discovered a brand of steam that steamed downwards, Silas would have introduced it.

Under the harsh shadows and highlights of Silas's jacket was an elegant affair of Edwardian curlicues and Baroque nonsense, entitled *Bells on Her Toes*. Which was Rupert Rouge being arch about vice. Rupert Rouge always seduced you into laughter for the first three pages. About Page Three you noticed that Rupert had learned from that very arch (but of course not vicious) creature George Bernard Shaw that the easiest way to sound witty was to use that cheap and convenient method, the paradox. After that you could see the jokes coming three sentences away.

The thing with a red gun-flash across a night-green cover was Oscar Oakley's latest. Toughs talking out of the corners of their mouths in synthetic American that had neither the wit nor the pungency of the real thing. Blondes, chromium bars, breakneck chases. Very remarkably bunk.

The Case of the Missing Tin-Opener, by John James Mark, had three errors of procedure in the first two pages, and had at least provided Grant with a pleasant five minutes while he composed an imaginary letter to its author.

He could not remember what the thin blue book at the bottom of the pile was. Something earnest and statistical, he thought. Tsetse flies, or calories, or sex behaviour, or something.

Even in that, you knew what to expect on the next page. Did no one, any more, no one in all this wide world, change their record now and then? Was everyone nowadays thirled to a formula? Authors today wrote so much to a pattern that their public expected it. The public talked about "a new Silas Weekley" or "a new Lavinia Fitch" exactly as they talked about "a new brick" or "a new hairbrush." They never said "a new book by" whoever it might be. Their interest was not in the book but in its newness. They knew quite well what the book would be like.

It might be a good thing, Grant thought as he turned his nauseated gaze away from the motley pile, if all the presses of the world were stopped for a generation. There ought to be a literary moratorium. Some Superman ought to invent a ray that would stop them all simultaneously. Then people wouldn't send you a lot of fool nonsense when you were flat on your back, and bossy bits of Meissen wouldn't expect you to read them.

He heard the door open, but did not stir himself to look. He had turned his face to the wall, literally and metaphorically.

He heard someone come across to his bed, and closed his eyes against possible conversation. He wanted neither Gloucestershire sympathy nor Lancashire briskness just now. In the succeeding pause a faint enticement, a nostalgic breath of all the fields of Grasse, teased his nostrils and swam about his brain. He savoured it and considered. The Midget smelt of lavender dusting powder, and The Amazon of soap and iodoform. What was floating expensively about his nostrils was *L'Enclos Numéro Cinq*. Only one person of his acquaintance used L'Enclos Number Five. Marta Hallard.

He opened an eye and squinted up at her. She had evidently bent over to see if he was

asleep, and was now standing in an irresolute way—if anything Marta did could be
said to be irresolute—with her attention on
the heap of all too obviously virgin publica-
tions on the table. In one arm she was carrying two new books, and in the other a
great sheaf of white lilac. He wondered
whether she had chosen white lilac because
it was her idea of the proper floral offering
for winter (it adorned her dressing-room at
the theatre from December to March) or
whether she had taken it because it would
not detract from her black-and-white chic.
She was wearing a new hat and her usual
pearls; the pearls which he had once been
the means of recovering for her. She looked
very handsome, very Parisian, and bless-
edly unhospital-like.

"Did I waken you, Alan?"

"No. I wasn't asleep."

"I seem to be bringing the proverbial
coals," she said, dropping the two books
alongside their despised brethren. "I hope
you will find these more interesting than you
seem to have found that lot. Didn't you even
try a little teensy taste of our Lavinia?"

"I can't read anything."

"Are you in pain?"

"Agony. But it's neither my leg nor my back."

"What then?"

"It's what my cousin Laura calls 'the prickles of boredom.' "

"Poor Alan. And how right your Laura is." She picked a bunch of narcissi out of a glass that was much too large for them, dropped them with one of her best gestures into the washbasin, and proceeded to substitute the lilac. "One would expect boredom to be a great yawning emotion, but it isn't, of course. It's a small niggling thing."

"Small nothing. It's like being beaten with nettles."

"Why don't you take up something?"

"Improve the shining hour?"

"Improve your mind. To say nothing of your soul and your temper. You might study one of the philosophies. Yoga, or something like that. But I suppose an analytical mind is not the best kind to bring to the consideration of the abstract."

"I did think of going back to algebra. I have an idea that I never did algebra justice, at school. But I've done so much geometry on that damned ceiling that I'm a little off mathematics."

"Well, I suppose it is no use suggesting jig-saws to someone in your position. How about cross-words. I could get you a book of them, if you like."

"God forbid."

"You could invent them, of course. I have heard that that is more fun than solving them."

"Perhaps. But a dictionary weighs several pounds. Besides, I always did hate looking up something in a reference book."

"Do you play chess? I don't remember. How about chess problems? White to play and mate in three moves, or something like that."

"My only interest in chess is pictorial."

"Pictorial?"

"Very decorative things, knights and pawns and what-not. Very elegant."

"Charming. I *could* bring you along a set to play with. All right, no chess. You could do some academic investigating. That's a sort of mathematics. Finding a solution to an unsolved problem."

"Crime, you mean? I know all the case-histories by heart. And there is nothing more that can be done about any of them. Certainly not by someone who is flat on his back."

"I didn't mean something out of the files at the Yard. I meant something more—what's the word?—something classic. Something that has puzzled the world for ages."

"As what, for instance?"

"Say, the casket letters."

"Oh, *not* Mary Queen of Scots!"

"Why not?" asked Marta, who like all actresses saw Mary Stuart through a haze of white veils.

"I could be interested in a bad woman but never in a silly one."

"*Silly*?" said Marta in her best lower-register Electra voice.

"*Very* silly."

"Oh, Alan, how can you!"

"If she had worn another kind of head-dress no one would ever have bothered about her. It's that cap that seduces people."

"You think she would have loved less greatly in a sun-bonnet?"

"She never loved greatly at all, in any kind of bonnet."

Marta looked as scandalised as a lifetime

in the theatre and an hour of careful make-up allowed her to.

"Why do you think that?"

"Mary Stuart was six feet tall. Nearly all out-size women are sexually cold. Ask any doctor."

And as he said it he wondered why, in all the years since Marta had first adopted him as a spare escort when she needed one, it had not occurred to him to wonder whether her notorious level-headedness about men had something to do with her inches. But Marta had not drawn any parallels; her mind was still on her favourite queen.

"At least she was a martyr. You'll have to allow her that."

"Martyr to what?"

"Her religion."

"The only thing she was a martyr to was rheumatism. She married Darnley without the Pope's dispensation, and Bothwell by Protestant rites."

"In a moment you'll be telling me she wasn't a prisoner!"

"The trouble with you is that you think of her in a little room at the top of a castle, with bars on the windows and a faithful old attendant to share her prayers with her. In actual fact she had a personal household of sixty persons. She complained bitterly when it was reduced to a beggarly thirty, and nearly died of chagrin when it was reduced to two male secretaries, several women, an embroiderer, and a cook or two. And Elizabeth had to pay for all that out of her own purse. For twenty years she paid, and for twenty years Mary Stuart hawked the crown of Scotland round Europe to anyone who would start a revolution and put her back on the throne that she had lost; or, alternatively, on the one Elizabeth was sitting on."

He looked at Marta and found that she was smiling.

"Are they a little better now?" she asked.

"Are what better?"

"The prickles."

He laughed.

"Yes. For a whole minute I had forgotten about them. That is at least one good thing to put down to Mary Stuart's account!"

"How do you know so much about Mary?"

"I did an essay about her in my last year at school."

"And didn't like her, I take it."

"Didn't like what I found out about her."

"You don't think her tragic, then."

"Oh, yes, very. But not tragic in any of the ways that popular belief makes her tragic. Her tragedy was that she was born a queen with the outlook of a suburban house-wife. Scoring off Mrs. Tudor in the next street is harmless and amusing; it may lead you into unwarrantable indulgence in hire-purchase, but it affects only yourself. When you use the same technique on kingdoms the result is disastrous. If you are willing to put a country of ten million people in pawn in order to score off a royal rival, then you end by being a friendless failure." He lay thinking about it for a little. "She would have been a wild success as a mistress at a girls' school."

"Beast!"

"I meant it nicely. The staff would have liked her, and all the little girls would have adored her. That is what I meant about her being tragic."

"Ah, well. No casket letters, it seems. What else is there? The Man in the Iron Mask?"

"I can't remember who that was, but I couldn't be interested in anyone who was being coy behind some tin-plate. I couldn't be interested in anyone at all unless I could see his face."

"Ah, yes. I forgot your passion for faces. The Borgias had wonderful faces. I should think they would provide a little mystery or two for you to dabble in if you looked them up. Or there was Perkin Warbeck, of course. Imposture is always fascinating. Was he or wasn't he? A lovely game. The balance can never come down wholly on one side or the other. You push it over and up it comes again, like one of those weighted toys."

The door opened and Mrs. Tinker's homely face appeared in the aperture surmounted by her still more homely and historic hat. Mrs. Tinker had worn the same hat since first she began to "do" for Grant, and he could not imagine her in any other. That she did possess another one he knew, because it went with something that she referred to as "me blue." Her "blue" was an occasional affair, in both senses, and never appeared at 19 Tenby Court. It was worn with a ritualistic awareness, and having been worn it was used in the event as a yardstick by which to judge the proceedings. ("Did you enjoy it, Tink? What was it like?" "Not worth putting on me blue for.")

She had worn it to Princess Elizabeth's wedding, and to various other royal functions, and had indeed figured in it for two flashing seconds in a newsreel shot of the Duchess of Kent cutting a ribbon, but to Grant it was a mere report; a criterion of the social worth of an occasion. A thing was or was not worth putting on "me blue" for.

"I 'eard you 'ad a visitor," said Mrs. Tinker, "and I was all set to go away again when I thought the voice sounded familiar like, and I says to meself: 'It's only Miss Hallard,' I says, so I come in."

She was carrying various paper bags and a small tight bunch of anemones. She greeted Marta as woman to woman, having been in her time a dresser and having therefore no exaggerated reverence for the goddesses of the theatre world, and looked askance at the beautiful arrangement of lilac sprays that had blossomed under Marta's ministrations. Marta did not see the glance but she saw the little bunch of anemones and took over the situation as if it were something already rehearsed.

"I squander my vagabond's hire on white lilac for you, and then Mrs. Tinker puts my nose out of joint by bringing you the Lilies of the Field."

"Lilies?" said Mrs. Tinker, doubtfully.

"Those are the Solomon in all his glory things. The ones that toiled not, neither did they spin."

Mrs. Tinker went to church only for weddings and christenings, but she belonged to a generation that had been sent to Sunday school. She looked with a new interest at the little handful of glory incased by her woollen glove.

"Well, now. I never knew that. Makes more sense that way, don't it? I always pictured them arums. Fields and fields of arums. Awful expensive, you know, but a bit depressing. So they was coloured? Well, why can't they say so? What do they have to call them lilies for!"

And they went on to talk about translation, and how misleading Holy Writ could be ("I always wondered what bread on the waters was," Mrs. Tinker said) and the awkward moment was over.

While they were still busy with the Bible, The Midget came in with extra flower vases. Grant noticed that the vases were designed to hold white lilac and not anemones. They were tribute to Marta; a passport to further communing. But Marta never bothered about women unless she had an immediate use for them; her tack with Mrs. Tinker had been mere *savoir faire;* a conditioned reflex. So The Midget was reduced to being functional instead of social. She collected the discarded narcissi from the washbasin and meekly put them back into a vase. The Midget being meek was the most beautiful sight that had gladdened Grant's eyes for a long time.

"Well," Marta said, having finished her arrangement of the lilac and placed the result where he could see it, "I shall leave Mrs. Tinker to feed you all the titbits out of those paper bags. It couldn't be, could it, Mrs. Tinker darling, that one of those bags contains any of your wonderful bachelor's buttons?"

Mrs. Tinker glowed.

"You'd like one or two maybe? Fresh outa me oven?"

"Well, of course I shall have to do penance for it afterwards—those little rich cakes are death on the waist—but just give me a couple to put in my bag for my tea at the theatre."

She chose two with a flattering delibera-
tion ("I like them a little brown at the
edges"), dropped them into her handbag,
and said: "Well, au revoir, Alan. I shall look
in, in a day or two, and start you on a sock.
There is nothing so soothing, I understand,
as knitting. Isn't that so, Nurse?"

"Oh, yes, indeed. A lot of my gentlemen
patients take to knitting. They find it whiles
away the time very nicely."

Marta blew him a kiss from the door and
was gone, followed by the respectful Midget.

"I'd be surprised if that hussy is any better
than she ought to be," Mrs. Tinker said, beginning to open the paper bags. She was
not referring to Marta.

Chapter 2

But when Marta came back two days later it was not with knitting needles and wool. She breezed in, very dashing in a Cossack hat worn at a casual rake that must have taken her several minutes at her mirror, just after lunch.

"I haven't come to stay, my dear, I'm on my way to the theatre. It's matinée day, God help me. Tea trays and morons. And we've got to the frightful stage when the lines have ceased to have any meaning at all for us. I don't think this play is ever coming off. It's going to be like those New York ones that run by the decade instead of by the year. It's too frightening. One's mind just won't stay on the thing. Geoffrey dried up in the middle of the second act last night. His eyes nearly popped out of his head. I thought for a moment he was having a stroke. He said afterwards that he had no recollection of anything that happened between his entrance and the point where he came to and found himself half-way through the act."

"A black-out, you mean?"

"No. Oh, no. Just being an automaton. Saying the lines and doing the business and thinking of something else all the time."

"If all reports are true that's no unusual matter where actors are concerned."

"Oh, in moderation, no. Johnny Garson can tell you how much paper there is in the house while he is sobbing his heart out on someone's lap. But that's different from being 'away' for half an act. Do you realise that Geoffrey had turned his son out of the house, quarrelled with his mistress, and accused his wife of having an affaire with his best friend all without being aware of it?"

"What *was* he aware of?"

"He says he had decided to lease his Park Lane flat to Dolly Dacre and buy that Charles the Second house at Richmond that the Latimers are giving up because he has got that Governor's appointment. He had thought about the lack of bathrooms and decided that the little upstairs room, with the eighteenth-century Chinese paper, would make a very good one. They could remove the beautiful paper and use it to decorate that dull little room downstairs at the back. It's full of Victorian paneling, the dull little room. He had also reviewed the drainage, wondered if he had enough money to take the old tiling off and replace it, and speculated as to what kind of cooking range they had in the kitchen. He had just decided to get rid of the shrubbery at the gate when he found himself face to face with me, on a stage, in the presence of nine hundred and eighty-seven people, in the middle of a speech. Do you wonder that his eyes popped? I see that you have managed to read at least one of the books I brought you—if the rumpled jacket is any criterion."

"Yes. The mountain one. It was a godsend. I lay for hours looking at the pictures. Nothing puts things in perspective as quickly as a mountain."

"The stars are better, I find."

"Oh, *no*. The stars merely reduce one to the status of an amoeba. The stars take the last vestige of human pride, the last spark of confidence, from one. But a snow mountain is a nice human-size yardstick. I lay and looked at Everest and thanked God that I wasn't climbing those slopes. A hospital bed was a haven of warmth and rest and security by comparison, and The Midget and The Amazon two of the highest achievements of civilisation."

"Ah, well, here are some more pictures for you."

Marta up-ended the quarto envelope she was carrying, and spilled a collection of paper sheets over his chest.

"What is this?"

"Faces," said Marta, delightedly. "Dozens of faces for you. Men, women, and children. All sorts, conditions, and sizes."

He picked a sheet off his chest and looked at it. It was an engraving of a fifteenth-century portrait. A woman.

"Who is this?"

"Lucrezia Borgia. Isn't she a duck?"

"Perhaps, but are you suggesting that there was any mystery about her?"

"Oh, yes. No one has ever decided whether she was her brother's tool or his accomplice."

He discarded Lucrezia, and picked up a second sheet. This proved to be the portrait of a small boy in late-eighteenth-century clothes, and under it in faint capitals were printed the words: Louis XVII.

"Now there's a *beautiful* mystery for you,"

Marta said. "The Dauphin. Did he escape or did he die in captivity?"

"Where did you get all these?"

"I routed James out of his cubby-hole at the Victoria and Albert, and made him take me to a print shop. I knew he would know about that sort of thing, and I'm sure he has nothing to interest him at the V. and A."

It was so like Marta to take it for granted that a Civil Servant, because he happened also to be a playwright and an authority on portraits, should be willing to leave his work and delve about in print shops for her pleasure.

He turned up the photograph of an Elizabethan portrait. A man in velvet and pearls. He turned the back to see who this might be and found that it was the Earl of Leicester.

"So that is Elizabeth's Robin," he said. "I don't think I ever saw a portrait of him before."

Marta looked down on the virile fleshy face and said: "It occurs to me for the first time that one of the major tragedies of history is that the best painters didn't paint you till you were past your best. Robin must have been quite a man. They say Henry the Eighth was dazzling as a young man, but

what is he now? Something on a playing
card. Nowadays we *know* what Tennyson
was like before he grew that frightful beard.
I must fly. I'm late as it is. I've been lunching
at the Blague, and so many people came up
to talk that I couldn't get away as early as I
meant to."

"I hope your host was impressed," Grant
said, with a glance at the hat.

"Oh, yes. She knows about hats. She took
one look and said, 'Jacques Tous, I take
it.' "

"She!" said Grant, surprised.

"Yes. Madeleine March. And it was I who
was giving her luncheon. Don't look so astonished: it isn't tactful. I'm hoping, if you
must know, that she'll write me that play
about Lady Blessington. But there was such
a to-ing and fro-ing that I had no chance to
make any impression on her. However, I
gave her a wonderful meal. Which reminds
me that Tony Bittmaker was entertaining a
party of seven. Magnums galore. How do
you imagine he keeps going?"

"Lack of evidence," Grant said, and she
laughed and went away.

In the silence he went back to considering

Elizabeth's Robin. What mystery was there about Robin?

Oh, yes. Amy Robsart, of course.

Well, he wasn't interested in Amy Robsart. He didn't care how she had fallen down stairs, or why.

But he spent a very happy afternoon with the rest of the faces. Long before he had entered the Force he had taken a delight in faces, and in his years at the Yard that interest had proved both a private entertainment and a professional advantage. He had once in his early days dropped in with his Superintendent at an identification parade. It was not his case, and they were both there on other business, but they lingered in the background and watched while a man and a woman, separately, walked down the line of twelve nondescript men, looking for the one they hoped to recognise.

"Which is Chummy, do you know?" the Super had whispered to him.

"I don't know," Grant had said, "but I can guess."

"You can? Which do you make it?"

"The third from the left."

"What is the charge?"

"I don't know. Don't know anything about it."

His chief had cast him an amused glance. But when both the man and the woman had failed to identify anyone and had gone away, and the line broke into a chattering group, hitching collars and settling ties preparatory to going back to the street and the world of every day from which they had been summoned to assist the Law, the one who did not move was the third man from the left. The third man from the left waited submissively for his escort and was led to his cell again.

"Strewth!" the Superintendent had said. "One chance out of twelve, and you made it. That was good going. He picked your man out of the bunch," he said in explanation to the local Inspector.

"Did you know him?" the Inspector said, a little surprised. "He's never been in trouble before, as far as we know."

"No, I never saw him before. I don't even know what the charge is."

"Then what made you pick him?"

Grant had hesitated, analysing for the first time his process of selection. It had not been a matter of reasoning. He had not said: "That man's face has this characteristic or that characteristic, therefore he is the accused person." His choice had been almost instinctive; the reason was in his subconscious. At last, having delved into his subconscious, he blurted: "He was the only one of the twelve with no lines on his face."

They had laughed at that. But Grant, once he had pulled the thing into the light, saw how his instinct had worked and recognised the reasoning behind it. "It sounds silly, but it isn't," he said. "The only adult entirely without face lines is the idiot."

"Freeman's no idiot, take it from me," the Inspector broke in. "A very wide-awake boy he is, believe me."

"I didn't mean that. I mean that the idiot is irresponsible. The idiot is the standard of irresponsibility. All those twelve men in that parade were thirty-ish, but only one had an irresponsible face. So I picked him at once."

After that it had become a mild joke at the Yard that Grant could "pick them at sight." And the Assistant Commissioner had once said teasingly: "Don't tell me that you believe that there is such a thing as a criminal face, Inspector."

But Grant had said no, he wasn't as simple as that. "If there was only one kind of crime, sir, it might be possible; but crimes being as wide as human nature, if a policeman started to put faces into categories he would be sunk. You can tell what the normal run of over-sexed women look like by a walk down Bond Street any day between five and six, and yet the most notorious nymphomaniac in London looks like a cold saint."

"Not so saintly of late; she's drinking too much these days," the A.C. had said, identifying the lady without difficulty; and the conversation had gone on to other things.

But Grant's interest in faces had remained and enlarged until it became a conscious study. A matter of case records and comparisons. It was, as he had said, not possible to put faces into any kind of category, but it was possible to characterise individual faces. In a reprint of a famous trial, for instance, where photographs of the principal actors in the case were displayed for the public's interest, there was never any doubt as to which was the accused and which the judge. Occasionally, one of the counsel might on looks have changed places with the prisoner in the dock—counsel were after all a mere cross-section of humanity, as liable to passion and greed as the rest of the world, but a judge had a special quality; an integrity and a detachment. So, even without a wig, one did not confuse him with the man in the dock, who had had neither integrity nor detachment.

Marta's James, having been dragged from his "cubby-hole," had evidently enjoyed himself, and a fine selection of offenders, or their victims, kept Grant entertained until The Midget brought his tea. As he tidied the sheets together to put them away in his locker his hand came in contact with one that had slipped off his chest and had lain all afternoon unnoticed on the counterpane. He picked it up and looked at it.

It was the portrait of a man. A man dressed in the velvet cap and slashed doublet of the late fifteenth century. A man about thirty-five or thirty-six years old, lean and clean-shaven. He wore a rich jewelled collar, and was in the act of putting a ring on the little finger of his right hand. But he was not looking at the ring. He was looking off into space.

Of all the portraits Grant had seen this afternoon this was the most individual. It was as if the artist had striven to put on canvas something that his talent was not sufficient to translate into paint. The expression in the eyes—that most arresting and individual expression—had defeated him. So had the mouth: he had not known how to make lips so thin and so wide look mobile, so the mouth was wooden and a failure. What he had best succeeded in was the bone structure of the face: the strong cheekbones, the hollows below them, the chin too large for strength.

Grant paused in the act of turning the thing over, to consider the face a moment longer. A judge? A soldier? A prince? Someone used to great responsibility, and responsible in his authority. Someone too conscientious. A worrier; perhaps a perfectionist. A man at ease in a large design, but anxious over details. A candidate for gastric ulcer. Someone, too, who had suffered ill-health as a child. He had that incommunicable, that indescribable look that childhood suffering leaves behind it, less positive than the look on a cripple's face, but as inescapable. This the artist had both understood and translated into terms of paint. The slight fullness of the lower eyelid, like a child that has slept too heavily; the texture of the skin; the old-man look in a young face.

He turned the portrait over to look for a caption.

On the back was printed: *Richard the Third. From the portrait in the National Portrait Gallery. Artist Unknown.*

Richard the Third.

So that was who it was. Richard the Third. Crouchback. The monster of nursery stories. The destroyer of innocence. A synonym for villainy.

He turned the paper over and looked again. Was that what the artist had tried to convey when he had painted those eyes? Had what he had seen in those eyes been the look of a man haunted?

He lay a long time looking at that face; at those extraordinary eyes. They were long eyes, set close under the brows; the brows slightly drawn in that worried, over-conscientious frown. At first glance they appeared to be peering; but as one looked one found that they were in fact withdrawn, almost absent-minded.

When The Midget came back for his tray he was still staring at the portrait. Nothing like this had come his way for years. It made La Gioconda look like a poster.

The Midget examined his virgin teacup, put a practised hand against the teapot's tepid cheek, and pouted. She had better things to do, she conveyed, than bring him trays for him to ignore.

He pushed the portrait at her.

What did she think of it? If that man were her patient what would be her verdict?

"Liver," she said crisply, and bore away the tray in heel-tapping protest, all starch and blond curls.

But the surgeon strolling in against her draught, kindly and casual, had other views. He looked at the portrait, as invited, and said after a moment's scrutiny:

"Poliomyelitis."

"Infantile paralysis?" Grant said; and re-membered all of a sudden that Richard III had a withered arm.

"Who is it?" the surgeon asked.

"Richard the Third."

"Really? That's interesting."

"Did you know that he had a withered arm?"

"Had he? I didn't remember that. I thought he was a hunchback."

"So he was."

"What I do remember is that he was born with a full set of teeth and ate live frogs. Well, my diagnosis seems to be abnormally accurate."

"Uncanny. What made you choose polio?"

"I don't quite know, now that you ask me to be definitive. Just the look of the face, I suppose. It's the look one sees on the face of a crippled child. If he was born hunchbacked that probably accounts for it and not polio. I notice the artist has left out the hump."

"Yes. Court painters have to have a modicum of tact. It wasn't until Cromwell that sitters asked for 'warts and all.' "

"If you ask me," the surgeon said, absentmindedly considering the splint on Grant's leg, "Cromwell started that inverted snobbery from which we are all suffering today. 'I'm a plain man, I am; no nonsense about *me*.' And no manners, grace, or generosity, either." He pinched Grant's toe with detached interest. "It's a raging disease. A horrible perversion. In some parts of the States, I understand, it's as much as a man's political life is worth to go to some constituencies with his tie and his coat on. That's being stuffed-shirt. The beau ideal is to be one of the boys. That's looking very healthy," he added, referring to Grant's big toe, and came back of his own accord to the portrait lying on the counterpane.

"Interesting," he said, "that about the polio. Perhaps it really was polio, and that accounts for the shrunken arm." He went on considering it, making no movement to go. "Interesting, anyhow. Portrait of a murderer. Does he run to type, would you say?"

"There isn't a murder type. People murder for too many different reasons. But I can't remember any murderer, either in my own experience, or in case-histories, who resembled him."

"Of course he was *hors-concours* in his class, wasn't he? He couldn't have known the meaning of scruple."

"No."

"I once saw Olivier play him. The most dazzling exhibition of sheer evil, it was. Always on the verge of toppling over into the grotesque, and never doing it."

"When I showed you the portrait," Grant said, "before you knew who it was, did you think of villainy?"

"No," said the surgeon, "no, I thought of illness."

"It's odd, isn't it? I didn't think of villainy either. And now that I know who it is, now that I've read the name on the back, I can't think of it as anything but villainous."

"I suppose villainy, like beauty, is in the eye of the beholder. Well, I'll look in again towards the end of the week. No pain to speak of now?"

And he went away, kindly and casual as he had come.

It was only after he had given the portrait further puzzled consideration (it piqued him to have mistaken one of the most notorious murderers of all time for a judge; to have transferred a subject from the dock to the bench was a shocking piece of ineptitude) that it occurred to Grant that the portrait had been provided as the illustration to a piece of detection.

What mystery was there about Richard III?

And then he remembered. Richard had murdered his two boy nephews, but no one knew how. They had merely disappeared. They had disappeared, if he remembered rightly, while Richard was away from London. Richard had sent someone to do the deed. But the mystery of the children's actual fate had never been solved. Two skeletons had turned up—under some stairs?—in Charles II's day, and had been buried. It was taken for granted that the skeletons were the remains of the young princes, but nothing had ever been proved.

It was shocking how little history remained with one after a good education. All he knew about Richard III was that he was the younger brother of Edward IV. That Edward was a blond six-footer with remarkable good looks and a still more remarkable way with women; and that Richard was a hunchback who usurped the throne on his brother's death in place of the boy heir, and arranged the death of that heir and his small brother to save himself any further trouble. He also knew that Richard had died at the battle of Bosworth yelling for a horse, and that he was the last of his line. The last Plantagenet.

Every schoolboy turned over the final page of Richard III with relief, because now at last the Wars of the Roses were over and they could get on to the Tudors, who were dull but easy to follow.

When The Midget came to tidy him up for

the night, Grant said: "You don't happen to have a history book, by any chance, do you?"

"A history book? No. What would I be doing with a history book." It was not a question, so Grant did not try to provide an answer. His silence seemed to fret her.

"If you really want a history book," she said presently, "you could ask Nurse Darroll when she brings your supper. She has all her school books on a shelf in her room and it's quite possible she has a history among them."

How like The Amazon to keep her school books! he thought. She was still homesick for school as she was homesick for Gloucestershire every time the daffodils bloomed. When she lumbered into the room, bearing his cheese pudding and stewed rhubarb, he looked at her with a tolerance that bordered on the benevolent. She ceased to be a large female who breathed like a suction-pump and became a potential dispenser of delight.

Oh, yes, she had a history book, she said. Indeed, she rather thought that she had two. She had kept all her school books, because she had loved school.

It was on the tip of Grant's tongue to ask her if she had kept her dolls, but he stopped himself in time.

"And of course I loved history," she said. "It was my favourite subject. Richard the Lionheart was my hero."

"An intolerable bounder," Grant said.

"Oh, no!" she said, looking wounded.

"A hyperthyroid type," Grant said pitilessly. "Rocketing to and fro about the earth like a badly made firework. Are you going off duty now?"

"Whenever I've finished my trays."

"Could you find that book for me tonight?"

"You're supposed to be going to sleep, not staying awake over history books."

"I might as well read history as look at the ceiling—which is the alternative. Will you get it for me?"

"I don't think I could go all the way up to the Nurses' Block and back again tonight for someone who is rude about the Lionheart."

"All right," he said. "I'm not the stuff that martyrs are made of. As far as I'm concerned Coeur-de-Lion is the pattern of chivalry, the *chevalier sans peur et sans re-*

proche, a faultless commander and a triple D.S.O. Now will you get the book?"

"It seems to me you've sore need to read a little history," she said, smoothing a mitred sheet-corner with a large admiring hand, "so I'll bring you the book when I come past. I'm going out to the pictures anyhow."

It was nearly an hour before she reappeared, immense in a camel-hair coat. The room lights had been put out and she materialised into the light of his reading-lamp like some kindly genie.

"I was hoping you'd be asleep," she said. "I don't really think you should start on these tonight."

"If there is anything that is likely to put me to sleep," he said, "it would be an English history book. So you can hold hands with a clear conscience."

"I'm going with Nurse Burrows."

"You can still hold hands."

"I've no patience with you," she said patiently and faded backwards into the gloom.

She had brought two books.

One was the kind of history book known as a Historical Reader. It bore the same relation to history as Stories from the Bible bears to Holy Writ. Canute rebuked his courtiers on the shore, Alfred burned the cakes, Raleigh spread his cloak for Elizabeth, Nelson took leave of Hardy in his cabin on the *Victory*, all in nice clear large print and one-sentence paragraphs. To each episode went one full-page illustration.

There was something curiously touching in the fact that The Amazon should treasure this childish literature. He turned to the flyleaf to see if her name was there. On the flyleaf was written:

Ella Darroll,
Form III
Newbridge High School
Newbridge,
Gloucestershire.
England
Europe,
The World
The Universe.

This was surrounded by a fine section of coloured transfers.

Did all children do that, he wondered. Write their names like that, and spend their time in class making transfers? He certainly had. And the sight of those squares of bright primitive colour brought back his childhood as nothing had for many years. He had forgotten the excitement of transfers. That wonderfully satisfying moment when you began the peeling-off and saw that it was coming perfectly. The adult world held few such gratifications. A clean smacking drive at golf, perhaps, was the nearest. Or the moment when your line tightened and you knew that the fish had struck.

The little book pleased him so much that he went through it at his leisure. Solemnly reading each childish story. This, after all, was the history that every adult remembered. This was what remained in their minds when tonnage and poundage, and ship money, and Laud's Liturgy, and the Rye House Plot, and the Triennial Acts, and all the long muddle of schism and shindy, treaty and treason, had faded from their consciousness.

The Richard III story, when he came to it, was called *The Princes in the Tower*, and it seemed that young Ella had found the Princes a poor substitute for Coeur-de-Lion, since she had filled every small O throughout the tale with neat pencil shading. The two golden-haired boys who played together in the sunbeam from the barred window in the accompanying picture had each been provided with a pair of anachronistic spectacles, and on the blank back of the picture-page someone had been playing Noughts and Crosses. As far as young Ella was concerned the Princes were a dead loss.

And yet it was a sufficiently arresting little story. Macabre enough to delight any child's heart. The innocent children; the wicked uncle. The classic ingredients in a tale of classic simplicity.

It had also a moral. It was the perfect cautionary tale.

But the King won no profit from his wicked deed. The people of England were shocked by his coldblooded cruelty and decided that they would no longer have him for King. They sent for a distant cousin of Richard's, Henry Tudor, who was living in France, to come and be crowned King in his stead. Richard died bravely in the battle which resulted, but he had made his name hated

throughout the country and many deserted him to fight for his rival.

Well, it was neat but not gaudy. Reporting
at its simplest.

He turned to the second book.

The second book was the School History
proper. The two thousand years of England's
story were neatly parcelled into compart-
ments for ready reference. The compart-
ments, as usual, were reigns. It was no wonder that one pinned a personality to a reign,
forgetful that that personality had known and
lived under other kings. One put them in
pigeon-holes automatically. Pepys: Charles II.
Shakespeare: Elizabeth. Marlborough: Queen
Anne. It never crossed one's mind that someone who had seen Queen Elizabeth could
also have seen George I. One had been conditioned to the reign idea from childhood.

However it did simplify things when you
were just a policeman with a game leg and
a concussed spine hunting up some information on dead and gone royalties to keep
yourself from going crazy.

He was surprised to find the reign of
Richard III so short. To have made oneself
one of the best-known rulers in all those two

thousand years of England's history, and to have had only two years to do it in, surely augured a towering personality. If Richard had not made friends he had certainly influenced people.

The history book, too, thought that he had personality.

Richard was a man of great ability, but quite unscrupulous as to his means. He boldly claimed the crown on the absurd grounds that his brother's marriage with Elizabeth Woodville had been illegal and the children of it illegitimate. He was accepted by the people, who dreaded a minority, and began his reign by making a progress through the south, where he was well received. During this progress, however, the two young Princes who were living in the Tower, disappeared, and were believed to have been murdered. A serious rebellion followed, which Richard put down with great ferocity. In order to recover some of his lost popularity he held a Parliament, which passed useful statutes against Benevolences, Maintenance, and Livery.

But a second rebellion followed. This

took the form of an invasion, with French troops, by the head of the Lancaster branch, Henry Tudor. He encountered Richard at Bosworth, near Leicester, where the treachery of the Stanleys gave the day to Henry. Richard was killed in battle, fighting courageously, leaving behind him a name hardly less infamous than that of John.

What on earth were Benevolences, Maintenance, and Livery?

And how did the English like having the succession decided for them by French troops?

But, of course, in the days of the Roses, France was still a sort of semi-detached part of England; a country much less foreign to an Englishman than Ireland was. A fifteenth-century Englishman went to France as a matter of course; but to Ireland only under protest.

He lay and thought about that England. The England over which the Wars of the Roses had been fought. A green, green England; with not a chimney-stack from Cumberland to Cornwall. An England still unhedged, with great forests alive with game, and wide marshes thick with wild-fowl. An England with the same small group of dwellings repeated every few miles in endless permutation: castle, church, and cottages; monastery, church, and cottages; manor, church, and cottages. The strips of cultivation round the cluster of dwellings, and beyond that the greenness. The unbroken greenness. The deep-rutted lanes that ran from group to group, mired to bog in the winter and white with dust in the summer; decorated with wild roses or red with hawthorn as the seasons came and went.

For thirty years, over this green uncrowded land, the Wars of the Roses had been fought. But it had been more of a blood feud than a war. A Montague and Capulet affair; of no great concern to the average Englishman. No one pushed in at your door to demand whether you were York or Lancaster and to hale you off to a concentration camp if your answer proved to be the wrong one for the occasion. It was a small concentrated war; almost a private party. They fought a battle in your lower meadow, and turned your kitchen into a dressing-station, and then moved off somewhere or other to fight a battle somewhere else, and a few weeks later you would hear what had happened at that battle, and you would have a family row about the result because your wife was probably Lancaster and you were perhaps York, and it was all rather like following rival football teams. No one persecuted you for being a Lancastrian or a Yorkist, any more than you would be persecuted for being an Arsenal fan or a Chelsea follower.

He was still thinking of the green England when he fell asleep.

And he was not a whit wiser about the two young Princes and their fate.

Chapter 3

"Can't you find something more cheerful to look at than that thing?" The Midget asked next morning, referring to the Richard portrait which Grant had propped up against the pile of books on his bed-side table.

"You don't find it an interesting face?"

"Interesting! It gives me the willies. A proper Dismal Desmond."

"According to the history books he was a man of great ability."

"So was Bluebeard."

"And considerable popularity, it would seem."

"So was Bluebeard."

"A very fine soldier, too," Grant said wickedly, and waited. "No Bluebeard offers?"

"What do you want to look at that face for? Who was he anyway?"

"Richard the Third."

"Oh, well, I ask you!"

"You mean that's what you expected him to look like."

"Exactly."

"Why?"

"A murdering brute, wasn't he?"

"You seem to know your history."

"Everyone knows that. Did away with his two little nephews, poor brats. Had them smothered."

"Smothered?" said Grant, interested. "I didn't know that."

"Smothered with pillows." She banged his own pillows with a fragile vigorous fist, and replaced them with speed and precision.

"Why smothering? Why not poison?" Grant inquired.

"Don't ask me. I didn't arrange it."

"Who said they were smothered?"

"My history book at school said it."

"Yes, but whom was the history book quoting?"

"Quoting? It wasn't quoting anything. It was just giving facts."

"Who smothered them, did it say?"

"A man called Tyrrel. Didn't you do any history, at school?"

"I attended history lessons. It is not the same thing. Who was Tyrrel?"

"I haven't the remotest. A friend of Richard's."

"How did anyone know it was Tyrrel?"

"He confessed."

"Confessed?"

"After he had been found guilty, of course. Before he was hanged."

"You mean that this Tyrrel was actually hanged for the murder of the two Princes?"

"Yes, of course. Shall I take that dreary face away and put up something gayer? There were quite a lot of nice faces in that bundle Miss Hallard brought you yesterday."

"I'm not interested in nice faces. I'm interested only in dreary ones; in 'murdering brutes' who are 'men of great ability.' "

"Well, there's no accounting for tastes," said The Midget inevitably. "And *I* don't have to look at it, thank goodness. But in my humble estimation it's enough to prevent bones knitting, so help me it is."

"Well, if my fracture doesn't mend you can put it down to Richard III's account. Another little item on that account won't be noticed, it seems to me."

He must ask Marta when next she looked in if she too knew about this Tyrrel. Her general knowledge was not very great, but she had been educated very expensively at a highly approved school and perhaps some of it had stuck.

But the first visitor to penetrate from the outside world proved to be Sergeant Williams, large and pink and scrubbed-looking; and for a little Grant forgot about battles long ago and considered wide boys alive today. Williams sat planted on the small hard visitors' chair, his knees apart and his pale blue eyes blinking like a contented cat's in the light from the window, and Grant regarded him with affection. It was pleasant to talk shop again; to use that elliptical, allusive speech that one uses only with another of one's trade. It was pleasant to hear the professional gossip, to talk professional politics; to learn who was on the mat and who was on the skids.

"The Super sent his regards," Williams said as he got up to go, "and said if there was anything he could do for you to let him know." His eyes, no longer dazzled by the light, went to the photograph propped against the books. He leant his head sideways at it. "Who's the bloke?"

Grant was just about to tell him when it

occurred to him that here was a fellow policeman. A man as used, professionally, to
faces as he was himself. Someone to whom
faces were of daily importance.

"Portrait of a man by an unknown
fifteenth-century painter," he said. "What do
you make of it?"

"I don't know the first thing about paint-
ing."

"I didn't mean that. I meant what do you
make of the subject?"

"Oh. Oh, I see." Williams bent forward and
drew his bland brows into a travesty of concentration. "How do you mean: make of it?"

"Well, where would you place him? In the
dock or on the bench?"

Williams considered for a moment, and
then said with confidence: "Oh, on the
bench."

"You would?"

"Certainly. Why? Wouldn't you?"

"Yes. But the odd thing is that we're both
wrong. He belongs in the dock."

"You surprise me," Williams said, peering
again. "Do you know who he was, then?"

"Yes. Richard the Third."

Williams whistled.

"So that's who it is, is it! Well, well. The

Princes in the Tower, and all that. The original Wicked Uncle. I suppose, once you know, you can see it, but offhand it wouldn't occur to you. I mean, that he was a crook. He's the spit of old Halsbury, come to think of it, and if Halsbury had a fault at all it was that he was too soft with the bastards in the dock. He used to lean over backwards to give them the benefit in his summing-up."

"Do you know how the Princes were murdered?"

"I don't know a thing about Richard III except that his mother was two years conceiving him."

"What! Where did you get that tale?"

"In my school history, I suppose."

"You must have gone to a very remarkable school. Conception was not mentioned in any history book of mine. That is what made Shakespeare and the Bible so refreshing as lessons; the facts of life were always turning up. Did you ever hear of a man called Tyrrel?"

"Yes; he was a con man on the P. & O. boats. Drowned in the *Egypt*."

"No; I mean in history."

"I tell you, I never knew any history except 1066 and 1603."

"What happened in 1603?" Grant asked, his mind still on Tyrrel.

"We had the Scots tied to our tails for good."

"Better than having them at our throats every five minutes. Tyrrel is said to be the man who put the boys out of the way."

"The nephews? No, it doesn't ring a bell. Well, I must be getting along. Anything I can do for you?"

"Did you say you were going to Charing Cross Road?"

"To the Phoenix, yes."

"You could do something for me."

"What is that?"

"Go into one of the bookshops and buy me a History of England. An adult one. And a Life of Richard III, if you can find one."

"Sure, I'll do that."

As he was going out he encountered The Amazon, and looked startled to find anything as large as himself in nurse's uniform. He murmured a good-morning in an abashed way, cast a questioning glance at Grant, and faded into the corridor.

The Amazon said that she was supposed to be giving Number Four her blanket bath but that she had to look in to see if he was convinced.

"Convinced?"

About the nobility of Richard Coeur-de-Lion.

"I haven't got round to Richard the First yet. But keep Number Four waiting a few moments longer and tell me what you know about Richard III."

"Ah, those poor lambs!" she said, her great cow's eyes soft with pity.

"Who?"

"Those two precious little boys. It used to be my nightmare when I was a kiddie. That someone would come and put a pillow over my face when I was asleep."

"Is that how it was done: the murder?"

"Oh, yes. Didn't you know? Sir James Tyrrel rode back to London when the court was at Warwick, and told Dighton and Forrest to kill them, and then they buried them at the foot of some stairs under a great mound of stones."

"But it doesn't say that in the book you lent me."

"Oh, that book is just history-for-exams, if you know what I mean. You don't get really interesting history in swot books like that."

"And where did you get the juicy gossip about Tyrrel, may one ask?"

"It isn't gossip," she said, hurt. "You'll find it in Sir Thomas More's history of his time. And you can't find a more respected or trustworthy person in the whole of history than Sir Thomas More, now can you?"

"No. It would be bad manners to contradict Sir Thomas."

"Well, that's what Sir Thomas says, and, after all, he was alive then and knew all those people to talk to."

"Dighton and Forrest?"

"No, of course not. But Richard, and the poor Queen, and those."

"The Queen? Richard's Queen?"

"Yes."

"Why 'poor'?"

"He led her an awful life. They say he poisoned her. He wanted to marry his niece."

"Why?"

"Because she was the heir to the throne."

"I see. He got rid of the two boys, and then wanted to marry their eldest sister."

"Yes. He couldn't marry either of the boys, you see."

"No, I suppose even Richard the Third never thought of that one."

"So he wanted to marry Elizabeth so as to feel safer on the throne. Actually, of course, she married his successor. She was Queen Elizabeth's grandmother. It always used to please me that Elizabeth was a little bit Plantagenet. I never was very fond of the Tudor side. Now I must go, or Matron will be here on her round before I have Number Four tidied up."

"That would be the end of the world."

"It would be the end of *me*," she said, and went away.

Grant took the book she had left him off the pile again, and tried to make head or tail of the Wars of the Roses. He failed. Armies marched and counter-marched. York and Lancaster succeeded each other as victors in a bewildering repetition. It was as meaningless as watching a crowd of dodgem cars bumping and whirling at a fair.

But it seemed to him that the whole trouble was implicit, the germ of it sown, nearly a hundred years earlier, when the direct line was broken by the deposition of Richard II. He knew all about that because he had in his youth seen *Richard of Bordeaux* at the New Theatre; four times he had seen it. For three generations the usurping Lancasters had ruled England: Richard of Bordeaux's Henry unhappily but with fair efficiency, Shakespeare's Prince Hal with Agincourt for glory and the stake for zeal, and his son in half-witted muddle and failure. It was no wonder if men hankered after the legitimate line again, as they watched poor Henry VI's inept friends frittering away the victories in France while Henry nursed his new foundation of Eton and besought the ladies at court to cover up their bosoms.

All three Lancasters had had an unlovely fanaticism which contrasted sharply with the liberalism of the Court which had died with Richard II. Richard's live-and-let-live methods had given place, almost overnight, to the burning of heretics. For three generations heretics had burned. It was no wonder if a less public fire of discontent had begun to smoulder in the heart of the man on the street.

Especially since there, before their eyes, was the Duke of York. Able, sensible, influential, gifted, a great prince in his own right, and by blood the heir of Richard II. They might not desire that York should take the place of poor silly Henry, but they did wish that he would take over the running of the country and clean up the mess.

York tried it, and died in battle for his pains, and his family spent much time in exile or sanctuary as a result.

But when the tumult and the shouting was all over, there on the throne of England was the son who had fought alongside him in that struggle, and the country settled back happily under that tall, flaxen, wenching, exceedingly beautiful but most remarkably shrewd young man, Edward IV.

And that was as near as Grant would ever come to understanding the Wars of the Roses.

He looked up from his book to find Matron standing in the middle of the room.

"I did knock," she said, "but you were lost in your book."

She stood there, slender and remote; as elegant in her way as Marta was; her white-cuffed hands clasped loosely in front of her narrow waist; her white veil spreading itself in imperishable dignity; her only ornament the small silver badge of her diploma. Grant wondered if there was anywhere in this world a more unshakable poise than that achieved by the matron of a great hospital.

"I've taken to history," he said. "Rather late in the day."

"An admirable choice," she said. "It puts things in perspective." Her eyes lighted on the portrait and she said: "Are you York or Lancaster?"

"So you recognise the portrait."

"Oh, yes. When I was a probationer I used to spend a lot of time in the National. I had very little money and very sore feet, and it was warm in the Gallery and quiet and it had plenty of seats." She smiled a very little, looking back from her present consequence to that young, tired, earnest creature she had been. "I liked the Portrait Gallery best because it gave one the same sense of proportion that reading history does. All those Importances who had made such a to-do over so much in their day. All just names. Just canvas and paint. I saw a lot of that portrait in those days." Her attention went back to the picture. "A most unhappy creature," she said.

"My surgeon thinks it is poliomyelitis."

"Polio?" She considered it. "Perhaps. I hadn't thought of it before. But to me it has always seemed to be intense unhappiness. It is the most desperately unhappy face that

I have ever encountered—and I have encountered a great many."

"You think it was painted later than the murder, then?"

"Oh, yes. Obviously. He is not a type that would do anything lightly. A man of that calibre. He must have been well aware of how—heinous the crime was."

"You think he belonged to the type who can't live with themselves any more."

"What a good description! Yes. The kind who want something badly, and then discover that the price they have paid for it is too high."

"So you don't think he was an out-and-out villain?"

"No; oh, no. Villains don't suffer, and that face is full of the most dreadful pain."

They considered the portrait in silence for a moment or two.

"It must have seemed like retribution, you know. Losing his only boy so soon after. And his wife's death. Being stripped of his own personal world in so short a time. It must have seemed like Divine justice."

"Would he care about his wife?"

"She was his cousin, and they had known each other from childhood. So whether he loved her or not, she must have been a companion for him. When you sit on a throne I suspect that companionship is a rare blessing. Now I must go and see how my hospital is getting on. I have not even asked the question that I came to ask. Which was how you felt this morning. But it is a very healthy sign that you have interest to spare for a man dead these four hundred years."

She had not moved from the position in which he had first caught sight of her. Now she smiled her faint, withdrawn smile, and with her hands still clasped lightly in front of her belt-buckle moved toward the door. She had a transcendental repose. Like a nun. Like a queen.

Chapter 4

It was after luncheon before Sergeant Williams reappeared, breathless, bearing two fat volumes.

"You should have left them with the porter," Grant said. "I didn't mean you to come sweating up here with them."

"I had to come up and explain. I had only time to go to one shop, but it's the biggest in the street. That's the best history of England they have in stock. It's the best there is anywhere, they say." He laid down a severe-looking sage-green tome, with an air of taking no responsibility for it. "They had no separate history of Richard III. I mean, no life of him. But they gave me this." This was a gay affair with a coat of arms on the wrapper. It was called *The Rose of Raby*.

"What is this?"

"She was his mother, it seems. The Rose in question, I mean. I can't wait: I'm due at the Yard in five minutes from now and the

Super will flay me alive if I'm late. Sorry I couldn't do better. I'll look in again, first time I'm passing, and if these are no good I'll see what else I can get."

Grant was grateful and said so.

To the sound of Williams's brisk departing footsteps he began his inspection of the "best history of England there is." It turned out to be what is known as a "constitutional" history; a sober compilation lightened with improving illustrations. An illumination from the Luttrell Psalter decorated the husbandry of the fourteenth century, and a contemporary map of London bisected the Great Fire. Kings and queens were mentioned only incidentally. Tanner's Constitutional History was concerned only with social progress and political evolution; with the Black Death, and the invention of printing, and the use of gunpowder, and the formation of the Trade Guilds, and so forth. But here and there Mr. Tanner was forced, by a horrid germaneness, to mention a king or his relations. And one such germaneness occurred in connection with the invention of printing.

A man called Caxton came out of the Weald of Kent as draper's apprentice to a future Lord Mayor of London, and then went to Bruges with the twenty marks his master left him in his will. And when, in the dreary autumn rain of the Low Countries, two young refugees from England fetched up on those low shores, in very low water, it was the successful merchant from the Weald of Kent who gave them succour. The refugees were Edward IV and his brother Richard; and when in the turn of the wheel Edward came back to rule England, Caxton came too, and the first books printed in England were printed for Edward IV and written by Edward's brother-in-law.

He turned the pages and marvelled how dull information is deprived of personality. The sorrows of humanity are no one's sorrows, as newspaper readers long ago found out. A *frisson* of horror may go down one's spine at wholesale destruction but one's heart stays unmoved. A thousand people drowned in floods in China are news: a solitary child drowned in a pond is tragedy. So Mr. Tanner's account of the progress of the English race was admirable but unexciting. But here and there where he could not avoid the personal his narrative flowered into a more immediate interest. In extracts from the Pastons' letters, for instance. The Pastons had a habit of sandwiching scraps of history between orders for salad oil and inquiries as to how Clement was doing at Cambridge. And between two of those domesticities appeared the small item that the two little York boys, George and Richard, were living in the Pastons' London lodgings, and that their brother Edward came every day to see them.

Surely, thought Grant, dropping the book for a moment on the counterpane and staring up at the now invisible ceiling, surely never before can anyone have come to the throne of England with so personal an experience of the ordinary man's life as Edward IV and his brother Richard. And perhaps only Charles II after them. And Charles, even in poverty and flight, had always been a King's son, a man apart. The two little boys who were living in the Pastons' lodgings were merely the babies of the York family. Of no particular importance at the best of times and at the moment when the Pastons' letter was written without a home and possibly without a future.

Grant reached for The Amazon's history book to find out what Edward was about in

London at that date, and learned that he was collecting an army. "London was always Yorkist in temper, and men flocked with enthusiasm to the banner of the youthful Edward," said the history book.

And yet young Edward, aged eighteen, idol of a capital city and on the way to the first of his victories, found time to come every day to see his small brothers.

Was it now, Grant wondered, that the remarkable devotion of Richard to his elder brother was born? An unwavering life-long devotion that the history books not only did not deny but actually used in order to point the moral. "Up to the moment of his brother's death Richard had been in all vicissitudes his loyal and faithful help-meet, but the opportunity of a crown proved too much for him." Or in the simpler words of the Historical Reader: "He had been a good brother to Edward but when he saw that he might become King greed hardened his heart."

Grant took a sideways look at the portrait and decided that the Historical Reader was off the beam. Whatever had hardened Richard's heart to the point of murder had not been greed. Or did the Historical Reader mean greed for power? Probably. Probably.

But surely Richard must have had all the power that mortal man could wish. He was the King's brother, and rich. Was that short step further so important that he could murder his brother's children to achieve it?

It was an odd set-up altogether.

He was still mulling it over in his mind when Mrs. Tinker came in with fresh pyjamas for him and her daily précis of the newspaper headlines. Mrs. Tinker never read past the third headline of a report unless it happened to be a murder, in which case she read every word and bought an evening paper for herself on the way home to cook Tinker's supper.

Today the gentle burble of her comment on a Yorkshire arsenic-and-exhumation case flowed over him unbroken until she caught sight of the morning paper lying in its virgin condition alongside the books on the table. This brought her to a sudden halt.

"You not feelin' so good today?" she asked in a concerned way.

"I'm fine, Tink, fine. Why?"

"You 'aven't as much as opened your paper. That's 'ow my sister's gel started her decline. Not takin' no notice of what was in the paper."

"Don't worry. I'm on the up-grade. Even my temper has improved. I forgot about the paper because I've been reading history stories. Ever heard of the Princes in the Tower?"

"*Everyone's* 'eard of the Princes in the Tower."

"And do you know how they met their end?"

"Course I do. He put a pillow on their faces when they was asleep."

"Who did?"

"Their wicked uncle. Richard the Third. You didn't ought to think of things like that when you're poorly. You ought to be reading something nice and cheerful."

"Are you in a hurry to get home, Tink, or could you go round by St. Martin's Lane for me?"

"No, I've plenty of time. Is it Miss Hallard? She won't be at the theatre till six-about."

"No, I know. But you might leave a note for her and she'll get it when she comes in."

He reached for his scribbling pad and pencil and wrote:

"For the love of Mike find me a copy of Thomas More's *History of Richard III*."

He tore off the page, folded it, and scribbled Marta's name on it.

"You can give it to old Saxton at the stage-door. He'll see that she gets it."

"If I can get near the stage-door what with the stools for the queue," Mrs. Tinker said; in comment rather than in truth. "That thing's going to run for ever."

She put the folded paper carefully away in the cheap pseudo-leather handbag with the shabby edges that was as much a part of her as her hat. Grant had, Christmas by Christmas, provided her with a new bag; each of them a work of art in the best tradition of English leatherworking, an article so admirable in design and so perfect in execution that Marta Hallard might have carried it to luncheon at the Blague. But that was the last he had ever seen of any of them. Since Mrs. Tinker regarded a pawnshop as one degree more disgraceful than prison, he absolved her from any suspicion of cashing in on her presents. He deduced that the handbags were safely laid away in a drawer somewhere, still wrapped up in the original tissue paper. Perhaps she took them out to show people sometimes, sometimes perhaps just to gloat over; or perhaps the knowledge that they were there enriched her, as the knowledge of "something put by for my funeral" might enrich another. Next Christmas he was going to open this shabby sack of hers, this perennial satchel *à toute faire*, and put something in the money compartment. She would fritter it away, of course, in small unimportances; so that in the end she would not know what she had done with it; but perhaps a series of small satisfactions scattered like sequins over the texture of everyday life was of greater worth than the academic satisfaction of owning a collection of fine objects at the back of a drawer.

When she had gone creaking away, in a shoes-and-corset concerto, he went back to Mr. Tanner and tried to improve his mind by acquiring some of Mr. Tanner's interest in the human race. But he found it an effort. Neither by nature nor by profession was he interested in mankind in the large. His bias, native and acquired, was towards the personal. He waded through Mr. Tanner's statistics and longed for a king in an oak tree, or a broom tied to a mast-head, or a Highlander hanging on to a trooper's stirrup in a charge. But at least he had the satisfaction of learning that the Englishman of the fifteenth century "drank water only as a penance." The English labourer of Richard III's day was, it seemed, the admiration of the continent. Mr. Tanner quoted a contemporary, writing in France.

The King of France will allow no one to use salt, but what is bought of himself at his own arbitrary price. The troops pay for nothing, and treat the people barbarously if they are not satisfied. All growers of vines must give a fourth to the King. All the towns must pay the King great yearly sums for his men-at-arms. The peasants live in great hardship and misery. They wear no woollen. Their clothing consists of little short jerkins of sackcloth, no trowse but from the knees up, and legs exposed and naked. The women all go barefoot. The people eat no meat, except the fat of bacon in their soup. Nor are the gentry much better off. If an accusation is brought against them they are examined in private, and perhaps never more heard of.

In England it is very different. No one can abide in another man's house without his leave. The King cannot put on taxes, nor alter the laws, nor make new ones. The English never drink water except for penance. They eat all sorts of flesh and fish. They are clothed throughout in good woollens, and are provided with all sorts of house-hold goods. An Englishman cannot be sued except before the ordinary judge.

And it seemed to Grant that if you were very hard up and wanted to go to see what your Lizzie's firstborn looked like it must have been reassuring to know that there was shelter and a hand-out at every religious house, instead of wondering how you were going to raise the train fare. That green England he had fallen asleep with last night had a lot to be said for it.

He thumbed through the pages on the fifteenth century, looking for personal items; for individual reports that might, in their single vividness, illumine the scene for him as a "spot" lights the desired part of a stage.

But the story was distressingly devoted to the general. According to Mr. Tanner, Richard III's only Parliament was the most liberal and progressive within record; and he regretted, did the worthy Mr. Tanner, that his private crimes should have militated against his patent desire for the common weal. And that seemed to be all that Mr. Tanner had to say about Richard III. Except for the Pastons, chatting indestructibly through the centuries, there was a dearth of human beings in this record of humanity.

He let the book slide off his chest, and searched with his hand until he found *The Rose of Raby*.

Chapter 5

The Rose of Raby proved to be fiction, but it was at least easier to hold than Tanner's Constitutional History of England. It was, moreover, the almost-respectable form of historical fiction which is merely history-with-conversation, so to speak. An imaginative biography rather than an imagined story. Evelyn Payne-Ellis, whoever she might be, had provided portraits and a family tree, and had made no attempt, it seemed, to what he and his cousin Laura used to call in their childhood "write forsoothly." There were no "by our Ladys," no "nathelesses" or "varlets." It was an honest affair according to its lights.

And its lights were more illuminating than Mr. Tanner.

Much more illuminating.

It was Grant's belief that if you could not find out about a man, the next best way to arrive at an estimate of him was to find out about his mother.

So until Marta could provide him with the sainted and infallible Thomas More's personal account of Richard, he would do very happily with Cicely Nevill, Duchess of York.

He glanced at the family tree, and thought that if the two York brothers, Edward and Richard, were, as kings, unique in their experience of ordinary life they were no less unique in their Englishness. He looked at their breeding and marvelled. Nevill, Fitzalan, Percy, Holland, Mortimer, Clifford, and Audley, as well as Plantagenet. Queen Elizabeth (who made it her boast) was all English; if one counted the Welsh streak as English. But among all the half-bred monarchs who had graced the throne between the Conquest and Farmer George—half-French, half-Spanish, half-Danish, half-Dutch, half-Portuguese—Edward IV and Richard III were remarkable in their home-bred quality.

They were also, he noted, as royally bred on their mother's side as on their father's. Cicely Nevill's grandfather was John of Gaunt, the first of the Lancasters; third son of Edward III. Her husband's two grandfathers were two other sons of Edward III. So

three of Edward III's five sons had contributed to the making of the two York
brothers.

"To be a Nevill," said Miss Payne-Ellis,
"was to be of some importance since
they were great landowners. To be a
Nevill was almost certainly to be handsome, since they were a good-looking
family. To be a Nevill was to have personality, since they excelled in displays
of both character and temperament. To
unite all three Nevill gifts, in their finest
quality, in one person was the good fortune of Cicely Nevill, who was the sole
Rose of the north long before that north
was forced to choose between White
Roses and Red."

It was Miss Payne-Ellis's contention that
the marriage with Richard Plantagenet,
Duke of York, was a love match. Grant received this theory with a scepticism border-
ing on scorn until he noticed the results of
that marriage. To have a yearly addition to
the family was not, in the fifteenth century,
evidence of anything but fertility. And the
long family produced by Cicely Nevill to her

charming husband augured nothing nearer love than co-habitation. But in a time when the wife's rôle was to stay meekly at home and see to her still-room, Cicely Nevill's constant travelings about in her husband's company were surely remarkable enough to suggest an abnormal pleasure in that company. The extent and constancy of that travel was witnessed to by the birthplaces of her children. Anne, her first, was born in Fotheringhay, the family home in Northamptonshire. Henry, who died as a baby, at Hatfield. Edward at Rouen, where the Duke was on active service. Edmund and Elizabeth also at Rouen. Margaret at Fotheringhay. John, who died young, at Neath in Wales. George in Dublin (and could it be, wondered Grant, that that accounted for the almost Irish perverseness of the ineffable George?). Richard at Fotheringhay.

Cicely Nevill had not sat at home in Northamptonshire waiting for her lord and master to visit her when it seemed good to him. She had accompanied him about the world of their inhabiting. There was a strong presumption in favour of Miss Payne-Ellis's theory. At the very canniest reckoning it was patently a very successful marriage.

Which perhaps accounted for the family devotion of those daily visits of Edward to his small brothers in the Pastons' lodgings. The York family, even before tribulations, was a united one.

This was borne out unexpectedly when, spurting the pages from under his thumb, he came on a letter. It was a letter from the two elder boys, Edward and Edmund, to their father. The boys were at Ludlow Castle, undergoing their education, and on a Saturday in Easter week, taking advantage of a courier who was going back, they burst out in loud complaint of their tutor and his "odiousness" and begged their father to listen to the tale of the courier, William Smyth, who was fully charged with the details of their oppression. This S.O.S. was introduced and ended in respectful padding, the formality of which was a little marred by their pointing out that it was nice of him to send the clothes but that he had forgotten their breviary.

The conscientious Miss Payne-Ellis had given the reference for this letter (one of the Cotton manuscripts, it appeared) and he thumbed more slowly, in search of more. Factual evidence was a policeman's meat.

He could not find any, but he came on a family tableau which held him for a moment.

The Duchess moved out into the thin sharp sunlight of a London December morning, and stood on the steps to watch them go: her husband, her brother, and her son. Dirk and his nephews brought the horses into the courtyard, scattering the pigeons and the fussing sparrows from the cobbles. She watched her husband mount, equable and deliberate as always, and thought that for all the emotion he showed he might be riding down to Fotheringhay to look at some new rams instead of setting out on a campaign. Salisbury, her brother, was being Nevill and temperamental; a little conscious of the occasion and living up to it. She looked at them both and smiled in her mind at them. But it was Edmund who caught at her heart. Edmund at seventeen, very slender, very untried, very vulnerable. Flushed with pride and excitement at this setting-out to his first campaigning. She wanted to say to her husband: "Take care of Edmund," but she could not do that. Her husband would not understand; and Edmund, if he were to suspect, would be furious. If Edward, only a year older, was commanding an army of his own on the borders of Wales at this very minute, then he, Edmund, was more than old enough to see a war at first-hand.

She glanced behind her at the three younger children who had come out in her wake; Margaret and George, the two solid fair ones, and behind them, a pace in the rear as always, her changeling baby, Richard; his dark brows and brown hair making him look like a visitor. Good-natured untidy Margaret watched with all the moist-eyed emotion of fourteen; George in a passionate envy and wild rebellion that he was only eleven and of no consequence in this martial moment. Thin little Richard showed no excitement at all, but his mother thought that he vibrated like a softly tapped drum.

The three horses moved out of the court-yard in a clatter of slipping hooves and jingling accoutrements, to join the servants waiting for them in the roadway, and the children called and danced and waved them out of the gate.

And Cicely, who in her time had seen so many men, and so many of her family, go off to war, went back to the house with an unaccustomed weight at her bosom. Which of them, said the voice in her unwilling mind, which of them was it who was not coming back?

Her imagination did not compass anything so horrible as the fact that none of them was coming back again. That she would never see any one of them again.

That before the year was ended her husband's severed head, crowned for insult with a paper crown, would be nailed above the Micklegate Bar in York, and the heads of her brother and her son on the two other gates.

Well, that might be fiction, but it was an illuminating glimpse of Richard. The dark one in a blond family. The one who "looked like a visitor." The "changeling."

He abandoned Cicely Nevill for the moment, and went hunting through the book for her son Richard. But Miss Payne-Ellis seemed not to be greatly interested in Richard. He was merely the tail-end of the family. The magnificent young creature who flourished at the other end was more to her taste. Edward was much to the fore. With his Nevill cousin Warwick, Salisbury's son, he won the battle of Towton, and, with the memory of Lancastrian ferocity still fresh and his father's head still nailed to the Micklegate Bar, gave evidence of that tolerance that was to be characteristic of him. There was quarter at Towton for all who asked. He was crowned King of England in Westminster Abbey (and two small boys, home from exile in Utrecht, were created respectively Duke of Clarence and Duke of Gloucester). And he buried his father and his brother Edmund with great magnificence in the church at Fotheringhay (though it was Richard, aged thirteen, who convoyed that sad procession from Yorkshire, through the bright glory of five July days, to Northamptonshire; nearly six years after he had stood on the steps of Baynard's Castle in London to watch them ride away).

It was not until Edward had been King for some time that Miss Payne-Ellis allowed Richard to come back into the story. He was then being educated with his Nevill cousins at Middleham, in Yorkshire.

As Richard rode into the shadow of the keep, out of the broad sunlight and flying winds of Wensleydale, it seemed to him that there was an atmosphere of strangeness about the place. The guards were talking in loud excitement in the gatehouse and seemed abashed at his presence. From their sudden silence he rode on into a silent court that should have been bustling with activity at this hour of the day. It would soon be supper time, and both habit and hunger brought all the inhabitants of Middleham home from their various occupations, as they were bringing him back from his hawking, for the evening meal. This hush, this desertion, was unusual. He walked his horse to the stables, but there was no one there to give it to. As he unsaddled he noticed a hard-ridden bay in the next stall; a horse that did not belong to Middleham; a horse so tired that he had not eaten up and his head hung in a despondent beaten way between his knees.

Richard wiped his horse down and rugged him, brought him some hay and fresh water, and left him; wondering about that beaten horse and the uncanny silence. As he paused in the doorway he could hear voices in the distance of the great hall; and debated whether he should go there and investigate before going upstairs to his own quarters. As he hesitated a voice from the stairs above him said: "Z-z-zt."

He looked up to see his cousin Anne's head peering over the banisters, her two long fair plaits hanging down like bell-ropes.

"Richard!" she said, half whispering. "Have you heard?"

"Is something wrong?" he asked. "What is it?"

As he moved up to her she grabbed his hand and dragged him upwards towards their schoolroom in the roof.

"But what is it?" he asked, leaning back in protest against her urgency. "What has happened? Is it something so awful that you can't tell me here?"

She swept him into the schoolroom and shut the door.

"It's Edward!"

"Edward? Is he ill?"

"No! *Scandal!*"

"Oh," said Richard, relieved. Scandal and Edward were never far apart. "What is it? Has he a new mistress?"

"Much worse than that! Oh, much, *much* worse. He's married."

"Married?" said Richard, so unbelieving that he sounded calm. "He can't be."

"But he is. The news came from London an hour ago."

"He can't be married," Richard insisted. "For a King marriage is a long affair. A matter of contracts, and agreements. A matter for Parliament, even, I think. What made you think he had got married?"

"I don't *think*," Anne said, out of patience at this sober reception of her broadside. "The whole family is raging together in the Great Hall over the affair."

"Anne! have you been listening at the door?"

"Oh, don't be so righteous. I didn't have to listen very hard, anyhow. You could hear them on the other side of the river. He has married Lady Grey!"

"Who is Lady Grey? Lady Grey of Groby?"

"Yes."

"But he can't. She has two children and she's quite old."

"She is five years older than Edward, and she is wonderfully beautiful—so I overhear."

"When did this happen?"

"They've been married five months. They got married in secret down in Northampton-shire."

"But I thought he was going to marry the King of France's sister."

"So," said Anne, in a tone full of meaning, "did my father."

"Yes; yes, it makes things very awkward for him, doesn't it; after all the negotiating."

"According to the messenger from London he is throwing fits. It isn't only the making him look a fool. It seems she has cohorts of relations and he hates every one of them."

"Edward must be possessed." In Richard's hero-worshipping eyes everything Edward did had always been right. This folly, this undeniable, this inexcusable folly, could come only from possession.

"It will break my mother's heart," he said. He thought of his mother's courage when his father and Edmund had been killed, and the Lancastrian army was almost at the gates of London. She had not wept nor wrapped herself in protective veils of self-pity. She had arranged that he and George should go to Utrecht, as if she were arranging for them to go away to school. They might never see each other again, but she had busied herself about warm clothes for their winter voyage across the Channel with a calm and dry-eyed practicality.

How would she bear this; this further blow? This destructive folly. This shattering foolishness.

"Yes," said Anne, softening. "Poor Aunt Cicely. It is monstrous of Edward to hurt everyone so. Monstrous."

But Edward was still the infallible. If Edward had done wrong it was because he was ill, or possessed, or bewitched. Edward still had Richard's allegiance; his heart-whole and worshipping allegiance.

Nor in after years was that allegiance—an adult allegiance of recognition and acceptance—ever less than heart-whole.

And then the story went on to Cicely Nevill's tribulation, and her efforts to bring some kind of order into the relations between her son Edward, half-pleased, half-ashamed, and her nephew Warwick, wholly furious. There was also a long description of that indestructibly virtuous beauty with the famous "gilt" hair, who had succeeded where more complaisant beauties had failed; and of her enthroning at Reading Abbey (led to the throne by a silently protesting Warwick, who could not but note the large array of Woodvilles, come to see their sister Elizabeth acknowledged Queen of England).

The next time Richard turned up in the tale he was setting out from Lynn without a penny in his pocket, in a Dutch vessel that happened to be in the harbour when it was needed. Along with him was his brother Edward, Edward's friend Lord Hastings, and a few followers. None of them had anything except what they stood up in, and after some argument the ship's captain agreed to accept Edward's fur-lined cape as fare.

Warwick had finally decided that the Woodville clan was more than he could stomach. He had helped to put his cousin Edward on the throne of England; he could just as easily unseat him. For the achievement of this he had the help of the whole Nevill brood; and, incredibly, the active assistance of the ineffable George. Who had decided that falling heir to half the lands of Montague, Nevill, and Beauchamp, by marrying Warwick's other daughter Isabel, was a better bet than being loyal to his brother Edward. In eleven days Warwick was master of a surprised England, and Edward and

Richard were squelching through the October mud between Alkmaar and The Hague.

From then on, Richard was always in the background of the story. Through that dreary winter in Bruges. Staying with Margaret in Burgundy—for that kind moist-eyed Margaret who had stood on the steps of Baynard's Castle with himself and George to watch their father ride away was now the very new Duchess of Burgundy. Margaret, kind Margaret, was saddened and dismayed—as many people in future were to be saddened and dismayed—by George's inexplicable conduct, and set herself to missionary work what time she got together funds for her two more admirable brothers.

Not even Miss Payne-Ellis's interest in the magnificent Edward allowed her to conceal that the real work of outfitting the ships hired with Margaret's money was done by Richard; a Richard not yet eighteen. And when Edward with an absurd handful of followers found himself once more camped in an English meadow, facing George with an army, it was Richard who went over to George's camp and talked the Margaret-weakened George into alliance again and so left the road to London open to them.

Not, Grant thought, that this last was any great achievement. George could obviously be talked into anything. He was the born missionee.

Chapter 6

He had not nearly exhausted *The Rose of Raby* and the illicit joys of fiction when, next morning about eleven, a parcel arrived from Marta containing the more respectable entertainment of history as recorded by the sainted Sir Thomas.

With the book was a note in Marta's large sprawling writing on Marta's stiff expensive notepaper.

Have to send this instead of bringing it. Frantically busy. Think I have got M.M. to the sticking point re Blessington. No T. More in any of the bookshops, so tried Public Library. Can't think why one never thinks of Public Libraries. Probably because books expected to be soupy. Think this looks quite clean and unsoupy. You get fourteen days. Sounds like a sentence rather than a loan. Hope this interest in Crouchback means that the prickles are less nettlish. Till soon.

Marta

The book did indeed look clean and unsoupy, if a little elderly. But after the light going of *The Rose* its print looked unexciting and its solid paragraphs forbidding. Nevertheless he attacked it with interest. This was, after all, where Richard III was concerned, "the horse's mouth."

He came to the surface an hour later, vaguely puzzled and ill at ease. It was not that the matter surprised him; the facts were very much what he had expected them to be. It was that this was not how he had expected Sir Thomas to write.

He took ill rest at nights, lay long waking and musing; sore wearied with care and watch, he slumbered rather than slept. So was his restless heart continually tossed and tumbled with the tedious impression and stormy remembrance of his most abominable deeds.

That was all right. But when he added that "this he had from such as were secret with his chamberers" one was suddenly re-pelled. An aroma of back-stair gossip and servants' spying came off the page. So that one's sympathy tilted before one was aware of it from the smug commentator to the tor-tured creature sleeping on his bed. The murderer seemed of greater stature than the man who was writing of him.

Which was all wrong.

Grant was conscious too of the same un-ease that filled him when he listened to a witness telling a perfect story that he knew to be flawed somewhere.

And that was very puzzling indeed. What could possibly be wrong with the personal account of a man revered for his integrity as Thomas More had been revered for four centuries?

The Richard who appeared in More's ac-count was, Grant thought, one that Matron would have recognised. A man highly-strung and capable of both great evil and great suffering. "He was never quiet in his mind, never thought himself secure. His eyes whirled about, his body was privily fenced, his hand ever on his dagger, his countenance and manner like one always ready to strike again."

And of course there was the dramatic, not to say hysterical, scene that Grant remembered from his school-days; that every schoolboy probably remembered. The council scene in the Tower before he laid claim to the crown. Richard's sudden challenge to Hastings as to what was the proper fate for a man who plotted the death of the Protector of the Kingdom. The insane claim that Edward's wife and Edward's mistress (Jane Shore) were responsible for his withered arm by their sorcery. The smiting of the table in his rage, which was the signal for his armed satellites to burst in and arrest Lord Hastings, Lord Stanley, and John Morton, Bishop of Ely. The rushing of Hastings down into the courtyard and his beheading on a handy log of wood after bare time to confess himself to the first priest who could be found.

That was certainly the picture of a man who would act first—in fury, in fear, in revenge—and repent afterwards.

But it seemed that he was capable of more calculated iniquity. He caused a sermon to be preached by a certain Dr. Shaw, brother of the Lord Mayor, at Paul's Cross, on June 22, on the text: "Bastard slips shall take no root." Wherein Dr. Shaw maintained that both Edward and George were sons of the Duchess of York by some unknown man, and that Richard was the only legitimate son of the Duke and Duchess of York.

This was so unlikely, so inherently absurd, that Grant went back and read it over again. But it still said the same thing. That Richard had traduced his mother, in public and for his own material advantage, with an unbelievable infamy.

Well, Sir Thomas More said it. And if anyone should know it would be Thomas More. And if anyone should know how to pick and choose between the credibilities in the reporting of a story it ought to be Thomas More, Lord Chancellor of England.

Richard's mother, said Sir Thomas, complained bitterly of the slander with which her son had smirched her. Understandably, on the whole, Grant thought.

As for Dr. Shaw, he was overcome with remorse. So much so that "within a few days he withered and consumed away."

Had a stroke, probably, Grant considered. And little wonder. To have stood up and told that tale to a London crowd must have taken some nerve.

Sir Thomas's account of the Princes in the Tower was the same as The Amazon's, but Sir Thomas's version was more detailed. Richard had suggested to Robert Brackenbury, Constable of the Tower, that it might be a good thing if the Princes disappeared, but Brackenbury would have no part in such an act. Richard therefore waited until he was at Warwick, during his progress through England after his coronation, and then sent Tyrrel to London with orders that he was to receive the keys of the Tower for one night. During that night two ruffians, Dighton and Forrest, one a groom and one a warder, smothered the two boys.

At this point The Midget came in with his lunch and removed the book from his grasp; and while he forked the shepherd's pie from plate to mouth he considered again the face of the man in the dock. The faithful and patient small brother who had turned into a monster.

When The Midget came back for his tray he said: "Did you know that Richard III was a very popular person in his day? Before he came to the throne, I mean."

The Midget cast a baleful glance at the picture.

"Always was a snake in the grass, if you ask me. Smooth, that's what he was: smooth. Biding his time."

Biding his time for what? he wondered, as she tapped away down the corridor. He could not have known that his brother Edward would die unexpectedly at the early age of forty. He could not have foreseen (even after a childhood shared with him in uncommon intimacy) that George's ongoings would end in attainder and the debarring of his two children from the succession. There seemed little point in "biding one's time" if there was nothing to bide for. The indestructible virtuous beauty with the gilt hair had, except for her incurable nepotism, proved an admirable Queen and had provided Edward with a large brood of healthy children, including two boys. The whole of that brood, together with George and his son and daughter, stood between Richard and the throne. It was surely unlikely that a man busy with the administration of the North of England, or campaigning (with dazzling success) against the Scots, would have much spare interest in being "smooth."

What then had changed him so fundamentally in so short a time?

Grant reached for *The Rose of Raby* to see what Miss Payne-Ellis had had to say about the unhappy metamorphosis of Cicely Nevill's youngest son. But that wily author had burked the issue. She had wanted the book to be a happy one, and to have carried it to its logical conclusion would have made it unredeemed tragedy. She had therefore wound it up with a fine resounding major chord by making her last chapter the coming-out of young Elizabeth, Edward's eldest child. This avoided both the tragedy of Elizabeth's young brothers and the defeat and death of Richard in battle.

So the book ended with a Palace party, and a flushed and happy young Elizabeth, very magnificent in a new white dress and her first pearls, dancing the soles out of her slippers like the princesses in the fairy-tale. Richard and Anne, and their delicate little son, had come up from Middleham for the occasion. But neither George nor Isabel was there. Isabel had died in childbirth years ago, obscurely and as far as George was concerned unmourned. George too had died obscurely, but with that perverseness that was so peculiarly George's, had by that very obscurity won for himself imperishable fame.

George's life had been a progression from one spectacular piece of spiritual extravagance to the next. Each time, his family must have said: "Well, that at last is the summit of frightfulness; even George cannot think of anything more fantastic than that." And each time George had surprised them. There was no limit to George's antic capacity.

The seed was perhaps sown when, during his first backsliding in the company of his father-in-law, Warwick had created him heir to the poor crazy puppet-King, Henry VI, whom Warwick had dumped back on the throne to spite his cousin Edward. Both Warwick's hopes of seeing his daughter a Queen and George's royal pretensions had gone down the drain on that night when Richard had gone over to the Lancastrian camp and talked to George. But the taste of importance had perhaps proved too much for a natural sweet-tooth. In the years to come the family were always heading George off from unexpected vagaries, or rescuing him from his latest caper.

When Isabel died he had been certain that

she had been poisoned by her waiting woman, and that his baby son had been poisoned by another. Edward, thinking the affair important enough to be tried before a London court, sent down a writ; only to find that George had tried them both at a petty sessions of his own magistrates and hanged them. The furious Edward, by way of rapping him over the knuckles, had two members of George's household tried for treason; but instead of taking the hint George declared that this was just judicial murder, and went about saying so in loud tones and a fine blaze of *lèse-majesté*.

Then he decided that he wanted to marry the richest heiress in Europe; who was Margaret's stepdaughter, young Mary of Burgundy. Kind Margaret thought that it would be nice to have her brother in Burgundy, but Edward had arranged to back Maximilian of Austria's suit, and George was a continual embarrassment.

When the Burgundy intrigue came to nothing, the family hoped for a little peace. After all, George owned half the Nevill lands and had no need to marry again either for fortune or children. But George had a new scheme for marrying Margaret, the sister of James III of Scotland.

At last his *folie de grandeur* graduated from secret negotiation undertaken on his own behalf with foreign courts to open display of the Lancastrian act of Parliament which had declared him heir to the throne after Henry VI. This, inevitably, landed him before another Parliament, and a much less amenable one.

The trial was chiefly remarkable for a flaming and wordy row between the two brothers, Edward and George, but when the expected attainder was passed, there was a pause. Depriving George of his standing was one thing: desirable and indeed necessary. But executing him was something else again.

As the days went by without sentence being carried out, the Commons sent a reminder. And next day it was announced that George, Duke of Clarence, had died in the Tower.

"Drowned in a butt of malmsey," said London. And what was merely a Cockney's comment on a drunkard's end passed into history and made the undeserving George immortal.

So George was not at that party at Westminster, and the emphasis in Miss Payne-Ellis's final chapter was not on Cicely Nevill as the mother of sons, but on Cicely Nevill the grandmother of a fine brood. George might have died discredited, on a dried-leaf heap of worn-out friendships, but his son, young Warwick, was a fine upstanding boy, and little Margaret at ten was already showing signs of the traditional Nevill beauty. Edmund, dead in battle at seventeen, might seem a wanton waste of young life, but there to balance it was the delicate baby whom she had never thought to rear; and he had a son to follow him. Richard in his twenties still looked as though one could break him in two, but he was as tough as a heather root, and perhaps his fragile-looking son would grow up to be as resilient. As for Edward, her tall blond Edward, his beauty might be blurring into grossness and his amiability into sloth, but his two small sons and his five girls had all the character and good looks of their combined ancestry.

As a grandmother she could look on that crowd of children with a personal pride, and as a Princess of England she could look on them with assurance. The crown was safe in the York line for generations to come.

If anyone, looking in a crystal ball at that party, had told Cicely Nevill that in four years not only the York line but the whole Plantagenet dynasty would have gone forever, she would have held it to be either madness or treason.

But what Miss Payne-Ellis had not sought to gloss over was the prevalence of the Woodville clan in a Nevill-Plantagenet gathering.

She looked round the room and wished that her daughter-in-law Elizabeth had been blessed either with a less generous heart or with fewer relations. The Woodville match had turned out far more happily than anyone had dared to hope; Elizabeth had been an admirable wife; but the by-products had not been so fortunate. It was perhaps inevitable that the governorship of the two boys should have gone to her eldest brother; and Rivers, if a little nouveau riche in his liking for display and a little too obviously ambitious, was a cultured creature and an admirable person to have the boys in charge during their schoolroom days at Ludlow. But as for the rest: four brothers, seven sisters, and two sons by her first hus-

band, were really too many by half to have
brought into the marriage market in her
wake.

Cicely looked across the laughing mêlée
of the children's blind man's buff to the
grown-ups standing round the supper table.
Anne Woodville married to the Earl of Essex's heir. Eleanor Woodville married to the
Earl of Kent's heir. Margaret Woodville married to the Earl of Arundel's heir. Catherine
Woodville married to the Duke of Buckingham. Jacquette Woodville to Lord Strange.
Mary Woodville to Lord Herbert's heir. And
John Woodville, disgracefully, to the Dowager of Norfolk who was old enough to be his
grandmother. It was good that new blood
should strengthen the old families—new
blood had always seeped in—but it was not
good that it should come suddenly and in a
flood from one particular source. It was like
a fever in the political blood of the country;
a foreign introduction, difficult to be assimilated. Unwise and regrettable.

However. There were long years ahead in
which that influx could be assimilated. This
new sudden power in the body politic would
cease to be so concentrated, would spread
out, would settle down, would cease to be

dangerous and upsetting. Edward for all his amiability had a shrewd common sense; he would keep the country on an even keel as he had kept it for nearly twenty years. No one had run England with a more despotic power or a lighter hand than her acute, lazy, woman-loving Edward.

It would be all right eventually.

She was about to rise and join them in their discussion of sweetmeats—they must not think that she was being critical or aloof—when her granddaughter Elizabeth came breathless and laughing out of the scrimmage and swept into the seat beside her.

"I am much too old for this sort of thing," she said between her gasps, "and it is ruinous to one's clothes. Do you like my dress, grandmother? I had to coax it out of Father. He said my old tawny satin would do. The one I had when Aunt Margaret came from Burgundy to visit us. That is the worst of having a father who notices what women wear. He knows too much about one's wardrobe. Did you hear that the Dauphin has jilted me? Father is in a pet, but I am so happy. I lighted ten candles to St. Catherine. It took all I had left of my allowance. I don't want to leave England. I want never to leave England ever. Can you arrange that for me, grandmother?"

Cicely smiled and said that she would try.

"Old Ankaret, who tells fortunes, says that I am to be a Queen. But since there is no prince to marry me I do not see how that may be." She paused, and added in a smaller voice: "She said Queen of England. But I expect she was just a little tipsy. She is very fond of hippocras."

It was unfair, not to say inartistic, of Miss Payne-Ellis to hint at Elizabeth's future as the wife of Henry VII if as author she was not prepared to face the unpleasantness that lay between. To presuppose in her readers a knowledge of Elizabeth's marriage to the first Tudor king, was also to presuppose their awareness of her brothers' murder. So that a dark reminding shadow fell across the festive scene with which she had chosen to end her story.

But on the whole, Grant thought, she had made a good enough job of the story, judging by what he had read of it. He might even go back sometime and read the bits he had skipped.

Chapter 7

Grant had switched off his bedside light that night, and was half asleep, when a voice in his mind said, "But Thomas More was Henry the Eighth."

This brought him wide awake. He flicked the light on again.

What the voice had meant, of course, was not that Thomas More and Henry the Eighth were one and the same person, but that, in that business of putting personalities into pigeon-holes according to reigns, Thomas More belonged to the reign of Henry the Eighth.

Grant lay looking at the pool of light that his lamp threw on the ceiling, and reckoned. If Thomas More was Henry VIII's Chancellor, then he must have lived through the whole of Henry VII's long reign as well as Richard III's. There was something wrong some-where.

He reached for More's *History of Richard*

III. It had as preface a short life of More which he had not bothered to read. Now he turned to it to find out how More could have been both Richard III's historian and Henry VIII's Chancellor. How old was More when Richard succeeded?

He was five.

When that dramatic council scene had taken place at the Tower, Thomas More had been five years old. He had been only eight when Richard died at Bosworth.

Everything in that history had been hearsay.

And if there was one word that a policeman loathed more than another it was hearsay. Especially when applied to evidence.

He was so disgusted that he flung the precious book on to the floor before he remembered that it was the property of a Public Library and his only by grace and for fourteen days.

More had never known Richard III at all. He had indeed grown up under a Tudor administration. That book was the Bible of the whole historical world on the subject of Richard III—it was from that account that Holinshed had taken his material, and from that that Shakespeare had written his—and except that More believed what he wrote to be true it was of no more value than what the soldier said. It was what his cousin Laura called "snow on their boots." A "gospel-true" event seen by someone other than the teller. That More had a critical mind and an admirable integrity did not make the story acceptable evidence. A great many otherwise admirable minds had accepted that story of the Russian troops passing through Britain. Grant had dealt too long with the human intelligence to accept as truth someone's report of someone's report of what that someone remembered to have seen or been told.

He was disgusted.

At the first opportunity he must get an actual contemporary account of the events of Richard's short reign. The Public Library could have Sir Thomas More back tomorrow and be damned to their fourteen days. The fact that Sir Thomas was a martyr and a Great Mind did not cut any ice at all with him, Alan Grant. He, Alan Grant, had known Great Minds so uncritical that they would believe a story that would make a con man blush for shame. He had known a great scientist who was convinced that a piece of butter muslin was his great-aunt Sophia because an illiterate medium from the back streets of Plymouth told him so. He had known a great authority on the Human Mind and Its Evolution who had been taken for all he had by an incurable knave because he "judged for himself and not on police stories." As far as he, Alan Grant, was concerned there was nothing so uncritical or so damn-silly as your Great Mind. As far as he, Alan Grant, was concerned Thomas More was washed out, cancelled, deleted; and he, Alan Grant, was beginning from scratch again tomorrow morning.

He was still illogically fuming when he fell asleep and he woke fuming.

"Do you know that your Sir Thomas More knew nothing about Richard III at all?" he said, accusing, to The Amazon the moment her large person appeared in the doorway.

She looked startled, not at his news but at his ferocity. Her eyes looked as if they might brim with tears at another rough word.

"But of *course* he knew!" she protested. "He *lived* then."

"He was eight when Richard died," Grant said, relentless. "And all he knew was what he had been told. Like me. Like you. Like Will Rogers of blessed memory. There is nothing hallowed at all about Sir Thomas More's history of Richard III. It's a damned piece of hearsay and a swindle."

"Aren't you feeling so well this morning?" she asked anxiously. "Do you think you've got a temperature?"

"I don't know about a temperature, but my blood pressure's away up."

"Oh, dear, dear," she said, taking this literally. "And you were doing so very well. Nurse Ingham will be so distressed. She has been boasting about your good recovery."

That The Midget should have found him a subject for boasting was a new idea to Grant, but it was not one that gave him any gratification. He resolved to have a temperature in earnest if he could manage it, just to score off The Midget.

But the morning visit of Marta distracted him from this experiment in the power of mind over matter.

Marta, it seemed, was pluming herself on his mental health very much as The Midget was pluming herself on his physical improvement. She was delighted that her pokings-about with James in the print shop had been so effective.

"Have you decided on Perkin Warbeck, then?" she asked.

"No. Not Warbeck. Tell me: what made you bring me a portrait of Richard III? There's no mystery about Richard, is there?"

"No. I suppose we took it as illustration to the Warbeck story. No, wait a moment. I remember, James turned it up and said: 'If he's mad about faces, there's one for him!' He said: 'That's the most notorious murderer in history, and yet his face is in my estimation the face of a saint.' "

"A saint!" Grant said; and then remembered something. " 'Over-conscientious,' " he said.

"What?"

"Nothing. I was just remembering my first impressions of it. Is that how it seemed to you: the face of a saint?"

She looked across to the picture, propped up against the pile of books. "I can't see it against the light," she said, and picked it up for a closer scrutiny.

He was suddenly reminded that to Marta, as to Sergeant Williams, faces were a professional matter. The slant of an eyebrow, the set of a mouth, was just as much an evidence of character to Marta as to Williams. Indeed she actually made herself faces to match the characters she played.

"Nurse Ingham thinks he's dreary. Nurse Darroll thinks he's a horror. My surgeon thinks he's a polio victim. Sergeant Williams thinks he's a born judge. Matron thinks he's a soul in torment."

Marta said nothing for a little. Then she said: "It's odd, you know. When you first look at it you think it a mean, suspicious face. Even cantankerous. But when you look at it a little longer you find that it isn't like that at all. It is quite calm. It is really quite a gentle face. Perhaps that is what James meant by being saintlike."

"No. No, I don't think so. What he meant was the subservience to conscience."

"Whatever it is, it is a *face*, isn't it! Not just a collection of organs for seeing, breathing, and eating with. A wonderful face. With very little alteration, you know, it might be a portrait of Lorenzo the Magnificent."

"You don't suppose that it *is* Lorenzo and that we're considering the wrong man altogether?"

"Of course not. Why should you think that?"

"Because nothing in the face fits the facts of history. And pictures have got shuffled before now."

"Oh, yes, of course they have. But that is Richard all right. The original—or what is supposed to be the original—is at Windsor Castle, James told me. It is included in Henry VIII's inventory, so it has been there for four hundred years or so. And there are duplicates at Hatfield and Albury."

"It's Richard," Grant said resignedly. "I just don't know anything about faces. Do you know anyone at the B. M.?"

"At the British Museum?" Marta asked, her attention still on the portrait. "No. I don't think so. Not that I can think of at the moment. I went there once to look at some Egyptian jewellery, when I was playing Cleopatra with Geoffrey—did you ever see Geoffrey's Antony? It was superlatively genteel—but the place frightens me rather. Such a garnering of the ages. It made me feel the way the stars make you feel: small and no-account. What do you want of the B. M.?"

"I wanted some information about history

written in Richard III's day. Contemporary accounts."

"Isn't the sainted Sir Thomas any good, then?"

"The sainted Sir Thomas is nothing but an old gossip," Grant said with venom. He had taken a wild dislike to the much-admired More.

"Oh, dear. And the nice man at the Library seemed so reverent about him. The Gospel of Richard III according to St. Thomas More, and all that."

"Gospel nothing," Grant said rudely. "He was writing down in a Tudor England what someone had told him about events that happened in a Plantagenet England when he himself was five."

"Five years old?"

"Yes."

"Oh, dear. Not exactly the horse's mouth."

"Not even straight from the course. Come to think of it, it's as reliable as a bookie's tips would be. He's on the wrong side of the rails altogether. If he was a Tudor servant he was on the laying side where Richard III was concerned."

"Yes. Yes, I suppose so. What do you

want to find out about Richard, when there is no mystery to investigate?"

"I want to know what made him tick. That is a more profound mystery than anything I have come up against of late. What changed him almost overnight? Up to the moment of his brother's death he seems to have been entirely admirable. And devoted to his brother."

"I suppose the supreme honour must always be a temptation."

"He was Regent until the boy came of age. Protector of England. With his previous history, you would think that would have been enough for him. You would have thought, indeed, that it would have been very much his cup of tea: guardian to both Edward's son and the kingdom."

"Perhaps the brat was unbearable, and Richard longed to 'larn' him. Isn't it odd how we never think of victims as anything but white innocents. Like Joseph in the Bible. I'm sure he was a quite intolerable young man, actually, and long overdue for that pushing into the pit. Perhaps young Edward was just sitting up and begging to be quietly put down."

"There were two of them," Grant reminded her.

"Yes, of course. Of course there isn't an explanation. It was the ultimate barbarism. Poor little woolly lambs! Oh!"

"What was the 'Oh' for?"

"I've just thought of something. Woolly lambs made me think of it."

"Well?"

"No, I won't tell you in case it doesn't come off. I must fly."

"Have you charmed Madeleine March into agreeing to write the play?"

"Well, she hasn't actually signed a contract yet, but I think she is sold on the idea. Au revoir, my dear, I shall look in soon again."

She went away, sped on her way by a blushing Amazon, and Grant did not remember anything about woolly lambs until the woolly lamb actually turned up in his room next evening. The woolly lamb was wearing horn-rimmed spectacles, which in some odd way emphasized the resemblance instead of detracting from it. Grant had been dozing, more at peace with the world than he had been for some time; history was, as Matron had pointed out, an excellent way of acquiring a sense of perspective. The tap at his door was so tentative that he had decided that he had imagined it. Taps on hospital doors are not apt to be tentative. But something made him say: "Come in!" and there in the opening was something that was so unmistakably Marta's woolly lamb that Grant laughed aloud before he could stop himself.

The young man looked abashed, smiled nervously, propped the spectacles on his nose with a long thin forefinger, cleared his throat, and said:

"Mr. Grant? My name is Carradine. Brent Carradine. I hope I haven't disturbed you when you were resting."

"No, no. Come in, Mr. Carradine. I am delighted to see you."

"Marta—Miss Hallard, that is—sent me. She said I could be of some help to you."

"Did she say how? Do sit down. You'll find a chair over there behind the door. Bring it over."

He was a tall boy, hatless, with soft fair curls crowning a high forehead and a much too big tweed coat hanging unfastened round him in negligent folds, American-wise. Indeed, it was obvious that he was in fact American. He brought over the chair, planted himself on it with the coat spread round him like some royal robe and looked at Grant with kind brown eyes whose luminous charm not even the horn-rims could dim.

"Marta—Miss Hallard, that is—said that you wanted something looked up."

"And are you a looker-upper?"

"I'm doing research, here in London. Historical research, I mean. And she said something about your wanting something in that line. She knows I work at the B. M. most mornings. I'd be very pleased, Mr. Grant, to do anything I can to help you."

"That's very kind of you; very kind indeed. What is it that you are working on? Your research, I mean."

"The Peasants' Revolt."

"Oh, Richard II."

"Yes."

"Are you interested in social conditions?"

The young man grinned suddenly in a very unstudent-like way and said: "No, I'm interested in staying in England."

"And you can't stay in England without doing research?"

"Not very easily. I've got to have an alibi.

My pop thinks I should go into the family business. It's furniture. Wholesale furniture. You order it by mail. Out of a book. Don't misunderstand me, Mr. Grant: it's very good furniture. Lasts for ever. It's just that I can't take much interest in furnishing-units."

"And, short of Polar exploration, the British Museum was the best hideaway you could think of."

"Well, it's warm. And I really do like history. I majored in it. And—well, Mr. Grant, if you really want to know, I just had to follow Atlanta Shergold to England. She's the dumb blonde in Marta's—I mean, in Miss Hallard's play. I mean she *plays* the dumb blonde. She's not at all dumb, Atlanta."

"No, indeed. A very gifted young woman indeed."

"You've seen her?"

"I shouldn't think there is anyone in London who hasn't seen her."

"No, I suppose not. It does go on and on, doesn't it? We didn't think—Atlanta and me—that it would run for more than a few weeks, so we just waved each other goodbye and said: See you at the beginning of the month! It was when we found that it was going on indefinitely that I just had to find an excuse to come to England."

"Wasn't Atlanta sufficient excuse?"

"Not for my pop! The family are very snooty about Atlanta, but Pop is the worst of the bunch. When he can bring himself to mention her he refers to her as 'that young actress acquaintance of yours.' You see, Pop is Carradine the Third, and Atlanta's father is very much Shergold the First. A little grocery store on Main Street, as a matter of fact. And the salt of the earth, in case you're interested. And of course Atlanta hadn't really done very much, back in the States. I mean, on the stage. This is her first big success. That is why she didn't want to break her contract and come back home. As a matter of fact it'll be quite a fight to get her back home at all. She says we never appreciated her."

"So you took to research."

"I had to think of something that I could do only in London, you see. And I had done some research at college. So the B. M. seemed to be what you call my cup of tea. I could enjoy myself and yet show my father that I was really working, both at the same time."

"Yes. It's as nice an alibi as ever I met with. Why the Peasants' Revolt, by the way?"

"Well, it's an interesting time. And I thought it would please Pop."

"Is *he* interested in social reform, then?"

"No, but he hates kings."

"Carradine the Third?"

"Yes, it's a laugh, isn't it? I wouldn't put it past him to have a crown in one of his safe deposit boxes. I bet he takes out the parcel every now and then and sneaks over to Grand Central and tries it on in the men's washroom. I'm afraid I'm tiring you, Mr. Grant; gabbing on about my own affairs like this. I didn't come for that. I came to—"

"Whatever you came for, you're manna straight from heaven. So relax, if you're not in a hurry."

"I'm never in a hurry," the young man said, unfolding his legs and laying them out in front of him. As he did it his feet, at the far extremity of his long limbs, touched the bedside table and shook the portrait of Richard III from its precarious position, so that it dropped to the floor.

"Oh, pardon me! That was careless of me. I haven't really got used to the length of my legs yet. You'd think a fellow would be used to his growth by twenty-two, wouldn't you?" He picked up the photograph, dusted it carefully with the cuff of his sleeve, and looked at it with interest. "Richardus III. Ang. Rex.," he read aloud.

"You're the first person to have noticed that background writing," Grant said.

"Well, I suppose it isn't visible unless you look into it. You're the first person I ever met who had a king for a pinup."

"No beauty, is he?"

"I don't know," said the boy slowly. "It's not a bad face, as faces go. I had a prof. at college who looked rather like him. He lived on bismuth and glasses of milk so he had a slightly jaundiced outlook on life, but he was the kindest creature imaginable. Is it about Richard that you wanted information?"

"Yes. Nothing very abstruse or difficult. Just to know what the contemporary authority is."

"Well, that should be easy enough. It isn't very far from my own time. I mean my research period. Indeed, the modern authority for Richard II—Sir Cuthbert Oliphant—stretches over both. Have you read Oliphant?" Grant said that he had read nothing but school books and Sir Thomas More.

"More? Henry VIII's Chancellor?"

"Yes."

"I take it that that was a bit of special pleading!"

"It read to me more like a party pamphlet," Grant said, realising for the first time that that was the taste that had been left in his mouth. It had not read like a statesman's account; it had read like a party throw-away.

No, it read like a columnist. Like a columnist who got his information below-stairs.

"Do you know anything about Richard III?"

"Nothing except that he croaked his nephews, and offered his kingdom for a horse. And that he had two stooges known as the Cat and the Rat."

"What!"

"You know: 'The Cat, the Rat, and Love Our Dog, Rule all England under a Hog.' "

"Yes, of course. I'd forgotten that. What does it mean, do you know?"

"No, I've no idea. I don't know that period very well. How did you get interested in Richard III?"

"Marta suggested that I should do some

academic investigating, since I can't do any practical investigating for some time to come. And because I find faces interesting she brought me portraits of all the principals. Principals in the various mysteries she suggested, I mean. Richard got in more or less by accident, but he proved the biggest mystery of the lot."

"He did? In what way?"

"He is the author of the most revolting crime in history, and he has the face of a great judge; a great administrator. Moreover he was by all accounts an abnormally civilised and well-living creature. He actually *was* a good administrator, by the way. He governed the North of England and did it excellently. He was a good staff officer and a good soldier. And nothing is known against his private life. His brother, perhaps you know, was—bar Charles II—our most wench-ridden royal product."

"Edward IV. Yes, I know. A six-foot hunk of male beauty. Perhaps Richard suffered from resentment at the contrast. And that accounts for his willingness to blot out his brother's seed."

This was something that Grant had not thought of.

"You're suggesting that Richard had a suppressed hate for his brother?"

"Why suppressed?"

"Because even his worst detractors admit that he was devoted to Edward. They were together in everything from the time that Richard was twelve or thirteen. The other brother was no good to anyone. George."

"Who was George?"

"The Duke of Clarence."

"Oh. Him! Butt-of-malmsey Clarence."

"That's the one. So there were just the two of them—Edward and Richard, I mean. And there was a ten-year gap in their ages. Just the right difference for hero worship."

"If I were a hunchback," young Carradine said musingly, "I sure would hate a brother who took my credit and my women and my place in the sun."

"It's possible," Grant said after an interval. "It's the best explanation I've come on so far."

"It mightn't have been an overt thing at all, you know. It mightn't have been even a conscious thing. It may just have all boiled up in him when he saw the chance of a crown. He may have said—I mean his blood may have said: 'Here's my chance! All those years of fetching and carrying and standing one pace in the rear, and no thanks for them. Here's where I take my pay. Here's where I settle accounts.' "

Grant noticed that by sheer chance Carradine had used the same imagined description of Richard as Miss Payne-Ellis. Standing one pace in the rear. That is how the novelist had seen him, standing with the fair, solid Margaret and George, on the steps of Baynard's Castle watching their father go away to war. One pace in the rear, "as always."

"That's very interesting, though, what you say about Richard being apparently a good sort up to the time of the crime," Carradine said, propping one leg of his horn-rims with a long forefinger in his characteristic gesture. "Makes him more of a person. That Shakespeare version of him, you know, that's just a caricature. Not a man at all. I'll be very pleased to do any investigating you want, Mr. Grant. It'll make a nice change from the Peasants."

"The Cat and the Rat instead of John Ball and Wat Tyler."

"That's it."

"Well, it's very nice of you. I'd be glad of

anything you can rake up. But at the moment all I pine for is a contemporary account of events. They must have been country-rocking events. I want to read a contemporary's account of them. Not what someone heard-tell about events that happened when he was five, and under another regime altogether."

"I'll find out who the contemporary historian is. Fabyan, perhaps. Or is he Henry VII? Anyway, I'll find out. And meanwhile perhaps you'd like a look at Oliphant. He's the modern authority on the period, or so I understand."

Grant said that he would be delighted to take a look at Sir Cuthbert.

"I'll drop him in when I'm passing tomorrow—I suppose it'll be all right if I leave him in the office for you?—and as soon as I find out about the contemporary writers I'll be in with the news. That suit you?"

Grant said that that was perfect.

Young Carradine went suddenly shy, reminding Grant of the woolly lamb which he had quite forgotten in the interest of this new approach to Richard. He said goodnight in a quiet smothered way, and ambled out of the room followed by the sweeping skirts of his topcoat.

Grant thought that, the Carradine fortune apart, Atlanta Shergold looked like being on a good thing.

Chapter 8

"Well," said Marta, when she came again, "what did you think of my woolly lamb?"

"It was *very* kind of you to find him for me."

"I didn't have to find him. He's continually underfoot. He practically lives at the theatre. He must have seen *To Sea in a Bowl* five hundred times; when he isn't in Atlanta's dressing-room he's in front. I wish they'd get married, and then we might see less of him. They're not even living together, you know. It's all pure idyll." She dropped her "actress" voice for a moment and said: "They're rather sweet together. In some ways they are more like twins than lovers. They have that utter trust in each other; that dependence on the other half to make a proper whole. And they never have rows— or even quarrels, that I can see. An idyll, as I said. Was it Brent who brought you this?"

She poked the solid bulk of Oliphant with a doubtful finger.

"Yes, he left it with the porter for me."

"It looks very indigestible."

"A bit unappetising, let us say. It is quite easily digested once you have swallowed it. History for the student. Set out in detailed fact."

"Ugh!"

"At least I've discovered where the revered and sainted Sir Thomas More got his account of Richard."

"Yes? Where?"

"From one John Morton."

"Never heard of him."

"Neither did I, but that's our ignorance."

"Who was he?"

"He was Henry VII's Archbishop of Canterbury. And Richard's bitterest enemy."

If Marta had been capable of whistling, she would have whistled in comment.

"So *that* was the horse's mouth!" she said.

"That was the horse's mouth. And it is on that account of Richard that all the later ones were built. It is on that story that Holinshed fashioned his history, and on that story that Shakespeare fashioned his character."

"So it is the version of someone who hated Richard. I didn't know that. Why did the sainted Sir Thomas report Morton rather than someone else?"

"Whoever he reported, it would be a Tudor version. But he reported Morton, it seems, because he had been in Morton's household as a boy. And of course Morton had been very much 'in on the act,' so it was natural to write down the version of an eye-witness whose account he could have at first hand."

Marta poked her finger at Oliphant again. "Does your dull fat historian acknowledge that it is a biassed version?"

"Oliphant? Only by implication. He is, to be honest, in a sad muddle himself about Richard. On the same page he says that he was an admirable administrator and general, with an excellent reputation, staid and good-living, very popular by contrast with the Woodville upstarts (the Queen's relations) and that he was 'perfectly unscrupulous and ready to wade through any depth of bloodshed to the crown which lay within his grasp.' On one page he says grudgingly: 'There are reasons for supposing that he was not destitute of a conscience' and then on a later page reports More's picture of a man so tormented by his own deed that he could not sleep. And so on."

"Does your dull fat Oliphant prefer his roses red, then?"

"Oh, I don't think so. I don't think he is consciously Lancastrian. Though now that I think of it he *is* very tolerant of Henry VII's usurpation. I can't remember his saying anywhere, brutally, that Henry hadn't a vestige of a shadow of a claim to the throne."

"Who put him there, then? Henry, I mean."

"The Lancastrian remnant and the upstart Woodvilles, backed, I suppose, by a country revolted by the boys' murder. Apparently anyone with a spice of Lancastrian blood in their veins would do. Henry himself was canny enough to put 'conquest' first in his claim to the throne, and his Lancaster blood second, '*De jure belli et de jure Lancastriae.*' His mother was the heir of an illegitimate son of the third son of Edward III."

"All I know about Henry VII is that he was fantastically rich and fantastically mean. Do you know the lovely Kipling story about his knighting the craftsman not for having done beautiful work but for having saved him the cost of some scroll-work?"

"With a rusty sword from behind the arras. You must be one of the few women who know their Kipling."

"Oh, I'm a very remarkable woman in many ways. So you are no nearer finding out about Richard's personality than you were?"

"No. I'm as completely bewildered as Sir Cuthbert Oliphant, bless his heart. The only difference between us is that I know I'm bewildered and he doesn't seem to be aware of it."

"Have you seen much of my woolly lamb?"

"I've seen nothing of him since his first visit, and that's three days ago. I'm beginning to wonder whether he has repented of his promise."

"Oh, no. I'm sure not. Faithfulness is his banner and creed."

"Like Richard."

"Richard?"

"His motto was 'Loyaulté me lie.' Loyalty binds me."

There was a tentative tap at the door, and in answer to Grant's invitation, Brent Carradine appeared, hung around with topcoat as usual.

"Oh! I seem to be butting in. I didn't know you were here, Miss Hallard. I met the Statue of Liberty in the corridor there, and she seemed to think you were alone, Mr. Grant."

Grant identified the Statue of Liberty without difficulty. Marta said that she was in the act of going, and that in any case Brent was a much more welcome visitor than she was nowadays. She would leave them in peace to pursue their search for the soul of a murderer.

When he had bowed her politely to the door Brent came back and sat himself down in the visitor's chair with exactly the same air that an Englishman wears when he sits down to his port after the women have left the table. Grant wondered if even the female-ridden American felt a subconscious relief at settling down to a stag party. In answer to Brent's inquiry as to how he was getting on with Oliphant, he said he found Sir Cuthbert admirably lucid.

"I've discovered who the Cat and the Rat were, incidentally. They were entirely respectable knights of the realm: William Catesby and Richard Ratcliffe. Catesby was Speaker of the House of Commons, and

Ratcliffe was one of the Commissioners of Peace with Scotland. It's odd how the very sound of words makes a political jingle vicious. The Hog of course was Richard's badge. The White Boar. Do you frequent our English pubs?"

"Sure. They're one of the things I think you do better than us."

"You forgive us our plumbing for the sake of the beer at the Boar."

"I wouldn't go as far as to say I forgive it. I discount it, shall we say?"

"Magnanimous of you. Well, there's something else you've got to discount. That theory of yours that Richard hated his brother because of the contrast between his beauty and Richard's hunchbacked state. According to Sir Cuthbert, the hunchback is a myth. So is the withered arm. It appears that he had no visible deformity. At least none that mattered. His left shoulder was lower than his right, that was all. Did you find out who the contemporary historian is?"

"There isn't one."

"None at *all*?"

"Not in the sense that you mean it. There *were* writers who were contemporaries of Richard, but they wrote after his death. For the Tudors. Which puts them out of court. There is a monkish chronicle in Latin somewhere that is contemporary, but I haven't been able to get hold of it yet. One thing I have discovered though: that account of Richard III is called Sir Thomas More's not because he wrote it but because the manuscript was found among his papers. It was an unfinished copy of an account that appears elsewhere in finished form."

"Well!" Grant considered this with interest. "You mean it was More's own manuscript copy?"

"Yes. In his own writing. Made when he was about thirty-five. In those days, before printing was general, manuscript copies of books were the usual thing."

"Yes. So, if the information came from John Morton, as it did, it is just as likely that the thing was written by Morton."

"Yes."

"Which would certainly account for the—the lack of sensibility. A climber like Morton wouldn't be at all abashed by back-stairs gossip. Do you know about Morton?"

"No."

"He was a lawyer turned churchman, and the greatest pluralist on record. He chose the Lancastrian side and stayed with it until it was clear that Edward IV was home and dried. Then he made his peace with the York side and Edward made him Bishop of Ely. And vicar of God knows how many parishes besides. But after Richard's accession he backed first the Woodvilles and then Henry Tudor and ended up with a cardinal's hat as Henry VII's Archbishop of—"

"Wait a minute!" said the boy, amused. "Of *course* I know Morton. He was Morton of 'Morton's Fork.' 'You can't be spending much so how about something for the King; you're spending such a lot you must be very rich so how about something for the King.' "

"Yes. That's Morton. Henry's best thumbscrew. And I've just thought of a reason why he might have a personal hatred for Richard long before the murder of the boys."

"Yes?"

"Edward took a large bribe from Louis XI to make a dishonourable peace in France. Richard was very angry about that—it really was a disgraceful affair—and washed his hands of the business. Which included refusing a large cash offer. But Morton was very much in favour both of the deal and the cash. Indeed he took a pension from Louis.

A very nice pension it was. Two thousand crowns a year. I don't suppose Richard's outspoken comments went down very well, even with good gold for a chaser."

"No. I guess not."

"And of course there would be no preferment for Morton under the strait-laced Richard as there had been under the easygoing Edward. So he would have taken the Woodville side, even if there had been no murder."

"About that murder—" the boy said; and paused.

"Yes?"

"About that murder—the murder of those two boys—isn't it odd that no one talks of it?"

"How do you mean; no one talks of it?"

"These last three days I've been going through contemporary papers; letters and what not. And no one mentions them at all."

"Perhaps they were afraid to. It was a time when it paid to be discreet."

"Yes; but I'll tell you something even odder. You know that Henry brought a Bill of Attainder against Richard, after Bosworth. Before Parliament, I mean. Well, he accuses

Richard of cruelty and tyranny but doesn't even mention the murder."

"What!" said Grant, startled.

"Yes, you may well look startled."

"Are you sure!"

"Quite sure."

"But Henry got possession of the Tower immediately on his arrival in London after Bosworth. If the boys were missing it is incredible that he should not publish the fact immediately. It was the trump card in his hand." He lay in surprised silence for a little. The sparrows on the windowsill quarrelled loudly. "I can't make sense of it," he said. "What possible explanation can there be for his omission to make capital out of the fact that the boys were missing?"

Brent shifted his long legs to a more comfortable position. "There is only one explanation," he said. "And that is that the boys weren't missing."

There was a still longer silence this time, while they stared at each other.

"Oh, no, it's nonsense," Grant said. "There must be some obvious explanation that we are failing to see."

"As what, for instance?"

"I don't know. I haven't had time to think."

"I've had nearly three days to think, and I still haven't thought up a reason that will fit. *Nothing* will fit the facts except the conclusion that the boys were alive when Henry took over the Tower. It was a completely unscrupulous Act of Attainder; it accused Richard's followers—the loyal followers of an anointed King fighting against an invader—of treason. Every accusation that Henry could possibly make with any hope of getting away with it was put into the Bill. And the very worst he could accuse Richard of was the usual cruelty and tyranny. The boys aren't even mentioned."

"It's fantastic."

"It's unbelievable. But it is fact."

"What it means is that there was *no contemporary accusation at all*."

"That's about it."

"But—but wait a minute. Tyrrel was *hanged* for the murder. He actually confessed to it before he died. Wait a minute." He reached for Oliphant and sped through the pages looking for the place. "There's a full account of it here somewhere. There was no mystery about it. Even the Statue of Liberty knew about it."

"Who?"

"The nurse you met in the corridor. It was Tyrrel who committed the murder and he was found guilty and confessed before his death."

"Was that when Henry took over in London, then?"

"Wait a moment. Here it is." He skimmed down the paragraph. "No, it was in 1502." He realised all of a sudden what he had just said, and repeated in a new, bewildered tone: "In—1502."

"But—but—but that was—"

"Yes. Nearly twenty years afterwards."

Brent fumbled for his cigarette case, took it out, and then put it hastily away again.

"Smoke if you like," Grant said. "It's a good stiff drink I need. I don't think my brain can be working very well. I feel the way I used to feel as a child when I was blindfolded and whirled round before beginning a blindman's-buff game."

"Yes," said Carradine. He took out a cigarette and lighted it. "Completely in the dark, and more than a little dizzy."

He sat staring at the sparrows.

"Forty million school books can't be wrong," Grant said after a little.

"Can't they?"

"Well, can they!"

"I used to think so, but I'm not so sure nowadays."

"Aren't you being a little sudden in your scepticism?"

"Oh, it wasn't this that shook me."

"What then?"

"A little affair called the Boston Massacre. Ever heard of it?"

"Of course."

"Well, I discovered quite by accident, when I was looking up something at college, that the Boston Massacre consisted of a mob throwing stones at a sentry. The total casualties were four. I was brought up on the Boston Massacre, Mr. Grant. My twenty-eight-inch chest used to swell at the very memory of it. My good red spinach-laden blood used to seethe at the thought of helpless civilians mowed down by the fire of British troops. You can't imagine what a shock it was to find that all it added up to in actual fact was a brawl that wouldn't get more than local reporting in a clash between police and strikers in any American lock-out."

As Grant made no reply to this, he

squinted his eyes against the light to see how Grant was taking it. But Grant was staring at the ceiling as if he were watching patterns forming there.

"That's partly why I like to research so much," Carradine volunteered, and settled back to staring at the sparrows.

Presently Grant put his hand out, wordlessly, and Carradine gave him a cigarette and lighted it for him.

They smoked in silence.

It was Grant who interrupted the sparrows' performance.

"Tonypandy," he said.

"How's that?"

But Grant was still far away.

"After all, I've seen the thing at work in my own day, haven't I?" He said, not to Carradine but to the ceiling, "It's Tonypandy."

"And what in heck is Tonypandy?" Brent asked. "It sounds like a patent medicine. Does your child get out of sorts? Does the little face get flushed, the temper short, and the limbs easily tired? Give the little one Tonypandy, and see the radiant results." And then, as Grant made no answer: "All right, then; keep your Tonypandy. I wouldn't have it as a gift."

"Tonypandy," Grant said, still in that sleep-walking voice, "is a place in the South of Wales."

"I knew it was some kind of physic."

"If you go to South Wales you will hear that, in 1910, the Government used troops to shoot down Welsh miners who were striking for their rights. You'll probably hear that Winston Churchill, who was Home Secretary at the time, was responsible. South Wales, you will be told, will never forget Tonypandy!"

Carradine had dropped his flippant air.

"And it wasn't a bit like that?"

"The actual facts are these. The rougher section of the Rhondda valley crowd had got quite out of hand. Shops were being looted and property destroyed. The Chief Constable of Glamorgan sent a request to the Home Office for troops to protect the lieges. If a Chief Constable thinks a situation serious enough to ask for the help of the military a Home Secretary has very little choice in the matter. But Churchill was so horrified at the possibility of the troops coming face to face with a crowd of rioters and having to fire on them, that he stopped the movement of the troops and sent instead a body of plain, solid Metropolitan Police, armed with nothing but their rolled-up mackintoshes. The troops were kept in reserve, and all contact with the rioters was made by unarmed London police. The only bloodshed in the whole affair was a bloody nose or two. The Home Secretary was severely criticised in the House of Commons incidentally for his 'unprecedented intervention.' That was Tonypandy. That is the shooting down by troops that Wales will never forget."

"Yes," Carradine said, considering. "Yes. It's almost a parallel to the Boston affair. Someone blowing up a simple affair to huge proportions for a political end."

"The point is not that it is a parallel. The point is that *every single man* who was there knows that the story is nonsense, and yet it has never been contradicted. It will never be overtaken now. It is a completely untrue story grown to legend while the men who knew it to be untrue looked on and said nothing."

"Yes. That's very interesting; very. History as it is made."

"Yes. History."

"Give me research. After all, the truth of anything at all doesn't lie in someone's account of it. It lies in all the small facts of the time. An advertisement in a paper. The sale of a house. The price of a ring."

Grant went on looking at the ceiling, and the sparrows' clamour came back into the room.

"What amuses you?" Grant said, turning his head at last and catching the expression on his visitor's face.

"This is the first time I've seen you look like a policeman."

"I'm feeling like a policeman. I'm *thinking* like a policeman. I'm asking myself the question that every policeman asks in every case of murder: Who benefits? And for the first time it occurs to me that the glib theory that Richard got rid of the boys to make himself safer on the throne is so much nonsense. Supposing he had got rid of the boys. There were still the boys' five sisters between him and the throne. To say nothing of George's two: the boy and girl. George's son and daughter were barred by their father's attainder; but I take it that an attainder can be reversed, or annulled, or something. If Richard's claim was shaky, all those lives stood between him and safety."

"And did they all survive him?"

"I don't know. But I shall make it my business to find out. The boys' eldest sister certainly did because she became Queen of England as Henry's wife."

"Look, Mr. Grant, let's you and I start at the very beginning of this thing. Without history books, or modern versions, or anyone's opinion about anything. Truth isn't in accounts but in account books."

"A neat phrase," Grant said, complimentary. "Does it mean anything?"

"It means everything. The real history is written in forms not meant as history. In Wardrobe accounts, in Privy Purse expenses, in personal letters, in estate books. If someone, say, insists that Lady Whosit never had a child, and you find in the account book the entry: 'For the son born to my lady on Michaelmas eve: five yards of blue ribbon, fourpence halfpenny' it's a reasonably fair deduction that my lady had a son on Michaelmas eve."

"Yes. I see. All right, where do we begin?"

"You're the investigator. I'm only the looker-upper."

"Research Worker."

"Thanks. What do you want to know?"

"Well, for a start, it would be useful, not to say enlightening, to know how the principals in the case reacted to Edward's death, Edward IV. I mean, Edward died unexpectedly, and his death must have caught everyone on the hop. I'd like to know how the people concerned reacted."

"That's straightforward and easy. I take it you mean what they did and not what they thought."

"Yes, of course."

"Only historians tell you what they thought. Research workers stick to what they did."

"What they did is all I want to know. I've always been a believer in the old saw that actions speak louder than words."

"Incidentally, what does the sainted Sir Thomas say that Richard did when he heard that his brother was dead?" Brent wanted to know.

"The sainted Sir Thomas (alias John Morton) says that Richard got busy being charming to the Queen and persuading her not to send a large bodyguard to escort the boy prince from Ludlow, meanwhile cooking up a plot to kidnap the boy on his way to London."

"According to the sainted More, then, Richard meant from the very first to supplant the boy."

"Oh, yes."

"Well, we shall find out, at least, who was where and doing what, whether we can deduce their intentions or not."

"That's what I want. Exactly."

"Policeman," jibed the boy. " 'Where were you at five P.M. on the night of the fifteenth inst.?' "

"It works," Grant assured him. "It works."

"Well, I'll go away and work too. I'll be in again as soon as I have got the information you want. I'm very grateful to you, Mr. Grant. This is a lot better than the Peasants."

He floated away into the gathering dusk of the winter afternoon, his train-like coat giving an academic sweep and dignity to his thin young figure.

Grant switched on his lamp, and examined the pattern it made on the ceiling as if he had never seen it before.

It was a unique and engaging problem

that the boy had dropped so casually into his lap. As unexpected as it was baffling.

What possible reason could there be for that lack of contemporary accusation?

Henry had not even needed proof that Richard was himself responsible. The boys were in Richard's care. If they were not to be found when the Tower was taken over, then that was far finer, thicker mud to throw at his dead rival than the routine accusations of cruelty and tyranny.

Grant ate his supper without for one moment being conscious either of its taste or its nature.

It was only when The Amazon, taking away his tray, said kindly: "Come now, that's a very good sign. Both rissoles all eaten up to the last crumb!" that he became aware that he had partaken of a meal.

For another hour he watched the lamp-pattern on the ceiling, going over the thing in his mind; going round and round it looking for some small crack that might indicate a way into the heart of the matter.

In the end he withdrew his attention altogether from the problem. Which was his habit when a conundrum proved too round and smooth and solid for immediate solution. If he slept on the proposition it might, tomorrow, show a facet that he had missed.

He looked for something that might stop his mind from harking back to that Act of Attainder, and saw the pile of letters waiting to be acknowledged. Kind, well-wishing letters from all sorts of people, including a few old lags. The really likable old lags were an outmoded type, growing fewer and fewer daily. Their place had been taken by brash young thugs with not a spark of humanity in their egocentric souls, as illiterate as puppies and as pitiless as a circular saw. The old professional burglar was apt to be as individual as the member of any other profession, and as little vicious. Quiet little domestic men, interested in family holidays and the children's tonsils; or odd bachelors devoted to cage-birds, or second-hand bookshops, or complicated and infallible betting systems. Old-fashioned types.

No modern thug would write to say that he was sorry that a "busy" was laid aside. No such idea would ever cross a modern thug's mind.

Writing a letter when lying on one's back is a laborious business, and Grant shied away from it. But the top envelope on the pile bore the writing of his cousin Laura, and Laura would become anxious if she had no answer at all from him. Laura and he had shared summer holidays as children, and had been a little in love with each other all through one Highland summer, and that made a bond between them that had never been broken. He had better send Laura a note to say that he was alive.

He read her letter again, smiling a little; and the waters of the Turlie sounded in his ears and slid under his eyes, and he could smell the sweet cold smell of a Highland moor in winter and he forgot for a little that he was a hospital patient and that life was sordid and boring and claustrophobic.

Pat sends what would be his love if he were a little older or just a little younger. Being nine, he says: "Tell Alan I was asking for him," and has a fly of his own invention waiting to be presented to you when you come on sick-leave. He is a little in disgrace at the moment in school, having learned for the first time that the Scots sold Charles the First to the English and having decided that he can no longer belong to such a nation. He is therefore, I understand, conducting a one-man protest strike against all things Scottish, and will learn no history, sing no song, nor memorise any geography pertaining to so deplorable a country. He announced going to bed last night that he has decided to apply for Norwegian citizenship.

Grant took his letter pad from the table and wrote in pencil:

Dearest Laura,
  Would you be unbearably surprised to learn that the Princes in the Tower survived Richard III?

As ever
Alan.

P.S. I am nearly well again.

Chapter 9

"Do you know that the Bill attainting Richard III before Parliament didn't mention the murder of the Princes in the Tower?" Grant asked the surgeon next morning.

"Really?" said the surgeon. "That's odd, isn't it?"

"Extremely odd. Can you think of an explanation?"

"Probably trying to minimise the scandal. For the sake of the family."

"He wasn't succeeded by one of his family. He was the last of his line. His successor was the first Tudor. Henry VII."

"Yes, of course. I'd forgotten. I was never any good at history. I used to use the history period to do my home algebra. They don't manage to make history very interesting in schools. Perhaps more portraits might help." He glanced up at the Richard portrait and went back to his professional inspection. "That is looking very nice and healthy, I'm glad to say. No pain to speak of now?"

And he went away, kindly and casual. He was interested in faces because they were part of his trade, but history was just something that he used for other purposes; something that he set aside in favour of algebra under the desk. He had living bodies in his care, and the future in his hands; he had no thought to spare for problems academic.

Matron, too, had more immediate worries. She listened politely while he put his difficulty to her, but he had the impression that she might say: "I should see the almoner about it if I were you." It was not her affair. She looked down from her regal eminence at the great hive below her buzzing with activity, all of it urgent and important; she could hardly be expected to focus her gaze on something more than four hundred years away.

He wanted to say: "But you of all people should be interested in what can happen to royalty; in the frailness of your reputation's worth. Tomorrow a whisper may destroy you." But he was already guiltily conscious that to hinder a Matron with irrelevances was to lengthen her already lengthy morning round without reason or excuse.

The Midget did not know what an Attainder was, and made it clear that she did not care.

"It's becoming an obsession with you, that thing," she said, leaning her head at the portrait. "It's not healthy. Why don't you read some of those nice books?"

Even Marta, to whose visit he had looked forward so that he could put this odd, new proposition to her and see her reaction, even Marta was too full of wrath with Madeleine March to pay attention to him.

"After practically promising me that she would write it! After all our get-togethers and my plans for when this endless thing finally comes to an end. I had even talked to Jacques about clothes! And now she decides that she must write one of her awful little detective stories. She says she must write it while it is fresh—whatever it is."

He listened to Marta's grieving with sympathy—good plays were the scarcest commodity in the world and good playwrights worth their weight in platinum—but it was like watching something through a window. The fifteenth century was more actual to him this morning than any ongoings in Shaftesbury Avenue.

"I don't suppose it will take her long to write her detective book," he said comfortingly.

"Oh, no. She does them in six weeks or so. But now that she's off the chain how do I know that I'll ever get her on again? Tony Savilla wants her to write a Marlborough play for him, and you know what Tony is when he sets his heart on something. He'd talk the pigeons off the Admiralty Arch."

She came back to the Attainder problem, briefly, before she took her leave.

"There's sure to be some explanation, my dear," she said from the door.

Of *course* there's an explanation, he wanted to shout after her, but what is it? The thing is against all likelihood and sense. Historians say that the murder caused a great revulsion of feeling against Richard, that he was hated for the crime by the common people of England, and that was why they welcomed a stranger in his place. And yet when the tale of his wrongdoing is placed before Parliament there is no mention of the crime.

Richard was dead when that complaint

was drawn up, and his followers in flight or exile; his enemies were free to bring against him any charge they could think of. And they *had not thought of that spectacular murder*.

Why?

The country was reputedly ringing with the scandal of the boys' disappearance. The very recent scandal. And when his enemies collected his alleged offences against morality and the State they had not included Richard's most spectacular piece of infamy.

Why?

Henry needed every small featherweight of advantage in the precarious newness of his accession. He was unknown to the country at large and he had no right by blood to be where he was. But he hadn't used the overwhelming advantage that Richard's published crime would have given him.

Why?

He was succeeding a man of great reputation, known personally to the people from the Marches of Wales to the Scots border, a man universally liked and admired until the disappearance of his nephews. And yet he omitted to use the one real advantage he had against Richard, the unforgivable, the abhorred thing.

Why?

Only The Amazon seemed concerned about the oddity that was engaging his mind; and she not out of any feeling for Richard but because her conscientious soul was distressed at any possibility of mistake. The Amazon would go all the way down the corridor and back again to tear off a page in a loose-leaf calendar that someone had forgotten to remove. But her instinct to be worried was less strong than her instinct to comfort.

"You don't need to worry about it," she said, soothing. "There'll be some quite simple explanation that you haven't thought of. It'll come to you sometime when you're thinking of something else altogether. That's usually how I remember where something I've mislaid is. I'll be putting the kettle on in the pantry, or counting the sterile dressings as Sister doles them out, and suddenly I'll think: 'Goodness, I left it in my Burberry pocket.' Whatever the thing was, I mean. So you don't have to worry about it."

Sergeant Williams was in the wilds of Essex helping the local constabulary to decide who had hit an old shop-keeper over the head with a brass scale-weight and left her dead among the shoelaces and liquorice all-sorts, so there was no help from the Yard.

There was no help from anyone until young Carradine turned up again three days later. Grant thought that his normal insouciance had a deeper tinge than usual; there was almost an air of self-congratulation about him. Being a well-brought-up child he inquired politely about Grant's physical progress, and having been reassured on that point he pulled some notes out of the capacious pocket of his coat and beamed through his horn-rims at his colleague.

"I wouldn't have the sainted More as a present," he observed pleasantly.

"You're not being offered him. There are no takers."

"He's way off the beam. Way off."

"I suspected as much. Let us have the facts. Can you begin on the day Edward died?"

"Sure. Edward died on April the 9th, 1483. In London. I mean, in Westminster; which wasn't the same thing then. The Queen and the daughters were living there, *and* the younger boy. I think. The young Prince was doing lessons at Ludlow Castle in charge of the Queen's brother, Lord Rivers. The Queen's relations are very much to the fore, did you know? The place is just lousy with Woodvilles."

"Yes, I know. Go on. Where was Richard?"

"On the Scottish border."

"What!"

"Yes, I said: on the Scottish border. Caught away off base. But does he yell for a horse and go posting off to London? He does not."

"What did he do?"

"He arranged for a requiem mass at York, to which all the nobility of the North were summoned, and in his presence they took an oath of loyalty to the young Prince."

"Interesting," Grant said dryly. "What did Rivers do? The Queen's brother?"

"On the 24th of April he set out with the Prince for London. With two thousand men and a large supply of arms."

"What did he want the arms for?"

"Don't ask me. I'm only a research worker. Dorset, the elder of the Queen's two sons by her first marriage, took over both the arsenal and the treasure in the Tower and began to fit up ships to command the Channel. And Council orders were issued *in the name of Rivers and Dorset—'avunculus Regis' and 'frater Regis uterinus'* respectively—with no mention of Richard. Which was decidedly off-colour when you remember—if you ever knew—that in his will Edward had appointed Richard guardian of the boy and Protector of the Kingdom in case of any minority. Richard alone, mind you, without a colleague."

"Yes, that is in character, at least. He must always have had complete faith in Richard. Both as a person and as an administrator. Did Richard come south with a young army too?"

"No. He came with six hundred gentlemen of the North, all in deep mourning. He arrived at Northampton on April the 29th. He had apparently expected to join up with the Ludlow crowd there; but that is report and you have only a historian's word for it. But the Ludlow procession—Rivers and the young Prince—had gone on to Stoney Stratford without waiting for him. The person who actually met him at Northampton was the Duke of Buckingham with three hundred men. Do you know Buckingham?"

"We have a nodding acquaintance. He was a friend of Edward's."

"Yes. He arrived post haste from London."

"With the news of what was going on."

"It's a fair deduction. He wouldn't bring three hundred men just to express his condolences. Anyhow a Council was held there and then—he had all the human material for a proper Council in his own train and Buckingham's, and Rivers and his three aides were arrested and sent to the North, while Richard went on with the young Prince to London. They arrived in London on the 4th of May."

"Well, that is very nice and clear. And what is clearest of all is that, considering time and distances, the sainted More's account of his writing sweet letters to the Queen to induce her to send only a small escort for the boy, is nonsense."

"Bunk."

"Indeed, Richard did just what one would expect him to do. He must of course have known the provisions of Edward's will. What his actions suggest is just what one would expect them to suggest, his own sorrow and his care for the boy. A requiem mass and an oath of allegiance."

"Yes."

"Where does the break in this orthodox pattern come? I mean: in Richard's behaviour."

"Oh, not for a long time. When he arrived in London he found that the Queen, the younger boy, the daughters, and her first-marriage son, Dorset, had all bolted into sanctuary at Westminster. But apart from that things seem to have been normal."

"Did he take the boy to the Tower?"

Carradine riffled through his notes. "I don't remember. Perhaps I didn't get that. I was only—Oh, yes, here it is. No, he took the boy to the Bishop's Palace in St. Paul's Churchyard, and he himself went to stay with his mother at Baynard's Castle. Do you know where that was? I don't."

"Yes. It was the Yorks' town house. It stood on the bank of the river just a little way west of St. Paul's."

"Oh. Well, he stayed there until June the 5th, when his wife arrived from the North and they went to stay in a house called Crosby Place."

"It is still called Crosby Place. It has been moved to Chelsea, and the window Richard put into it may not still be there—I haven't seen it lately—but the building is there."

"It is?" Carradine said, delighted. "I'll go and see it right away. It's a very domestic tale when you think of it, isn't it? Staying with his mother until his wife gets to town and then moving in with her. Was Crosby Place theirs, then?"

"Richard had leased it, I think. It belonged to one of the Aldermen of London. So there is no suggestion of opposition to his Protectorship, or of change of plans, when he arrived in London."

"Oh, no. He was acknowledged Protector before he ever arrived in London."

"How do you know that?"

"In the Patent Rolls he is called Protector on two occasions—let me see—April 21st (that's less than a fortnight after Edward's death) and May the 2nd (that's two days before he arrived in London at all)."

"All right; I'm sold. And no fuss? No hint of trouble?"

"Not that I can find. On the 5th of June he gave detailed orders for the boy's coronation on the 22nd. He even had letters of summons sent out to the forty squires who would be made knights of the Bath. It seems it was the custom for the King to knight them on the occasion of his coronation."

"The 5th," Grant said musingly. "And he fixed the coronation for the 22nd. He wasn't leaving himself much time for a switch-over."

"No. There's even a record of the order for the boy's coronation clothes."

"And then what?"

"Well," Carradine said, apologetic, "that's as far as I've got. Something happened at a Council—on the 8th of June, I think—but the contemporary account is in the *Mémoires* of Philippe de Comines and I haven't been able to get hold of a copy so far. But someone promised to let me see a copy of Mandrot's 1901 printing of it tomorrow. It seems that the Bishop of Bath broke some news to the Council on June the 8th. Do you know the Bishop of Bath? His name was Stillington."

"Never heard of him."

"He was a fellow of All Souls, whatever that is, and a Canon of York, whatever *that* may be."

"Both learned and respectable, it appears."

"Well, we'll see."

"Have you turned up any contemporary historians—other than Comines?"

"Not any, so far, who wrote before Richard's death. Comines has a French bias but not a Tudor one, so he's more trustworthy than an Englishman writing about Richard under the Tudors would be. But I've got a lovely sample for you of how history is made. I found it when I was looking up the contemporary writers. You know that one of the things they tell about Richard III is that he killed Henry VI's only son in cold blood after the battle of Tewkesbury? Well, believe it or not, that story is made up out of whole cloth. You can trace it from the very time it was first told. It's the perfect answer to people who say there's no smoke without fire. Believe me, this smoke was made by rubbing two pieces of dry stick together."

"But Richard was just a boy at the time of Tewkesbury."

"He was eighteen, I think. And a very bonny fighter by all contemporary accounts. They were the same age, Henry's son and Richard. Well, *all* the contemporary accounts, of whatever complexion, are unanimous in saying that he was killed during the battle. Then the fun begins."

Carradine fluttered through his notes impatiently.

"Goldarn it, what did I do with it? Ah. Here we are. Now. Fabyan, writing for Henry VII, says that the boy was captured and brought before Edward IV, was struck in the face by Edward with his gauntlet and immediately slain by the King's servants. Nice? But Polydore Virgil goes one better. He says that the murder was done in person by George, Duke of Clarence, Richard, Duke of Gloucester, and William, Lord Hastings. Hall adds Dorset to the murderers. But that didn't satisfy Holinshed: Holinshed reports that it was Richard, Duke of Gloucester, who struck the first blow. How do you like that? Best quality Tonypandy, isn't it?"

"Pure Tonypandy. A dramatic story with not a word of truth in it. If you can bear to listen to a few sentences of the sainted More, I'll give you another sample of how history is made."

"The sainted More makes me sick at the stomach but I'll listen."

Grant looked for the paragraph he wanted, and read:

Some wise men also ween that his drift [that is, Richard's drift] covertly conveyed, lacked not in helping forth his brother Clarence to his death; which he resisted openly, howbeit somewhat, as men deemed, more faintly than he that were heartily minded to his weal. And they who deem thus think that he, long time in King Edward's life, forethought to be King in case that the King his brother (whose life he looked that evil diet should shorten) should happen to decease (as indeed he did) while his children were young. And they deem that for this intent he was glad of his brother Clarence's death, whose life must needs have hindered him so intending whether the same Clarence had kept true to his nephew the young King or enterprised to be King himself. But of all this point there is no certainty, and whoso divineth upon conjectures may as well shoot too far as too short.

"The mean, burbling, insinuating old bastard," said Carradine sweetly.

"Were you clever enough to pick out the

one positive statement in all that speculation?"

"Oh, yes."

"You spotted it? That was smart of you. I
had to read it three times before I got the
one unqualified fact."

"That Richard protested openly against
his brother George being put to death."

"Yes."

"Of course, with all that 'men say' stuff,"
Carradine observed, "the impression that is
left is just the opposite. I told you. I wouldn't
have the sainted More as a present."

"I think we ought to remember that it is
John Morton's account and not the sainted
More's."

"The sainted More sounds better. Besides, he liked the thing well enough to be
copying it out."

Grant, the one-time soldier, lay thinking of
the expert handling of that very sticky situation at Northampton.

"It was neat of him to mop up Rivers's two
thousand without any open clash."

"I expect they preferred the King's brother
to the Queen's brother, if they were faced
with it."

"Yes. And of course a fighting man has a

better chance with troops than a man who writes books."

"Did Rivers write books?"

"He wrote the first book printed in England. Very cultured, he was."

"Huh. It doesn't seem to have taught him not to try conclusions with a man who was a brigadier at eighteen and general before he was twenty-five. That's one thing that has surprised me, you know."

"Richard's qualities as a soldier?"

"No, his youth. I'd always thought of him as a middle-aged grouch. He was only thirty-two when he was killed at Bosworth."

"Tell me: when Richard took over the boy's guardianship, at Stoney Stratford, did he make a clean sweep of the Ludlow crowd? I mean, was the boy separated from all the people he had been growing up with?"

"Oh, no. His tutor, Dr. Alcock, came on to London with him, for one."

"So there was no panic clearing-out of everyone who might be on the Woodville side: everyone who might influence the boy against him."

"Seems not. Just the four arrests."

"Yes. A very neat, discriminating operation altogether. I felicitate Richard Plantagenet."

"I'm positively beginning to like the guy. Well. I'm going along now to look at Crosby Place. I'm tickled pink at the thought of actually looking at a place he lived in. And tomorrow I'll have that copy of Comines, and let you know what he says about events in England in 1483, and what Robert Stillington, Bishop of Bath, told the Council in June of that year."

Chapter 10

What Stillington told the Council on that summer day in 1483 was, Grant learned, that he had married Edward IV to Lady Eleanor Butler, a daughter of the first Earl of Shrewsbury, before Edward married Elizabeth Woodville.

"Why had he kept it to himself so long?" he asked when he had digested the news.

"Edward had commanded him to keep it secret. Naturally."

"Edward seems to have made a habit of secret marriages," Grant said dryly.

"Well, it must have been difficult for him, you know, when he came up against unassailable virtue. There was nothing for it but marriage. And he was so used to getting his own way with women—what with his looks and his crown—that he couldn't have taken very resignedly to frustration."

"Yes. That was the pattern of the Woodville marriage. The indestructibly virtuous beauty with the gilt hair, and the secret wedding. So Edward had used the same formula on a previous occasion, if Stillington's story was true. Was it true?"

"Well, in Edward's time, it seems, he was in turn both Privy Seal and Lord Chancellor, and he had been an ambassador to Brittany. So Edward either owed him something or liked him. And he, on his part, had no reason to cook up anything against Edward. Supposing he was the cooking sort."

"No, I suppose not."

"Anyway, the thing was put to Parliament so we don't have to take just Stillington's word for it."

"To Parliament!"

"Sure. Everything was open and above board. There was a very long meeting of the Lords at Westminster on the 9th. Stillington brought in his evidence and his witnesses, and a report was prepared to put before Parliament when it assembled on the 25th. On the 10th Richard sent a letter to the city of York asking for troops to protect and support him."

"Ha! Trouble at last."

"Yes. On the 11th he sent a similar letter to

his cousin Lord Nevill. So the danger was real."

"It must have been real. A man who dealt so economically with that unexpected and very nasty situation at Northampton wouldn't be one to lose his head at a threat."

"On the 20th he went with a small body of retainers to the Tower—did you know that the Tower was the royal residence in London, and not a prison at all?"

"Yes, I knew that. It got its prison meaning only because nowadays being sent to the Tower has one meaning only. And of course because, being the royal castle in London, and the only strong keep, offenders were sent there for safe keeping in the days before we had His Majesty's Prisons. What did Richard go to the Tower for?"

"He went to interrupt a meeting of the conspirators, and arrested Lord Hastings, Lord Stanley, and one John Morton, Bishop of Ely."

"I thought we would arrive at John Morton sooner or later!"

"A proclamation was issued, giving details of the plot to murder Richard, but apparently no copy now exists. Only one of the conspirators was beheaded, and that one, oddly enough, seems to have been an old friend of both Edward and Richard. Lord Hastings."

"Yes, according to the sainted More he was rushed down to the courtyard and beheaded on the nearest log."

"Rushed nothing," said Carradine disgustedly. "He was beheaded a week later. There's a contemporary letter about it that gives the date. Moreover, Richard couldn't have done it out of sheer vindictiveness, because he granted Hastings's forfeited estates to his widow, and restored the children's right of succession to them—which they had automatically lost."

"No, the death of Hastings must have been inevitable," said Grant, who was thumbing through More's *Richard III*. "Even the sainted More says: 'Undoubtedly the Protector loved him well, and was loth to have lost him.' What happened to Stanley and to John Morton?"

"Stanley was pardoned—what are you groaning about?"

"Poor Richard. That was his death warrant."

"Death warrant? How could pardoning Stanley be his death warrant?"

"Because it was Stanley's sudden decision to go over to the other side that lost Richard the battle of Bosworth."

"You don't say."

"Odd to think that if Richard had seen to it that Stanley went to the block like his much-loved Hastings, he would have won the battle of Bosworth, there would never have been any Tudors, and the hunchbacked monster that appears in Tudor tradition would never have been invented. On his previous showing he would probably have had the best and most enlightened reign in history. What was done to Morton?"

"Nothing."

"Another mistake."

"Or at least nothing to signify. He was put into gentlemanly detention under the care of Buckingham. The people who did go to the block were the heads of the conspiracy that Richard had arrested at Northampton: Rivers and Co. And Jane Shore was sentenced to do penance."

"Jane Shore? What on earth has she got to do with the case? I thought she was Edward's mistress?"

"So she was. But Hastings inherited her from Edward, it seems. Or rather—let me see—Dorset did. And she was go-between the Hastings side of the conspiracy and the Woodville side. One of Richard's letters existing today is about her. About Jane Shore."

"What about her?"

"His Solicitor-General wanted to marry her; when he was King, I mean."

"And he agreed?"

"He agreed. It's a lovely letter. More in sorrow than in anger—with a kind of twinkle in it."

" 'Lord, what fools these mortals be!' "

"That's it exactly."

"No vindictiveness there, either, it seems."

"No. Quite the opposite. You know, I know it isn't my business to think or draw deductions—I'm just the Research Worker—but it does strike me that Richard's ambition was to put an end to the York-Lancaster fight once and for all."

"What makes you think that?"

"Well, I've been looking at his coronation lists. It was the best-attended coronation on record, incidentally. You can't help being struck by the fact that practically nobody stayed away. Lancaster *or* York."

"Including the weather-cock Stanley, I suppose."

"I suppose so. I don't know them well enough to remember them individually."

"Perhaps you're right about his wanting a final end to the York-Lancaster feud. Perhaps his lenience with Stanley was due to that very thing."

"Was Stanley a Lancastrian, then?"

"No, but he was married to an abnormally rabid one. His wife was Margaret Beaufort, and the Beauforts were the reverse side, so to speak—the illegitimate side—of the Lancaster family. Not that her by-blow side worried her. *Or* her son."

"Who was her son?"

"Henry VII."

Carradine whistled, long and low.

"You actually mean to say that Lady Stanley was Henry's mother."

"She was. By her first husband Edmund Tudor."

"But—but Lady Stanley had a place of honour at Richard's coronation. She carried the Queen's train. I noticed that because I thought it quaint. Carrying the train, I mean. In our country we don't carry trains. It's an honour, I take it."

"It's a thundering great honour. Poor Richard. Poor Richard. It didn't work."

"What didn't?"

"Magnanimity." He lay thinking about it while Carradine shuffled through his notes. "So Parliament accepted the evidence of Stillington."

"They did more. They incorporated it into an Act, giving Richard the title to the crown. It was called Titulus Regius."

"For a holy man of God, Stillington wasn't cutting a very glorious figure. But I suppose that to have talked sooner would have been to compass his own ruin."

"You're a bit hard on him, aren't you? There wasn't any need to talk sooner. No harm was being done anyone."

"What about Lady Eleanor Butler?"

"She died in a convent. She's buried in the Church of the White Carmelites at Norwich, in case you're interested. As long as Edward was alive no wrong was being done anyone. But when it came to the question of succession, then he *had* to talk, whatever kind of figure he cut."

"Yes. Of course you're right. So the children were proclaimed illegitimate, in open Parliament. And Richard was crowned. With all the nobility of England in attendance. Was the Queen still in sanctuary?"

"Yes. But she had let the younger boy join his brother."

"When was that?"

Carradine searched through his notes. "On June the 16th. I've put: 'At the request of the Archbishop of Canterbury. Both boys living at the Tower.' "

"That was after the news had broken. The news that they were illegitimate."

"Yes." He tidied his notes into some kind of neatness and put them away in the enormous pocket. "That seems to be all, to date. But here's the pay-off." He gathered his train from either side of him on to his knees with a gesture that both Marta and King Richard might have envied. "You know that Act, that Titulus Regius."

"Yes; what about it?"

"Well, when Henry VII came to the throne he ordered that the Act should be repealed, without being read. He ordered that the Act itself should be destroyed, and forbade any copies to be kept. Anyone who kept a copy was to be fined and imprisoned during his pleasure."

Grant stared in great astonishment.

"*Henry VII!*" he said. "Why? What possible difference could it make to him?"

"I haven't a glimmer of an idea. But I mean to find out before I'm much older. Meanwhile, here is something to keep you amused till the Statue of Liberty brings your British tea."

He dropped a paper on to Grant's chest.

"What is this?" Grant said, looking at the torn-out page of a note-book.

"It's that letter of Richard's about Jane Shore. I'll be seeing you."

Left alone by himself in the quiet, Grant turned over the page and read.

The contrast between the sprawling childish handwriting and the formal phrases of Richard's imagining was piquant in the extreme. But what neither the untidy modern script nor the dignified phrases could destroy was the flavour of the letter. The bouquet of good humour that came up from the page as a bouquet comes up from a good-humoured wine. Translated into modern terms it said:

I hear to my great astonishment that Tom Lynom wants to marry Will Shore's wife. Apparently he is infatuated with her, and is quite determined about it. Do, my dear Bishop, send for him and see if you can talk some sense into his silly head. If you can't, and if there is no bar to their marriage from the Church's point of view, then I agree to it, but tell him to postpone the marriage till I am back in London. Meanwhile this will suffice to secure her release, on surety for her good behaviour, and I suggest that you hand her over for the time being to the care of her father, or anyone else who seems good to you.

It was certainly, as young Carradine had said, "more in sorrow than in anger." Indeed, considering that it was written about a woman who had done him a deadly wrong, its kindness and good temper were remarkable. And this was a case where no personal advantage could come to him from magnanimity. The broadmindedness that had sought for a York-Lancaster peace might not have been disinterested; it would have been enormously to his advantage to have a united country to rule. But this letter to the Bishop of Lincoln was a small private matter, and the release of Jane Shore of no importance to anyone but the infatuated Tom Lynom. Richard had nothing to gain by his generosity. His instinct to see a friend happy was apparently greater than his instinct for revenge.

Indeed, this instinct for revenge seemed to be lacking to a degree that would be surprising in any red-blooded male, and quite astonishing in the case of that reputed monster Richard III.

Chapter 11

The letter lasted Grant very nicely until The Amazon brought his tea. He listened to the twentieth-century sparrows on his windowsill and marvelled that he should be reading phrases that formed in a man's mind more than four hundred years ago. What a fantastic idea it would have seemed to Richard that anyone would be reading that short, intimate letter about Shore's wife, and wondering about him, four hundred years afterwards.

"There's a letter for you, now isn't that nice?" The Amazon said, coming in with his two pieces of bread-and-butter and a rock bun.

Grant took his eyes from the uncompromising healthiness of the rock bun and saw that the letter was from Laura.

He opened it with pleasure.

Dear Alan [said Laura]
Nothing (repeat: nothing) would sur-

prise me about history. Scotland has large monuments to two women martyrs drowned for their faith, in spite of the fact that they weren't drowned at all and neither was a martyr anyway. They were convicted of treason—fifth column work for the projected invasion from Holland, I think. Anyhow on a purely civil charge. They were reprieved *on their own petition* by the Privy Council, and the reprieve is in the Privy Council Register to this day.

This, of course, hasn't daunted the Scottish collectors of martyrs, and the tale of their sad end, complete with heart-rending dialogue, is to be found in every Scottish bookcase. Entirely different dialogue in each collection. And the gravestone of one of the women, in Wigtown churchyard, reads:

> Murdered for owning Christ supreme
> Head of his Church, and no more crime
> But her not owning Prelacy
> And not abjuring Presbytry
> Within the sea tied to a stake
> She suffered for Christ Jesus sake.

They are even a subject for fine Presbyterian sermons, I understand—though on that point I speak from hearsay. And tourists come and shake their heads over the monuments with their moving inscriptions, and a very profitable time is had by all.

All this in spite of the fact that the original collector of the material, canvassing the Wigtown district only forty years after the supposed martyrdom and at the height of the Presbyterian triumph, complains that "many deny that this happened"; and couldn't find any eyewitnesses at all.

It is very good news that you are convalescent, and a great relief to us all. If you manage it well your sick leave can coincide with the spring run. The water is very low at the moment, but by the time you are better it should be deep enough to please both the fish and you.

Love from us all,
Laura

P.S. It's an odd thing but when you tell someone the true facts of a mythical tale they are indignant not with the teller but with you. They don't *want* to have their ideas upset. It rouses some vague uneasiness in them, I think, and they resent it. So they reject it and refuse to think about it. If they were merely indifferent it would be natural and understandable. But it is much stronger than that, much more positive. They are annoyed.

Very odd, isn't it?

More Tonypandy, he thought.

He began to wonder just how much of the school book which up to now had represented British history for him was Tonypandy.

He went back, now that he knew a few facts, to read the sainted More again. To see how the relevant passages sounded now.

If, when he had read them merely by the light of his own critical mind, they had seemed to him curiously tattling, and in places absurd, they now read plain abominable. He was what Laura's small Pat was in the habit of calling "scunnered." And he was also puzzled.

This was Morton's account. Morton the eyewitness, the participant. Morton must have known with minute accuracy what took place between the beginning and end of June that year. And yet there was no mention of Lady Eleanor Butler; no mention of Titulus Regius. According to Morton, Richard's case has been that Edward was previously married to his mistress Elizabeth Lucy. But Elizabeth Lucy, Morton pointed out, had denied that she was ever married to the King.

Why did Morton set up a ninepin just to knock it down again?

Why the substitution of Elizabeth Lucy for Eleanor Butler?

Because he could deny with truth that Lucy was ever married to the King, but could not do the same in the case of Eleanor Butler?

Surely the presumption was that it was very important to someone or other that Richard's claim that the children were illegitimate should be shown to be untenable.

And since Morton—in the handwriting of the sainted More—was writing for Henry VII, then that someone was presumably Henry VII. The Henry VII who had destroyed Titulus Regius and forbidden anyone to keep a copy.

Something Carradine had said came back into Grant's mind.

Henry had caused the Act to be repealed *without being read*.

It was so important to Henry that the contents of the Act should not be brought to mind that he had specially provided for its unquoted destruction.

Why should it be of such importance to Henry VII?

How could it matter to *Henry* what Richard's rights were? It was not as if he could say: Richard's claim was a trumped-up one, therefore mine is good. Whatever wretched small claim Henry Tudor might have was a Lancastrian one, and the heirs of York did not enter into the matter.

Then why should it have been of such paramount importance to Henry that the contents of Titulus Regius should be forgotten?

Why hide away Eleanor Butler, and bring in her place a mistress whom no one ever suggested was married to the King?

This problem lasted Grant very happily till just before supper, when the porter came in with a note for him.

"The front hall says that young American

friend of yours left this for you," the porter said, handing him a folded sheet of paper.

"Thank you," said Grant. "What do you know about Richard the Third?"

"Is there a prize?"

"What for?"

"The quiz."

"No, just the satisfaction of intellectual curiosity. What *do* you know about Richard III?"

"He was the first multiple murderer."

"Multiple? I thought it was two nephews?"

"No, oh, no. I don't know much history but I do know that. Murdered his brother, and his cousin, and the poor old King in the Tower, and then finished off with his little nephews. A wholesale performer."

Grant considered this.

"If I told you that he never murdered anyone at all, what would you say?"

"I'd say that you're perfectly entitled to your opinion. Some people believe the earth is flat. Some people believe the world is going to end in A.D. 2000. Some people believe that it began less than five thousand years ago. You'll hear far funnier things than that at Marble Arch of a Sunday."

"So you wouldn't even entertain the idea for a moment?"

"I find it entertaining all right, but not what you might call very plausible, shall we say? But don't let me stand in your way. Try it out on a better bombing range. You take it to Marble Arch one Sunday, and I'll bet you'll find followers aplenty. Maybe start a movement."

He made a gay sketchy half-salute with his hand and went away humming to himself, secure and impervious.

So help me, Grant thought, I'm not far off it. If I get any deeper into this thing I *will* be standing on a soapbox at Marble Arch.

He unfolded the message from Carradine, and read: "You said that you wanted to know whether the other heirs to the throne survived Richard. As well as the boys, I mean. I forgot to say: would you make out a list of them for me, so that I can look them up. I think it's going to be important."

Well, if the world in general went on its humming way, brisk and uncaring, at least he had young America on his side.

He put aside the sainted More, with its Sunday-paper accounts of hysterical scenes and wild accusations, and reached for the sober student's account of history so that he might catalogue the possible rivals to Richard III in the English succession.

And as he put down More-Morton, he was reminded of something.

That hysterical scene during the Council in the Tower which was reported by More, that frantic outburst on Richard's part against the sorcery that had withered his arm, had been against Jane Shore.

The contrast between the reported scene, pointless and repellent even to a disinterested reader, and the kind, tolerant, almost casual air of the letter that Richard had actually written about her, was staggering.

So help me, he thought again, if I had to choose between the man who wrote that account and the man who wrote that letter I'd take the man who wrote the letter, whatever either of them had done besides.

The thought of Morton made him postpone his listing of the York heirs until he had found out what eventually became of John Morton. It seemed that, having used his leisure as Buckingham's guest to organise a joint Woodville-Lancastrian effort (in which Henry Tudor would bring ships and troops from France and Dorset and the rest of the

Woodville tribe would meet him with what English malcontents they could induce to follow them), he escaped to his old hunting ground in the Ely district, and from there to the continent. And did not come back until he came in the wake of a Henry who had won both Bosworth and a crown; being himself on the way to Canterbury and a cardinal's hat and immortality as Morton of "Morton's Fork." Almost the only thing that any schoolboy remembered about his master Henry VII.

For the rest of the evening Grant pottered happily through the history book, collecting heirs.

There was no lack of them. Edward's five, George's boy and girl. And if these were discounted, the first through illegitimacy and the second through attainder, there was another possible: his elder sister Elizabeth's boy. Elizabeth was Duchess of Suffolk, and her son was John de la Pole, Earl of Lincoln.

There was, too, in the family, a boy whose existence Grant had not suspected. It appeared that the delicate child at Middleham was not Richard's only son. He had a love-child; a boy called John. John of Gloucester. A boy of no importance in rank but acknowledged and living in the household. It was an age when a bend sinister was accepted without grief. Indeed the Conqueror had made it fashionable. And conquerors from then on had advertised its lack of disadvantage. By way of compensation, perhaps.

Edward
Edward,
   Prince of
   Wales
Richard,
   Duke of
   York
Elizabeth
Cicely
Anne
Katherine
Bridget

Elizabeth
John de la
   Pole, Earl
   of Lincoln

George
Edward, Earl
   of Warwick

Margaret,
    Countess
    of Salisbury

Richard
John of
    Gloucester

He copied it out again for young Carradine's use, wondering how it could ever have occurred to anyone, Richard most of all, that the elimination of Edward's two boys would have kept him safe from rebellion. The place was what young Carradine would call just lousy with heirs. Swarming with focuses (or was it foci?) for disaffection.

It was brought home to him for the first time not only what a useless thing the murder of the boys would have been, but what a *silly thing*.

And if there was anything that Richard of Gloucester was not, beyond a shadow of doubt, it was silly.

He looked up Oliphant to see what Oliphant had to say on this obvious crack in the story.

"It is strange," said Oliphant, "that Richard

does not seem to have published any version of their deaths."

It was more than strange: it was incomprehensible.

If Richard had wanted to murder his brother's sons then he most certainly would have done it expertly. They would have died of a fever, and their bodies would have been exposed to the public gaze as royal bodies habitually were, so that all men would know that they were in fact departed from this life.

No one can say that a man is incapable of murder—after long years on the Embankment Grant knew that only too well—but one can be sure to within one degree of the absolute when a man is incapable of silliness.

Oliphant had no doubts about the murder, nevertheless. Richard, according to Oliphant, was Richard the Monster. Perhaps when an historian was covering a field as large as the Middle Ages and the Renaissance he had no time to stop and analyse detail. Oliphant accepted the sainted More, even while he paused in flight to wonder at an oddity here and there. Not seeing that

the oddities ate away at the very founda-
tions of his theory.

Having Oliphant in his hand, he went on
with Oliphant. On through the triumphal
progress through England after the coronation. Oxford, Gloucester, Worcester, Warwick. No dissentient voice was recorded on
that tour. Only a chorus of blessing and
thanksgiving. A rejoicing that good government was to be the order of the day for a
lifetime to come. That, after all, Edward's
sudden death had not condemned them to
years of faction and a new civil struggle
over the person of his son.

And yet it was during this triumph, this
unanimous acclamation, this universal ho-
sanna, that (according to Oliphant, riding in
the pocket of the sainted More) Richard
sent Tyrrel back to London to make away
with the boys who were doing lessons in the
Tower. Between July 7th and 15th: At Warwick. In the very summer of his safety, in the
heart of the York country on the borders of
Wales, he planned the destruction of two
discredited children.

It was a highly unlikely story.

He began to wonder whether historians
were possessed of minds any more com-

monsensical than those Great Minds he had encountered, who had been so credulous.

He must find out without delay why, if Tyrrel did that job in 1485, he wasn't brought to book until twenty years afterwards. Where had he been in the meantime?

But Richard's summer was like an April day. Full of a promise that came to nothing. In the autumn he had to face that Woodville-Lancastrian invasion which Morton had cooked up before leaving these shores himself. The Lancastrian part of the affair did Morton proud: they came with a fleet of French ships and a French army. But the Woodville side could provide nothing better than sporadic little gatherings in widely separated centres: Guildford, Salisbury, Maidstone, Newbury, Exeter, and Brecon. The English wanted no part of Henry Tudor, whom they knew only too well. Even the English weather would have none of them. And Dorset's hope of seeing his half-sister Elizabeth queen of England as Henry Tudor's wife was washed away in Severn floods. Henry tried to land in the West, but found Devon and Cornwall up in indignant arms at the idea. He therefore sailed away to France again, to wait for a luckier day. And Dorset went to join in the growing crowd of Woodville exiles hanging around the French court.

So Morton's plan was washed away in autumn rain and English indifference, and Richard could be at peace for a little; but with the spring came a grief that nothing could wash away. The death of his son.

"The King is said to have shown signs of desperate grief; he was not such an unnatural monster as to be destitute of the feeling of a father," said the historian.

Nor of a husband, it seemed. The same marks of suffering were reported of him less than a year later, when Anne died.

And after that there was nothing but the waiting for the renewal of the invasion that had failed; the keeping of England in a state of defence, and the anxiety that that drain on the Exchequer brought him.

He had done what good he could. He had given his name to a model Parliament. He had made peace at last with Scotland and arranged a marriage between his niece and James III's son. He had tried very hard for a peace with France, but had failed. At the

French court was Henry Tudor, and Henry Tudor was France's white-headed boy. It would be only a matter of time before Henry landed in England, this time with better backing.

Grant suddenly remembered Lady Stanley, the ardent Lancastrian mother of Henry. What part had Lady Stanley had in that autumn invasion that had put paid to Richard's summer?

He hunted through the solid print until he found it.

Lady Stanley had been found guilty of treasonable correspondence with her son.

But again Richard had proved too lenient for his own good, it seemed. Her estates were forfeit, but they were handed over to her husband. And so was Lady Stanley. For safe keeping. The bitter joke being that Stanley had almost certainly been as knowledgeable about the invasion as his wife.

Truly, the monster was not running according to form.

As Grant was falling asleep a voice said in his mind: "If the boys were murdered in July, and the Woodville-Lancastrian invasion took place in October, why didn't they use the murder of the children as a rallying call?"

The invasion had, of course, been planned before there was any question of murder; it was a full-dress affair of fifteen ships and five thousand mercenaries and must have taken a long time to prepare. But by the time of the rising the rumours of Richard's infamy must have been widespread if there were any rumours at all. Why had they not gone shouting his crime through England, so that the horror of it brought men flocking to their cause?

Chapter 12

"Cool off, cool off," he said to himself when he woke next morning, "you're beginning to be partisan. That's no way to conduct an investigation."

So, by way of moral discipline, he became prosecutor.

Supposing that the Butler story was a frame-up. A story concocted with Stillington's help. Supposing that both Lords and Commons were willing to be hoodwinked in the hope of stable Government to come.

Did that bring one any nearer the murder of the two boys?

It didn't, did it?

If the story was false, the person to be got rid of was Stillington. Lady Eleanor had died in her convent long ago, so was not there to blow Titulus Regius to pieces any time she had a mind. But Stillington could. And Stillington evidently showed no difficulty in going on living. He survived the man he had put on the throne.

The sudden jar in the proceedings, the abrupt break in the pattern of the coronation preparation, was either wonderful stage-managing or just what one would expect if the thunderclap of Stillington's confession descended on unprepared ears. Richard was—what? Eleven? Twelve?— when the Butler contract was signed and witnessed; it was unlikely that he knew anything of it.

If the Butler story was an invention to oblige Richard, then Richard must have rewarded Stillington. But there was no sign of Stillington's being obliged with a cardinal's hat, or preferment, or office.

But the surest evidence that the Butler story was true lay in Henry VII's urgent need to destroy it. If it were false, then all he had to do to discredit Richard was to bring it into the open and make Stillington eat his words. Instead he hushed it up.

At this point Grant realised with disgust that he was back on the Defence side again. He decided to give it up. He would take to Lavinia Fitch, or Rupert Rouge, or some other of the fashionable authors lying in such expensive neglect on his table, and forget Richard Plantagenet until such time as young Carradine appeared to renew the inquisition.

He put the family-tree sketch of Cicely Nevill's grandchildren into an envelope and addressed it to Carradine, and gave it to The Midget to post. Then he turned down the portrait that was leaning against the books, so that he should not be seduced by that face which Sergeant Williams had placed, without hesitation, on the bench, and reached for Silas Weekley's *The Sweat and the Furrow*. Thereafter he went from Silas's seamy wrestlings to Lavinia's tea-cups, and from Lavinia's teacups to Rupert's cavortings in the *coulisses*, with a growing dissatisfaction, until Brent Carradine once more turned up in his life.

Carradine regarded him anxiously and said: "You don't look so bright as last time I saw you, Mr. Grant. You not doing so well?"

"Not where Richard is concerned, I'm not," Grant said. "But I've got a new piece of Tonypandy for you."

And he handed him Laura's letter about the drowned women who were never drowned.

Carradine read it with a delight that grew on him like slow sunlight coming out, until eventually he glowed.

"My, but that's wonderful. That's very superior, first growth, dyed-in-the-wool Tonypandy, isn't it? Lovely, lovely. You didn't know about this before? And you a Scotsman?"

"I'm only a Scot once removed," Grant pointed out. "No; I knew that none of these Covenanters died 'for the Faith,' of course; but I didn't know that one of them—or rather, two of them—hadn't died at all."

"They didn't die for their Faith?" Carradine repeated, bewildered. "D'you mean that the *whole thing's* Tonypandy?"

Grant laughed. "I suppose it is," he said, surprised. "I never thought about it before. I've known so long that the 'martyrs' were no more martyrs than that thug who is going to his death for killing that old shopkeeper in Essex, that I've ceased to think about it. No one in Scotland went to his death for anything but civil crime."

"But I thought they were very holy people—the Covenanters, I mean."

"You've been looking at nineteenth-century pictures of conventicles. The reverent little gathering in the heather listening to the preacher; young rapt faces, and white hair blowing in the winds of God. The Covenanters were the exact equivalent of the I.R.A. in Ireland. A small irreconcilable minority, and as bloodthirsty a crowd as ever disgraced a Christian nation. If you went to church on Sunday instead of to a conventicle, you were liable to wake on Monday to find your barn burned or your horses ham-strung. If you were more open in your disapproval you were shot. The men who shot Archbishop Sharp in his daughter's presence, in broad daylight on a road in Fife, were the heroes of the movement. 'Men of courage and zeal for the cause of God,' according to their admiring followers. They lived safe and swaggering among their Covenanting fans in the West for years. It was a 'preacher of the gospel' who shot Bishop Honeyman in an Edinburgh street. And they shot the old parish priest of Carsphairn on his own doorstep."

"It does sound like Ireland, doesn't it?" Carradine said.

"They were actually worse than the I.R.A. because there was a fifth column element on it. They were financed from Holland, and their arms came from Holland. There was nothing forlorn about their movement, you know. They expected to take over the Government any day, and rule Scotland. All their preaching was pure sedition. The most violent incitement to crime you could imagine. No modern Government could afford to be so patient with such a menace as the Government of the time were. The Covenanters were continually being offered amnesties."

"Well, well. And I thought they were fighting for freedom to worship God their own way."

"No one ever stopped them from worshipping God any way they pleased. What they were out to do was to impose their method of church government not only on Scotland but on England, believe it or not. You should read the Covenant some day. Freedom of worship was not to be allowed to anyone according to the Covenanting creed—except the Covenanters, of course."

"And all those gravestones and monuments that tourists go to see—"

"All Tonypandy. If you ever read on a gravestone that John Whosit 'suffered death for his adherence to the Word of God and Scotland's Covenanted work of Reformation,' with a touching little verse underneath about 'dust sacrificed to tyranny,' you can be sure that the said John Whosit was found guilty before a properly constituted court, of a civil crime punishable by death and that his death had nothing whatever to do with the Word of God." He laughed a little under his breath. "It's the final irony, you know, that a group whose name was anathema to the rest of Scotland in their own time should have been elevated into the position of saints and martyrs."

"I wouldn't wonder if it wasn't onomatopoeic," Carradine said thoughtfully.

"What?"

"Like the Cat and the Rat, you know."

"What are you talking about?"

" 'Member you said, about that Cat and Rat lampoon, that rhyme, that the sound of it made it an offence?"

"Yes; made it venomous."

"Well, the word dragoon does the same thing. I take it that the dragoons were just the policemen of the time."

"Yes. Mounted infantry."

"Well, to me—and I suspect to every other

person reading about it—dragoons sound dreadful. They've come to mean something that they never were."

"Yes, I see. Force majeure in being. Actually the Government had only a tiny handful of men to police an enormous area, so the odds were all on the Covenanters' side. In more ways than one. A dragoon (read policeman) couldn't arrest anyone without a warrant (he couldn't stable his horse without the owner's permission, if it comes to that), but there was nothing to hinder a Covenanter lying snug in the heather and picking off dragoons at his leisure. Which they did, of course. And now there's a whole literature about the poor ill-used saint in the heather with his pistol; and the dragoon who died in the course of his duty is a Monster."

"Like Richard."

"Like Richard. How have you been getting on with our own particular Tonypandy?"

"Well, I still haven't managed to find out why Henry was so anxious to hush up that Act as well as repeal it. The thing *was* hushed up and for years it was forgotten, until the original draft turned up, just by chance, in the Tower records. It was printed in 1611. Speed printed the full text of it in his *History of Great Britain*."

"Oh. So there's no question at all about Titulus Regius. Richard succeeded as the Act says, and the sainted More's account is nonsense. There never was an Elizabeth Lucy in the matter."

"Lucy? Who's Elizabeth Lucy?"

"Oh, I forgot. You weren't on in that act. According to the sainted More, Richard claimed that Edward was married to one of his mistresses, one Elizabeth Lucy."

The disgusted look that the mention of the sainted More always caused on young Carradine's mild face made him look almost nauseated.

"That's nonsense."

"So the sainted More smugly pointed out."

"Why did they want to hide Eleanor Butler?" Carradine said, seeing the point.

"Because she really had married Edward, and the children really were illegitimate. And if the children really were illegitimate, by the way, then no one could rise in their favour and they were no danger to Richard. Have you noticed that the Woodville-Lancastrian invasion was in Henry's favour, and not in the boys'—although Dorset was their half-brother? And that was before any rumours of their nonexistence could have reached him. As far as the leaders of the Dorset-Morton rebellion were concerned the boys were of no account. They were backing Henry. That way, Dorset would have a brother-in-law on the throne of England, and the Queen would be his half-sister. Which would be a nice reversal of form for a penniless fugitive."

"Yes. Yes, that's a point, all right; that about Dorset not fighting to restore his half-brother. If there had been a chance at all that England would have accepted the boy, he surely would have backed the boy. I'll tell you another interesting thing I found. The Queen and her daughters came out of sanctuary quite soon. It's your talking about her son Dorset that reminded me. She not only came out of sanctuary but settled down as if nothing had happened. Her daughters went to festivities at the Palace. And do you know what the pay-off is?"

"No."

"That was *after the Princes had been 'murdered.'* Yes, and I'll tell you something else. With her two boys done to death by their wicked uncle, she writes to her other son, in France—Dorset—and asks him to come home and make his peace with Richard, who will treat him well."

There was silence.

There were no sparrows to talk today. Only the soft sound of the rain against the window.

"No comment," Carradine said at last.

"You know," Grant said, "from the police point of view there is no case against Richard at all. And I mean that literally. It isn't that the case isn't good enough. Good enough to bring into court, I mean. There, quite literally, isn't any case against him at all."

"I'll say there isn't. Especially when I tell you that every single one of those people whose names you sent me were alive and prosperous, and *free*, when Richard was killed at Bosworth. They were not only free, they were very well cared for. Edward's children not only danced at the Palace, they had pensions. He appointed one of the crowd his heir when his own boy died."

"Which one?"

"George's boy."

"So he meant to reverse the attainder on his brother's children."

"Yes. He had protested about his being condemned, if you remember."

"According to even the sainted More, he did. So all the heirs to the throne of England were going about their business, free and unfettered, during the reign of Richard III, the Monster."

"They were more. They were part of the general scheme of things. I mean, part of the family and the general economy of the realm. I've been reading a collection of York records by a man Davies, records of the town of York, I mean; not the family. Both young Warwick—George's son—and his cousin, young Lincoln, were members of the Council. The town addressed a letter to them. In 1485, that was. What's more, Richard knighted young Warwick at the same time as he knighted his own son, at a splendid 'do' at York." He paused a long moment, and then blurted out: "Mr. Grant, do you want to write a book about this?"

"A book!" Grant said, astonished. "God forbid. Why?"

"Because I should like to write one. It

would make a much better book than the Peasants."

"Write away."

"You see, I'd like to have something to show my father. Pop thinks I'm no good because I can't take an interest in furniture, and marketing, and graphs of sales. If he could actually handle a book that I had written he might believe that I wasn't so hopeless a bet after all. In fact, I wouldn't put it past him to begin to boast about me for a change."

Grant looked at him with benevolence.

"I forgot to ask you what you thought of Crosby Place," he said.

"Oh, fine, fine. If Carradine the Third ever sees it he'll want to take it back with him and rebuild it in the Adirondacks somewhere."

"If you write that book about Richard, he most certainly will. He'll feel like a part-owner. What are you going to call it?"

"The book?"

"Yes."

"I'm going to borrow a phrase from Henry Ford, and call it *History Is the Bunk*."

"Excellent."

"However, I'll have a lot more reading to

do and a lot more research, before I can start writing."

"Most assuredly you have. You haven't arrived yet at the real question."

"What is that?"

"Who *did* murder the boys?"

"Yes, of course."

"If the boys were alive when Henry took over the Tower what happened to them?"

"Yes. I'll get on to that. I still want to know why it was so important to Henry to hush up the contents of Titulus Regius."

He got up to go, and then noticed the portrait that was lying on its face on the table. He reached over and restored the photograph to its original place, propping it with a concerned care against the pile of books.

"You stay there," he said to the painted Richard. "I'm going to put you back where you belong."

As he went out the door, Grant said:

"I've just thought of a piece of history which is *not* Tonypandy."

"Yes?" said Carradine, lingering.

"The massacre of Glencoe."

"That really did happen?"

"That really did happen. And—Brent!"

Brent put his head back inside the door. "Yes?"

"The man who gave the order for it was an ardent Covenanter."

Chapter 13

Carradine had not been gone more than twenty minutes when Marta appeared, laden with flowers, books, candy, and goodwill. She found Grant deep in the fifteenth century as reported by Sir Cuthbert Oliphant. He greeted her with an absent-mindedness to which she was not accustomed.

"If your two sons had been murdered by your brother-in-law, would you take a handsome pension from him?"

"I take it that the question is rhetorical," Marta said, putting down her sheaf of flowers and looking round to see which of the already occupied vases would best suit their type.

"Honestly, I think historians are all mad. Listen to this:

The conduct of the Queen-Dowager is hard to explain; whether she feared to be taken from sanctuary by force, or whether she was merely tired of her forlorn existence at Westminster, and had resolved to be reconciled to the murder of her sons out of mere callous apathy, seems uncertain."

"Merciful Heaven!" said Marta, pausing with a delft jar in one hand and a glass cylinder in the other, and looking at him in wild surmise.

"Do you think historians really *listen* to what they are saying?"

"Who was the said Queen-Dowager?"

"Elizabeth Woodville. Edward IV's wife."

"Oh, yes. I played her once. It was a 'bit.' In a play about Warwick the Kingmaker."

"Of course I'm only a policeman," Grant said. "Perhaps I never moved in the right circles. It may be that I've met only nice people. Where would one have to go to meet a woman who became matey with the murderer of her two boys?"

"Greece, I should think," Marta said. "*Ancient* Greece."

"I can't remember a sample even there."

"Or a lunatic asylum, perhaps. Was there

any sign of idiocy about Elizabeth Woodville?"

"Not that anyone ever noticed. And she
was Queen for twenty years or so."

"Of course the thing is farce, I hope you
see," Marta said, going on with her flower
arranging. "Not tragedy at all. 'Yes, I know
he did kill Edward and little Richard, but he
really is a rather charming creature and it is
so bad for my rheumatism living in rooms
with a north light.' "

Grant laughed, and his good temper came
back.

"Yes, of course. It's the height of absurdity. It belongs to Ruthless Rhymes, not to
sober history. That is why historians surprise me. They seem to have no talent for
the *likeliness* of any situation. They see history like a peepshow; with two-dimensional
figures against a distant background."

"Perhaps when you are grubbing about
with tattered records you haven't time to
learn about people. I don't mean about the
people in the records, but just about People. Flesh and blood. And how they react to
circumstances."

"How would you play her?" Grant asked,

remembering that the understanding of motive was Marta's trade.

"Play who?"

"The woman who came out of sanctuary and made friends with her children's murderer for seven hundred marks per annum and the right to go to parties at the Palace."

"I couldn't. There is no such woman outside Euripides or a delinquents' home. One could only play her as a rag. She'd make a very good burlesque, now I think of it. A take-off of poetic tragedy. The blank verse kind. I must try it sometime. For a charity matinée, or something. I hope you don't hate mimosa. It's odd, considering how long I've known you, how little I know your likes and dislikes. Who invented the woman who became buddies with her sons' murderer?"

"No one in vented her. Elizabeth Woodville did come out of sanctuary, and did accept a pension from Richard. The pension was not only granted, it was paid. Her daughters went to parties at the Palace and she wrote to her other son—her first-marriage son—to come home from France and make his peace with Richard. Oliphant's only suggestion as to the reason for this is that she was either frightened of being dragged out of sanctuary (did you ever know of anyone who was dragged out of sanctuary? The man who did that would be excommunicated—and Richard was a very good son of Holy Church) or that she was bored with sanctuary life."

"And what is your theory about so odd a proceeding?"

"The obvious explanation is that the boys were alive and well. No one at that time ever suggested otherwise."

Marta considered the sprays of mimosa. "Yes, of course. You said that there was no accusation in that Bill of Attainder. After Richard's death, I mean." Her eyes went from the mimosa to the portrait on the table and then to Grant. "You think, then, you really soberly think, as a policeman, that Richard didn't have anything to do with the boys' deaths."

"I'm quite sure that they were alive and well when Henry took over the Tower on his arrival in London. There is *nothing* that would explain his omission to make a scandal of it if the boys were missing. Can you think of anything?"

"No. No, of course not. It is quite inexplicable. I have always taken it for granted that there was a terrific scandal about it. That it would be one of the main accusations against Richard. You and my woolly lamb seem to be having a lovely time with history. When I suggested a little investigation to pass the time and stop the prickles I had no idea that I was contributing to the rewriting of history. Which reminds me. Atlanta Shergold is gunning for you."

"For me? I've never even met her."

"Nevertheless she is looking for you with a gun. She says that Brent's attitude to the B. M. has become the attitude of an addict to his drug. She can't drag him away from it. If she takes him away from it physically, he spends the time harking back to it in his mind; so that she mightn't exist as far as he is concerned. He has even stopped sitting through *To Sea in a Bowl*. Do you see much of him?"

"He was here a few minutes before you came. But I don't expect to hear from him again for some days to come."

But in that he was wrong.

Just before supper-time the porter appeared with a telegram.

Grant put his thumb under the dainty Post

Office lick on the flap and extracted two sheets of telegram. The telegram was from Brent.

Hell and damnation an awful thing has happened (stop) you know that chronicle in Latin I talked about (stop) the chronicle written by the monk at Croyland Abbey (stop) well I've just seen it and the rumour is there the rumour about the boys being dead (stop) the thing is written before Richard's death so we are sunk aren't we and I specially am sunk and that fine book of mine will never be written (stop) is anyone allowed to commit suicide in your river or is it reserved for the British

Brent

Into the silence the voice of the porter said: "It's reply-paid, sir. Do you want to send an answer?"

"What? Oh. No. Not right away. I'll send it down presently."

"Very good, sir," said the porter, looking respectfully at the two sheets of telegram—in the porter's family a telegram was confined to one sheet only—and went away, not humming this time.

Grant considered the news conveyed with such transatlantic extravagance in the matter of telegraphic communication. He read the thing again.

"Croyland," he said, considering. Why did that ring a bell? No one had mentioned Croyland so far in this case. Carradine had talked merely of a monkish chronicle somewhere.

He had been too often, in his professional life, faced with a fact that apparently destroyed his whole case to be dismayed now. He reacted as he would have reacted in a professional investigation. He took out the upsetting small fact and looked at it. Calmly. Dispassionately. With none of poor Carradine's wild dismay.

"Croyland," he said again. Croyland was somewhere in Cambridgeshire. Or was it Norfolk? Somewhere on the borders there, in the flat country.

The Midget came in with his supper, and propped the flat bowl-like plate where he could eat from it with a modicum of comfort, but he was not aware of her.

"Can you reach your pudding easily from

there?" she asked. And as he did not answer: "Mr. Grant, can you reach your pudding if I leave it on the edge there?"

"*Ely!*" he shouted at her.

"What?"

"Ely," he said, softly to the ceiling.

"Mr. Grant, aren't you feeling well?"

He became conscious of The Midget's well-powdered and concerned little face as it intruded between him and the familiar cracks.

"I'm fine, fine. Better than I've ever been in my life. Wait just a moment, there's a good girl, and send a telegram down for me. Give me my writing-pad. I can't reach it with that mess of rice pudding in the way."

She gave him the pad and pencil, and on the reply-paid form he wrote:

Can you find me a similar rumour in France at about the same date?

Grant

After that he ate his supper with a good appetite, and settled down to a good night's sleep. He was floating in that delicious half-way stage on the way to unconsciousness when he became aware that someone was leaning over to inspect him. He opened his eyes to see who it might be, and looked straight into the anxious yearning brown irises of The Amazon, looking larger and more cowlike than ever in the soft lamplight. She was holding in her hand a yellow envelope.

"I didn't quite know what to do," she said. "I didn't want to disturb you and yet I didn't know whether it mightn't be important. A telegram, you know. You never can tell. And if you didn't have it tonight it would mean a whole twelve hours' delay. Nurse Ingham has gone off duty, so there was no one to ask till Nurse Briggs comes on at ten. I hope I haven't wakened you up. But you weren't really asleep, were you?"

Grant assured her that she had done the right thing and she let out a sigh that nearly blew the portrait of Richard over. She stood by while he read the telegram, with an air of being ready to support him in any evil news that it might contain. To The Amazon all telegrams conveyed evil tidings.

The telegram was from Carradine.

It said: "You mean you want repeat want that there should be another repeat another accusation question-mark—Brent."

Grant took the reply-paid form and wrote: "Yes. Preferably in France."

Then he said to The Amazon: "You can turn out the light, I think. I'm going to sleep until seven tomorrow morning."

He fell asleep wondering how long it would be before he saw Carradine again, and what the odds were against that much desired instance of a second rumour.

But it was not so long after all until Carradine turned up again, and he turned up looking anything but suicidal. Indeed he seemed in some queer way to have broadened out. His coat seemed less of an appendage and more of a garment. He beamed at Grant.

"Mr. Grant, you're a wonder. Do they have more like you at Scotland Yard? Or do you rate special?"

Grant looked at him almost unbelieving. "Don't tell me you've turned up a French instance!"

"Didn't you want me to?"

"Yes. But I hardly dared hope for it. The odds against seemed tremendous. What form did the rumour take in France? A chronicle? A letter?"

"No. Something much more surprising.

Something much more dismaying, actually. It seems that the Chancellor of France, in a speech to the States-General at Tours, spoke of the rumour. Indeed he was quite eloquent about it. In a way, his eloquence was the one scrap of comfort I could find in the situation."

"Why?"

"Well, it sounded more to my mind like a Senator being hasty about someone who had brought in a measure his own people back home wouldn't like. More like politics than State, if you know what I mean."

"You should be at the Yard, Brent. What did the Chancellor say?"

"Well, it's in French and my French isn't very good so perhaps you'd better read it for yourself."

He handed over a sheet of childish writing and Grant read:

Regardez, je vous prie, les événements qui après la mort du roi Edouard sont arrivés dans ce pays. Contemplez ses enfants, déjà grands et braves, massacrés impunément, et la couronne transportée à l'assassin par la faveur des peuples.

" 'Ce pays,' " said Grant. "Then he was in full flood against England. He even suggests that it was with the will of the English people that the boys were 'massacred.' We are being held up as a barbarous race."

"Yes. That's what I meant. It's a Congressman scoring a point. Actually, the French Regency sent an embassy to Richard that same year—about six months later—so they had probably found that the rumour wasn't true. Richard signed a safe-conduct for their visit. He wouldn't have done that if they had been still slanging him as a murdering untouchable."

"No. Can you give me the dates of the two libels?"

"Sure. I have them here. The monk at Croyland wrote about events in the late summer of 1483. He says that there was a rumour that the boys had been put to death but no one knew how. The nasty slap in the meeting of the States-General was in January 1484."

"Perfect," said Grant.

"*Why* did you want there to have been another instance of rumour?"

"As a cross-check. Do you know where Croyland is?"

"Yes. In the Fen country."

"In the Fen country. Near Ely. And it was in the Fen country that Morton was hiding out after his escape from Buckingham's charge."

"Morton! Yes, of course."

"If Morton was the carrier, then there had to be another outbreak on the Continent, when he moved on there. Morton escaped from England in the autumn of 1483, and the rumour appears promptly in January 1484. Croyland is a very isolated place, incidentally; it would be an ideal place for a fugitive bishop to hide out till he could arrange transport abroad."

"Morton!" said Carradine again, rolling the name over on his tongue. "Wherever there's hanky-panky in this business you stub your toe against Morton."

"So you've noticed that too."

"He was the heart of that conspiracy to murder Richard before he could be crowned, he was in the back of the rebellion against Richard once he *was* crowned, and his trail to the Continent is sticky as a snail's with—with subversion."

"We-ll, the snail part is mere deduction. It wouldn't stand up in court. But there's no peradventure about his activities once he was across the channel. He settled down to a whole-time job of subversion. He and a buddy of his called Christopher Urswick worked like beavers in Henry's interest; 'sending preuie letters and cloked messengers' to England to stir up hostility to Richard."

"Yes? I don't know as much as you about what stands up in court and what won't but it seems to me that that snail's trail is a very allowable deduction—if you'll allow me. I don't suppose Morton waited till he was overseas before beginning his undermining."

"No. No, of course he didn't. It was life and death to Morton that Richard should go. Unless Richard went, John Morton's career was over. He was finished. It wasn't even that there would be no preferment for him now. There would be nothing. He would be stripped of his numerous livings and be reduced to his plain priest's frock. He, John Morton. Who had been within touching distance of an archbishopric. But if he could help Henry Tudor to a throne then he might still become not only Archbishop of Canterbury but a Cardinal besides. Oh, yes; it was desperately, overwhelmingly important to Morton that Richard should not have the governing of England."

"Well," said Brent, "he was the right man for a job of subversion. I don't suppose he knew what a scruple was. A little rumour like infanticide must have been child's play to him."

"There's always the odd chance that he believed it, of course," Grant said, his habit of weighing evidence overcoming even his dislike of Morton.

"Believed that the boys were murdered?"

"Yes. It may have been someone else's invention. After all, the country must have been swarming with Lancastrian tales, part mere ill-will, part propaganda. He may have been merely passing on the latest sample."

"Huh! I wouldn't put it past him to be paving the way for their future murder," Brent said tartly.

Grant laughed. "I wouldn't, at that," he said. "What else did you get from your monk at Croyland?"

"A little comfort, too. I found after I had written that panic wire to you that he wasn't at all to be taken as gospel. He just put down what gossip came his way from the outer world. He says, for instance, that Richard had a second coronation, at York; and that of course just isn't true. If he can be wrong about a big, known fact like a coronation, then he's not to be trusted as a reporter. But he did know about Titulus Regius, by the way. He recorded the whole tenor of it, including Lady Eleanor."

"That's interesting. Even a monk at Croyland had heard who Edward was supposed to have been married to."

"Yes. The sainted More must have dreamed up Elizabeth Lucy a good deal later."

"To say nothing of the unspeakable story that Richard based his claim on his mother's shame."

"What?"

"He says that Richard caused a sermon to be preached claiming that Edward and George were his mother's sons by some other father, and that he, Richard, was the only legitimate son and therefore the only true heir."

"The sainted More might have thought up a more convincing one," young Carradine said dryly.

"Yes. Especially when Richard was living

in his mother's house at the time of the libel!"

"So he was. I'd forgotten that. I don't have a proper police brain. That's very neat, what you say about Morton being the carrier of the rumour. But suppose the rumour turns up somewhere else, even yet?"

"It's possible, of course. But I'm willing to lay you fifties to any amount that it won't. I don't for one moment believe that there was any general rumour that the boys were missing."

"Why not?"

"For a reason that I hold to be unanswerable. If there had been any general uneasiness, any obviously subversive rumours or action, Richard would have taken immediate steps to checkmate them. When the rumour went round, later, that he was proposing to marry his niece Elizabeth—the boys' eldest sister—he was on to it like a hawk. He not only sent letters to the various towns denying the rumour in no uncertain terms, he was so furious (and evidently thought it of such importance that he should not be traduced) that he summoned the 'heid yins' of London to the biggest hall he could find (so that he could get them all in at one time) and told them face to face what he thought about the affair."

"Yes. Of course you're right. Richard would have made a public denial of the rumour if the rumour was general. After all, it was a much more horrifying one than the one that he was going to marry his niece."

"Yes; actually you could get a dispensation to marry your niece in those days. Perhaps you still can, for all I know. That's not my department at the Yard. What is certain is that if Richard went to such lengths to contradict the marriage rumour then he most certainly would have gone to much greater lengths to put a stop to the murder one, if it had existed. The conclusion is inevitable; there *was* no general rumour of disappearance or foul play where the boys were concerned."

"Just a thin little trickle between the Fens and France."

"Just a thin little trickle between the Fens and France. Nothing in the picture suggests any worry about the boys. I mean: in a police investigation you look for any abnormalities in behaviour among the suspects in a crime. Why did X, who always goes to the movies on a Thursday night, decide on that night of all nights not to go? Why did Y take a return half as usual and very unusually not use it? That sort of thing. But in the short time between Richard's succession and his death everyone behaves quite normally. The boys' mother comes out of sanctuary and makes her peace with Richard. The girls resume their court life. The boys are presumably still doing their lessons that their father's death had interrupted. Their young cousins have a place on the Council and are of sufficient importance for the town of York to be addressing letters to them. It's all quite a normal, peaceful scene, with everyone going about their ordinary business, and no suggestion anywhere that a spectacular and unnecessary murder has just taken place in the family."

"It looks as if I might write that book after all, Mr. Grant."

"Most certainly you will write it. You have not only Richard to rescue from calumny; you have to clear Elizabeth Woodville of the imputation of condoning her sons' murder for seven hundred marks a year and perks."

"I can't write the book and leave it in the air like that, of course. I'll have to have at least a theory as to what became of the boys."

"You will."

Carradine's mild gaze came away from the small woolly clouds over the Thames and considered Grant with a question in it.

"Why that tone?" he asked. "Why are you looking like a cat with cream?"

"Well, I've been proceeding along police lines. During those empty days while I was waiting for you to turn up again."

"Police lines?"

"Yes. Who benefits, and all that. We've discovered that it wouldn't be a pin's-worth of advantage to Richard that the boys should die. So we go on looking round to see whom, in that case, it *would* benefit. And this is where Titulus Regius comes in."

"What has Titulus Regius got to do with the murder?"

"Henry VII married the boys' eldest sister. Elizabeth."

"Yes."

"By way of reconciling the Yorkists to his occupation of the throne."

"Yes."

"By repealing Titulus Regius, he made her legitimate."

"Sure."

"But by making the children legitimate he automatically made the two boys heir to the throne before her. In fact, by repealing Titulus Regius he made the elder of the two King of England."

Carradine made a little clicking sound with his tongue. His eyes behind their horn-rims were glowing with pleasure.

"So," said Grant, "I propose that we proceed with investigation along those lines."

"Sure. What do you want?"

"I want to know a lot more about that confession of Tyrrel's. But first, and most of all, I'd like to know how the people concerned acted. What happened to them; not what anyone reported of anyone. Just as we did in the case of Richard's succession after Edward's unexpected death."

"Fine. What do you want to know?"

"I want to know what became of all the York heirs that Richard left so alive and well and prosperous. Every single one of them. Can you do that for me?"

"Sure. That's elementary."

"And I could bear to know more about Tyrrel. About the man himself, I mean. Who he was, and what he had done."

"I'll do that." Carradine got up with such an on-with-the-charge air that for one moment Grant thought that he was actually going to button his coat. "Mr. Grant, I'm so grateful to you for all this—this—"

"This fun and games?"

"When you're on your feet again, I'll—I'll—I'll take you round the Tower of London."

"Make it Greenwich-and-back by boat. Our island race have a passion for the nautical."

"How long do they reckon it will be before you're out of bed, do you know?"

"I'll probably be up before you come back with the news about the heirs and Tyrrel."

Chapter 14

Grant was not, as it happened, out of bed when Carradine came again, but he was sitting up.

"You can't imagine," he said to Brent, "how fascinating the opposite wall looks, after the ceiling. And how small and queer the world looks right way up."

He was touched by Carradine's obvious pleasure in this progress and it was some time before they got down to business. It was Grant who had to say: "Well, how did the York heirs make out under Henry VII?"

"Oh, yes," said the boy, pulling out his usual wad of notes and drawing up a chair by hooking his right toe in the crossbar. He sat down on the chair. "Where shall I begin?"

"Well, about Elizabeth we know. He married her, and she was Queen of England until she died and he made a bid for the mad Juana of Spain."

"Yes. She was married to Henry in the spring of 1486—in January, rather; five months after Bosworth—and she died in the spring of 1503."

"Seventeen years. Poor Elizabeth. With Henry it must have seemed like seventy. He was what is euphemistically referred to as 'unuxorious.' Let us go on down the family. Edward's children, I mean. Fate of the two boys unknown. What happened to Cicely?"

"She was married to his old uncle Lord Welles, and sent away to live in Lincolnshire. Anne and Katherine, who were children, were married when they were old enough to be good Lancastrians. Bridget, the youngest, became a nun at Dartford."

"Orthodox enough, so far. Who comes next? George's boy."

"Yes. Young Warwick. Shut up for life in the Tower, and executed for allegedly planning to escape."

"So. And George's daughter? Margaret."

"She became the Countess of Salisbury. Her execution by Henry VIII on a trumped-up charge is apparently the classic sample of judicial murder."

"Elizabeth's son? The alternative heir?"

"John de la Pole. He went to live with his aunt in Burgundy until—"

"To live with Margaret, Richard's sister."

"Yes. He died in the Simnel rising. But he had a younger brother that you didn't put in that list. He was executed by Henry VIII. He had surrendered to Henry VII under a safe-conduct, so Henry, I suppose, thought that it might break his luck to ignore that. In any case he had about used up his quota. Henry VIII took no chances. He didn't stop at de la Pole. There were four more that you missed out of that list. Exeter, Surrey, Buckingham, and Montague. He got rid of the lot."

"And Richard's son? John? The bastard one."

"Henry VII granted him a pension of £20 a year, but he was the first of the lot to go."

"On what charge?"

"On having been suspected of receiving an invitation to go to Ireland."

"You're joking."

"I'm not. Ireland was the focus of loyalist rebellion. The York family were very popular in Ireland, and to get an invitation from that direction was as good as a death warrant in Henry's eyes. Though I can't think why even Henry would have bothered about young

John. 'An active, well-disposed boy,' he was, by the way, according to the 'Foedera.' "

"His claim was better than Henry's," Grant said, very tart. "He was the illegitimate only son of a King. Henry was the great-grandson of an illegitimate son of a younger son of a King."

There was silence for some time.

Then Carradine, out of the silence, said: "Yes."

"Yes to what?"

"To what you are thinking."

"It does look like it, doesn't it? They're the only two who are missing from the list."

There was another silence.

"They were all judicial murders," Grant said presently. "Murders under the form of law. But you can't bring a capital charge against a pair of children."

"No," agreed Carradine, and went on watching the sparrows. "No, it would have to be done some other way. After all, they were the important ones."

"The vital ones."

"How do we start?"

"As we did with Richard's succession. Find out where everyone was in the first months of Henry's reign and what they were doing. Say the first year of his reign. There will be a break in the pattern somewhere, just as there was a break in the preparations for the boy's coronation."

"Right."

"Did you find out anything about Tyrrel? Who he was?"

"Yes. He wasn't at all what I had imagined. I'd imagined him as a sort of hanger-on; hadn't you?"

"Yes, I think I did. Wasn't he?"

"No. He was a person of importance. He was Sir James Tyrrel of Gipping. He had been on various—committees, I suppose you'd call them, for Edward IV. And he was created a Knight Banneret, whatever that is, at the siege of Berwick. And he did well for himself under Richard, though I can't find that he was at the battle of Bosworth. A lot of people came too late for the battle—did you know?—so I don't suppose that means anything particular. Anyhow, he wasn't that lackey-on-the-make person that I'd always pictured."

"That's interesting. How did he make out under Henry VII?"

"Well, that's the *really* interesting thing.

For such a very good and successful servant of the York family, he seems to have fairly blossomed under Henry. Henry appointed him Constable of Guisnes. Then he was sent as ambassador to Rome. He was one of the Commissioners for negotiating the Treaty of Etaples. And Henry gave him a grant for life of the revenues of some lands in Wales, but made him exchange them for revenues of the county of Guisnes of equal value—I can't think why."

"I can," said Grant.

"You can?"

"Has it struck you that all his honours and his commissions are outside England? Even the reward of land revenues."

"Yes, so they are. What does that convey to you?"

"Nothing at the moment. Perhaps he just found Guisnes better for his bronchial catarrh. It is possible to read too much into historical transactions. Like Shakespeare's plays, they are capable of almost endless interpretations. How long did this honeymoon with Henry VII last?"

"Oh, quite a long time. Everything was just grand until 1502."

"What happened in 1502?"

"Henry heard that he had been ready to help one of the York crowd in the Tower to escape to Germany. He sent the whole garrison of Calais to besiege the castle at Guisnes. That wasn't quick enough for him, so he sent his Lord Privy Seal—know what that is?"

Grant nodded.

"Sent his Lord Privy Seal—what names you English have dreamed up for your Elks officials—to offer him safe conduct if he would come aboard a ship at Calais and confer with the Chancellor of the Exchequer."

"Don't tell me."

"I don't need to, do I? He finished up in a dungeon in the Tower. And was beheaded 'in great haste and without trial' on May 6, 1502."

"And what about his confession?"

"There wasn't one."

"What!"

"Don't look at me like that. I'm not responsible."

"But I thought he confessed to the murder of the boys."

"Yes, according to various accounts. But

they are accounts of a confession, not—not a transcript, if you see what I mean."

"You mean, Henry didn't publish a confession?"

"No. His paid historian, Polydore Virgil, gave an account of how the murder was done. After Tyrrel was dead."

"But if Tyrrel confessed that he murdered the boys at Richard's instigation, why wasn't he charged with the crime and publicly tried for it?"

"I can't imagine."

"Let me get this straight. Nothing was heard of Tyrrel's confession until Tyrrel was dead."

"No."

"Tyrrel confesses that way back in 1483, nearly twenty years ago, he pelted up to London from Warwick, got the keys of the Tower from the Constable—I forget his name—"

"Brackenbury. Sir Robert Brackenbury."

"Yes. Got the keys of the Tower from Sir Robert Brackenbury for one night, murdered the boys, handed back the keys, and reported back to Richard. He confesses this, and so puts an end to what must have been a much canvassed mystery, and yet nothing public is done with him."

"Not a thing."

"I'd hate to go into court with a story like that."

"I wouldn't even consider it, myself. It's as phony a tale as ever I heard."

"Didn't they even bring Brackenbury in to affirm or deny the story of the keys being handed over?"

"Brackenbury was killed at Bosworth."

"So he was conveniently dead too, was he?" He lay and thought about it. "You know, if Brackenbury died at Bosworth, then we have one more small piece of evidence on our side."

"How? What?"

"If that had really happened; I mean: if the keys were handed over for a night on Richard's order, then a lot of junior officials at the Tower must have been aware of it. It is quite inconceivable that one or other of them wouldn't be ready to tell the tale of Henry when he took over the Tower. Especially if the boys were missing. Brackenbury was dead. Richard was dead. The next in command at the Tower would be expected to produce the boys. When they weren't producible, he *must* have said: 'The Constable handed over the keys, one night, and since then the boys have not been seen.' There would have been the most ruthless hue and cry after the man who had been given the keys. He would have been Exhibit A in the case against Richard, and to produce him would have been a feather in Henry's cap."

"Not only that, but Tyrrel was too well known to the people at the Tower to have passed unrecognised. In the small London of that day he must have been quite a well-known figure."

"Yes. If that story were true Tyrrel would have been tried and executed for the boys' murder, openly, in 1485. He had no one to protect him." He reached for his cigarettes. "So what we're left with is that Henry executed Tyrrel in 1502, and then announced by way of his tame historians that Tyrrel had confessed that twenty years before he had murdered the Princes."

"Yes."

"And he didn't offer, anywhere, at any time, any reason for trying Tyrrel for this atrocious thing he had confessed."

"No. Not as far as I can make out. He was

sideways as a crab, you know. He never went straight at anything, even murder. It had to be covered up to look like something else. He waited years to find some sort of legal excuse that would camouflage a murder. He had a mind like a corkscrew. Do you know what his first official action as Henry VII was?"

"No."

"To execute some of the men fighting for Richard at Bosworth *on a charge of treason.* And do you know how he managed to make it legally treason? By dating his reign from the day before Bosworth. A mind that was capable of a piece of sharp practice of that calibre was capable of anything." He took the cigarette that Grant was offering him. "But he didn't get away with it," he added, with sober joy. "Oh, no, he didn't get away with it. The English, bless them, drew the line at that. They told him where he got off."

"How?"

"They presented him, in that nice polite English way, with an Act of Parliament that said that no one serving the Sovereign Lord of the land for the time being should be convicted of treason or suffer either forfeiture or imprisonment, and they made him consent to it. That's terribly English, that ruthless politeness. No yelling in the street or throwing stones because they didn't like his little bit of cheating. Just a nice polite reasonable Act for him to swallow and like it. I bet he did a slow burn about that one. Well, I must be on my way. It's sure nice to see you sitting up and taking notice. We'll be having that trip to Greenwich in no time at all, I see. What's at Greenwich?"

"Some very fine architecture and a fine stretch of muddy river."

"That all?"

"And some good pubs."

"We're going to Greenwich."

When he had gone Grant slid down in bed and smoked one cigarette after another while he considered the tale of those heirs of York who had prospered under Richard III, and gone to their graves under Henry VII.

Some of them may have "asked for it." Carradine's report had, after all, been a précis; innocent of qualification, insusceptible to half-tones. But it was surely a thundering great coincidence that all the lives who stood between the Tudors and the throne had been cut short so conveniently.

He looked, with no great enthusiasm, at

the book that young Carradine had brought him. It was called *The Life and Reign of Richard III*, by someone named James Gairdner. Carradine had assured him that he would find Dr. Gairdner well worth his while. Dr. Gairdner was, according to Brent, "a scream."

The book did not appear to Grant to be markedly hilarious, but anything about Richard was better than something about anyone else, so he began to glance through it, and presently he became aware just what Brent had meant by saying that the good Doctor was a "scream." Dr. Gairdner obstinately believed Richard to be a murderer, but since he was a writer honest, learned, and according to his lights impartial, it was not in him to suppress facts. The spectacle of Dr. Gairdner trying to make his facts fit his theory was the most entertaining thing in gymnastics that Grant had witnessed for some time.

Dr. Gairdner acknowledged with no apparent sense of incongruity Richard's great wisdom, his generosity, and his courage, his ability, his charm, his popularity, and the trust that he inspired even in his beaten enemies; and in the same breath reported his vile slander of his mother and his slaughter of two helpless children. Tradition says, said the worthy Doctor; and solemnly reported the horrible tradition and subscribed to it. There was nothing mean or paltry in his character, according to the Doctor—but he was a murderer of innocent children. Even his enemies had confidence in his justice— but he murdered his own nephews. His integrity was remarkable—but he killed for gain.

As a contortionist Dr. Gairdner was the original boneless wonder. More than ever Grant wondered with what part of their brains historians reasoned. It was certainly by no process of reasoning known to ordinary mortals that they arrived at their conclusions. Nowhere in life had he met any human being remotely resembling either Dr. Gairdner's Richard or Oliphant's Elizabeth Woodville.

Perhaps there was something in Laura's theory that human nature found it difficult to give up preconceived beliefs. That there was some vague inward opposition to, and resentment of, a reversal of accepted fact. Certainly Dr. Gairdner dragged like a frightened child on the hand that was pulling him towards the inevitable.

That charming men of great integrity had committed murder in their day Grant knew only too well. But not that kind of murder and not for that kind of reason. The kind of man whom Dr. Gairdner had drawn in his *Life and History of Richard III* would commit murder only when his personal life had been *bouleversé* by some earthquake. He would murder his wife for unfaithfulness suddenly discovered, perhaps. Or kill the partner whose secret speculation had ruined their firm and the future of his children. Whatever murder he committed would be the result of acute emotion, it would never be planned; and it would never be a base murder.

One could not say: Because Richard possessed this quality and that, therefore he was incapable of murder. But one could say: Because Richard possessed these qualities, therefore he is incapable of this murder.

It would have been a silly murder, that murder of the boy Princes; and Richard was a remarkably able man. It was base beyond description; and he was a man of great integrity. It was callous; and he was noted for his warm-heartedness.

One could go through the catalogue of his acknowledged virtues, and find that each of them, individually, made his part in the murder unlikely in the extreme. Taken together they amounted to a wall of impossibility that towered into fantasy.

Chapter 15

"There was one person you forgot to ask for," Carradine said, breezing in, very gay, some days later. "In your list of kind inquiries."

"Hullo. Who was that?"

"Stillington."

"Of course! The worthy Bishop of Bath. If Henry hated Titulus Regius, as a witness of Richard's integrity and his own wife's illegitimacy, he must still more have disliked the presence of its instigator. What happened to old Stillington? Judicial murder?"

"Apparently the old boy wouldn't play."

"Wouldn't play what?"

"Henry's pet game. Out goes he. Either he was a wily old bird, or he was too innocent to see the snare at all. It's my belief—if a mere Research Worker is entitled to a belief—that he was so innocent that no agent provocateur could provoke him to anything.

Not anything that could be made a capital charge, anyhow."

"Are you telling me that he defeated Henry?"

"No. Oh, no. No one ever defeated Henry. Henry put him on a charge and conveniently forgot to release him. And never home came he. Who was that? Mary on the sands of Dee?"

"You're very bright this morning, not to say exhilarated."

"Don't say it in that suspicious tone. They're not open yet. This effervescence that you observe in me is intellectual carbonisation. Spiritual rejoicing. An entirely cerebral scintillation."

"Well? Sit down and cough up. What is so good? I take it that something is?"

"Good is hardly the proper word. It's beautiful, perfectly-holy beautiful."

"I think you *have* been drinking."

"I couldn't drink this morning if I tried. I'm bung full, full up to the gullet's edge, with satisfaction."

"I take it you found that break in the pattern we were looking for."

"Yes, I found it, but it was later than we had thought. Later in time, I mean. Further on. In the first months everyone did what you would expect them to do. Henry took over—not a word about the boys—and cleaned up, got married to the boys' sister. Got his own attainder reversed by a Parliament of his own attainted followers—no mention of the boys—and got an act of attainder through against Richard and his loyal subjects whose service was so neatly made treason by that one day's antedating. That brought a fine heap of forfeited estates into the kitty in one go. The Croyland monk was terribly scandalised, by the way, at Henry's sharp practice in the matter of treason. 'O God,' he says, 'what security are our kings to have henceforth in the day of battle if their loyal followers may in defeat be deprived of life, fortune, and inheritance?' "

"He reckoned without his countrymen."

"Yes. He might have known that the English would get round to that matter sooner or later. Perhaps he was an alien. Anyhow, everything went on just as you would expect things to go with Henry in charge. He succeeded in August of 1485, and married Elizabeth in the following January. Elizabeth had her first child at Winchester, and her mother was there with her and was present at the baptism. That was in September 1486. Then she came back to London—the Queen-Dowager, I mean—in the autumn. And in February—hold on to everything—in February she was shut up in a convent for the rest of her life."

"*Elizabeth Woodville?*" Grant said, in the greatest astonishment. This was the very last thing he had expected.

"Yes. Elizabeth Woodville. The boys' mother."

"How do you know that she didn't go voluntarily?" Grant asked, when he had thought of it for a little. "It was not an uncommon thing for great ladies who were tired of court life to retire into an Order. It was not a severe existence, you know. Indeed, I have an idea it was fairly comfortable for rich women."

"Henry stripped her of everything she owned, and ordered her into the nunnery at Bermondsey. And that, by the way, *did* create a sensation. There was 'much wondering,' it appears."

"I'm not surprised. What an extraordinary thing. Did he give a reason?"

"Yes."

"What did he say he was ruining her for?"

"For being nice to Richard."

"Are you serious?"

"Sure."

"Is that the official wording?"

"No. That's the version of Henry's pet historian."

"Virgil?"

"Yes. The actual order of council that shut her up, said it was 'for various considerations.' "

"Are you quoting?" asked Grant, incredulous.

"I'm quoting. That's what it said: 'For various considerations.' "

After a moment Grant said: "He had no talent for excuses, had he? In his place I would have thought up six better ones."

"Either he couldn't be bothered or he thought other people very credulous. Mark you, her niceness to Richard didn't worry him until eighteen months after he succeeded Richard. Up till then everything had apparently been smooth as silk. He had even given her presents, manors and what not, when he succeeded Richard."

"What was his real reason? Have you any suggestion?"

"Well, I've another little item that may give you ideas. It certainly gave me one hell of a big idea."

"Go on."

"In June of that year—"

"Which year?"

"The first year of Elizabeth's marriage. 1486. The year when she was married in January and had Prince Arthur at Winchester in September, with her mother dancing attendance."

"All right. Yes."

"In June of that year, Sir James Tyrrel received a general pardon. On the 16th June."

"But that means very little, you know. It was quite a usual thing. At the end of a period of service. Or on setting out on a new one. It merely meant that you were quit of anything that anyone might think of raking up against you afterwards."

"Yes, I know. I know that. The first pardon isn't the surprising one."

"The *first* pardon? Was there a second one?"

"Yes. That's the pay-off. There was a second general pardon to Sir James exactly a month later. To be exact on the 16th of July, 1486."

"Yes," Grant said, thinking it over. "That really is extraordinary."

"It's highly unusual, anyway. I asked an old boy who works next to me at the B. M.—he does historical research and he's been a wonderful help to me I don't mind telling you—and he said he had never come across another instance. I showed him the two entries—in the *Memorials of Henry VII*—and he mooned over them like a lover."

Grant said, considering: "On the 16th June, Tyrrel is given a general pardon. On the 16th July he is given a second general pardon. In November or thereabouts the boys' mother comes back to town. And in February she is immured for life."

"Suggestive?"

"Very."

"You think he did it? Tyrrel."

"It could be. It's very suggestive, isn't it, that when we find the break in the normal pattern that we've been looking for, Tyrrel is there, on the spot, with a most unconscionable break in his own pattern. When did the rumour that the boys were missing first become general? I mean, something to be talked openly about."

"Quite early in Henry's reign, it would seem."

"Yes; it fits. It would certainly explain the thing that has puzzled us from the beginning in this affair."

"What do you mean?"

"It would explain why there was no fuss when the boys disappeared. It's always been a puzzling thing, even to people who thought that Richard did it. Indeed, when you come to think of it it would be impossible for Richard to get away with it. There was a large, and very active, and very powerful opposition party in Richard's day, and he left them all free and scattered up and down the country to carry on as they liked. He had all the Woodville-Lancaster crowd to deal with if the boys had gone missing. But where interference or undue curiosity was concerned Henry was sitting pretty. Henry had got *his* opposition party safely in jail. The only possible danger was his mother-in-law, and at the very moment when she becomes capable of being a prying nuisance she too is put under hatches and battened down."

"Yes. Wouldn't you think that there was *something* she could have done? When she found that she was being prevented from getting news of the boys."

"She may never have known that they were missing. He may just have said: 'It is my wish that you should not see them. I think you are a bad influence on them: you who came out of sanctuary and let your daughters go to that man's parties!' "

"Yes, that's so, of course. He didn't have to wait until she actually became suspicious. The whole thing might have been one move. 'You're a bad woman, and a bad mother; I am sending you into a convent to save your soul and your children from the contamination of your presence.' "

"Yes. And where the rest of England were concerned, he was as safe as any murderer ever could be. After his happy thought about the 'treason' accusation, no one was going to stick his neck out by inquiring particularly about the boys' health. Everyone must have been walking on eggs as it was. No one knowing what Henry might think of next to make into a retrospective offence that would send their lives into limbo and their estates into Henry's kitty. No, it was no time to be overcurious about anything that didn't directly concern oneself. Not that it would be easy, in any case, to satisfy one's curiosity."

"With the boys living at the Tower, you mean."

"With the boys living in a Tower officialled by Henry's men. There was none of Richard's get-together live-and-let-live attitude about Henry. No York-Lancaster alliance for Henry. The people at the Tower would be Henry's men."

"Yes. Of course they would. Did you know that Henry was the first English King to have a bodyguard? I wonder what he told his wife about her brothers."

"Yes. That would be interesting to know. He may even have told her the truth."

"*Henry!* Never! It would cost Henry a spiritual struggle, Mr. Grant, to acknowledge that two and two were four. I tell you, he was a crab; he never went straight at anything."

"If he were a sadist he could tell her with impunity, you know. There was practically nothing she could do about it. Even if she wanted to. She mightn't have wanted to all that much. She had just produced an heir to the throne of England and was getting ready to produce another. She might not have the spare interest for a crusade; especially a crusade that would knock the ground from under her own feet."

"He wasn't a sadist, Henry," young Carradine said sadly. Sad at having to grant Henry even a negative virtue. "In a way he was just the opposite. He didn't enjoy murder at all. He had to pretty it up before he could bear the thought of it. Dress it up in legal ribbons. If you think that Henry got a kick out of boasting to Elizabeth in bed about what he had done with her brothers, I think you're wrong."

"Yes, probably," Grant said. And lay thinking about Henry. "I've just thought of the right adjective for Henry," he said presently. "Shabby. He was a shabby creature."

"Yes. Even his hair was thin and scanty."

"I didn't mean it physically."

"I know you didn't."

"Everything that he did was shabby. Come to think of it, 'Morton's Fork' is the shabbiest piece of revenue-raising in history. But it wasn't only his greed for money. Everything about him is shabby, isn't it?"

"Yes. Dr. Gairdner wouldn't have any trouble in making *his* actions fit his character. How did you get on with the Doctor?"

"A fascinating study. But for the grace of God I think the worthy Doctor might have made a living as a criminal."

"Because he cheated?"

"Because he didn't cheat. He was as honest as the day. He just couldn't reason from B to C."

"All right, I'll buy."

"Everyone can reason from A to B—even a child. And most adults can reason from B to C. But a lot can't. Most criminals can't. You may not believe it—I know it's an awful come-down from the popular conception of the criminal as a dashing and cute character—but the criminal mind is an essentially silly one. You can't imagine how silly sometimes. You'd have to experience it to believe their lack of reasoning powers. They arrive at B, but they're quite incapable of making the jump to C. They'll lay two completely incompatible things side by side and contemplate them with the most unquestioning content. You can't make them see that they can't have both, any more than you can make a man of no taste see that bits of plywood nailed on to a gable to simulate Tudor beams are impossible. Have you started your own book?"

"Well—I've made a sort of tentative beginning. I know the way I *want* to write it. I mean the form. I hope you won't mind."

"Why should I mind?"

"I want to write it the way it happened. You know; about my coming to see you, and our starting the Richard thing quite casually and not knowing what we were getting into, and how we stuck to things that actually happened and not what someone reported afterwards about it, and how we looked for the break in the normal pattern that would indicate where the mischief was, like bubbles coming up from a diver way below, and that sort of thing."

"I think it's a grand idea."

"You do?"

"I do indeed."

"Well, that's fine, then. I'll get on with it. I'm going to do some research on Henry, just as garnish. I'd like to be able to put their actual records side by side, you see. So that people can compare them for themselves. Did you know that Henry invented the Star Chamber?"

"Was it Henry? I'd forgotten that. Morton's Fork and the Star Chamber. The classic sample of sharp practice, and the classic sample of tyranny. You're not going to have any difficulty in differentiating the rival portraits, are you? Morton's Fork and the Star Chamber make a nice contrast to the granting of the right to bail, and the prevention of the intimidation of juries."

"Was that Richard's Parliament? Golly, what a lot of reading I have to do. Atlanta's not speaking to me. She hates your marrow. She says I'm about as much use to a girl as last year's *Vogue*. But honestly, Mr. Grant, this is the first time in my life that anything exciting has happened to me. Important, I mean. Not exciting meaning exciting. Atlanta's exciting. She's all the excitement I ever want. But neither of us is important, the way I mean important—if you can understand what I mean."

"Yes, I understand. You've found something worth doing."

"That's it. I've found something worth doing. And it's me that's doing it; that's what's wonderful about it. Me. Mrs. Carradine's little boy. I come over here with Atlanta, with no idea about anything but using that research gag as an alibi. I walked into the B. M. to get me some dope to keep Pop quiet, and I walk out with a mission. Doesn't that shake you!" He eyed Grant in a considering way. "You're quite sure, Mr. Grant, that you don't want to write this book yourself? After all, it's quite a thing to do."

"I shall *never* write a book," Grant said firmly. "Not even *My Twenty Years at the Yard*."

"What! Not even your autobiography?"

"Not even my autobiography. It is my considered opinion that far too many books are written as it is."

"But this is one that must be written," Carradine said, looking slightly hurt.

"Of course it is. This one must be written. Tell me: there's something I forgot to ask you. How soon after that double did Tyrrel get that appointment in France? How soon after his supposed service to Henry in July 1486 did he become Constable of the Castle of Guisnes?"

Carradine stopped looking hurt and looked as malicious as it was possible for his kind woolly-lamb face to look.

"I was wondering when you were going to ask that," he said. "I was going to throw it at you on my way out if you forgot to ask. The answer is: almost right away."

"So. Another appropriate little pebble in

the mosaic. I wonder whether the constableship just happened to be vacant, or whether it was a French appointment because Henry wanted him out of England."

"I bet it was the other way about, and it was Tyrrel who wanted to get out of England. If I were being ruled by Henry VII, I'd sure prefer to be ruled by remote control. Especially if I had done a secret job for Henry that might make it convenient for Henry if I didn't live to too venerable an age."

"Yes, perhaps you're right. He didn't only go abroad, he stayed abroad—as we have already observed. Interesting."

"He wasn't the only one who stayed abroad. John Dighton did too. I couldn't find out who all the people who were supposed to be involved in the murder actually were. All the Tudor accounts are different, I suppose you know. Indeed most of them are so different that they contradict each other flat. Henry's pet historian, Polydore Virgil, says the deed was done when Richard was at York. According to the sainted More it was during an earlier trip altogether, when Richard was at Warwick. And the personnel changes with each account. So that it's dif-

ficult to sort them out. I don't know who Will
Slater was—Black Will to you, and another
piece of onomatopoesis—or Miles Forrest.
But there *was* a John Dighton. Grafton says
he lived for long at Calais 'no less disdained
than pointed at' and died there in great misery. How they relished a good moral, didn't
they? The Victorians had nothing on them."

"If Dighton was destitute it doesn't look as
if he had done any job for Henry. What was
he by trade?"

"Well, if it's the same John Dighton, he was
a priest, and he was anything but destitute. He
was living very comfortably on the proceeds
of a sinecure. Henry gave a John Dighton the
living of Fulbeck, near Grantham—that's in
Lincolnshire—on the 2nd of May, 1487."

"Well, well," Grant said, drawling. "1487.
And he, too, lives abroad and in comfort."

"Uh-huh. Lovely, isn't it?"

"It's beautiful. And does anyone explain
how the much-pointed-at Dighton wasn't
haled home by the scruff of his neck to hang
for regicide?"

"Oh, no. Nothing like that. Tudor historians
didn't any of them think from B to C."

Grant laughed. "I see you're being educated."

"Sure. I'm not only learning history, I'm sitting at the feet of Scotland Yard on the subject of the human mind. Well, that will be about all for now. If you feel strong enough I'll read you the first two chapters of the book next time I come." He paused and said: "Would you mind, Mr. Grant, if I dedicated it to you?"

"I think you had better dedicate it to Carradine the Third," Grant said lightly.

But Carradine apparently did not feel it to be a light matter.

"I don't use soft soap as a dedication," he said, with a hint of stiffness.

"Oh, not soft soap," Grant said in haste. "A matter of policy merely."

"I'd never have started on this thing if it hadn't been for you, Mr. Grant," Carradine said, standing in the middle of the floor all formal and emotional and American and surrounded by the sweeping folds of his topcoat, "and I should like to make due acknowledgement of my indebtedness."

"I should be delighted, of course," murmured Grant, and the royal figure in the middle of the floor relaxed to boyhood again and the awkward moment was over. Carradine went away joyous and light-footed as he had come, looking thirty pounds heavier and twelve inches more round the chest than he had done three weeks ago.

And Grant took out the new knowledge that had been given him, hung it on the opposite wall, and stared at it.

Chapter 16

She had been shut away from the world, that indestructibly virtuous beauty with the gilt hair.

Why gilt, he wondered for the first time. Silver-gilt probably; she had been radiantly fair. A pity that the word blonde had degenerated to the point where it had almost a secondary meaning.

She had been walled up to end her days where she could be no trouble to anyone. An eddy of trouble had moved with her all through her life. Her marriage to Edward had rocked England. She had been the passive means of Warwick's ruin. Her kindnesses to her family had built a whole new party in England and had prevented Richard's peaceful succession. Bosworth was implicit in that scanty little ceremony in the wilds of Northamptonshire when she became Edward's wife. But no one seemed to have borne her malice. Even the sinned-against

Richard had forgiven her her relations' enormities. No one—until Henry came.

She had disappeared into obscurity. Elizabeth Woodville. The Queen-Dowager who was mother of the Queen of England. The mother of the Princes in the Tower, who had lived free and prosperous under Richard III.

That was an ugly break in the pattern, wasn't it?

He took his mind away from personal histories and began to think police-fashion. It was time he tidied up his case. Put it ship-shape for presenting. It would help the boy with his book, and better still it would clear his own mind. It would be down in black and white where he could see it.

He reached for his writing-pad and pen, and made a neat entry:

CASE: Disappearance of two boys (Edward, Prince of Wales; Richard, Duke of York) from the Tower of London, 1485 or thereabouts.

He wondered whether it would be better to do the two suspects in parallel columns or successively. Perhaps it was better to finish with Richard first. So he made another neat headline, and began on his summing-up:

RICHARD III

Previous Record:
Good. Has excellent record in public service, and good reputation in private life. Salient characteristic as indicated by his actions: good sense.

In the matter of the presumed crime:
(a) He did not stand to benefit; there were nine other heirs to the house of York, including three males.
(b) There is no contemporary accusation.
(c) The boys' mother continued on friendly terms with him until his death, and her daughters attended Palace festivities.
(d) He showed no fear of the other heirs of York, providing generously for their upkeep and granting all of them their royal state.
(e) His own right to the crown was unassailable, approved by Act of Parliament and public acclamation; the boys

were out of the succession and of no danger to him.

(f) If he had been nervous about disaffection then the person to have got rid of was not the two boys, but the person who really was next in succession to him: young Warwick. Whom he publicly created his heir when his own son died.

HENRY VII

Previous Record:
An adventurer, living at foreign courts. Son of an ambitious mother. Nothing known against his private life. No public office or employment. Salient characteristic as indicated by his actions: subtlety.

In the matter of the presumed crime:
(a) It was of great importance to him that the boys should not continue to live. By repealing the Act acknowledging the children's illegitimacy, he made the elder boy King of England, and the youngest boy the next heir.

(b) In the Act which he brought before Parliament for the attainting of Richard he accused Richard of the conventional tyranny and cruelty but made no mention of the two young Princes. The conclusion is inevitable that at that time the two boys were alive and their whereabouts known.

(c) The boys' mother was deprived of her living and consigned to a nunnery eighteen months after his succession.

(d) He took immediate steps to secure the persons of all the other heirs to the crown, and kept them in close arrest until he could with the minimum of scandal get rid of them.

(e) He had no right whatever to the throne. Since the death of Richard, young Warwick was *de jure* King of England.

It occurred to Grant for the first time, as he wrote it out, that it had been within Richard's power to legitimise his bastard son John, and foist him on the nation. There was no lack of precedent for such a course. After all, the whole Beaufort clan (including Henry's mother) were the descendants not only of an illegitimate union but of a double adultery. There was nothing to hinder Richard from legitimising that "active and well-disposed" boy who lived in recognised state in his household. It was surely the measure of Richard that no such course had apparently crossed his mind. He had appointed as his heir his brother's boy. Even in the destitution of his own grief, good sense was his ruling characteristic. Good sense and family feeling. No base-born son, however active and well-disposed, was going to sit in the Plantagenets' seat while his brother's son was there to occupy it.

It was remarkable how that atmosphere of family feeling permeated the whole story. All the way from Cicely's journeyings about in her husband's company to her son's free acknowledgement of his brother George's boy as his heir.

And it occurred to him too for the first time in full force just how that family atmosphere strengthened the case for Richard's innocence. The boys whom he was supposed to have put down as he would put down twin foals were Edward's sons, children he must have known personally and well. To Henry, on the other hand, they were mere symbols. Obstacles on a path. He may never even have set eyes on them. All questions of character apart, the choice between the two men as suspects might almost be decided on that alone.

It was wonderfully clearing to the head to see it neat and tidy as *(a)*, *(b)*, and *(c)*. He had not noticed before how doubly suspect was Henry's behaviour over Titulus Regius. If, as Henry had insisted, Richard's claim was absurd, then surely the obvious thing to do was to have the thing reread in public and demonstrate its falsity. But he did no such thing. He went to endless pains to obliterate even the memory of it. The conclusion was inevitable that Richard's title to the crown as shown in Titulus Regius was unassailable.

Chapter 17

On the afternoon when Carradine reappeared in the room at the hospital Grant had walked to the window and back again, and was so cock-a-hoop about it that The Midget was moved to remind him that it was a thing that a child of eighteen months could do. But nothing could subdue Grant today.

"Thought you'd have me here for months, didn't you?" he crowed.

"We are very glad to see you better so quickly," she said primly; and added: "We are, of course, very glad, too, to have your bed."

And she clicked away down the corridor, all blond curls and starch.

Grant lay on his bed and looked at his little prison room with something approaching benevolence. Neither a man who has stood at the Pole nor a man who has stood on Everest has anything on a man who has stood at a window after weeks of being merely twelve stones of destitution. Or so Grant felt.

Tomorrow he was going home. Going home to be cosseted by Mrs. Tinker. He would have to spend half of each day in bed and he would be able to walk only with the aid of sticks, but he would be his own man again. At the bidding of no one. In tutelage to no half-pint piece of efficiency, yearned over by no lump of outsized benevolence.

It was a glorious prospect.

He had already unloaded his hallelujahs all over Sergeant Williams, who had looked in on the completion of his chore in Essex, and he was now yearning for Marta to drop in so that he could peacock in front of her in his new-found manhood.

"How did you get on with the history books?" Williams had asked.

"Couldn't be better. I've proved them all wrong."

Williams had grinned. "I expect there's a law against that," he said. "MI 5 won't like it. Treason or lèse-majesté or something like that it might turn out to be. You never know nowadays. I'd be careful if I was you."

"I'll never again believe anything I read in

a history book, as long as I live, so help me."

"You'll have to make exceptions," Williams pointed out with Williams's dogged reasonableness. "Queen Victoria was true, and I suppose Julius Caesar did invade Britain. And there's 1066."

"I'm beginning to have the gravest doubts about 1066. I see you've tied up the Essex job. What is Chummy like?"

"A thorough little bastard. Been treated soft all his life since he started stealing change from his Ma at the age of nine. A good belting at the age of twelve might have saved his life. Now he'll hang before the almond blossoms' out. It's going to be an early spring. I've been working every evening in the garden this last few days, now that the days are drawing out. You'll be glad to sniff fresh air again."

And he had gone away, rosy and sane and balanced, as befitted a man who was belted for his good in his youth.

So Grant was longing for some other visitor from the outside world that he was so soon to be a part of again, and he was delighted when the familiar tentative tap came on his door.

"Come in, Brent!" he called, joyfully.

And Brent came in.

But it was not the Brent who had last gone out.

Gone was the jubilation. Gone was his newly acquired breadth.

He was no longer Carradine the pioneer, the blazer of trails.

He was just a thin boy in a very long, very large overcoat. He looked young, and shocked, and bereaved.

Grant watched him in dismay as he crossed the room with his listless uncoordinated walk. There was no bundle of paper sticking out of his mail-sack of a pocket today.

Oh, well, thought Grant philosophically; it had been fun while it lasted. There was bound to be a snag somewhere. One couldn't do serious research in that light-hearted amateur way and hope to prove anything by it. One wouldn't expect an amateur to walk into the Yard and solve a case that had defeated the pros; so why should he have thought himself smarter than the historians. He had wanted to prove to himself that he was right in his face-reading of the portrait; he had wanted to blot out the shame of having put a criminal on the bench instead of in the dock. But he would have to accept his mistake, and like it. Perhaps he had asked for it. Perhaps, in his heart of hearts, he had been growing a little pleased with himself about his eye for faces.

"Hullo, Mr. Grant."

"Hullo, Brent."

Actually it was worse for the boy. He was at the age when he expected miracles to happen. He was still at the age when he was surprised that a balloon should burst.

"You look saddish," he said cheerfully to the boy. "Something come unstuck?"

"Everything."

Carradine sat down on the chair and stared at the window.

"Don't these damned sparrows get you down?" he asked, fretfully.

"What is it? Have you discovered that there was a general rumour about the boys before Richard's death, after all?"

"Oh, much worse than that."

"Oh. Something in print? A letter?"

"No, it isn't that sort of thing at all. It's something much worse. Something quite— quite fundamental. I don't know how to tell you." He glowered at the quarrelling sparrows. "These damned birds. I'll never write that book now, Mr. Grant."

"Why not, Brent?"

"Because it isn't new to anyone. Everyone has known all about those things all along."

"Known? About what?"

"About Richard not having killed the boys at all, and all that."

"They've *known*? Since when!"

"Oh, hundreds and hundreds of years."

"Pull yourself together, chum. It's only four hundred years altogether since the thing happened."

"I know. But it doesn't make any difference. People have known about Richard's not doing it for hundreds and hundreds—"

"Will you stop that keening and talk sense. When did this—this rehabilitation first begin?"

"Begin? Oh, at the first available moment."

"When was that?"

"As soon as the Tudors were gone and it was safe to talk."

"In Stuart times, you mean?"

"Yes, I suppose—yes. A man Buck wrote a vindication in the seventeenth century. And Horace Walpole in the eighteenth. And someone called Markham in the nine-teenth."

"And who in the twentieth?"

"No one that I know of."

"Then what's wrong with your doing it?"

"But it won't be the same, don't you see? It won't be a great discovery!" He said it in capitals. A Great Discovery.

Grant smiled at him. "Oh, come! You can't expect to pick Great Discoveries off bushes. If you can't be a pioneer what's wrong with leading a crusade?"

"A crusade?"

"Certainly."

"Against what?"

"Tonypandy."

The boy's face lost its blankness. It looked suddenly amused, like someone who has just seen a joke.

"It's the damnedest silliest name, isn't it!" he remarked.

"If people have been pointing out for three hundred and fifty years that Richard didn't murder his nephews and a school book can still say, in words of one syllable and with-out qualification, that he did, then it seems to me that Tonypandy has a long lead on you. It's time you got busy."

"But what can *I* do when people like Walpole and those have failed?"

"There's that old saying about constant water and its effect on stone."

"Mr. Grant, right now I feel an awfully feeble little trickle."

"You look it, I must say. I've never seen such self-pity. That's no mood to start bucking the British public in. You'll be giving enough weight away as it is."

"Because I've not written a book before, you mean?"

"No, that doesn't matter at all. Most people's first books are their best anyway; it's the one they wanted most to write. No, I meant that all the people who've never read a history book since they left school will feel themselves qualified to pontificate about what you've written. They'll accuse you of whitewashing Richard: 'whitewashing' has a derogatory sound that 'rehabilitation' hasn't, so they'll call it whitewashing. A few will look up the *Britannica*, and feel themselves competent to go a little further in the matter. These will slay you instead of flaying you. And the serious historians won't even bother to notice you."

"By God, I'll make them notice me!" Carradine said.

"Come! That sounds a little more like the spirit that won the Empire."

"We haven't got an Empire," Carradine reminded him.

"Oh, yes, you have," Grant said equably. "The only difference between ours and yours is that you acquire yours, economically, in the one latitude, while we got ours in bits all over the world. Had you written any of the book before the awful knowledge of its unoriginality hit you?"

"Yes, I'd done two chapters."

"What have you done with them? You haven't thrown them away, have you?"

"No. I nearly did. I nearly threw them in the fire."

"What stopped you?"

"It was an electric fire." Carradine stretched out his long legs in a relaxing movement and began to laugh. "Brother, I feel better already. I can't wait to land the British public one in the kisser with a few home truths. Carradine the First is just raging in my blood."

"A very virulent fever, it sounds."

"He was the most ruthless old blackguard that ever felled timber. He started as a log-ger and ended up with a Renaissance castle, two yachts, and a private car. Railroad car, you know. It had green silk curtains with bobbles on them and inlay woodwork that had to be seen to be believed. It has been popularly supposed, not least by Carradine the Third, that the Carradine blood was growing thin. But right now I'm all Carradine the First. I know just how the old boy felt when he wanted to buy a particular forest and someone said that he couldn't have it. Brother, I'm going to town."

"That's nice," Grant said, mildly. "I was looking forward to that dedication." He took his writing-pad from the table and held it out. "I've been doing a policeman's summing-up. Perhaps it may help you when you come to your peroration."

Carradine took it and looked at it with respect.

"Tear it off and take it with you. I've finished with it."

"I suppose in a week or two you'll be too busy with real investigations to care about a—an academic one," Carradine said, a little wistfully.

"I'll never enjoy one more than I've enjoyed this," Grant said, with truth. He glanced sideways at the portrait which was still propped against the books. "I was more dashed than you would believe when you came in all despondent, and I thought it had come to pieces." He looked back at the portrait and said: "Marta thinks he is a little like Lorenzo the Magnificent. Her friend James thinks it is the face of a saint. My surgeon thinks it is the face of a cripple. Sergeant Williams thinks he looks like a great judge. But I think, perhaps, Matron comes nearest the heart of the matter."

"What does she say?"

"She says it is a face full of the most dreadful suffering."

"Yes. Yes, I suppose it is. And would you wonder, after all?"

"No. No, there was little he was spared. Those last two years of his life must have happened with the suddenness and weight of an avalanche. Everything had been going along so nicely. England on an even keel at last. The civil war fading out of mind, a good firm government to keep things peaceful and a good brisk trade to keep things prosperous. It must have seemed a good outlook, looking out from Middleham across

Wensleydale. And in two short years—his wife, his son, and his peace."

"I know one thing he was spared."

"What?"

"The knowledge that his name was to be a hissing and a byword down the centuries."

"Yes. That would have been the final heart-break. Do you know what I personally find *the* convincing thing in the case for Richard's innocence of any design for usurpation?"

"No. What?"

"The fact that he had to send for those troops from the North when Stillington broke his news. If he had any foreknowledge of what Stillington was going to say, or even any plans to concoct a story with Stillington's help, he would have brought those troops with him. If not to London then to the Home Counties where they would be handy. That he had to send urgently first to York and then to his Nevill cousins for men is proof that Stillington's confession took him entirely unawares."

"Yes. He came up with his train of gentlemen, expecting to take over the Regency. He met the news of the Woodville trouble when he came to Northampton, but that didn't rattle him. He mopped up the Woodville two thousand and went on to London as if nothing had happened. There was still nothing but an orthodox Coronation in front of him as far as he knew. It wasn't until Stillington confessed to the council that he sends for troops of his own. And he has to send all the way to the North of England at a critical moment. Yes, you're right, of course. He was taken aback." He propped the leg of his spectacles with a forefinger in the old tentative gesture, and proffered a companion piece. "Know what I find the convincing thing in the case for Henry's guilt?"

"What?"

"The mystery."

"Mystery?"

"The mysteriousness. The hush-hush. The hole-and-corner stuff."

"Because it is in character, you mean?"

"No, no; nothing as subtle as that. Don't you see: Richard had no need of any mystery; but Henry's whole case depended on the boys' end being mysterious. No one has ever been able to think up a reason for such a hole-and-corner method as Richard